No One Gets Out Alive

ADAM NEVILL

No One Gets Out Alive

ST. MARTIN'S GRIFFIN
NEW YORK

NO ONE GETS OUT ALIVE. Copyright © 2014 by Adam Nevill. All rights reserved. Printed in the United States of America. For information, address St. Martin's Press, 175 Fifth Avenue, New York, N.Y. 10010.

www.stmartins.com

The Library of Congress has cataloged the hardcover edition as follows:

Nevill, Adam L. G.
No one gets out alive : a novel / Adam Nevill. — First U.S. edition.
    p. cm.
ISBN 978-1-250-04128-9 (hardcover)
ISBN 978-1-4668-3739-3 (e-book)
1. Young women—England—Fiction. 2. Haunted houses—England—Fiction. I. Title.
PR6114.E92N6 2015
823'.92—dc23

2015002463

ISBN 978-1-250-09238-0 (trade paperback)

Our books may be purchased in bulk for promotional, educational, or business use. Please contact your local bookseller or the Macmillan Corporate and Premium Sales Department at 1-800-221-7945, extension 5442, or by e-mail at MacmillanSpecialMarkets@macmillan.com.

First published in Great Britain by Pan Books, an imprint of Pan Macmillan, a division of Macmillan Publishers Limited

First St. Martin's Griffin Edition: August 2016

10 9

For my little girl, Iona.
One day your old Dad is going to have a lot
of explaining to do about these books.

And in memory of two of my favourite writers:

Joel Lane (1963–2013):
Birmingham's finest writer of the weird tale.

Colin Wilson (1931–2013):
whose ideas have always been such an inspiration to me.

No One Gets Out Alive

CLOSER BY DARKNESS THAN LIGHT

The most dreadful thing of all – the figure materialized at my bedside and actually spoke to me. I remember the words, which he repeated twice before he vanished: 'Come and get me, Dod.'

Blackwoods Magazine, 1840
(letter from a reader)

DAY ONE

ONE

The dream receded quickly and Stephanie recalled little of it, beside an anxious desire to leave a cold, greyish place; a narrow space in which people stood too close to her. One of them had been crying.

Into the unsettling moments, trailing the end of sleep, came a relief that only her panic lingered from the nightmare. The respite was twinned with a sense of loss for something important, yet indefinable and left incomplete. And she was cold. Where her head poked out of the duvet it stiffened, as though her bed had been placed outside of the building.

Stephanie's eyes were open. She was lying on her back and could see nothing above. But inside the darkness was a voice, a muffled continuous voice surrounding her waking thoughts. Not a single word was loud or clear enough to be understood, but she was horribly certain the muttering could not be part of the dream because she was fully awake. There was no urgency to the voice, or particular emphasis, or even emotion; the tone suggested monotony, a monologue.

The voice issued from the side of the room, near the fireplace that she couldn't make out in the dark. Even with

5

the lights off, not even an ambient glimmer peeked around the thick curtains.

A radio? In another room?

Though the more she considered the voice, the greater was her impression that someone was speaking behind the wall on the other side of the room. But there was nothing on the other side because the house was detached. So perhaps a television was switched on – *yes, don't forget those* – in the room below her own, and the sound was travelling up through the chimney.

When the voice in the fireplace began sobbing, Stephanie felt like joining in. It was a strange kind of broadcast that allowed one person to speak continuously before breaking down on air.

Could be another tenant. In a nearby room someone might have been talking to themselves and was now crying. This sound of genuine anguish introduced a picture into Stephanie's mind of a woman kneeling on the floor beside an open fireplace, clutching her face.

She could not go and ask after them. She disliked herself for feeling embarrassed by another's distress, but it was the middle of her first night in the house and she wasn't confident enough to offer that kind of gesture to a stranger.

But thank God it's only a neighbour. For a moment I thought—

The tension returned to her body and her mind so quickly and with such force that she sucked in her breath as if she'd stepped into cold water. Because no radio or television or heartbroken tenant could possibly account for the scratching that began beneath her bed.

She might have risen from the bedclothes screaming had she not arrived at a new hope: that the grating noise against timber was issuing from beneath the floorboards, as opposed to the wooden slats on the underside of the bedframe.

Mice! There were mice here; she had seen two little cardboard traps, the type containing a blob of poisonous blue bait, on the first floor landing and the second floor toilet. When she was shown around the house yesterday morning the sight of the traps had shocked her; they were another symbol of diminishing choices, of being compromised by poverty – a side to freedom improperly considered before independence was achieved, or exchanged for a different kind of captivity. But she'd lived in a building infested with mice before, and seen similar traps in the warehouse where she worked last summer.

And during your first night in the darkness and unfamiliarity of a new room in a strange building, the sound of mice was bound to be alarming and to seem too *large* a disturbance for small animals. When you lay alone in bed, the sound of tiny claws were amplified in the silence of deep night, *everyone knows that*. Only in these circumstances could such a noise suggest the activity of determined human hands beneath your bed.

The mice were having a go at something that was rustling. *Polythene. Maybe. Yes, it must be polythene.* There could be a plastic carrier bag under there and the mice, or rats – *don't even go there* – were having a go at the bag, or tearing something under the floorboards. *Yes, that is a better idea.*

Beneath her bed the sound of rustling increased in

volume and ardour and her imagination swamped her thoughts again with the notion that these were, in fact, human fingers pulling at polythene. She was just about to sit up and reach for the bedside lamp – the one she'd read by before she fell asleep, satisfied she'd found a new room so quickly – when everything suddenly got worse and she was filled with the kind of fear that was mindless, that was madness. Because Stephanie could now hear a fresh intrusion of noise inside her room.

Beyond the foot of her bed, between the two large sash window frames, was a table and chair. On the table were her unpacked bags. And from this area came a rustling, a rummaging, as if someone's hands were going through her rucksack. The painted floorboards beneath the rug creaked as the intruder shifted its weight.

Behind the fireplace a woman wept.

Under the bed fingers pulled at polythene.

The darkness was filling with sound.

Stephanie could see nothing. The air was so cold she shivered. She desperately wanted to reach for the bedside light, but that would creak the old bedframe. She didn't want to make a sound, any sound at all.

And what will I do if I turn the light on and someone is standing there?

The door to her room was locked. The key was inside the lock. *Had they come in through a window?* Could she get off the bed and reach the door, and hold the key in her fingers, and turn the key in the lock, and open the door, and step through the doorway . . . before *it* reached her?

Can I fight? Should I start screaming?

She had no strength for screaming, let alone defence.

Everything inside her was frigid with a fear so vast she was nothing but terror; she became stone from the hair on her head to the toes on her feet.

Unwelcome images flashed: cotton buds being used to take swabs, police officers in plastic overalls collecting hairs from a carpet, a gurney covered with a sheet being loaded into an ambulance, watched by a woman in the doorway of a nearby house.

Stephanie sat up and reached for the bedside table. The bedframe made the sound of an old wooden ship.

The rifling of her bags stopped.

She slapped a hand around the bedside table. The wooden surface was cold under her mostly useless fingers. She found the rubber cable with the light switch attached to it, then lost the cable, sensed it swing away from her fingertips in the darkness.

Footsteps creaked across the floor towards her bed.

She groped for the cable again and found the metal stem of the lamp instead. When she located the cable her desperate fingers twitched their way to the plastic switch.

Beneath her feet the mattress dipped as someone sat down.

Through the darkness she was sure a face was moving closer to her own.

She snapped the lamp on and turned to confront the intruder sitting on the end of her bed.

'Oh God, oh God, oh God, shit, shit, shit, oh God.'

TWO

Stephanie sat in the pre-dawn darkness with the duvet grasped under her chin. Through the open curtains the sky turned from black-blue to mackerel-grey. The bedside light was switched on. The overhead light was switched on. In the palm of one hand her mobile phone was cloudy with the heat from her tight grip. On the bedside cabinet the small travel clock clicked towards six a.m.

When she'd turned the bedside light on, there had been no one sitting on her bed and no one in her room. When she'd summoned the courage to look under the bed, she'd seen large balls of greyish dust on painted floorboards, but no plastic bag. Her door key was still hanging from the lock of the secured door. The sash windows were closed and held tight with metal clasps. Only her clothes occupied the walnut-veneered wardrobe. She couldn't be sure that someone had actually interfered with her bags during the night either, because she'd left them unzipped and gaping before she went to bed.

The scratching under the bed must have stopped when the light came on, though she couldn't recall the exact moment the noise ceased. When she put an end to the darkness there had been no voice in the fireplace either.

The fireplace grate and surround were made from

metal, thickly coated in black paint and dusty. The chimney flue was no more than a few inches across. She'd moved her ear close to the fireplace and heard what sounded like a distant wind, nothing more.

Stephanie looked at the walls around her more closely. They had not been decorated in years, not since the yellowing paper, carrying the impression of bamboo stalks and leaves, had been pasted upon them. The room was as depressing as the others she had lived in since leaving home; small capsules of space left stranded by the onward surge of life, untouched by modernization and a source of revulsion for those of means. These rooms were now home to those who were only one more misfortune away from homelessness, and so close to dropping out of the statistics of the unemployed and into the statistics of those with no fixed address, or those reported missing.

Stephanie squeezed the duvet until her nails pressed through the fabric and hurt the palms of her hands.

Thoughts of the MDMA she'd once taken came back to her with the full weight and pressure of an accusation, as did memories of the skunk weed she'd smoked a few times, and the magic mushroom tea she'd once drunk – all three years ago in her first year at college. She wondered if those brief and fledgling experiments with drugs had been the cause of the hallucinations; some kind of delayed reaction.

And as she sat in bed, waiting for the morning, it began to seem a long time since she had woken in a room loud with intrusive sound. Most of her mind now insisted that the experience was part of the indistinct nightmare, that had continued in the form of footsteps crossing the room, followed by the impression of someone sitting on the bed. All of it could have been imagined.

Must have been.

But what she had so recently heard in the dark didn't feel like the lingering effects of a dream. After she had slapped the lights on and finished her inspection of her sealed room, she'd thought about ghosts for a long time. And she remembered a story her dad had told her. Long before her natural mother died, her dad told her that his own mother, Stephanie's paternal grandmother, once appeared beside his bed and asked, 'Are you coming?' The following morning her dad was called on the phone by his sister to say their mother had died the night before, in her bed, in her home, on the other side of town. The story had enthralled Stephanie, but also given her a hope that death was not the end. What she'd just endured made her wish that death was, in fact, final.

Her dad also used to call her 'my miracle girl' because she'd come close to death as a toddler after swallowing seawater. She had no memory of the incident, but had briefly wondered, when she was small, if nearly dying had made her special. Because at the funerals of both her grandfathers, in a way she still could not explain, she remembered being engulfed by a sense of them around her, and inside her head, at the terrible moment their coffins rolled behind the red curtains in the same crematorium chapel in Stoke.

But this was the sum total of her experience with the supernatural. Stephanie hadn't watched a horror film since she was sixteen and she wasn't religious. She'd always assumed she needed to sort out her place in this world before she thought of the next.

Looking back on the episode that had so recently occurred in her new room, she was struck by a notion that two very different places had opened onto each other, or come together.

The sky turned from mackerel to white-grey.

Exhaustion lay heavy inside her body, but the fatigue helped the shock dwindle. Listless memories of the previous day drifted through her mind as the sun rose.

There was a blister on the little toe of her right foot and her calf muscles bulged with aches; both reminders of the three trips she had made on foot from a tiny rented room in another sub-divided house in Handsworth to this one. She'd carried her bags three miles through quiet, identical streets choked with parked cars. Her new room was the same price but much bigger than her last place – a room she had called *the cell*. She'd nearly gone mad inside 'the cell' during her first few months in Birmingham.

Weariness from the move and from the weekend's two twelve-hour shifts, working as a steward in the reception of a caravan show, had put her to sleep before ten p.m. She'd awoken more frightened than she could remember between two and three. In one hour, un-refreshed and tense, she would need to leave for work.

How did I get here? Why is this happening to me?

She ran through the seemingly ordinary sequence of events that led to her sitting up in bed, terrified and praying for the dawn light to hurry into the sky. The day before, an overly friendly man she had found it hard to like, a Mr McGuire, or 'Knacker', had guided her round 82 Edgehill Road: an old, neglected, but otherwise ordinary house with rooms he let out to lodgers scratching around the bottom of the rental market.

Knacker was the landlord and lived on the top floor in a private flat. He had shown her this large room with high ceilings that she had been so excited to find at forty pounds per week. It had been advertised on a card in the window of a local grocer's: BIG ROOM. 40 QUID FOR WEAK. GIRLS ONLY. SHARD BAFROOM, KICHEN. V CLEEN. There had been a mobile phone number too, and she had grinned at the misspellings and imagined the house was let by migrants for whom English was still a mystifying second language. Many of the big Victorian houses in the area were sub-divided into bedsits. Her ex-boyfriend, Ryan, who was working in Coventry, knew Birmingham well and had said Perry Barr was mostly an Asian area, but increasingly popular with Eastern European migrants and students from the City of Birmingham University. He'd said it was really cheap, and really cheap was all she had the budget for. But at least this place was only let to females, and in the most deprived areas of town that was an asset among such unappealing pickings.

There was nothing extraordinary about the circumstances of her being here; anyone in the same position could have ended up in the same room and, therefore, experienced the same thing. But sitting in a strange bed, in an unfathomable building, made her feel that her life resembled a landscape pitted with bad decisions and unfortunate situations created by circumstances she had no control over. And the craters of hasty choices, or impacts made by fate, were interspersed with the shadows of anxiety about her immediate future.

Did she always bring these situations upon herself? Her stepmother had always said as much. *Bitch*. But how is *it* done, how is control over your life possible when you have no money, and no prospect of getting more than a little to survive on? *To exist on* was closer to the truth. *Because that is what you are doing: existing, not living.*

A familiar suspicion revived itself: that she hadn't even started in life and was still outside it somehow, looking in, drifting, or being blown about its fringes, while trapped in places where anything could happen to her.

Regret had become tangible overnight and was now a lump in her throat and a cold weight in her tummy; it made her face literally feel too long. Taking the room had been impulsive, as was handing over £320 in cash as a deposit and first month's rent to a man who made her wary.

She now seriously regretted not calling Ryan and asking if he knew anything about the street, or even to come down to get his sense of the landlord. She hadn't spoken to Ryan in a month, but didn't know anyone else well enough to ask them to perform such a task on her behalf. Her friends were mostly at home with their parents, applying for jobs, retaking A Levels and signing on in Stoke.

Now that she wanted to leave the house and move on again after only one night, Stephanie worried she might not get her deposit back from Knacker McGuire. She would need the deposit to pay for the next room, or there would be no next room. Until she was paid for the temp work she had this week, she was down to fourteen pounds and change. Fourteen pounds and thirty-two pence to be exact, because when you are skint you do count every penny.

According to the text message she'd received from the temp agency yesterday afternoon, while she lugged her bags between the two houses, she would spend the next three days giving out food samples in a shopping centre. So when today's eight-hour shift finished, unless she retrieved her deposit and found a new room that didn't require a reference, she would have to return to this house. To this very room. There was nowhere else for her to go.

She didn't know what to do. Stephanie cried as quietly as she could, her wet face pressed into the duvet. She thought of the woman she'd heard in the night.

House of tears.

The sky's brief glow was smothered by charcoal clouds full of rain. She would have to get ready for work soon.

At ten minutes past six the world reinserted itself into her isolation and introversion. Hot water pipes and the solitary radiator beside her bed gurgled reassuringly. The air about her face warmed. In the distance of the house, downstairs she thought, a door closed. Soon after a toilet flushed. In the room behind hers, at the end of the corridor and overlooking the street, the heavy footsteps of a stranger announced themselves and remained an active presence until her alarm sounded at half past six.

In the cluttered concrete yard beneath her windows, a dog stirred and moved its short chain. Far off, a police car raced through the dawn streets. The dog barked a gruff, angry retort, then whistled through its nose and fell silent.

Stephanie got out of bed and found her robe, her towel and her washbag. The rug was crispy beneath the soles of her bare feet. She unlocked the door and felt her skin prickle and shrink in the cold air of the unlit corridor outside her room. By the light that fell from the doorway of her room, she watched the other two doors on her floor. The occupants had fallen silent. No light bled from beneath their doors. She did not know who lived in the rooms around her, and that ignorance made her feel small and vulnerable and nervous. She'd not long stopped crying, but her eyes burned again.

She looked at the fly-specked lightshade above her, noted the forlorn silence of the unlit stairwell. The place was a refuge for transients like her. The dismal corridor seemed to confirm that this was where she belonged now: a place of indifference, anonymous neighbours, coughs in the night from gruff throats, creaks of worn bedframes, and televisions murmuring behind closed doors; hidden histories, disparate accents and alien languages, the awkwardness of meeting strangers in shabby corridors with dressing gowns tucked under their chins. This was a place of stale air and overfull bins, compromised privacy, petty thefts, and new faces as worn but disingenuously watchful as the last crowd.

She'd seen it all before in the six months since she'd left home. Not yet twenty and her eyes should never have looked upon this side of life. If her dad was still alive he'd have been furious with Val, her stepmother, who'd thrown her out. 'You don't want to find yourself down there.

Down there with the rest of them,' he'd said while she studied for her A levels, specifically to escape a home traumatized by her stepmother's personality disorder – an instability that had raged daily beneath the roof of Val's house until Stephanie was gone from it. There was no going back there.

Yesterday, when she'd asked about the other tenants in the house, Knacker had sniffed and said, 'Uvver girls. Stoodents mostly. All kinds, Powls – all kinds bin in 'ere over the years.' Knacker had come up from Essex to take care of his family home, but claimed to be a Brummy originally, and constantly sniffed up his long, bony nose during the interview. 'All over. Bin all over, me. Like to move around, yeah? Spain, you name it. Bin everywhere, me. Done it all.'

Though he hadn't said much specifically about himself or the house, he had asked her a lot of questions. With hindsight, once he had the deposit, she wondered if he'd actually been evasive about the other tenants, while she'd mistaken his brief non-committal replies for disinterest. His big washed-out eyes had slid all over her but darted away when she looked directly at him.

She didn't want to think about his face. She didn't want to be here. Not for the first time since she left Stoke, with her stepmother ranting behind her, she asked herself, *What have you done?*

THREE

The bathroom was cold enough to make her think twice about a shower. The air bit her face, her ankles and feet. Even with the water splashing hot inside the tub and creating steam, the mere thought of removing her gown was an anticipation of pain.

Grit and fluff had stuck to the soles of her feet when she'd flitted down one flight of stairs to the communal bathroom on the first floor. She wished she'd worn her trainers, or ended her resistance to slippers; they had their uses.

She checked the radiator. It burned red hot but failed to transfer any heat into the cramped space.

The room was bone dry and dusty. A red carpet, as stiff and desiccated as the rug in her room, crackled under her feet. Plain paper painted a watery yellow covered the walls. In the corners above the toilet and sink, a rash of black spores erupted from damp plaster. Around the sink, old black whiskers had fossilized under the overflow hole. She wondered if she would have become a resident if she'd properly inspected the bathroom during her tour yesterday. Though to be honest, she'd used worse.

Sitting on the toilet to pee, she sensed being on the edge of a bad smell that wouldn't fully reveal its source. There was a strong odour of damp and old carpet in the air of the bathroom, but the ripe sweetness of meat in deep bins suggested itself too.

Wiping the grimy and discoloured enamel of the bath with sodden toilet paper was a delaying tactic for actually stepping into the shower. When was the last time the bath had been cleaned?

Up on the second floor there was only a toilet on the landing, without a sink, so there was no alternative to this bathroom in such a large building. But the sink and the toilet seat had been dusty before she used them, which was odd because she had heard this toilet flush a little while ago, so someone must have been in here.

As far as she could tell there was a self-contained flat on the ground floor, another on the third floor, and six bedrooms in the communal section of the building: three bedrooms on the first floor, three on the second floor, but only one complete bathroom. Grim. The idea of someone not washing their hands after using the toilet this morning made her wince. *What sort of people lived here?*

She checked the time on her phone. *Better get a move on.*

She laid her shampoo and conditioner bottles behind the blotchy taps at the top of the bath. When the room was sufficiently cloudy with steam to give an impression of heat, she braved the cold and removed her robe, her t-shirt and underwear. She didn't shiver as much as shake. By the time she stepped into the cascade of water, her feet and fingers were numb.

The window was closed, the heating was on. How could it be so cold?

20

As dawn struggled through a cleaner portion of the window, daylight revealed an aperture blocked with painted iron bars, fixed to the exterior wall.

What would you do in a fire?

The windows in her room were not barred, so maybe this was a security feature of the lower floors – something else she hadn't noticed yesterday in her determination to get out of the cell. But it was yet another reason to get out of here. The very idea of moving again was exhausting, but she couldn't remain here. She wanted to run someplace familiar.

Ryan.

Whenever fear and anxiety had overrun her since she'd arrived in Birmingham, her first thought was always to call her ex, Ryan, and ask him if she could return to his room – at least until she found work in Coventry, or somewhere nearby. But that wouldn't be possible until the weekend, because she needed the next three days' work giving out the samples. She'd make £120. And a return to Coventry would also be an act of outright desperation; the very idea made her feelings crawl around on all fours in the form of guilt and grief.

She didn't want to go through all that again. She didn't want to be with Ryan. There wasn't a doubt in her mind about that. Her being at his place would be inappropriate and near unbearable. And a sorry-faced return to Ryan's life would involve her sleeping on Ryan's bed *again*, while he fidgeted on the floor in a sleeping bag.

Going back to his room, but not back to him, would mean tears, mostly his, and a revival of the discomfort and awkwardness that would overwhelm a few nights in his room. His desperate need for them to get back together would take him over. It was one of the main reasons she'd shifted down to Birmingham to find work: to cut them off from each other.

Stephanie thought herself into brief surges of hope, which sank into a familiar cycle of stifling frustrations and ended in dread. *Nothing new there.* She always seemed to be inside houses owned by other people, restless with anxiety or paralyzed by regret. How could she have been so foolish as to believe she could make it on her own in a strange city?

Conscious of the time, she washed her hair quickly, constantly rotating her body under the water that struggled to escape the limescale-encrusted shower head. After a few uncomfortable minutes, she climbed out of the bathtub and wrapped herself in the towel while her teeth chattered.

Not having to use the bathroom for much longer was the only relief she could draw from the experience. She could pick up a scourer and cleaning spray on her way home from work, from a pound shop, and just use the sink until she moved out. No one need know. As she thought about how bearable she could make her time at 82 Edgehill Road, she heard a voice.

The cold forgotten for a moment, Stephanie stepped away from the bath, because she was sure the voice had come from the tub.

Steam clouded to the ceiling. She swiped her hands before her face to clear her vision.

Silence.

And then she heard it again: a faint voice down by the

floor. But not one directed at her; the speaker seemed to be talking into a corner, or even at the floor. Maybe from under the floor?

She followed the direction of the voice and wondered if there were tenants on the ground floor and some weird acoustic or cavity in the building was throwing voices into the nearby rooms.

She lowered herself to her hands and knees. But the carpet was filthy enough to make her rear back to her heels and bat the gathered hairs and grit from her damp hands.

'What is my name?'

Stephanie stood up and backed against the nearest wall. Opened the bathroom door to let the steam escape so she could see the woman who had spoken, and only a few feet from her face at that.

What is my name? The question had risen as if someone lying inside the tub had spoken out loud.

And whoever was speaking now continued to mumble as if they were drifting away. Stephanie could almost catch the words that appeared to originate, impossibly, from beneath the bathtub. She moved closer, swallowed the constriction in her throat, and knocked on the bath, hoping that would make it stop. 'Hello? Can you—'

The speaker either didn't hear her or ignored her and continued to talk in a quick stream of words, to herself, or to someone else she could not see. It was a woman urgently communicating something to someone that wasn't Stephanie.

On all fours, Stephanie moved her hands around the carpet at the base of the bath, though she wasn't sure what she was looking for. A waft of wet rags and a hint of sewage buffeted her face. The room below must have a hole in the ceiling and she was overhearing a one-sided conversation or a television.

Stephanie's ear touched the side panel of the bath's surround.

'. . . before here . . . that time. Nowhere . . . to where the other . . . the cold . . . is my name?'

A television, it must be, or a radio play, overheard from a room beneath the bathroom. The voice had to be coming from below. She didn't want to believe it could be coming from anywhere else.

Stephanie gathered up her things and hurried into the warmer corridor of the first floor. She came to a standstill on the landing, sluggish with shock and bewilderment, and wondered what on God's earth she had moved into.

FOUR

When she left her room, dressed for work in boots, her last pair of smart black trousers and a white shirt under her coat, the interior of the house was still dark enough to require lights in the communal landings and on the staircase.

The ceiling lights were on timers and didn't remain switched on for long. They came on for a few seconds to reveal dated green wallpaper, torn down to plaster in places, or interspersed with long panels of newer paper, painted white. There were scuffed skirting boards and ancient wainscoting so thickly covered in paint it was impossible to determine the original decorative features. And if she was quick enough, she could reach the next circular light switch before the darkness fell with a horrible suddenness behind her. Not a building she would want to move through at night. She suppressed the thought.

Uncomfortably eager to leave the building, Stephanie jogged down the stairs. She wondered if she would ever have the courage to cross the threshold later when she finished work, even if it was just to collect her stuff and . . . *go where?*

As she turned into the last flight of uncarpeted stairs leading to the hall, she heard the scuffle of leather-soled feet on the floor tiles: footsteps preceding the unlatching and the creak of the front door. It gave her a start until she realized it could be one of the other tenants leaving the building ahead of her. She sensed a man. But this place was for girls only, so maybe this was the landlord.

If she could share her experiences, she might receive an explanation about the noises in the house. Stephanie hurried down.

The front door closed before she made the bottom step. She raced along the ground floor passageway, the heels of her boots scraping and clattering across the tiles, to struggle with the front door.

Outside, the world was reluctant to reach whatever served for light in this grey time of year, but there was no one on the path and the gate was closed. She could not be that far behind whoever had just left the building.

On the short front path six wet rubbish bins stood sentinel on either side of the little rusty gate that rose as high as her hips. The rest of the front yard was a combination of broken paving slabs, litter and long weeds. Clumps of wet leaves, drooping from unkempt trees, flopped against the ground floor windows and concealed the lower storey of the house, which was why she hadn't noticed the security bars yesterday. Behind the ancient white cages of iron bars, all she could see behind the windows were black curtains. Rain rustled the pennants of crisp packets and plastic bags caught up in the unruly privet hedge that screened the front of the house from the street.

Gripped with a need for human contact, Stephanie unlatched the gate and stepped into Edgehill Road. Traffic from the T-junction at the end of the road became loud around her head. She looked left and right. The streetlights glowed yellow and lit up the vertical descent of the rain that had fallen for hours. The road surface appeared oily, the cars heavy with a second skin of water, the trees tense with cold. The dim and miserable world was soaked but empty. So where had the man gone?

Stephanie looked at the house. Sooty red bricks running with dirty water. Black drainpipes. Old wooden sash window frames on the second floor, visible above the trees. Faded curtains. Only the top floor windows boasted venetian blinds. Not a flicker of light escaped the interior. The building appeared deserted. She could not recall it looking this way yesterday. Must be the light and weather, or her lack of sleep. Had the sun not briefly appeared for yesterday's viewing she doubted she would have even set foot inside.

Huddled into herself, with her head dipped from the rain, she made her way to the top of the road to find the bus stop and typed a quick text message to Ryan:

I'VE MADE A TERRIBLE MISTAKE [AGAIN!].
CAN YOU HELP ME?

FIVE

Stephanie arrived back at the house after seven. The rain continued to fall hard upon North Birmingham. The streetlights in Edgehill Road were spaced so far apart, and issued such thin light, they made the houses exude a vaguer, more inhospitable aspect than they had done that morning. Or perhaps they seemed menacing now that she had something to feel intimidated by. She wasn't sure. But she wondered if there had been any daylight here at all while she'd worked indoors at the vast Bullring shopping centre in the city, a world of steel, glass, marble, white electric light, and the trappings of affluence that ejected her into the rain once her day's servitude was complete.

The people she had worked with, and the location, had felt impersonal and never close to familiarity, as if to communicate the message: *Don't get used to it*. She couldn't help taking that to heart.

Usually she made friends on temp jobs, during the long hours of boredom and repetition that always felt more stressful than important work. In the past, she'd even exchanged phone numbers and email addresses with the other girls she'd worked with in warehouses, factories and while stewarding live events. But the bright lights and designer clothes shops of the Bullring had given airs to the other two girls she'd worked with, an attitude demon-strated by many of the shoppers as if they were all accustomed to, and unimpressed by, the opulence. Her two colleagues both considered themselves to be models.

And what recession? Amongst crowds laden down with logo-emblazoned paper bags with string handles, expen-sive hair styles, new clothes, smart phones, the shopping centre had suggested an exclusive annexe existing beyond any world she was familiar with. While she had resorted to blacking-out the scuffs on her one pair of boots with an eyeliner pencil, others seemed to exist in effortless afflu-ence. It mystified her like magic. Where were all the people, like her, who had no money? Were they hiding themselves away in wretched buildings like she was?

Beside the thirty-minute break, when she'd sat on a bench in the Bullring and watched silent news reports on a huge television screen about flooding in Cornwall, York-shire and Wales, she had been on her feet for the best part of eight hours. She'd become so tired she'd begun to slur her 'Hello, sir, would you like to try our new Italiano range of wrap? Only two hundred calories per . . .' She'd called two women 'sir', and the edges of her vision had started to flicker by late afternoon. She needed eight hours' sleep but had had less than three the night before. Her stomach burned with hunger.

Relief that the working day was over plummeted at the sight of the house. The building appeared wetter, grub-bier and even more derelict than when she'd hurried away from it that morning. The whole place seemed sullen and eager to be left alone in the cold darkness. What-ever optimism and comfort the building once possessed was long gone. The house's character seemed so obvious now.

Don't think like that.

She paused in the hallway to turn on the light and inspect the post: fliers for Asian mini-markets, fried chicken and pizza delivery services mingled with cards for local taxi companies. There was nothing addressed to the tenants, beside one final demand from British Gas for a Mr Bennet. Everything else in a white envelope was addressed to 'Dear Homeowner'.

Not having notified the bank or the doctor's surgery of her change of address was a small mercy. She'd do all of that when she found a new room in another building. And if she stood any longer looking at the faded walls, the uncarpeted stairs leading to the first floor, and the solitary closed door at the end of the ground floor hall, she worried she might not get up the stairs to her room.

Stick to the plan. She'd rehearsed it all day. *Eat, then go and see the landlord and give notice on the room. Ask if you can leave your bags here until Monday morning. Get your deposit back. Find a new place this weekend. Accept that the month's rent paid in advance might be gone, but still try to get a refund so you can stay in a cheap B&B over the weekend until you find a new room.*

If she could not get the rent back she would have to stay in the house until Monday.

Stop! Don't think about it . . . One thing at a time.

You can do it. You can do it. You can do it.

Reciting the silent mantra throughout the day to deter self-pity had felt absurd. But now she was back inside the building, the house suggested the implacable, with an entrapping power that would drain any resistance to itself.

'It's what you make of it,' Knacker had said yesterday, grinning through his gappy teeth. But that was a cliché. It was incorrect. After six months away from the family home, she knew it was how these demoralizing places changed you that needed to be resisted. And she always resisted them. 'Character building', others might have said about her experiences. But that was also a cliché, and easy to say when it wasn't your character being built by adversity.

'You're a smart girl. And beautiful too. You'll make it all come right,' her dad once said after a dispiriting week-end together in Aberystwyth, when she knew she couldn't afford to go to university, no matter how good her A Levels had been.

Why didn't you come and see me the night you died, Daddy, and tell me what the fuck to do?

She briefly wondered what the ground floor was used for. Maybe it held tenants too? She hurried past the silent first floor and ran up the carpeted stairs to the second storey, slapping the lights on as she moved, running to the next switch before the lights behind her winked out.

She paused outside her room long enough to disappear into the abrupt darkness produced by the three-second timer on the overhead light reaching the end of its pathetic cycle. *What kind of mean bastard would try and save electricity like this?*

Only the ambient glow of a distant street lamp, seeping through the window on the stairwell between the first and second floors, offered any illumination.

Stephanie held the long room key lightly between her fingertips and listened intently.

All was silent on the other side of the door to her room.

She struggled to control her bottom lip's tremble when she recalled the tug and rustle of plastic beneath the bed, the mournful voice, the bed springs depressing as a new weight added itself to the mattress. *What happened in this room last night?*

Could the floorboards of an old building correct at night, as a building moved upon its foundations, to suggest a footfall? Had she heard a radio in another room, or a conversation, maybe someone talking to themselves? Were there mice under the bed? And what about the bathroom that morning? Was she losing her mind?

Schizophrenia. Psychosis.

Stephanie pushed the door to her room open with more force than she'd intended, and reached inside to slap the light on.

SIX

All was as she had left it: a chipped Formica table, the old bed concealed by her purple duvet, a red rug on floorboards painted with brown emulsion, the hideous gold and black curtains, the white bedside cabinet at odds in style and time with the imitation walnut wardrobe. The room looked like the scene of a potential suicide following an occupant's long period of depression, isolation and poverty, cobbled together out of oddments of junkshop furniture. Plaster wainscoting, an iron fireplace and hardwood skirting boards suggested bourgeoisie grandeur so faded as to be almost undetectable behind the tat. Sparse, but somehow too lived in. Overcrowded with the past, but left barren by neglect. *Despair*: an installation created by stuff given away on Gumtree. It could win the Turner Prize without breaking a sweat. The smile on her lips surprised Stephanie, and she realized she was looking at the room with new eyes; with the scrutiny afforded by the death of wishful thinking.

She dropped her handbag and supermarket bag on the bed, but kept her boots on because the floors were dusty and because they made noises, *and had voices in them that she could not account for*.

She killed the thought. Plugged in her phone to

recharge. Slapped her iPod into another socket. Locked her room and went down to the kitchen with her Tesco Express bag. A carton of salad that had to be eaten that day and a pasty with the same imminent expiry bumped against her hip as she descended the staircase.

The kitchen was on the first floor landing, opposite the bathroom; both communal rooms were set before the staircase. The other doors in the first floor corridor sank away from the landing towards the front of the house and into darkness.

Beneath a bedroom door on the right hand side she could see a warm and welcome strip of electric light. No sound came from beyond the door.

Inside the kitchen the orange and lemon coloured lino peeled up skirting boards black-rimmed with dust. A table had been shoved into one corner. A quick wipe of a finger across the vast L-shaped counter blackened the pad with dust. The plastic swing-lid bin was empty and smelled of ancient bleach. Detergent and limescale traces had evolved into white powdery rimes in the arid kitchen sink. Puzzled, she went to the ancient fridge and opened the door. Completely empty save the wire-frame shelves. Old stains darkened the bottom of a tray that promised to be a 'Vegetable Crisper'. The fridge had been emptied at some point but not cleaned. The freezer compartment was a solid brick of ice that had broken the hinges of the ice box door.

Black spills around the electric cooking rings were ancient too. She snapped two of them off the enamelled metal. They looked like flattened, desiccated worms.

Like the bathroom, the kitchen had not been used in a long time, nor had it been cleaned recently. Even the mouse traps were old, the bait long gone. In the corners the petrified black rice of mouse droppings were suspended in a grey fur of dust, gathering as if the spoor had been absorbed by a monstrous fungus.

Knacker had said there were other people living here, so what did they do to prepare food? Eat out? Takeaways went with the territory, especially if the household was male-oriented, but this one was supposedly all female. Certainly didn't look like it. And who could afford takeaways every day? Not someone who lived here. Stephanie's last vestige of illusion that she might have sat in here with other girls, and bitched about work over coffee, as communal stir-fries sizzled on the stove, doused like the final spark in a cold fireplace.

Yet as she plugged the microwave in to see if it still worked, and then fiddled with the buttons to change the setting from HELLO . . . DEFROST . . . ADD WEIGHT, she heard footsteps outside: high heels on the tiles of the ground floor before they began to rise up the stairs to the first floor.

A girl!

With her warmest smile primed in anticipation, Stephanie headed for the kitchen doorway. 'Hey! Hello there,' she called out.

The footsteps softened as they hit the carpeted landing of the first floor, before continuing on to the second floor without slowing down. Wasn't Birmingham supposed to be friendly? The big heart of England? She would have to crawl out of its arse before she found its heart.

'Hello. Hi,' Stephanie said as she came into the corridor outside the kitchen.

35

The girl turned on the first part of the staircase to the second floor. Stephanie didn't see much beyond a slender silhouette moving across the undraped window of the stairwell.

She lives on my floor. The idea made Stephanie so excited she desperately slapped at the light switch on the wall outside the kitchen. But the woman was already rising up the stairs to the second floor, leaving Stephanie with only the sounds of muted high heels.

'Hello. Sorry. I just wanted to introduce . . .'

Engulfed in the woman's perfumed wake, Stephanie followed the footsteps. The scent was strong but pleasant. She thought she recognized it and must have once smelled a sample in Debenhams. When Stephanie turned the staircase and the second floor came into sight, the light below clicked off and left her in darkness.

'Hi. Hello!' An edge had come into her voice; she just wanted to say hello to a neighbour. The woman must have heard her. And it was odd that the girl had walked up these stairs so swiftly without turning the lights on. She must have been living here a while to cross the terrain so confidently.

Stephanie made the second floor and reached for the nearest light switch. In the darkness ahead of her the swish of clothing and thump of high heels moved away, and quickly too, as if in flight. A key rattled inside a lock.

'Hello,' Stephanie repeated, and more loudly this time as she snapped the corridor light on, which briefly revealed a woman entering the room opposite hers in the middle of the corridor. A glimpse of long blonde hair, a pale face, tight jeans and dark high heels was all she received before the door closed and was locked. Inside the room a light clicked on.

'Suit yourself.'

Stephanie walked back to the kitchen, her footsteps accompanied by the angry bark of the dog outside. The draught around the stairwell window smelled of the wet yard and she shivered. The woman had been anxious not to make contact; her movement through the dark had actually sped up when Stephanie spoke. An evasion. What was that about?

You won't be here long so don't sweat it. She might fancy herself as a glamour puss but she lives the fuck here.

In the kitchen Stephanie tugged open the cabinet doors beside the stove and found two plates. She washed them in hot water as there was no washing up liquid, then slid her pasty into the microwave. She'd eat in her room. It was that kind of place.

The rude girl in the dark revived her fighting spirit. Once she got this food down she'd go and face the land-lord. No wonder he kept a low profile, renting out this hole. He'd been delighted by her interest in the room, and her pitiful enthusiasm had made her an easy mark. He had positively shivered with glee when she handed over the three twenty.

Three hundred and twenty quid!

SEVEN

The door to 'Knacker' McGuire's flat was ornate, like the grand entrance of a house owned by the West Midlands rich. There was a brass knocker and a spyhole and a glare of blonde wood to suggest a visitor had arrived *somewhere* and probably underestimated the importance of the people inside. The sight of the landlord's door also re-inforced her feelings that all of her assumptions about the building and the people inside might be entirely wrong.

What was even stranger was the small CCTV camera attached high on the wall above the top of the door. It was not a new camera, but one of the old ones that looked like a Super-8 cine-camera fixed into a bracket.

Nearly a minute passed after Stephanie knocked before several locks were unbolted and a chain slid through a latch on the other side. The door shifted a few inches to become ajar. One large eye presented itself, the blue iris so pale as to suggest marine life, and with it a nose reminis-cent of a horse – not regally equine, but more nag-like and knuckled from hard labour and scraps. Dim light shone around a halo of curly hair. 'Yeah?'

Stephanie moved her eyes up to the camera. 'It's OK, I'm not here to rob you.'

Knacker didn't smile. 'What's the problem? It's the

evenin'. I should have said that anyfing that needs fixin' you need to tell me before six.'

Where do I start? Stephanie bit back on recommending demolition. 'Oh, no, it's not that. I just need to speak with you. Something's come up. I, er . . . I need to leave.'

'Eh? What you talkin' about?' It was more of a belligerent challenge than a question and her resolve tottered as though it had suddenly hit black ice. Just as quickly she tightened all over with irritation at his tone.

The door opened a full foot. Knacker's face filled the gap, followed by one bare shoulder and arm. He wasn't wearing a shirt, just silky tracksuit bottoms with the waistband of Calvin Klein underwear visible. All of his clothes looked new; they hadn't yesterday.

The landlord had the kind of body she'd seen on drug addicts and women with eating disorders: supple skin pulled tight on knobbly features and sinewy limbs. Old man bony in a younger body. She always wondered if people worked at that 'look' or if it was genetic. They seemed to have made a lifelong enemy of body fat and ended up striking but unattractive. The hair had not been starved of nutrition, however: it was thick and so well groomed she feared a wig. Big curly locks around an ageing face. A middle-aged man dressed like a teenager.

'I've changed my mind. About the room. I've come about the deposit.'

Knacker's eyes narrowed and she knew in a heartbeat she'd struck a nerve. He quickly relaxed his expression, sniffed, and changed his tack. He had some persuading to do, some ducking and diving – she'd seen that look all her life. 'That's not something I'm prepared to discuss now. I'll come and see you tomorrow—'

She cut his bullshit off before it could get airborne. 'I'm at work tomorrow. Early start. This won't take long.'

Yesterday, at the time of the interview, she'd disliked him immediately, but knew most landlords of sub-lets were bastards; they went with the territory. Buy-to-let summoned the spiv. But what had been immediately and abundantly clear was that he liked the sound of his own voice, liked to give flight to his opinions and 'foughts', without really answering questions.

She guessed he'd also been showing off because she was young and attractive and he had wanted to appear worldly. She hadn't planned on staying for long, no more than a few months before she landed a job in London, so she'd reasoned she could put up with him. He was small too, and hadn't exuded lechery or hostility. And there were other girls living here, he had said so, and that fact had reassured her. But how much effort had she really put into an assessment of Knacker, when so desperate to find another room at no more than forty pounds a week? After only one night beneath the roof of 82 Edgehill Road, the awareness that she'd suppressed her suspicions and instincts gnawed at her accusingly. Her chest burned with an indigestion of frustration.

He'd also kept control of the exchanges yesterday afternoon, and she'd let him. They'd both been disingenuously upbeat and exuded positive energy, because he was close to money and she *so* wanted the room. A not unusual barter of self-interest that she loathed herself for now.

When she'd asked about central heating, a shower, he'd

seemed amused, half smiled and said, 'All of that, all of that' – *that* pronounced *vat* – 'has been put in. Done it myself. One of the fings my dad taught me. How to be handy, like.'

But tonight, Knacker's temperament had undergone a change as he continued to try and get rid of her from his doorstep. 'I'm busy. I like to relax in the evenin's. Not get bovvered by people. You'll find I'm a very private person. You wouldn't want me knockin' on your door when you was settled down for the evenin'.'

She suspected he was also selling an idea of himself while telling her off. She hated that about older men who knew they were unappealing to her. He liked the word *evening* too. She suspected he thought it gave him gravitas, civility, respectability. A chav with airs.

She spoke slowly but couldn't keep the edge out of her voice. 'I'm sorry. But it's not even nine. I've been at work all day. And I need to get this resolved now.'

'You need to get it *resolved*,' he recited the word back at her sarcastically, and she caught a glimpse of gappy teeth between thick lips that were incongruously sensual amidst all the bony hollows of his face. 'It's neither the time nor the place to *resolve* fings of this nature.' He played at a contrived intelligence and thought he was clever. It made her more determined to retrieve both the rent and deposit. 'I mean I ain't got no shirt on,' he added and thought this was funny. He revealed more of his torso and was proud of it. Though thin, his body was deeply muscle-cut and he wanted her to notice his abs. 'But I'll tell you what I'll do. I'll come down and see you in a bit.'

She filled with anger that was actually red and hot like people say it is. 'It won't take long. We can—'

'I ain't talking on a doorstep when I'm 'alf naked, girl. I gotta fink this frough, like. You was very happy to take that room. Practically snatched the key out me hand. And now you is on my doorstep asking for money that, let's be honest wiv each other, ain't yours no more.'

'I made a mistake. Things change. I need . . .' She stopped, furious with herself for introducing *need* into the exchange; she'd already lost ground.

Delighted with her irritation, Knacker looked down at her and smiled. He was mocking her. *No skirt would get the better of him over money.*

Stephanie turned to descend the stairs but was so emotional she momentarily lost her balance.

'Careful, you won't be going nowhere if you break your leg.'

'Then get the place bloody lit properly!' It was out of her mouth before she could give it a moment's consideration.

Knacker's smile became a sneer. Even in the dark his face appeared paler. 'You's got a nerve, girl.'

'It's not safe.' Her voice had lost its edge.

'Criticizin' and complainin' and using that language in my muvver's house. You not been here five minutes. What's wrong wiv you?'

'Nothing. There's nothing wrong with me. I don't like it here. I was wrong about it. I've changed my mind. People can change their minds.'

'Just as well you ain't a bloke.' He said this in a soft tone and one far worse than a spittle-propelled bark.

Stephanie stiffened all over. She seemed to grasp the most obvious fact about the situation right then: she was arguing with a thick bully, and an unscrupulous, half-naked reptile on the stairs of a dark house in which no one wanted to know her.

He smiled again, the sneer gone, happy he had made his point and belittled and intimidated her. 'As I said, I will make an exception to my rules, and I will come down and see you when I am ready.'

Stephanie turned away to hide the tears of rage and frustration filming her eyes. She returned to her room.

EIGHT

She'd stopped crying by the time Knacker knocked on her door, but she knew her eyes were still red. It was after ten. He'd let her sweat it out. She'd never before cried to get sympathy from a man who hadn't been a boyfriend, and even then it wasn't something she made a habit of. She hadn't been crying to manipulate Knacker McGuire; her distress was genuine, but she didn't mind him knowing that she was upset if it helped return her deposit and some of the rent. The realization made her feel even lower, but what did she have to bargain with beside tears?

She opened the door and stood aside. 'Please.'

He came in from the musty darkness of the corridor. The lights had clicked off while he waited for her to wipe her nose and compose herself.

The soft, unappealing scent of the house was masked by the pungency of his aftershave. She prayed he hadn't put it on for her sake.

'Awright. I hope you is in a better mood. Fought I'd let you cool off a bit. I don't like aggro in me own home.'

'I'm sorry I lost my temper . . . I'm under a bit of strain right now.'

'I'd never have guessed, darlin'.' Wearing a white muscle vest to complement his jogging bottoms, Knacker sauntered in. On his feet he wore box-fresh trainers. They were lime green and looked expensive. A tag hung from a lace as if he had just been trying them on before he made up his mind. He peered about the room, satisfied with what he saw. 'Place is awright. At that price you won't do better. Don't know why you is complaining.'

She would have to lie. 'It's not the room so much. I've got a new job. In Coventry. I only found out today—'

'What doin?'

'I need to move up there this weekend—'

'To do what?'

'Call centre. It's—'

'Wonder why you bother with all that. Shit, innit. Shit jobs. You'll never make any money doin' that. Mind if I sit down?'

He pulled the chair out from under the table and stared at her bags that were all packed and ready for evacuation. 'You didn't waste any time, did ya?'

'I need to be in Coventry by next Monday night.'

'Next Mundee! You ain't shy about takin' the piss, is you? So you is demanding a deposit back, and you don't like the place, but you was lookin' to stay here 'til next week?'

'No, just my bags. I'll stay somewhere else until then.'

'Suiting yourself, like. As I told you when you come to see the place, one mumf's notice. I don't let this by the week. It's not that kind of place.'

'I know, but this job just came up and—'

'Bit convenient. I mean, the day after you move in, you get another job? Sorry, darlin', but I fink you is lying. Telling porkies.'

'What does it matter? I can leave if I want to. I don't have to give you a reason. But I wanted to explain why I needed to go, out of consideration. I've already paid you a month's rent in advance, so why would next Monday be a problem? I've paid for this room for four weeks. And there's no damage. But I need my deposit to pay for a new place. I don't think I'm being unreasonable. I can't write that much money off. I'm not in a position to.'

'No you ain't, that's right, otherwise you wouldn't be coming to me looking for a place to stay for forty quid a week. This ain't some five star hotel where you come and go cus you has paid premium, like. And what do you mean, *my* deposit? Let me explain something to you: when you gave me that deposit, the money was no longer yours. It's mine until the mumf is up, like. We had an agreement for one mumf's notice. And I'm in business. I don't like getting mucked about. I'm a busy man.'

'Please. I need . . . I want to take this job.'

'What's that got to do wiv me? That's your business. This house is my business. You pays your money, you takes your risks. Fings change. Don't I know it. But business is business and you agreed to the conditions of the contract.'

'There is no contract. I never signed any contract. You said you don't "bovver wiv all vat". If I was to go to the police . . .'

A transformation spread swiftly across his face, then through his body. She could barely process the alteration in his expression, complexion, body language, and what it meant. It was the same change she'd incited upstairs when she'd resisted his argument, but now she'd mentioned the police and mimicked his voice.

The flesh of Knacker's face blanched, not white but to a greyish colour, like putty. And he looked past her into the distance. Stood up. His hands were shaking. He paced back and forth, one step forward, one step back. A terrible silence seemed to swell and thicken around her.

Like a boxer, Knacker McGuire rotated his head and tensed his arms. The muscles in his forearms and biceps corded like rope. His eyes shut to slits but the glimmer of colour in his irises became brighter against the pallid surrounding skin; even his eyelids bleached, and his brown hair appeared darker, almost woolly, which made his face more cadaverous than it already was. It was the kind of face that nutted and spat and bit; she recognized it from the bad pubs around Stoke.

Stephanie tensed and felt an urgent need to talk him down and get him out of the room she was so desperate to leave herself. The situation suddenly felt like the end of a road. Something deep inside her had started to murmur and it sounded like panic. The distance from the bed she sat upon to the front door of the building continued forever in her imagination. 'I apologize. I never meant for this to get complicated.'

'You is taking advantage.' His voice was slightly breathless but taut with emotion. 'You is taking me for a *cunt*.' The word seemed to unblock whatever served to restrain his anger. He started to nod his head and his tight curls trembled, as if in agreement with this Damascene moment, as if a great betrayal had been uncovered. He'd been taken for one of these *things* before and she assumed the consequences had been awful.

The scars on the bridge of his nose, one cheekbone, and in the big dimple in his long chin whitened to reinforce what he needed to say. 'I've done you a solid and you turn around and treat *me* like a cunt.' Now the word sounded like the philosopher's name: Kant. His own philosophy of total self-interest had been rejected, which reminded her of her stepmother: the emphasis on the all-mighty *me*.

Her legs felt like they were filling with warm water. She realized that when women laughed at that kind of face they had their own smashed. She imagined eyes so bruised they were black and blind.

Where had that come from?

A complete realization of her status as a girl, on her own, being confronted by an unstable male stranger took her breath away. This is how *those things* happen to women. She would have to let him rant, but not let him burn himself into an animal rage like her stepmum and her last boyfriend. Thank God he wasn't drunk; it was the only thing she had going for her.

'You don't know nuffin' about me. Nuffin' about me and my background. My family. If you did you wouldn't be givin' it all this.' In the air he made a snapping mouth with his bony fingers. 'Eh? Eh? Eh?' He was almost too enraged to speak. 'You've gone very quiet.'

His observation suggested to Stephanie that he often confronted people who disagreed with him and made them *go quiet*. And he just loved to point it out to them too, to add humiliation to their fear.

An urge to speak quivered in her throat and trembled

through her jaw. Her vision blurred hot. 'Stop! Stop it! I don't care . . . I just want to go . . .' Her final words seemed to come out in heavy globs. She pressed the ball of tissue in her hand against her nose as a last attempt at preserving dignity. The building seemed intent on snatching that away.

'Awright, awright. Cut it out. Yeah? Cut that out. I don't like people cryin', yeah?'

She wasn't sure if it was sympathy or disgust that he was now expressing, but at least it wasn't rage.

His body seemed to relax just as quickly as it had tensed. 'Fuck's sake, girl. What a state to get yourself into. You don't try it on wiv honest people unless you can take the grief, yeah? Didn't no one never tell you that? Eh? My word, what was you finking, tryin' to rob me blind? There's plenty who's learned you don't try it on wiv McGuires.'

'I wasn't . . . I wasn't . . .'

'Yeah, yeah, don't give me none of that. I'll tell you what you was finking, you was finking that I was some kinda mug, yeah? Who you can mess around. Yeah? Who would fall for a pretty face that batters her eyelashes, yeah? It's not about money. I earn good money. Eighty, ninety grand some years. Bet you didn't even fink that? It's the principal of the matter that I am trying to get into your head. I don't care if it's a pound or a grand, the same principle applies. My father taught me that. Shame your own parents were negligent on that front.'

Stephanie stopped crying. Not only was he a bully, he was rude and a boor. And she wanted to tell him that he was all of those things, and worse. She'd met repellent men in her time, in most of the dreadful jobs she'd endured and in every bar she'd worked behind. But right now she couldn't remember ever meeting a fouler man than Knacker McGuire. As a human being he was right up there with her stepmother. She recalled the superficial show of geniality he'd put on when they first met . . . *just like Val.*

'Now, I am a reasonable man. I don't wanna see you upset. What kind of person do you take me for? You ain't got no money, anyone can see that. We all have hard times. One sixty is nuffin' to me. I blow that on clothes every week and don't fink nuffin' of it.'

Stephanie eyed the new sports shoes on his feet, their fluorescent green the colour of insolence, and she guessed her deposit was no longer available.

'Some of us got more sense than to be wasting our lives in call centres, or giving out bits of food in the Bullring.' He snorted with laughter and seemed to expect her to join in. She'd forgotten she'd told him that. What else had she told him?

'You've had a hard time. You don't even need to tell me, yeah? It's written all over ya. Your mum don't want you round no more. Ain't really a surprise considering the mouth on ya, if I'm totally frank. Your poor old dad's dead. I can understand that. And you're skint. I didn't even want anyone living in my house. I forgot that ad was in the window of that raghead shop. But when you called I could tell – here is a young girl in a spot of bother. Even her boyfriend's fucked her off. She's short of a bit a luck, like. So I fought I'd help her out. Not the first time my family have taken in strays either. And then you goes and takes me for a mug. Just as well my cousin ain't 'ere. He's not as reasonable as me in these situations. He's a hard man.'

He watched the fear return to her eyes; the fear she couldn't keep out of them.

Knacker smiled. 'Don't worry, he ain't around. He's takin' care of some business down south while I sort this place out. Ain't no one lived in it since me mum and dad passed.' At the thought of them his eyes misted. 'This is my family home. You gotta understand it's a place I don't want disrespected. Means a lot to me. You disrespect this house you disrespect me mum and me dad, and you disrespect me. I don't want dossers in here. I was brought up here. I don't let just anyone froo that door. Me mum and dad had lodgers and I fought one little girl on the run won't hurt.'

Stephanie cut short her outrage. The sense of futility that seemed to paralyze her larynx, and everything else that wound about her head and heart on a spin cycle, transformed into suspicion. She frowned. 'But you said there were other girls living here. How many?'

He seemed embarrassed by his own garrulousness now that he was at full steam and had a captive audience. 'Like I said, people come and go. I help people out. Don't need to. Don't need the money when you make what I do. But it's in my nature to be helpful. A family trait. Always has been. But you rub us up the wrong way and you'll know about it, let me tell you that for nothing. We got big hearts in this family. My mum . . .'

She couldn't stand to hear another word. They seemed to grind inside her and make her gape in stupefied silence as she listened to his self-aggrandizing lies. She knew more than she needed to know about him. They'd only spoken three times, and now the trilogy of face-to-face meetings was complete, he made her feel sick with anger. Sick to her stomach. She hated herself for crying, for letting him make her cry so easily, for being stupid enough to be here, and for telling him so much about herself.

Had she? What had she been thinking?

'Please leave.'

Knacker looked at the door, then moved a few feet to the side to block it. 'Hang on, hang on. No need for the drama. You only just got here. You need to give the old place a bit a time, like. Settle in. Tell you what I'll do—'

'No. I'm going.'

'One fing I can't stand, girl, is people interrupting when I'm talking. You follow? I fought I made my point that I have limits on rudeness, yeah?'

Stephanie glared at him but kept quiet. She could be out of here in ten minutes. She'd call a cab. Eleven pounds would get her to the city centre.

But what then? If she spent her money on a cab she would be penniless until she was paid on Friday.

'Now I know it could do wiv a lick a paint and some smartnin' up. Whole house. Which is why the price is commensurate wiv its current condition, yeah? Which is why I am up here, back in the old home town. And when I'm done wiv this place it will be restored, yeah? To its former glory. You won't recognize this place no more. Me and me cousin ain't just pretty faces. But in the meantime, yeah, I'll make this a bit more comfortable for you. How's that? Can't say fairer. Maybe a TV. We got some spare. A comfy chair. Something nice to sit in, something to look at, yeah?'

'No thanks. I need to go. The job . . .'

'Ain't no job. We already established that. You got nuffin' but the clothes you is standing up in. And they ain't much to look at, darlin', if the truth be told. And you won't find a job lookin' like a pauper wiv no address. That's a non-starter right off. But you got yourself a decent place now. The job comes next. There's no more jobs in Coventry than there is here. Same all over. Country's fucked. Least for them that don't know how to go about fings. To help themselves, like. Cus no one is gonna help you in this life. My mother made sure I learned that. Your own probably tried to tell you the same fing, but you're all mouf. Time to start finkin' like an adult, like. Time to start listenin'. And where you gonna go runnin' to at this time a night, eh? Boyfriend? Some bloke that chucked you out? Smart move.'

'Stop! You don't know me. You don't know anything about me.'

'You'd be surprised what I know about all kinds of fings. Only a fool would fink otherwise about a McGuire, girl. And who's the one sitting pretty in a six-bedroom house wiv a loft conversion, eh? Wiv his own business? Me. Not you. You got nuffin'. But I'm reaching out. Offerin' a helpin' hand. First rung on the ladder. Last fing you want to do is take me finger off, sister.'

'Monday. That's my last day.'

'My you are a stubborn one. Don't know what's good for ya. But go on then, Monday it is. Suit yourself. You paid for a mumf, you can stay a mumf, or fuck off tonight. I can do without the grief, quite frankly. But you ain't having the deposit back. That's non-negotiable. You's broken the contract. I mean, what am I, a charity?'

Knacker grinned at her. She endured a long silence while he stood there with his eyebrows raised, waiting for her to argue. 'You've gone all quiet on me again. Cus you know you ain't got a leg to stand on, sister.' He sidled through the door, bouncing on his heels, the curly-haired head cocked with satisfaction.

Stephanie scrambled up from the bed and slammed the door.

Outside, she heard Knacker's footsteps pause as if he was thinking of coming back to address the slamming door, like she was a teenager having a tantrum. She thought again of Val, her stepmother, and wanted to scream.

Stephanie turned the key in the lock so quickly she twisted her wrist and then waited, pressed against the door, until she heard his feet creak up the stairs to his flat. In the distance a door closed.

She lay on the bed and clasped her hands over her face.

NINE

As Stephanie undressed for bed, the tenant in the room across the hallway began to cry.

It had to be the same girl Stephanie had glimpsed earlier. The tall woman with the lovely perfume was now producing a shuddery weeping sound that travelled through two walls to Stephanie, the kind of despair that came from the bottom of the lungs, when a throat burned with the taste of a swim in the sea. A sound that felt complementary to her own situation and the very house, as if this building was a place where misery flourished.

All of Stephanie's resentment at the girl's refusal to acknowledge her vanished. The grief she could hear heaved with everything that made life temporarily unbearable.

No good. She wouldn't be able to just lie in bed, swimming in her own self-pity, while listening to that. The girl across the hall was really hurting. Her distress might also explain why she hadn't spoken to Stephanie earlier, or even paused in her headlong charge back to her room; maybe the woman had simply been unable to face anyone.

But was this also the same woman she had heard behind the fireplace last night?

It couldn't have been, because the voice in the fireplace

had come from a different direction, seemingly from the other side of the house. So there could be two deeply unhappy women here. Three if she counted herself.

Another idea struck Stephanie. The other tenant might be in the same situation as her: broke, a victim of coercion, under the threat of violence for defiance, stuck, trapped . . . Was she being dramatic or had that been the subtext of her most recent exchange with the landlord?

BIG ROOM. 40 QUID FOR WEAK. GIRLS ONLY. *Why?*

Stephanie opened the door to her room and stepped into the hallway.

And came to a standstill before reaching for the light switch.

The sensation was akin to stepping outside the building without a coat. There was a plummet in the air temperature – a terrible cold that registered the moment she was engulfed by the thick darkness. And a smell that brought her to a halt – an odour akin to being inside a wooden space, fragranced by emptiness, dust and old timber, like a wooden shed. She was overwhelmed by the notion that she had just stepped into a different building. Or the same place altered so profoundly that it may as well have been somewhere else.

A solitary streetlight beyond the garden offered a meagre glow to silhouette the wooden handrail and a pallid patch of staircase wall. A strip of light fell out of Stephanie's room and suggested a dark carpet, some scuffed skirting board. The red door opposite her own was barely visible.

But these vague suggestions of the building's scruffy interior were oddly welcome, because they were real, while she felt . . . Yes, she could better identify it now . . . she felt an acute *anguish*. Abandonment. Like the first morning after her dad passed away. A hopelessness fully realized and suffocating and exhausting at the same time: something that would drive you insane if it didn't pass within minutes; if it wasn't relieved. But the feeling tonight, outside her room, was worse, because the overwhelming solitude wouldn't end for whoever was truly experiencing it. And that was the strangest thing of all.

This atmosphere, or sensation, that occupied the physical space of the passageway was not recognizable as being of her own making, as being generated by her own emotions. And this notion that she had been engulfed by someone else's distress, in effect stepped into its orbit, as irrational as it was, did not feel imagined either.

Or was it?

Now she was beyond the reach of a balanced state of mind herself, and what felt like actual physical safety after no more than a single step outside of her room, she heard herself whimper. And the shock of hearing her own small cry, in the cold and half blindness that was so vast it gave her vertigo, made her strike out at the light switch on the wall.

But the horrid feelings persisted through the sudden coming of light to the corridor, which also did nothing to stem the cries of the grief-stricken girl.

No light escaped from the room opposite her own. The occupant was weeping in the dark.

Stephanie forced herself to cross the corridor to go to the crying woman. She knocked on the door. 'Hello.

Please. Miss. Miss, please. Can I help?' She knocked again, twice, and stepped back.

But the girl was inconsolable, undeterred and undisturbed by the sound of a neighbour.

Stephanie tried again and spoke at the door. 'I just want you to know that you can talk to me. If you want to. I'm just across the hall. In the room opposite.'

The girl began to talk, but not to her and not in English. It sounded like Russian. A language as hard and fast as the Russian she'd heard spoken before, the words struggling through sobs.

'English? Do you speak English?' *Just open the door*, she wanted to shout. *We can communicate with our eyes, our faces. I'll even hold you. But please stop. It's too much . . . too much for me . . .*

Outside the house, Knacker's dog barked and leaped against the full extent of its chain.

Inside the building, from two floors down, footsteps erupted and skittered in haste against the tiled floor.

The footsteps bumped up the stairs to the first floor. Then began a scrabbling, urgent ascent to the second storey.

Stephanie didn't move, was not sure what to do. Though she was curious as to the appearance of another tenant, she was intimidated by the swift and loud nature of the movement up through the house, that also suggested the motion had been evoked by the woman's distress.

The light on the second floor landing clicked out. Stephanie turned for the light switch but only succeeded in covering her mouth because of . . . what? The gust. The sudden pall of . . . what was it? Sweat? Old male or animal sweat.

She gasped to keep the stench out of her lungs. Remembered the fungal scent when she'd sat on a bus behind a man with no grasp of personal hygiene. The smell in this house suggested a lather had been worked up by anger and alcohol. It was accompanied by a sudden, unpleasant sensation of herself twisting within thickly haired arms while she struggled to breathe. She didn't know why she had imagined this, and was too panicked to understand, but a determined muscular violence seemed to be driving the odour through the house.

The hot animal smell, now spiced with what she recognized as gum disease, replaced the scent of aged and unfinished wood, and so entirely that she doubted the underfloor cavity scent had ever existed.

Instinct informed her that if she didn't get inside her room and lock the door swiftly, something terrible, and perhaps final, would happen to her this very night. Irrational to think this, like she was a child running up the stairs to her bedroom all over again, so convinced something was following her that she'd often heard footsteps behind. But she did move, and fast, through the doorway of her room, to fall against the inside of the door. She turned the key the moment the door banged shut.

Upstairs a window opened and she heard Knacker roar, 'Shat up!' at the dog, which fell to whining and then silence.

Outside her room the footsteps reached the second floor and stopped, as if the owner had paused to catch his breath, before the bangs of his angry feet commenced down the hallway, *to her room* . . .

Stephanie stepped away from the door, on the verge of a scream.

The footsteps stopped outside.

A fist banged on the door of the room opposite her own.

Thank God it's her he wants and not me.

The door across the hall opened.

'No,' she whispered. *Don't let him in!* she screamed inside her head.

Silence.

Not moving, she stood in her room, a few feet behind the locked door, her hands over her mouth, her eyes watering from the strain of not blinking, her head aching from the strain of incomprehension.

At the end of her hearing a bed began to creak vigorously, back and forth. The noise failed to conceal the accompanying sound of rhythmic grunts.

TEN

After Stephanie checked inside the wardrobe, under the desk, behind the curtains and beneath the bedframe, she climbed under her duvet and lay awake with the lights on. She'd moved the bedside lamp closer to the edge of the bedside cabinet, with the metal shade angled upwards to add power to the ceiling light, and to make it more accessible for one of her arms in an emergency.

The noise of sex across the hall had been frenzied but brief. The girl had not made a sound during the encounter. Stephanie had feared that she'd heard a rape, because why would a woman so distressed consent to sex with another tenant, and one whose movements through the house implied aggression?

It could not have been Knacker in the girl's room because he was upstairs; she'd heard him shout at the dog. She wondered if the man that had thundered up through the house was the owner of the leather-soled shoes that she had heard leaving the house that morning. Not catching up with him may have proven to be a lucky escape. The first break she had caught here.

Distaste mixed with her fear of sexual assault as she considered the nature of the relationship between the girl and the man that smelled like an animal. Had the girl

ADAM NEVILL

offered a whimper of resistance, Stephanie would have called the police. But her neighbour hadn't made any sound, as if she were no longer even present in the room across the hall.

The man was still with her too, perhaps lying with her as if they were lovers. Maybe they were lovers entangled insanely in one of those love-hate relationships fuelled by aggression, and the girl had grown used to his smell. Stephanie squeezed her eyes shut at all of the horror in that thought.

She opened her eyes and tried to make sense of the atmosphere that had engulfed her out in the corridor: the cold emptiness, fragranced like an uninhabited wooden space, all around her. But she never came close to an understanding of the scent, beyond entertaining a brief and unconvincing notion that she had smelled stale air rising, *but rising from where?*

The same bewilderment applied to her attempt to understand the bestial smell. From whom could such a powerful gust of raw and feral maleness have risen? For how long would you have to avoid soap and water to cultivate such an odour?

She wondered if her interpretation of the male presence had been affected by her confrontation with Knacker. Maybe their argument had tainted her into believing she was in danger from men in this building. She didn't know. Didn't really know anything about this place, or anyone inside it. All she knew was that she was tense and frightened and anxious and exhausted, with nowhere else to go. But she also realized that no matter how bad her life seemed, the life of someone nearby was probably worse.

The memory of the woman's grief still made her nerves jangle. She imagined being in another country and in the same situation as the girl; a country in which she didn't know the language and couldn't even understand an offer of help at her door.

How did I get here?

All she'd wanted was a room and a job. Maybe that was all her neighbour had wanted too.

She told herself that she only needed to get through this night, just one more night, and if she heard anything around her bed, she would grab her most essential bag, call a taxi and go straight to the city centre. She would walk around in the dark until the Bullring opened.

Outside her window the thick mass of foliage that engulfed the neglected garden shook, rustled and sighed in the wind. Stephanie imagined a foul sea lapping against the back of the house, an attempt to reclaim the old bricks, stained cement and creaking timbers, to cover it all with the vines and thorns and skeletal deciduous tangles she could see from her window by daylight. It was an unruly vegetation that rose as high as the top of the fence, on all sides of the garden, like a tidal surge over coastal walls.

Her eyelids gradually became heavy from fatigue, from the near sleepless night before. Eventually she relaxed over the edge of sleep.

But only for short periods, from which she would jerk awake to find herself lying in the same position in a lit room, with the garden's noise still active beneath her window. Once, as she came round from being half asleep, she was sure the window was open because the thrash and scrape of bushes and tree branches below seemed unpleas-antly loud and active around the bed.

The final time she awoke, she realized the room had somehow become dark as she'd dozed.

ELEVEN

And within the darkness she heard a voice. A woman's voice. The voice in the fireplace. Only the voice was louder than it had been the night before. And now Stephanie better understood the tone to be comprised of weariness and resignation, a tired voice that seemed to be recounting grievances.

Snatches reached her ears. 'And then you said . . . I said . . . I wouldn't . . . unreasonable . . . but who was I . . . you, you told me . . . you swore . . . it was . . . meant something . . . a sign . . . frightened, the more I . . . and now I know . . .'

Stephanie lay still and acknowledged that her desire to know what the woman was saying exceeded her reluctant curiosity about why she could even hear the voice. This speech wasn't aimed at her; she was overhearing something, like a phone call further down a train carriage, or someone talking to themselves who didn't realize you were within earshot.

'. . . involved . . . you are . . . you said . . . not that simple . . . must understand . . .'

The monotony, the continuous nature of the dialogue, also suggested a preoccupation with something unresolved that a mind was making audible to itself, as if a relentless communication with oneself might lead to an answer. Stephanie had often walked in on her stepmother doing the same thing, or stood in great discomfort outside a room while Val worked herself into a volatile state through imaginary conversations, either with her, her dead father, people she knew, people she didn't know but knew of, while always playing herself as the injured party.

Only when polythene crinkled beneath the bed did Stephanie stop listening to the voice in the fireplace. Alarming as the voice was, there was something passive and disinterested about the tone. The sounds under her bed were incalculably worse. Particularly tonight, because they immediately suggested that something much bigger than a mouse had roused mere feet beneath where she lay.

The activity was reminiscent of rustling caused by whatever the polythene was wrapped around gradually shifting inside its coverings. And she'd happily accept a rat as an explanation right now. But as the only legitimate resident of a room that was so cold, either chilled to the bone by her fear, or naturally bereft of even a vestige of warmth because the central heating was off, she felt a scream build as her thoughts fragmented.

She looked down her body but couldn't see the duvet she lay beneath, and just peered, unblinking, into the lightless space that began on the surface of her eyes and seemed to continue into a freezing forever.

For a moment she suspected she was upside down and that the top of her head was level with the floor. The suspicion became belief as her mind failed to orientate the position of her body. And into the maelstrom of half thoughts, instincts and imaginings that her mind struggled to be more than, she received an impression that there was no floor at all and that she hung in space, revolving and adrift from solidity.

Dead. This is death.

She desperately wanted to move to regain a sense of the physical world she must have woken into. But if she moved she was terrified the other things in the darkness would be alerted to her presence: predators with blank eyes and gaping maws, changing course to follow a vibration in the depths of a freezing black ocean.

Her scream only added itself to the room when a floorboard shifted and groaned at the end of her bed, mere inches from her feet.

Into her awareness the missing dimensions of the physical world reassembled, prompted by the sound of the intruder, as if gravity itself had made a sudden reappearance inside the black space. An understanding that she was lying down, flat on her back, and not turning in the air should have been a blessing. But how could it when someone stood at the foot of her bed? An intruder who leaned forward, poised to climb onto the mattress with her. The bed coverings dipped on either side of her ankles.

Stephanie thrust one arm out from the covers and seized the lamp beside the bed. 'No. Don't,' was all she could manage in a quiet, almost resigned, tone of voice.

She found the rubber cord, the switch.

Held her breath.

When she saw the face her heart would stop. Which made her wonder if it would be better to endure this within darkness . . . whatever *this* was.

Stephanie switched on the light.

TWELVE

She gulped at the air like she had been holding her breath under cold water for a dangerous length of time. She drew her arms and legs into herself and shuffled up the bed and into the corner, dragging the bedclothes with her. Being uncovered within the room was unbearable.

She stared at the walls and the furnishings, peeked around the edges of the bed, and saw only those outmoded articles of furniture within the tacky, scruffy walls, and nothing else. There was no one on her bed and no one in her room.

At least no one you can see.

She stood up on the bed. Took the duvet with her and tottered down the mattress to hit the light switch on the wall beside the door to get the ceiling light on.

Leaning her back against the wall, she peered into the space under the desk, scrutinized the gap between the bedside cabinet and the mattress, assessed the curtains for a bulge in case someone had tried to conceal themselves against the locked windows.

There were no bulges, and no one crouched under the desk or lying on the floor beside her bed. The room was as empty as it had been before she fell asleep *with the lights on.*

The lights!

Who had switched the lights off? Someone had been in here.

A presence.

A presence that could kill the light.

What else could it kill?

Stephanie looked down at the sheets. Nothing rustled beneath her bed anymore. Nothing had crawled out from under there. The room was sealed. The room was locked.

And you're locked inside it.

She leapt off the bed and made sure to land clear of an area that an arm might reach into from under the bed-frame, with a hand swiping about.

She stared into the empty space beneath her bed: floor-boards, a multitude of dust rabbits, a section of red rug, the plain wall in shadow.

She moved to the curtains and yanked them aside to look at the grubby glass of two locked sash windows.

Bent over, her hands placed on the table to support her weight, she breathed in deeply, exhaled, breathed in. She stared at the empty black grate of the fireplace. At the long unused iron hearth, set between two Doric pillars of hard-wood, painted a creamy colour. Impossibly, just impossibly, the voice had come out of *there*.

Across the hallway, her neighbour's door opened, swung inwards and banged against an item of furniture.

Stephanie flinched and clasped her hands to her mouth. Her face screwed up but she was too frightened to cry. The coming together of noises and movements and energy that should not be, that could not be, seemed to merge into a critical mass around her.

Heavy footsteps crossed the dark corridor and paused outside her door. The round door knob quickly turned: once, twice, three times. The plastic handle rattled loosely inside the wood.

'Who is it?' she said to the door in a voice she barely recognized as her own.

There was no answer. But whoever had turned the handle, whoever had tried to enter her room, must still be there, outside, listening. She'd heard no footsteps retreat.

DAY TWO

THIRTEEN

'Awright, nice day at work? What flavour was them crusts you was giving out today? Don't know how you can stand a job like that. Demeaning, ain't it?' Knacker grinned as if triumphant at her return to the house. He came out of the room at the end of the second floor corridor, quickly pulling the door closed behind him. The hallway lights winked out.

Stephanie had only returned to collect as much as she could carry, and to make the most difficult phone call of her life to Ryan, before heading to New Street train station to buy a single ticket to Coventry with the last of her money, so she could put the disaster that had been her new start in Birmingham out of its misery.

Ryan hadn't picked up her calls so far, or responded to her text messages, but if he allowed her to return to his place, and if she travelled to Coventry tonight, the deposit and advance rent were gone for good, something she'd begrudgingly accepted that day like the removal of a front tooth to permanently destroy her smile. Ryan would then have to accompany her to this house at the weekend to pick up the rest of her bags, while also needing to sub her with cash.

Either that or she left the building this evening and

walked around Birmingham city centre all night until the Bullring opened.

Not even six full months away from her stepmother, after fleeing what she had known as the family home since the age of eleven, but a house that now belonged to Val, and she'd already sunk to last resorts: no money, borrowed beds, an ex-boyfriend's mercy.

'Fack's sake. Put them fings on again, will ya?'

Stephanie hit the switch quickly, her speed motivated by the thought of being inside a lightless passage with Knacker. She opened the door to her room and stepped inside.

'Hang on, hang on, I need to speak wiv you.'

'I have nothing to say to you.'

'Suit yourself. Just wanted to show you somefing.'

Stephanie dropped her bag on the bed and turned to close the door at the precise moment Knacker appeared in the doorway to deter her. The lights went out behind him. He shook his head with irritation and slapped them on again. It struck her as odd that he would be annoyed with his own policy of timed lighting. Maybe it was his parents' innovation.

His presence made her tense and nervous, but he made no move to enter the room. He sniffed up his long nose; the bones at the top were thickened by poorly healed breaks. 'I know the conversation we had last night was awkward.'

Awkward? She stared at him, aghast.

'We might have got off on the wrong foot and all that. So I've been having a fink today. And fought I was probably being a bit harsh last night.' Clearly delighted he had her full attention, he immediately resumed his tedious loquaciousness. 'I fought, have a heart, Knacker. Girl's on her own and all that. New city. No fella. No friends . . .'

'*What?* What do you want?' She couldn't bare him outlining the downsides of her life; she'd stuff hot wax in her own ears before she listened to another word.

The lights clicked out. She wished *he* would click out. Knacker slapped them on again. When the light returned he looked startled at having been plunged into such a heavy darkness. Then his eyes lidded, like a crafty serpent she thought, but the half-smile never left his face. Very slowly he said, 'I was getting to that. If you'd let me finish.'

She raised her hands. 'What? I can have my deposit, can I?'

He raised a finger as if talking to a naughty child. 'Ah, ah, ah. Don't put words in my mouf.'

'Then what do you want?'

'If you would care to follow me, I will show you.'

'Why would I go anywhere with you?'

'My, my, someone's had a bad day, but don't take it out on me, yeah, when I'm trying to do you a favour.'

Stephanie closed her eyes. Another night feeling terrified without sleep, followed by another eight hours on her feet, holding a tray of muffin fragments outside a coffee shop, gave her a sense that something inside her had finally broken and that nothing would be able to fix it. She opened her eyes and when she spoke there was no bite or strength left in her voice. 'Favour? My deposit is the only favour I want.'

'You're like a broken record, you are.' He broke into a bad falsetto to mimic her voice, in revenge she presumed.

'Deposit. Deposit. Deposit.' Then he grinned and showed her his peg teeth. 'Some fings are worth putting a down payment on, yeah? Holding deposit. You don't wanna look a gift horse in the mouf, sister. So follow me and see what you fink a this. No pressure. I ain't trying to sell you nuffin'. I'm doing you a favour. You don't want it, I'll even help you carry them bags down to the street, cus that might be your only other option, yeah? Else why would you be here?'

She wanted to be a man; she wanted to punch his face. But she was a girl denied even rudeness because he was unstable.

'Come on, come on. This way, darlin'.' Knacker stepped away and into the corridor, beaming at her. At the new distance his eyes appeared weird, like they were too close together, and a fraction of a second too slow to move, like he'd spent a significant amount of his life frying his brains with skunk weed or glue.

The lights clicked off and returned him to the darkness.

FOURTEEN

'What you fink of this then?'

The sight of the room made her feel more awake than she'd been all day. It was on the first floor and didn't appear to be a part of the same building that housed her room, the kitchen or the bathroom. The latter dismal place she'd not even been able to bear that morning; before leaving the house she'd just put new make-up on in her room and dressed in the previous day's clothes.

And like a replay of yesterday morning, as she'd made her way out of the building she'd heard a man shuffle across the tiles of the hall; he must live on the ground floor, because she was certain there had been no sound of movement on the staircase as she descended from the second floor to the first. So the man must have coincidentally come out of a ground floor door and left the house at the same time as her on two consecutive days. Only this morning her paranoia suggested that he was not running from her but circling her.

Stephanie had paused on the stairs when she heard the footsteps, and not moved until the front door had shut behind him. If the man leaving the building had been throwing himself into the crying Russian girl the night before, then Stephanie had not wanted to so much as glimpse the back of his head. Because he would have been the same man that had stood outside the door of her room, listening, after he'd finished with the Russian.

While Stephanie had waited on the stairs for the male tenant to leave the building, she'd also noticed a strip of yellow light under the door of the bathroom on the first floor. So maybe another tenant had been inside the bathroom getting ready for their day. It could not have been the Russian girl, because Stephanie had not heard her neighbour's door open at any time during her mostly sleepless early morning vigil.

With the man standing outside her room the night before, she'd sat with her back against the door for two hours before sleep overcame her around one a.m. And within those two hours of tense, alert wakefulness, she had not heard him creep away. Not heard any sound in the corridor outside her room. Or, *thank God*, inside it either.

Even as the sky lightened at dawn, after she stirred, near concussed with sleep deprivation, when Stephanie eventually inched the door open there had been no one in the corridor and not a trace of the smells or the atmosphere she'd encountered in the night. The Russian girl's room had been quiet and unlit.

Knacker stood and grinned by the foot of the bed in the first floor room that he was so keen to show her.

Stephanie never passed through the doorway. 'I don't understand.'

Knacker's big hyena grin evolved into a mucky laugh thickened by catarrh. 'It's yours, girl. If you want it. Same price an' everyfing. Least 'til the whole house is done up.

Fought it might be a bit more comfortable, like. You know, might help wiv your current dilemma.'

'What . . .' She didn't know what to say, or what to make of the offer, or the room. This was a room you might see in an eighties film. Two triple-bulb spotlights cast an icy glow over black walls and the starkness of a white carpet and ceiling, but without fully lighting the room. Mirrored wardrobe doors gave the impression the room was much bigger.

'As I told you, I've been fixin' the place up, room by room. This kind of job takes time, darlin'. I finished it up today. There's nuffin' I can't do wiv these hands. You know the Dorchester, yeah, on Park Lane? I did a total refit there. That kind of craftsmanship don't come cheap neither.'

He carried on talking but his voice barely registered while Stephanie stared at the room. She heard snatches: 'Bloke said . . . how much . . . I said, get out of it, what you fink I am?'

The bed was enormous, the iron ends decorative and painted white. There was a mirrored glass table with chrome edges set under the window, that appeared to have come from a hairdresser's that thought itself classy. Across the room from the bed was a bulky television set, with a case made from grey plastic. She remembered the style from years ago.

'Then I was finking about me old mum and dad's place . . . Lot of work, but me and me cousin . . . what they always did, have lodgers, like . . .'

Stephanie was aware of the chemical odours of carpet cleaner and air freshener hanging in what smelled like an older space. Because that's what it was: an unaired musty room, with dated décor that gave the impression it had been sealed away for some time, left unused and unchanged. Knacker might have made an attempt at cleaning it, but the paintwork was old, sallow in places on the ceiling. There was no smell or sign of recent decoration or refurbishments. Knacker was lying. But the room was still a vast improvement on the one she had; a room she would not be able to spend another night inside.

'Don't have to make up your mind straightaway, but my phone's been ringing all day. Rooms here is getting a lot of interest. This one will get snapped up by the first person that sees it. But I fought being as you was already here and paid up for the first mumf . . .'

If it were possible for her to tolerate one more night at this address, in this room, and to go to work Friday, then she could leave tomorrow night with three days' pay. And she wouldn't have to make that call to Ryan tonight.

She could be frightened in this building, and anxious about her safety amongst at least two male presences, or try and get to Coventry tonight, where she had never even found a single day's work, while dead on her feet and broke, and plunge into another kind of emotional manipulation from an ex-boyfriend. That was the choice.

One more night?

At least this was a new room; it wasn't *that* room. No two rooms could be alike.

Could they?

Knacker was manipulative, but his only desire, she was sure, was money. The other one's business was not clear, but she'd not even seen him, and his dealings were with the Russian girl up on the second floor. This room was even on a different floor of the house.

'OK. Thanks.' As soon as she'd spoken, she began worrying that her desperate acceptance might be another mistake she would pay for dearly in the very near future.

'Fought you'd see sense. Young girl like you don't wanna be movin' about all the time, dossin' on floors, like—'

'Who lived in here before?'

'What's that matter? She ain't here no more. Place is vacant.'

'The other room. The one I have. It's . . .'

His bony face turned to her quickly, the chin raised. 'What about it?'

Stephanie didn't know what to say. *I won't stay inside the room because it's haunted*, was not an option. That morning, as soon as she'd put some distance between herself and the house, *haunted* became a word coated in an absurd skin; it didn't even have to leave her mouth to make her feel ludicrous.

Stephanie studied Knacker's face, and suspected there might be a trace of apprehension in his expression over her line of enquiry. Either that or it was the defensive posture he adopted about the house. But while so tired and confused, she wasn't sure she could trust any of her perceptions. Perhaps no one could help her, save a priest or a psychiatrist, but the need to talk to someone about the room, to escape the prison of paranoia that her mind had become, became compulsive. 'It . . . the room. It's not right.'

'Eh? What you talkin' about? Place is old. Might need

a tart-up, but nuffin' major, like. This whole place is sound as—'

'No, I didn't mean that. I heard something. In my room. At night.'

Knacker grinned. 'Got spooked, did ya?' He was thinking of laughing at her.

She cut him off. 'I wasn't just frightened. It was worse than that.'

Knacker narrowed his eyes as if he was hooding them so she couldn't read them. He sniffed. 'Not sure I am comfortable with what you are suggesting.'

'Why?'

'I don't have patience wiv all that crap.'

'But I heard a voice in my room. Two nights running.'

He laughed. 'You heard a TV. Coulda been mine. Fink I had it on.'

'Didn't sound like a TV. And the sound . . . under the bed, I thought they were mice, but I'm not sure—'

'Fack's sake, girl. You jumpin' at the sound a mice. Not that I'm saying there is any here. I cleared them all out. The house's been empty for a while, that's all. They get into empty houses, see. Cus of the cold. Maybe there's still one left.'

'But that wouldn't explain—'

'You're pullin' my leg, you are. What you after, rent reduction? I've heard it all now.'

'Someone was inside my room.'

Knacker stopped laughing and sniffed. He looked wary.

'I heard someone. Twice. Both nights. But they weren't there when I turned the light on. Who lived in that—'

'As I said, I would fank you, yeah, I would appreciate

you not making remarks about me mum and dad's house, yeah? I got no time for none of that rubbish. So you is out of line.'

'Sorry.' She said it automatically, though she wasn't sorry at all.

'How would you like it, if I came round your mam's house, and I started going on about all of this, yeah? So I'll fank you to not talk about it again. This place is gonna be somefing, I can tell you, when it's all done up, so I don't want none of that, yeah, about my house. Reputation and all that.' He sniffed loudly and relaxed his shoulders. Getting his own way was important to Knacker.

It struck her as odd that he wouldn't put a name to the subject, but told herself to just focus on getting through the night. Even if it only meant a few hours' sleep. *Get your pay tomorrow. Grab your bags and take off. You can do it*. If she upset Knacker now he'd put her back in her old room, or on the street, and she'd spend the next few hours chasing after Ryan, and trying to get a train to another city, to stay in another place she didn't want to be. And there was no guarantee she even could crash at Ryan's place. He'd still not been in touch.

Towards the landlord she now felt the edge of an emotion that gave her a shudder of self-loathing: *gratitude*.

'Anyway, you got a new place. Best room in the house. Even fought about taking this one myself. But I like my privacy upstairs.'

'But can you at least tell me who lived in this room?'

His frown told her the question was unwelcome. 'How should I know? Place was empty when I took it on, like. Me mum and dad had all kinds here. Lodgers. Stoodents.

Girls. You know. Gave them somewhere decent to stay, like. I'm just carrying on the family tradition.'

'Are all the rooms different?'

'Yeah. A bit, like.'

'You never came here to visit your parents?'

'What is this, the fird degree? What's it matter to you? Specially when you is getting in here on the ground, in a new development, like. Gonna be a show home when I'm froo with it.'

'That girl in the room opposite me was really upset last night. The Russian girl. I think she is Russian. How many people live here? There's a man on the ground floor, isn't there? I heard him go into that Russian girl's room last night, I—'

'Bit nosy, ain't ya?' Again he tensed up but wouldn't meet her eye.

'That girl might need help.'

'My advice to you is don't interfere with fings that don't concern you, yeah?'

'I was just worried about her.'

'What am I, a social worker? People's business is their business. Long as people pay and keep themselves to themselves, I ain't their keeper.' Then he broke into a big grin to change the subject. 'Oh, I forgot to tell you somefing. You is getting a bit a company soon. Uvver girls, like. There's two movin' in very soon. Comin' up with my cousin.'

'Great,' she said, without any conviction, and immediately felt sorry for the future tenants. 'Coming up' was an odd expression too. *From where?* As Knacker spoke she also developed a suspicion that he'd been unable to let the rooms for long periods because of the disturbances. If she had experienced strange things here then surely others would have done too. *Experienced what though?* And hadn't he also said that he'd forgotten the 'Room for Rent' advert was in the grocer's window, and that he'd decided not to let the place? That he'd only taken pity on her? His story had changed twice in three days, because now 'uvver girls' were moving in. He had lied. Again.

'Wait there, yeah. I'll bring your bags down. See, I ain't all bad, sister.'

'It's OK, I can do it.'

Before she finished speaking Knacker's new trainers were bumping away into the darkness of the first floor corridor.

FIFTEEN

Stephanie rushed a shower and moved her head out of the cascade of water every few seconds to look over the side of the bath tub. *Just in case*.

But no one muttered beneath her feet.

It felt better, felt *safer*, to shower and wash her hair before she went to bed, rather than in the morning before work. She had no idea how she would feel by the time the sun rose and whether she would have the courage to wash herself. She refused to go another day without a shower and the water's heat was a small comfort she was greedy for.

She'd not been able to look up the stairwell as she'd walked down the first floor passage to the bathroom, but repeatedly reminded herself that she now had a different room on a different floor of the house, desperately wringing as much reassurance as possible from the thin new truth.

She felt lightheaded and still hadn't eaten. Back in her room she had crisps, a Double Decker chocolate bar, some supermarket sandwiches in a plastic carton – half price because they expired today. Something she'd snatched up before catching the bus home, unable to face the dirty kitchen and microwave preparation.

Home? Don't call it that. It is not home.

When one of her colleagues at the shopping centre had said, 'Thank God it's nearly Friday', and then recited her plans for the weekend that seemed to be entirely constructed out of *home, boyfriend, friends, home, boyfriend, friends,* each word had struck Stephanie with pangs of envy that wilted to a sadness as thick as the mumps inside her throat. She'd needed to busy herself inside her rucksack, looking for a bottle of water that she didn't need, so the other two girls didn't see the tears welling in her eyes.

Home. She had nothing that resembled a home, which in turn reminded her of her stepmother on that final day: the bleached and lined face, the lips sucked into the mouth, the jaw trembling and eyelids flickering, the complexion turning red, but then so bloodless at the point of no self-restraint, while her eyes purpled with rage before the screaming and shaking and slapping. It was something she'd seen too many times since her father died: the ranting that could continue all night.

She recalled Christmas. Val had screamed at her, through a door, for three hours without cease, until her voice gave out. Stephanie had pushed her bed against the door to keep the maniac outside. But Val had run downstairs and used a paring knife to cut Stephanie's clothes that were drying on a rack, before snapping her CDs in half. Val had then smashed every plate and glass in the kitchen until her fury puttered into sobs.

Against her will she revisited the most enduring memory of her youth, when her dad had held her stepmother by the shoulders and demanded to know what she'd done with Stephanie's guinea pig. The next day he'd taken his thirteen-year-old daughter to Dawlish for a week, where they'd felt like crying all of the time, and sometimes did, with their heads together.

Home.

Her plans for the weekend revolved around adding Pay-as-you-go credit to her phone, and doing sums to work out how little she would need to spend on food and bus fare to scrape another month's rent together.

The other two girls she'd worked with already had jobs lined up for the following week: *modelling*, or standing by a sports car in another shopping centre, wearing red satin shorts and trying to sell raffle tickets. But Stephanie still hadn't heard from the agency, and all the girls used the same firm.

Shivering, she switched off the shower, climbed out of the bath and yanked her towel from the radiator. The radiator was hot and her towel was warm. She clutched it around her shoulders and nearly wept from the pleasure it gave her.

The room was cold again. She looked to the window and wouldn't have been surprised to see the glass encased in ice.

'What is my name?'

'Oh God, no. No. No. No,' she whispered into the steam that hung like a mist about her face.

'What is my name?' There it was again, a voice rising from where she had just been standing in the bath. And the notion that she had just woken someone was hard to shift.

Stephanie opened the bathroom door and darted outside. Steam from her shower drifted out behind her and into the unlit corridor. The darkness of the house seemed vast.

The bathroom gradually took shape through the thinning steam: speckled mirror, grubby sink unit, grimy windows, red carpet flecked with bits, bath tub. And out of this dismal space came the voice again.

'. . . before here . . . that time. Nowhere . . . to where the other . . . the cold . . . is my name? . . . I can't . . .'

Stephanie's thoughts scrabbled through a nonsense of panic; chaos filled with a child-like begging for all to be as it was and not like this.

A recording?

This was the same thing she'd heard yesterday morning. Only it was louder now. So it could indeed be a recording. A trick. A joke. Something – some device – was under the bath and playing the same recording. Maybe this was just someone's attempt to freak the new girl out.

'What is my name?'

Stephanie strode inside the bathroom and stamped a foot on the floor. 'Stop it! Stop it now!' Stamped her foot again and didn't care who heard her. 'Enough!'

'I . . . don't . . . can you find . . . where . . . where . . . this . . . am I?'

The speaker, a girl, a teenager maybe, began to cry. And so did Stephanie as a terrible feeling of fear and misery enshrouded and then seeped through her until she was saturated with anguish.

But not her own anguish.

The grim sensations that occupied the physical space of the bathroom did not belong to her. With what presence of mind she retained, Stephanie was certain of this: the tangible misery of the room was contagious, unnatural and fast acting.

Stephanie lowered herself to her hands and knees and crawled across the hard, dry carpet towards the side of the bath. 'Who are you? Can you hear me? Please, tell me?'

SIXTEEN

Stephanie lay awake in her bed. Overhead, a dim white glow filtered more than shone from the spotlights. The bulbs were thick with dust but their illumination was augmented by her bedside reading lamp at floor level. With the volume muted, the television set provided some extra light. There was no Freeview so the set had five channels; Channel 5 was mostly static and shadows.

Knacker's cat-lick clean of the room had not extended above head height or involved dusting. The carpet had been vacuumed and the top of the mirrored table had been wiped clean, but on closer inspection not much else had been done to improve the condition of a long unoccupied space.

Stephanie wondered what kind of person would have painted walls so dark and had a white carpet. There was something immature about the style, something masculine too, like it had been put together by a Lothario to attract women, but a long time ago. She couldn't imagine a mature, working-class couple, with a son like Knacker, was responsible for the décor. Maybe a lodger had personalized the room.

From the bed Stephanie looked about the area she had just searched like a forensic detective. She'd found no trace of the previous occupant, beside a sachet of the tiny crystals included with new garments, and three plastic coat hangers that didn't match. These oddments were inside the vast mirrored wardrobe. There was nothing under the bed beside the large dust rabbits similar to those in her second floor room.

Her pile of bags rested against the wall beneath the barred window.

Were barred windows even legal?

It wasn't even ten p.m. and the encroach of sleep was the anticipation of a coma. But her sluggish thoughts returned to the voice of the girl in the bathroom. Whoever had been speaking hadn't answered her, or even seemed to hear her, despite an uncomfortable assumption that the speaker had been aware of her.

She'd nearly gone downstairs and knocked on the solitary door of the ground floor, which must open onto an apartment beneath the bathroom, but she had not found the courage because the smelly man lived down there.

After a while the voice beneath the bath had faded, and moved further away until it stopped. Only to start up again at a distance, far beneath the floor of the bathroom. The voice, she had ultimately decided, must have been a recording. Same with the voice in the fireplace of her first room. She tried her best to believe that a sophisticated practical joke with a sinister motive, rather than the presence of the supernatural, was responsible for the sounds. And sometimes she did believe this. Mostly, she didn't know what to believe.

Her attempt at an explanation did not account for

how sad and miserable the voice had made her feel. Just being close to it had made her heart break. Nor did her theories account for the plummet in the bathroom's temperature compared with the draughty but heated corridor outside. Once the voice had stopped and she'd left the bathroom, the remainder of the first floor had felt like a greenhouse.

The side panel of the white chipboard frame that encased the bath tub had come away in her hands after a few tugs. Damp had turned the board at the corners of the panel to what looked like sodden Weetabix. Under the tub she'd found wooden floorboards, balls of grey dust, wood shavings, a screw, an empty paint tin, a curl of tar paper, and a smell of mildew mingled with a trace of the rotten bin smell. It was the same odour she'd detected when she'd first sat on the dusty toilet the day before.

There had been nothing electrical in the visible spaces around the fibre glass tub: no little speakers, no holes or trapdoor in the floorboards, and no wires or electrical paraphernalia. Once the side panel was off, the voice had not been any louder either, or easier to hear, but had sounded as if it were rising from deeper inside the house, from downstairs.

If she heard it again she would go and get Knacker and make him stand in the bathroom and listen to it. She would make him tell her where the voice came from.

Stephanie set the alarm. Squashed herself against the wall and waited for sleep. She was tired enough to hallucinate, but told herself the room was unfamiliar, that she was on edge and she would surely wake at the first strange noise that announced itself. She would not be taken unawares again.

Beneath her pillow lay a blunt vegetable paring knife she had appropriated from the kitchen.

SEVENTEEN

The sound that roused Stephanie from sleep was the door to the neighbouring room opening. This was followed by the sound of feet padding out of the room and into the passage.

Stephanie rolled out of bed and ran to the door of her room.

She was sure the room beside hers was empty. There had been no light beneath the door when she passed the room to go to and from the bathroom earlier. To her knowledge, no one had entered the room since, and not a sound had passed through the shared wall. In fact, all evening following her shower, the entire first floor had remained silent.

Opening her own door a few inches she peered into the unlit corridor. All she could see was the distant stairwell window, nothing more than a dim rectangle of ambient light. But she could still hear the pad of feet, a sound issuing from further down the corridor.

Realizing the light in her room would alert her position to whoever was in the corridor, she opened her door wider, to fully reveal herself and to not appear sneaky. The flood of light from her room showed Stephanie an empty corridor and a lifeless landing at its end. Her entire coating of skin seemed to shrink as each hair follicle made itself known with a prickle of static.

How could this be?

The bathroom door shut.

Stephanie jumped.

Presumably it had been closed by her neighbour who must have just left the corridor to approach the bathroom from the landing. And been out of sight from the doorway of Stephanie's room?

Possible.

Her neighbour might also have been asleep when Knacker had shown her the room earlier. Or had returned to the room while Stephanie showered or slept. The idea that she was meant to wake now, and had been awoken, had to be supressed.

She went back inside her room and retrieved her phone from the floor beside the bed. The time was twenty to eleven. So she hadn't even been asleep for thirty minutes and immediately felt cheated by time; she dearly wished that dawn was only minutes away.

Stephanie returned to the door of her room and narrowed the gap, but left it ajar in the doorframe so she could better hear the neighbour come out of the bathroom. She was sure it was a young woman because of the lightness of the step.

She sat on the end of her bed to wait for the bathroom door to reopen; waited long enough to become uncomfortable with her own door remaining ajar for so long. While she waited, Stephanie pondered what the woman could be doing in the bathroom. *Shower? Bath? Constipation?* She waited another twenty minutes before becoming impatient, and then she marched through the passageway to the bathroom. She would not sleep tonight until she knew who was living in the room next door.

Outside of the bathroom, Stephanie cleared her throat. 'Excuse me? Miss? I wonder how long you will be. I need to use the bathroom.'

There was no answer.

Stephanie knocked on the door.

No response.

Stephanie turned the plastic door handle. It was unlocked and opened onto an unlit room. Behind her, the landing light clicked out.

She turned in panic. Rushed across the landing in near darkness to flail at the wall with her hands, but could not find the switch that was somewhere beside the open kitchen door. She shuffled back to the outline of the bathroom doorframe, yanked at the light cord and lit up the empty, silent room.

Where are you?

This wasn't possible. She'd heard her neighbour's feet and the bathroom door close.

The other bedrooms were further up the corridor towards the front of the house. So had the girl crept back to her room and re-entered it without Stephanie hearing?

Not possible.

Stephanie hurriedly returned to her own room. Closed the door and locked it. She climbed back into bed and stared at the television without noticing what was on the screen.

Within minutes footsteps padded down the corridor, from the direction of the bathroom. Stephanie did not move. She held her breath so as to not make any sound at all.

The door of the room next door opened and closed.

EIGHTEEN

The space was narrow, dim and lined with old grey pipes. In parts, a furry cladding was wrapped around the pipes and secured with electrical tape that was so old the tape had crisped and begun to peel away.

The walls Stephanie's shoulders squeezed through were made of plasterboard. Some words had been written on them with chalk. Stephanie read 'Misha is a slag', and hurried past to follow her stepmother through the tunnel. Val turned her head and said, 'Will you keep up. You've already made me late!'

Stephanie found herself to be a girl again, and she recognized her clothes from the faded pictures in the family photograph albums; pictures mostly taken at that unhappy time when her stepmum made a first unwelcome appearance into her young life. Back then, Val had been all smiles and permed red hair with matching red spectacle frames – which is how she looked right now. And despite her size, Val had no trouble moving through the narrow space.

Stephanie worried her stepmother was pulling too far away. Her own quilted coat kept getting stuck on things – a pipe bracket, a timber joist.

Val disappeared round a corner at the end of the narrow space.

Stephanie shuffled sideways to reach the end of the passage. At the turn the gap sloped into darkness. The space between these walls was just as narrow as before, but Stephanie could not see or hear her stepmother inside the darkness any longer.

She didn't have much time to query Val's disappearance because her own feet slipped down the passage and she batted her hands against the walls that were now made of galvanized metal and offered nothing to grab hold of. Her sphincter tingled as her feet slid faster and faster across the metal floor. She wondered if she should sit down before she fell.

Stephanie slipped into a room with dark brown and orange wallpaper, a big floral velour settee and two matching armchairs. The lightshades were made from pearlescent glass bowls. On the circular coffee table was a stack of magazines. The top one was called *Fiesta* and a woman with lots of make-up and big hair was sucking one of her fingers. Stephanie looked away.

Her stepmother stood before the window, talking to herself with her hands clasped over her face.

'Where's Daddy?' Stephanie asked Val.

The door behind opened. An elderly man came into the room. He wore a black three piece suit and had a long white face and near black eyes. He carried a large wooden box and placed it upon the magazines. A purple velvet curtain hung over the front of the box as if the box was a tiny stage.

Stephanie didn't like the box. It smelled of a museum she had once been to with her dad; inside the museum there had been a long room containing bits of people in rags, their remains squeezed inside wooden boxes that looked like canoes.

A distant doorbell chimed; it was the sound of her family home's bell when she was a child. She hadn't thought of it once until now.

'They're here,' the man in the black suit said and left the room.

When Stephanie turned around her stepmother was no longer inside the room, which was now entirely black and lit by a line of candles on a sideboard made from dark wood. A black curtain hung over the windows. Even the furniture had changed. There was now a large dining table with carven legs and four chairs.

Stephanie could not see her feet in the darkness and ran across the room and through the door the man had left open. As she ran, the candles on the sideboard winked out, one by one, until she felt she was fleeing a nothingness that swelled like a cold wave behind her back.

She ran into another room, a pink bedroom with floral bed-linen, pink curtains and big pink roses printed on the wallpaper. The only window was fussy with net curtains. Under her feet the carpet was thick and freshly scented with a cleaning product.

On the far side of the bed she could hear rustling plastic, like someone was on their hands and knees and rummaging inside a box full of polythene.

She said, 'I want to go now. Will you get my dad?'

From the floor beside the bed someone stood up and said, 'What's the time?' They were covered by a near opaque polythene sheet. Where her naked breasts and thighs pressed against the plastic, the woman's skin was brownish and mottled with liver spots. There was no hair on her head.

Stephanie sat up in bed and inhaled sharply, then fell to panting and realized she must have been holding her breath while asleep.

The person inside the polythene faded to an outline against the thick black curtains, like an after-image vanishing from her retina. The definition and clarity of the mirrored wardrobe, the furniture and the spotlights smarted against her startled vision.

There was nobody inside her room, which was still lit.

With an incalculable relief, she knew she had only been dreaming and was awake in the same room she had fallen asleep inside, but the nightmare had shaken her enough to make her feel like a child while she dreamed.

Stephanie looked at her alarm clock. Midnight.

No, that was too early. She couldn't have been asleep for only an hour.

In the room next to her own someone was talking, a young woman's voice, one too muffled for her to understand what the girl was saying. A recollection of the footsteps from an hour or so earlier brought a tremble to Stephanie's bottom lip.

She couldn't bear the idea of going back to sleep because it was taking most of her conscious mind to suppress what she remembered from the nightmare.

Stephanie climbed out of bed and wrapped herself in her towelling dressing gown and stood by the door. Unlocked it quietly. Feeling as uncomfortable as if she were looking at the night from inside a lit room, by moving her door wider she increased the amount of light falling into the passage outside. The corridor was empty. The room beside hers, from which she could hear the talking girl, was unlit.

Stephanie clawed her fingers down her face and left them over her mouth.

Not again. Not again. Not again.

Staring into the half-light of the corridor, she could just make out the landing at the end. Beyond this area was the stairwell, but it was too dark to see that part of the house with any clarity. And while peering down there Stephanie fought the instinctive notion of an alteration in the air temperature, a perceptible lowering from cool to cold.

Beyond the rear of the building, Knacker's dog began to bark.

Soon the cold air pricked her face and numbed her bare feet. Gripped by an apprehension that she was about to see movement down by the unlit stairs, Stephanie pushed her door shut. The sense of a profound stillness in the corridor, and the ache of solitude that seemed to pass from it and into her stiffening body, didn't pass with the closing of her door.

This can't go on.

Feeling flickers of anger at the situation, at her continuing powerless within it, Stephanie yanked open her door, left her room and stood outside her neighbour's door. She knocked. 'Hello, Miss. Miss?'

No answer.

Stephanie stepped away from the door and looked nervously towards the unlit stairwell, unwilling to acknowledge why she kept looking down there, while her imagination persisted in its attempt to insert the idea that a figure was standing on the stairs, watching her from inside a concealing darkness.

The voice of the girl in the neighbouring room thickened with tears until she began a pitiful sobbing, as though the woman had just heard terrible news. Stephanie even hoped that her knock at the door was the cause of the surge of grief, because that would mean there was an actual living occupant inside the room.

'If you don't want to talk, I understand. I just want to help. That's all.'

The girl sniffed, then whimpered. She never spoke, but her reaction felt like a response. A minimal response that would not develop.

Stephanie returned to her room, closed her door and sat on the bed. She stared at herself in the mirrored doors of the wardrobe opposite. She looked dreadful and would soon have two black eyes from lack of sleep. Her face also appeared as if it were incapable of a smile; she looked older, worn down, undernourished. She covered her face with her hands and listened to the sound of the girl next door, weeping inside what appeared to be an empty room.

Stephanie climbed back into bed and shuffled closer to the wall to listen to the girl. It didn't matter if nothing here made sense; she was just so tired. She didn't care any more. Just like the girl next door.

Stephanie put her hand on the wall. She wiped her eyes and said, 'Dad. Make it stop. Help me. Dad, please.'

The girl kept crying.

Eventually, Stephanie rolled over and closed her eyes.

DAY THREE

NINETEEN

As the duration of her journey from the bus stop to 82 Edgehill Road dwindled to a matter of minutes, Stephanie felt the growth of an anxiety that made her near nauseous. After her first night in the house, each time she'd returned to the anonymous street she'd felt increasingly vulnerable. Mostly unlit, the buildings and their watching windows struck her this evening as being strongly averse to her presence in the street.

Her phone trilled. Frantic to speak with Ryan, Stephanie yanked the handset out of her pocket. He'd sent a text that afternoon:

@ WORK. WILL CALL LATER.

There had been no characteristic X to end the message, and she believed it was the most unfeeling and abrupt message he'd ever sent her in the two years she'd known him. Her disappointment at the brevity of the text message had made her sullen for most of her last afternoon of work at the Bullring, where she'd been giving out bite-size portions of large cookies to shoppers for eight hours. Her sulk was soon overwhelmed by the next crisis, when she discovered that her debit card was missing from her purse.

She'd upended her bag on the staff room floor and scattered her fingers through the contents, on the verge of tears throughout a frantic search that failed to recover her bank card. There was nothing in her account to withdraw and she had no arranged overdraft, so couldn't recall the last time she'd noticed her card in her purse. After she'd calmed down, she realized the last time she'd used it was four days previously, when she'd withdrawn her last thirty pounds to feed herself and cover bus fare until she was paid at the end of this week.

She'd called the bank and cancelled the card; another would be on its way, but in six working days. Ryan might now have to provide her with more than temporary accommodation, if he was willing. But who had taken the card? She wanted to accuse everyone: the two stupid girls she'd worked with, the indifferent supervisor, the customers, that guy who had come back three times for samples, until she'd told him it was one per customer, and he'd responded by asking her out on a date.

She'd then thought of the house, of the landlord, the other tenants she'd failed to properly meet; someone could have entered her room while she was in the bathroom. Stuff was always going missing in shared accommodation.

It wouldn't stop, it just would not stop: the bad luck, the horrible slide that just kept sending her further down, faster and faster, while she gathered a momentum of misfortune.

This caller's number on her phone screen was unfamiliar. Not Ryan, but the last of five landlords she'd called that lunchtime to arrange viewings of rooms in shared houses. This would be the call back from the message she'd left.

She stopped walking to take the call, and then finished it with a tremor in her voice. All of the respective rooms on offer at the address were immediately available, but all required one month's rent in advance and a deposit, with no exceptions. Three days in the Bullring had put £120 in her bank account, but that didn't even cover half of what she needed to move. The word *hostel* had made an unwelcome appearance in her thoughts throughout the day. She'd have to find out where the nearest hostels were. At least she could withdraw cash across the bank counter tomorrow to provide enough money if she had to evacuate Edgehill Road in a hurry.

As if her voice in the street had provoked a reaction from the scarce evidence of the living about her, a black BMW slowed to a halt. The window slid down. From inside, a young man grinned at her. In the passenger seat, another man leaned forward to crowd the driver. There was someone in the back seat, though she couldn't see their face.

'Get in, luv,' the driver said. 'Get in.'

Stephanie didn't react beyond staring at what she interpreted as an insolent grin on the driver's face.

'Got a phone number, yeah?' the passenger in the front seat added.

When she came to an understanding of the communal intent of the car's passengers, she took a step away from the car.

'Slag,' the passenger said.

'Fuck off, twat!' she shouted at the open window and hurried away in the direction of the house.

The car pulled away to the heavy thump of interior music she hoped had been started to cover the embarrassment of the car's occupants. She'd often used the same response in Stoke, to some effect in the same situation, as she walked to and from college.

Her unappealing contact with the outside world was only just beginning. 'You's got a room then?' The voice came out of the front yard neighbouring the unruly privet hedge of number 82. A portly man in a dark waterproof grinned at her from behind the front wall of another untidy house. In one hand he held a black plastic bag that he was about to place inside a rubber dustbin.

'Er, yes.'

Inside the cavernous hood of his coat, the man's pink face was shiny with rain; the broad bifocal lenses of his glasses were speckled with droplets of moisture and disguised eyes she sensed more than saw.

'Nice to see the place up and running.' His Brummy accent was thick. 'The son still around then? You with him?'

'Sorry, what? No. I've just moved in—'

'Not seen him for a bit. He's been ill. Better now then? Fought so.' The neighbour seemed happier to do the talking, or the telling. He rolled his eyes knowingly. 'I wondered when he'd get his act togever. You the first then?'

What did he mean, the first new tenant? 'Er . . .' But then Stephanie realized she did not want to give the man the impression that she was the only girl in the house. And she wasn't, was she? 'No. There's others. And another two are coming. Moving in.' She felt flustered and didn't like his overfamiliar smile that could also have been a smirk, one she was unable to meet with anything but wariness. 'My boyfriend—'

'Good to hear it. His dad been gone a while. Him carrying on the family tradition, eh?' The man seemed to find this comment about Knacker extremely funny and guffawed to himself for longer than was necessary; he didn't seem to be aware that Stephanie wasn't encouraging his mirth. 'Might pop round, eh, and see you all some night soon. Bin quiet round here, like, since his dad died.'

She had no answer, or anything to contribute to the mystifying conversation and its intrusive tone, and began to wonder if the man was crazy. 'Gotta get on.'

'Ta-ra! Might I say I'm very impressed, like, if this keeps up.'

Stephanie didn't look back. She hurried on, still shaky from the confrontation with the youths and now confused by the neighbour.

As she closed the front door of number 82 she made a wish that all strangers would leave her alone forever. But of her encounters so far this evening, all in less than one hundred yards of the house, she quickly understood that another engagement with a stranger awaited, and this would be the oddest and most sinister contact yet.

The tall figure at the end of the hallway, a man she had never seen before, did not move his head as she came into the house more hastily than usual.

The man continued to stare intently at the solitary door at the foot of the ground floor corridor, situated on the right hand side. His long neck reached out of the scruffy brown puffer jacket, his forehead placed close to the ivory paintwork. He seemed to be listening with his eyes closed, while also issuing the weird suggestion of reverence, or prayer, his gangly body remaining perfectly still.

Stephanie picked up the post from the floor. It was stacked inside a red rubber band. Though none of the mail could possibly have been for her, she just felt a need to do something other than stand uncomfortably still.

She turned the light on. 'Hi,' she said to get the man's attention, though she wasn't entirely sure she wanted it.

The man did not speak or move. What light seeped through the hallway revealed short red hair, pale skin and a freakish height. His thin neck was distinguished by a pointed Adam's apple, the skin of his jaw coated in shaving rash and a fuzz of coppery stubble. From his long feet, clad in dirty white trainers, to his gingery head, he must have been six foot seven or more.

As the period of time in which he ignored her lengthened and became acutely uncomfortable to endure, Stephanie's thoughts filled with reminders of the voice in the bathroom, her invisible neighbour, her first room, and the mysterious male footsteps that walked this floor each morning, and possibly bolted up the stairs to the Russian girl's room on the second floor. And for a painful moment, she genuinely wondered whether the man was real, or another one of *them*: heard and even seen, but who didn't seem entirely *here*.

What is here?

The man turned his entire body to face Stephanie so quickly that she flinched and dropped the post. At the sight of her, his bony face didn't soften its expression of pitiless distaste. This was an unkind face with unsmiling blue eyes; a face still vaguely boyish but toughened to an inflexibility, or limited range of expression, by hard times. A *street* face.

Stephanie cleared her throat. She retrieved the post from where she'd dropped it, then stared at the man without smiling.

His gaze did not waver, and remained severe, as if her presence in the hall was a great inconvenience.

She felt too light on her feet, ungainly, muted, horribly chastened. But by what? She'd only come home from work to the building where she rented a room. Who the hell was *he* to make her feel awkward and tense? Stephanie glared at the man before walking quickly to the staircase. He watched her without speaking.

As she climbed the stairs he laughed in a deep, forced way that almost became verbal: a 'Ho, ho, ho' accompanied by a mocking grin she didn't look at for long. When he cut off the contrived laugh, he settled for staring at her until she passed from sight.

There had been nothing amorous in the intensity of his attention, but something that seemed far worse. When Stephanie reached her room she was grinding her teeth and clenching her fists, one of them around a stack of post that wasn't for her. 'Shit.' She wasn't taking the post back down there, where *he* was. *But at least he's real.* There was no other comfort to draw from the encounter.

TWENTY

Stephanie waited in her room for over an hour but Ryan didn't call. Eventually she phoned him.

'Thanks for calling,' she said when he picked up.

'Steph, you OK?'

She remained silent for a few seconds. The sound of his voice brought a lump to her throat. 'Not really.'

'What's going on? Your message worried me.'

But not that much.

She looked at the door; beyond her room the house was having one of its quiet periods. 'I'm in a bind. A real bind here. Look . . . I'm sorry, how are things with you?'

'All right. You know, still doing the night shifts. Contract, but it's still work . . .' He said other things but she found herself unable to pay attention; she was too engaged with trying to work out how to explain her situation to him. He finished what he had been saying with, 'You? Workwise?'

'Bits and pieces. Shit mostly. Nothing changed there.'

'So what's this mistake?'

'This house. This . . . place that I'm staying in . . .' She kept her narrative to details about Knacker being 'unstable', and things of that nature: the deposit he would not return, her parlous financial state, the missing bank card,

114

and her need to move out fast. And though some of Ryan's old protectiveness towards her reappeared, she was disappointed that he didn't immediately offer money; at one time he would have done so, confident that she was good for a loan, that she was not dishonest and hated dishonesty. With the little bit of money her dad left her, she had also helped him by covering the deposit and a few months' rent on their first place together. Had he forgotten? She'd never asked him for anything else, besides to let her go, and repeatedly during the last three months of their time together.

He must suspect that if she was calling him she had no one else to turn to. But if she wasn't mistaken Ryan's voice was different now: quieter, less tight with emotion, as it had been whenever they'd spoken closer to the time of their split. She also intuited a wariness because she had made contact with him. *How things change.* 'You're seeing someone?' she blurted.

He went quiet for at least three seconds. 'Yeah.'

It hurt, but only as a residual instinctive jealousy, as an infuriating sense of proprietorship over someone you didn't want to be with anymore. Though she'd never stopped loving Ryan, she didn't want him back. Not long ago, she'd even prayed he would meet someone else. All the same, she couldn't prevent her ego getting mixed up in his romantic affairs, particularly now she needed his help.

'Steph, can you blame me? I mean, you broke up with me.'

'I'm fine. Totally fine with it. I thought you might be anyway.'

'You?' he said, and his voice tensed as he entertained *that* thought.

'Few one night stands and a gangbang but nothing serious.' He knew this was not true, but Stephanie sensed a bristling from his side of the phone. 'I'm joking. There's been no one. It's not something I even think about.' At least that was the truth. 'Hardly a priority in my current situation.'

'Good,' he said too quickly to have thought out his response.

'But I need to get out of here and you've already answered my question. I'm sorry I bothered you.'

'Don't be like that.'

'I'm not being like anything. I only thought . . . wondered if I could crash at yours until I can save a deposit on a room. But that would be complicated.'

'Steph, you know I would help you out. No question. But things are tight here.'

She hadn't asked him for money.

'We're saving too,' he added.

'Don't tell me you live together? You've only just met her.' She wished she could take it back and hated herself for wanting to hurt him. In her mind she'd built Ryan into a guaranteed escape route – albeit an unwise one fraught with emotional attrition. But she now had one less safety net; the call confirmed it and the idea made her feel limp. Thank God she hadn't fled to him after her first night at the house, loaded down with bags. It would have been awful. *But worse than this?*

'Sometimes you just know,' he said, his tone subdued

by a combination of sullenness and passive antagonism she remembered only too well.

This was going nowhere. 'Sure. Look, I better get off. I need the credit on my phone to look for rooms.' Her voice was starting to break, which would only get worse the longer she stayed on the line.

No, wait, don't go. I'll call you back. He used to say things like that all the time, but they were way past all that now. Instead, he said, 'Try Joanie. Or Philippa. Bekka.' And that really sobered her.

'They're in Stoke. I'm not going back there.' *I'm never going back near her: near Val.*

For Ryan to even suggest she return to her home town was another example of him no longer truly thinking about her. Or even worse, no longer caring about her much. They were truly moving on and forgetting each other.

'You'll be all right,' he said, and sounded relieved the conversation was closing. 'You're a clever girl, Steph. Don't need me to tell you that. Something will turn up.'

'That's what I'm worried about. In my fucking room.'

'What? This bastard landlord trying it on with you?'

'No.' *Not yet.* 'Look, I wouldn't have called if I wasn't desperate.'

'Cheers.'

'I didn't mean it like that. But . . . No one would believe me. This house.' Her voice dropped to a whisper. 'It's not right. It's all wrong. There's people . . . girls who keep talking and crying, but I don't know if they are there. I can't find them.'

'What?'

Stephanie began to cry. She sniffed. 'Things are going on here.'

'What things?'

'I don't know. Someone was in my room, Ryan. My room!'

'What? Where is this place?'

'Edgehill Road. I can't stay here.'

'What number?'

'Eighty-two. Can you help, please?'

'But who was in your room? I don't understand.'

'They weren't there when I switched the light on. In the bathroom . . . another one . . . a voice. Everything is wrong.'

'What? Are you saying—'

The credit on her phone ran out with a bleep and it took all of her scant composure to resist throwing the handset against the wall.

She bit down on a stream of curses before they left her mouth – obscenities that would have made her feel even more desperate – just as someone announced themselves with three playful raps on the door.

TWENTY-ONE

It was Knacker. 'Awright, darlin'.' He was holding a bottle of wine and two glasses. 'Didn't like the fought of you being on your own down here on Friday night. Fought you might like to celebrate moving in, like. House warming.'

Had he been listening outside her door? The thought of Knacker knowing Ryan was no longer an alternative for accommodation chilled her. 'No. Not a good time. But thanks.'

Reeking of aftershave, Knacker stepped into the room without invitation, his body moving at her and around her at the same time. He came so close she pulled back as if from a blow.

'Don't be like that. I can see from a mile away that you been crying again. Somefing upset ya?' He raised the wine glasses. 'Nuffin' funny, like. No offence, sister, but you ain't my type and I don't mix business wiv pleasure. It's not like I'm short a that kind a fing anyway.' He spoke as though he were rejecting a proposition from her. 'Just offering a bit a hospitality, like.'

She could not refuse him entrance. It wasn't really her room, but a token of his charity; she'd been in it for one night and her ownership of the space hadn't been established. The realization prompted a vision of his face going

119

stiff and white with rage if she told him to piss off; followed by another of her standing outside in the rain with her bags at her feet.

'Mind if I sit?' Even if she had minded it wouldn't have done any good, and when he sat heavily on her bed she shivered with revulsion. He was steadily erasing the last vestiges of her resistance. Deliberately too, and with relish, and she hated him for it.

'No wonder you can't keep a fella, girl. Face like that. Who'd wanna look at that all day?'

'You . . .' Her voice died when Knacker raised his chin provocatively. He was wearing a new red Helly Hansen ski jacket and Diesel jeans with his pristine green trainers. A peacock hooligan; she'd never liked them.

'I hear you met Fergal. Me cousin. Said he seen you downstairs.' As he spoke his eyes slid about as he scoped out the room behind her. 'That the post?' He rose and snatched it off the little table. 'What you doing wiv it?'

'I . . . picked it up.'

Every trace of mocking humour vanished from his eyes so quickly it shocked her. 'I can see that, but it ain't yours.'

'I know.' She swallowed. 'Your cousin, he . . .'

'What?'

'Startled me. And I forgot I had it in my hand.'

Knacker was delighted and sat down again. 'Startled you! I like that, "startled". You don't hear that much. You's got a nice way of putting fings, girl. You just need to smile a bit and the world's your oyster.'

'What was he doing? Downstairs, by that door?'

Knacker frowned. 'It's his house as well as mine. He can do what he likes.'

It struck her as odd that a cousin would be a co-owner of the house. 'Who lives down there?'

Knacker started to sniff. 'No one. Out of bounds.' He uncapped the wine bottle. 'That whole part of the house is.'

'Why?'

'We need to do a bit of work on it. Here, you want some a this booze or not? Don't often touch it much meself. Loopy juice. I get a couple in me and people's holding me back, like. Does somefing to me head. I prefer a bit a weed, bit a coke. But I don't fink one glass will hurt.'

Knacker's cousin, Fergal, resting his head against the door in an unlit corridor, as if meditating, had not appeared like preparation for renovations. And Knacker was trying to change the subject.

'Decorating?' she said as a prompt.

'Bigger job, love. Structural work first, like. We gonna have our hands full.'

'A man lives down there though? I've heard him go out in the morning. Or was that your cousin?'

Knacker avoided her eyes, sniffed. 'Probably.' He passed a glass brimming with white wine at her. 'Here you are, time to stop nosing about and start drinking.'

Stephanie took the glass and resigned herself to using the coffee table as a seat.

For the next thirty minutes, stupefied by her own awkwardness and reticence, and never offering more than monosyllabic answers if she could help it, Stephanie fielded the landlord's quick-fire questions about her temporary work, her stepmother, her friends, what she studied, with Knacker taking a special interest in her psychology A level: 'Been finking about doing somefing like that meself'.

She did her best to mentally screen the bragging monologues that formed the majority share of his discourse, and mostly looked at the floor with a dazed expression on her face, hoping her lack of engagement would cut short the duration of his visit. He didn't seem to notice, and his face grew redder from the wine. As well as his fondness for undermining her, he found selling an idea of himself as a wily, tough, financially successful man even more delightful. He claimed he had been a paratrooper, that he had property 'all over', he was a builder, did 'electrics', and once had a nightclub in the rave scene. Spain was a popular topic. He'd done 'a bit of everyfing. You name it, done it. All of it.'

He wanted to impress her. Which was futile as she hated him and considered him ridiculous. She found his expectation of approval astounding, considering how he had bullied and insulted her from her first day at the house; a memory of his taunts made her stomach writhe at the very sight of him. But Knacker appeared unable to accept her evident dislike. Either that or he was stubbornly resisting her signals, which made her nervous.

As his self-aggrandizing gathered momentum, she found herself acknowledging, with difficulty, that permanent roles had already been assigned: he had the upper hand and would not take kindly to her digressing from this position. Just like the bullies she'd encountered in casual work. Just like her stepmother. In her unfortunate experience of what she understood to be a form of narcissism – because her stepmother had been diagnosed with a narcissistic personality disorder while her dad was still alive – her only real defence would be a retreat and a removal of herself from his presence. Only that wasn't possible until she had more money. She wondered if her frustration was contributing to her perception of him and the house, and perhaps even warping that perception.

'. . . You see, girl. Life is what you make it. End of the day, like, what you need to remember . . .'

What to do? She had no work lined up for the following week, and only £120 to her name. Once Knacker the arsehole left her room, she would call her friends in Stoke, like Ryan suggested, and see if she could borrow a sofa tomorrow. *But for how long? Indefinitely?* The work situation in her home town was as impossible as anywhere she'd known, and her stepmother was there. Going back to Stoke would not only be an admission of defeat but a dead end. She wondered if she would ever have the strength to leave it a second time, and alone, without Ryan.

It would take six days for her new cash card to arrive. She couldn't stay here that long. But if she went to Stoke she'd still have to come back here to collect the new card. *What to do?* She wanted to scream and keep on screaming.

'End of the day, when all is said and done, like, I'm a fighter, me . . . You'll never . . . a McGuire . . .'

She began to eye her uninvited visitor's new clothes and she pondered the absence of any evidence of renovation in the property. Knacker had lied about this room being newly decorated. In fact, he'd told so many lies she doubted even he could keep track of them, but he would become instantly hostile if she pointed out contradictions. Her thoughts were throttling her; they'd been a noose all day and most days for months now.

'Problem with most people—'

'What's her story? The girl next door.' She asked the question to prevent Knacker from giving her any more advice about life.

'What you talking about? Who lives here, who lives there? What's it to ya?'

'Perfectly natural to want to know who you're living next to in shared accommodation. And you seem to have an interest in your tenants.' She opened the palms of her hands to indicate his increasingly sprawled posture, or lack of posture, on her bed.

And that was going too far, because now he'd started to go pale, and his eyes were lidding. There was also a shrug as he sat upright, and a rustle as both shoulders rotated inside the ski jacket.

She kept her tone of voice level, struggling to suppress the sarcasm. 'It's just that I keep hearing them. Girls. Upset. But they won't speak to me. In the bathroom—'

'I don't get you. I don't get you at all. You get the best room in the house for forty quid a week. Which, I might add, may come under review sooner than you fink if you keep this up. Who lives here, who lives there? Other people's mail in your hand. It's none of your fuckin' business. You is prying. What's your game, eh?'

'I don't have one. I'm just—'

He wasn't listening. He was working himself up. She

remembered what he'd said about the effect alcohol had upon him. She swallowed.

'I'll tell you what your game is—'

The door opened so quickly they both jumped.

TWENTY-TWO

A ginger head thrust into the room. The neck behind the head was absurdly long and ribbed with cartilage visible through pasty skin. Without invitation, Knacker's cousin, Fergal, stepped inside.

'Fuck's sake, Fergal! You nearly give me a heart attack!' Knacker started to grin. But Fergal didn't acknowledge him. Instead he stared at Stephanie with what she took to be a limitless malevolence. It was similar to his expression when she'd first seen him downstairs, only this was worse. There was so much hatred and rage in the man's bloodless face she couldn't breathe, became dizzy, scratched around her mind for any reason she might have angered him.

Stephanie was sure he was going to hit her because he walked right at her. It took all of her will not to cringe or flinch. Her hands shook, so she squeezed them into fists.

Fergal halted one step away from her. He bent over so his face was no more than an inch from hers. And stared at her with such aggressive intensity, she looked away, and to Knacker for an explanation.

Knacker appeared anxious too, which made Stephanie's terror ratchet even higher.

'Come on, mate. Got some plonk here. Have a glass.'

There was a conciliatory tone to Knacker's entreaty that did nothing to restore Stephanie's confidence.

Up close, Fergal smelled unwashed, oily, sebaceous. His jeans were greasy, stained, the hems trodden down to a black mush of fabric and filth under the heels of his dirty trainers. He looked and smelled as if he had been sleeping in the street.

Fergal finally grinned into Stephanie's face and revealed yellow and brown teeth. As quickly as he'd entered, he took a long stride backwards and sat heavily on the bed, then thrust his legs apart, as if claiming territory, and knocked Knacker's knees together. Knacker stiffened, then quickly grinned and clapped his cousin on the back.

Fergal snatched the bottle from Knacker's hand. Inside his long spidery fingers and prominent knuckles, the bottle appeared to diminish in size, as well as being instantly stripped of any of the civilized values that accompany the drinking of wine. The man put the bottle to his lips and gulped at it; his sharp Adam's apple moved unpleasantly in his throat as he swallowed like a savage.

Determined to find the man's behaviour hilarious, Knacker started a slight bouncing of his buttocks on the bed. 'He was doing that fing, that fing, wiv his face. Classic it is. Shits everyone up. When we was in the Scrubs he—'

Fergal turned and thrust his face close to Knacker's. 'Shat it,' he said in a slow, deep voice.

Knacker did. He must have been ten years older than the younger man, but was clearly intimidated by Fergal. And Knacker now tried to maintain his smile, as if to drag his confederate back into the camaraderie, while proving to Stephanie that it was all harmless role play. She wasn't fooled, and not even Knacker seemed as menacing or problematic any more compared to the younger man.

There was something terribly wrong here, with them, with them being here. Not just inside her room, but inside the house. She sensed a disconnect between the vast inhospitable building and this pair of unstable men sitting on her bed. They were the most unusual and absurd landlords. And they weren't even from the Midlands.

How did I get here?

Surreal but dangerous, without a shred of humour she could glean, the situation wasn't making sense in comparison to anything she'd ever experienced. Nothing did in the building. Even without the voices and the crying women it was bizarre. It was a mad house and she felt as if she were the only sane thing here . . . *the only clean thing, civilized thing*.

She'd already swallowed the large glass of wine and the effects expanded her imagination into an ever more sinister darkness. It rendered her mute; her confusion was becoming unbearable. And what was Scrubs?

Her mind was made up; it would be stupid to remain in a building with Fergal, let alone Knacker. She'd seen enough, wanted to get them out of the room fast. She needed to call a cab to take her to New Street Station, and then start putting in calls to her friends while on the move back to Stoke. She found it staggering that she was even still here, *again*, in this building, a place that refused to settle into a recognizable condition. She worried that her despair, apathy and listlessness, that came from being exhausted and demoralized, were now her biggest enemies.

Fergal pulled a comical facial expression and nodded in

Stephanie's direction while keeping his eyes on Knacker. 'This the best you could do?'

Knacker suppressed a grin which suggested they privately shared a joke about her.

Seeing her reaction, Knacker struck his cousin's thigh gently as if to kill the jest because it had gone too far. 'Just helping a girl out, ain't I. She's doing her best. Trying to get by, like. I respect that. These is tough times.'

Fergal turned his head in an exaggerated fashion, as if he were a ventriloquist's dummy operated by the older man, and stared at Stephanie with his mouth open, feigning idiocy. He crossed his eyes. When Knacker spoke again, Fergal swivelled his head back in the older man's direction, his big mouth still hanging open.

'She ain't finding much work, like,' Knacker said. 'Struggling. Nothing we ain't seen before.' When he noticed his cousin's face mocking him with the imbecilic expression, he shouted, 'Cut it out!'

Stephanie stood up. She *needed* to get them out of her room. 'I need to get ready. Early start.'

Fergal swung his face back in her direction, a hideous, mocking, wrecking ball of a head. 'Don't let us stop ya.' They both found this funny and started laughing, Fergal in that deep, forced manner, Knacker with a hissy titter through his big lips.

'Not much of a party, is it?' Fergal said.

'She ain't the partying type like we's used to, mate,' Knacker replied, as the horrid nature of their coercive double act tried to take shape in her room.

The entire world felt criminally hostile. She thought of what she had read about rich people retreating into gated communities and prohibitively expensive areas of the country, and why they sent their children to private schools and Russell Group universities. To never brush shoulders with *this*, ever. Society was splitting, was less cohesive than ever, like her dad had said. The rich created the inequality and then fled the scene, or so he had constantly told her. She'd wondered what happened to all those people who got left behind, because they had no money and couldn't defend themselves – *like her*.

Victims.

'Mind if I skin up?' Fergal asked, his voice suddenly softer, even polite, as though another personality had risen to the surface.

'No. Don't,' she said, as if the appearance of drugs in her room was an invitation for terrible things to take place.

Ignoring her, Fergal took a Golden Virginia tobacco tin out of the pocket of his dirty jacket and opened it. Removed a packet of extra-long cigarette papers, a ball of skunk weed shrink-wrapped in plastic, a lighter. His movements were deliberately slow, if not purposefully antagonizing.

'Bit a draw. Can't beat a bit a draw,' Knacker said.

Stephanie stood up. 'Stop!' She was surprised at the strength of her own voice.

They shared her shock and looked stunned, mouths open, smiles gone, eyes blinking.

'I don't like this,' she said quietly, and her voice was shaking. 'You're making me nervous.'

'Nervous?' Fergal said after a long uncomfortable moment when no one seemed to know what to say.

'Nervous?' he repeated with a frown, and then forced a stupid laugh from deep inside his stomach. Another role, another voice. He thought he was the joker of the pack, only his material, like him, stank.

'I fink we is outstaying our welcome.' Knacker rose, smiling, hands outstretched, like he was trying to stop a fist-fight in the street. 'No harm done. Everyfing is cool, yeah. Just a bit a fun, like. I apologize. We never meant to frighten you. Not our style that. Makes me feel a right twat. I'm ashamed.' His act was delivered with such sincerity that she almost believed, for half a second, that he was genuinely contrite.

Fergal packed his gear away, clutched the wine bottle and stood up. Then looked at the wine bottle in his hand, still frowning, as if he was surprised to find it there.

'Leave it with her, like,' Knacker said, now playing his version of the man of manners and expansive generosity, and with such enthusiasm that Stephanie wanted to scream with laughter. 'It's hers. I give it her. House warming present. There you go, darlin'. Have a drink on us. In peace. We will take ourselves elsewhere.'

Fergal grinned and showed his discoloured teeth. 'And get caned.'

The fact that they were leaving filled her with so much relief she felt unsteady on her feet.

Knacker hovered by the door. 'No one gonna bovver you in your own room, like. Not that kind of house. This is totally on the level, right? You know that. Yeah? Yeah?' he repeated as he ushered his gangly cousin out of the room. 'Just a misunderstanding, that's all. But there's something I need to speak with you about. I was going to mention it earlier . . .'

Her face must have dropped back into despair so dramatically because Knacker cut himself off. 'But it can wait, yeah. Til tomorrow. But you is gonna wanna to hear it, like. In the morning, I'll tell ya. But an answer to your troubles ain't far away, like. On the level, yeah.'

'Yeah, totally legit,' his cousin chimed in from the darkness of the corridor. 'Much money is going to be made. Very soon. Right here.'

Knacker grinned like an excited boy. 'That's right, yeah. Tomorrow, darlin'. Have a glass a wine, courtesy of the house. Put the box on. No one is gonna bovver you no more. You's can relax now.'

His apologetic reassurance was starting to grind, but she was baffled about what they might be up to. She thought them capable of anything and nothing at the same time. She wondered if she should call the police and . . . *say what?*

Stephanie hurried to the door and attempted to push it shut. But a large, dirty trainer appeared and stopped it closing. Fergal's face thrust back into her room so quickly she gasped.

He looked up at the ceiling and at the walls in a mock conspiratorial manner and whispered, 'Don't worry about them. They can't hurt you.' Then he slipped away, into the unlit corridor, gently pulling the door closed behind him.

TWENTY-THREE

Stephanie sat on the bed and stared into space. It had been two hours since Knacker and Fergal had left her room, but Fergal's final comment had eclipsed her lingering horror at having to endure their company.

Fergal knew something about the strange nature of the house. The same thing she half-knew, suspected, denied, suppressed, and ultimately resisted; suspicions more than facts that were prone to being side-lined as soon as she left the building, because of her desperation to earn money to get out of there. But Fergal had made an admission she'd been unable to prise out of Knacker. So why had he admitted to what was tantamount to the building being haunted?

Had he?

She recalled the tall, thin figure leaning into the ground floor door.

What was that about?

She wanted to believe the two men were merely socially inept, unaccustomed to the role of landlord, and unable to rent out the rooms because of their awful natures. Or perhaps there were actual people living here too: a girl next door, a Russian girl upstairs, a smelly man on the ground floor, a woman somewhere below the bathroom? Illegal immigrants? Such an idea would actually bring her comfort. And maybe Fergal had been referring to the other tenants?

Or perhaps something far more sinister was at work inside the house, something the cousins were able to ignore, or even colluded with for reasons not yet disclosed. Maybe something had happened here that they were covering up. The latter scenario she tried to deny and repress, because it was an idea best considered once she'd permanently removed herself from the address. Nothing here was certain, but if she were honest with herself, the McGuires now frightened her more than anything she'd heard through the walls, under her mattress, or sensed sitting upon her bed in her first room.

'They can't hurt you.' *But we can.* Was that the subtext of Fergal's parting shot? And that horrible, angry stare: was that an act?

Knacker was evasive, disingenuous, quick to anger if she hinted at what she'd experienced, but he was a bullshitter, playing second fiddle to his maniac, druggie cousin. She knew that much now. She sensed that Fergal considered her a nuisance while Knacker was keen for her to stay. *Money.* She couldn't bear to think that Knacker's motivation could be anything else. Unless he was preparing the ground by circling her, working on her, hoping to erode her resistance to his concealed intentions. *Amorous intentions.* Stephanie stopped the train of thought before it brought her closer to nausea.

She went and checked the corridor outside her room.

Empty and silent; the rooms either side of her own emitted no light from beneath their respective doors, and no sound. Her instincts persisted in suggesting they were unoccupied and had been since she'd arrived at the address.

So what made the noises?

From the next floor up, seeping down the stairwell from the landlord's flat, came the distant thump of a bass drum.

She thought of her remaining friends in Stoke, none of whom she had heard from in a few months. She was still without the internet; the connection was impossibly slow on her old phone, and her stepmother, she suspected, had disabled her laptop before she left home. Val hadn't been able to stand her using it, though Stephanie was never sure why. The machine had not worked since she left home and she'd not had enough money to get it fixed. Her friends must all communicate on Facebook, Skype and Twitter. Either that or no one called her any more. Stephanie hoped they still thought of her. Their silence might simply be the result of their preoccupation with their own struggles, while they waited for news from her. Is that how it worked with home town friends? When she'd torn out of Stoke she hadn't looked back. Which now felt like a horrible mistake.

If her three friends in Stoke couldn't accommodate her, she would have to tolerate the situation at Edgehill Road for a bit longer. *And endure what was inside the house.* Or spend what she had at a hostel. How many nights would £120 cover? Maybe a week until it was all gone. She'd then have to work every day next week to pay for the following week, or she'd have no money and nowhere to stay come Friday.

Maybe if she stayed outside the building all day Saturday and Sunday, without spending much money, that might help. She could stay awake at night and take naps in a park. And if she refused to open her door to Knacker again, and only spoke through the door, he might get the message.

She'd only had a nightmare last night. *Hardly surprising*. But at least there had been nothing in her room. Nothing under the bed . . .

Stop now!

The confused voice in the bathroom, that may or may not have been a recording, was just a voice and offered no physical threat.

This room had no disused fireplace either.

The girl next door – the presence, if that's what it was – only cried and walked up and down the hall.

It's not so bad. Psychological damage she just might have to risk for the time being.

Even thinking in these terms, and weighing up so many earthly and unearthly considerations, struck her as absurd. But then her life was just that. She was being coerced into thinking in terms of the impossible and the unnatural to such an extent, she wondered again if she were schizophrenic. Her reality was becoming warped and she was hearing voices. Maybe even seeing things that were not there.

Stephanie checked the time: ten forty-five p.m. Too late to call one of her friends back in Stoke. But she would do, in the morning, to assess her options should she need to leave here in a hurry. If one of them would take her in tomorrow, on Saturday, then tonight could be her last night here.

Her room still smelled of Fergal and the uncapped wine. She opened a window. Turned her duvet around and upside down, so the part he had been sitting on would be near the foot of the mattress. Took the wine bottle to the kitchen and emptied it down the sink, all the time wincing at the memory of Fergal's uncouth mouth gulping from it. She tried not to touch the glass where his mouth had been.

Back in her room the travel clock told her the time had now passed eleven p.m. She set her alarm for eight in the morning. Once she was up she could head into the city centre and check in with the stores, pubs, bars and cafés where she'd already left her CV.

Leaving all of the lights and the muted television switched on, Stephanie undressed to her underwear and climbed into bed. She lay still and continued to think herself into ever decreasing circles to avoid any contemplation of another night in the building.

TWENTY-FOUR

The footsteps that slowly roused Stephanie from the dream moved swiftly down the corridor outside her room and continued inside her room, as if the door had been left open.

As she came awake a second set of heavier footsteps followed the first, as if in eager pursuit, but stopped outside her door, suggesting reluctance, or merely an inquisitive pause.

With her own sharp intake of breath loud inside her head, she broke from the last tendril of dream and burst out from under the bedcovers.

The sound of her shock appeared to bring everything to an abrupt end – the footsteps as well as the hurtful words that had been chattering from her stepmother's mouth in the dream; accusations accompanied by horrible grins on the faces of people she hadn't recognized, who'd all sat around a black table. People holding hands in a dark space with candles set in distant corners. Yet the surreal vestiges of the bad dream were dwarfed by the realization that someone may have entered her room.

The footsteps.

The ceiling lights and floor lamp were still on, and it didn't take Stephanie long to discover she was alone between the black walls and mirrors. The door to her room was still closed. She remained upright in bed, hands pressed to her cheeks, her chest rising and falling like she'd just struggled to get to the surface of deep water.

In the distance she could hear Knacker's dog barking at the rear of the house. It now sounded like a bellow combined with a cough.

Feeling her sanity was at stake, she quickly tried to rationalize the nightmare. Being intimidated by strangers in a room with black walls had a clear connection to the evening she'd endured earlier, and being tormented by her stepmother was a constant.

But the footsteps . . . About those she was all out of ideas.

What little calm she felt at being awake was soon obliterated.

In the room next door the heavier set of footsteps returned to life, bumping about the room in an uncoordinated and clumsy fashion. *Pisshead feet. Shit-faced feet you hide from.*

Stephanie turned to the wall her bed was pressed against. She hadn't heard the door to her neighbour's room open, but the sound of thumps and clatters now travelled through to her, as if determined hands had begun to scatter small objects and cast aside items of furniture in the room next door. The footsteps would occasionally pause, then speed up and stagger in another direction to continue what sounded like someone vandalizing the room.

When the footsteps banged towards the wall nearest to her, Stephanie flinched and seized up, and knew she would let go of a scream if whoever was next door managed to continue their antics on her side of the wall, which didn't seem impossible.

She heard mattress springs creak and a rubbing of fabric directly against the wall, followed by a woman's small cry announced into the very bricks and plaster that divided the two rooms.

A bang of wood and a clatter of bedsprings followed, and Stephanie received the impression that a bed had just been raised from the floor and then dropped. The woman must have been hiding beneath the bed. Her neighbour's cries worsened, giving the impression that the woman was now being pulled, or dragged across the floor and deeper into the room beyond.

The whimpers became sobs, until the woman grunted softly after each muffled thud and fleshy slap she received; the blows were all too audible and interspersed with the sound of the man's heavy feet adjusting their balance as he went to work.

Petrified with shock, and sickened enough by what she was hearing to know she'd never been truly repulsed before, Stephanie was unable to react.

A female stranger was being beaten. The sounds made her feel giddy and strengthless, as if she were seeing violence, or as if it were happening to her instead. Even her stepmum's boyfriend, the little bespectacled runt that had liked to stand in her doorway when drunk, leering at her every time he came upstairs to use the toilet, hadn't come close to disgusting her as much as what she could hear in the room next door.

Stephanie climbed off the bed, as quietly as possible,

wincing at every creak of mattress spring and then each squeak of floorboard. She approached the door on tiptoe.

So was there a girl next door after all, and had Fergal gone to her?

It could have been you.

She went back to her bedside and picked up her phone. Tapped in 999. Then paused with her thumb over the CALL button when she remembered her inability to catch sight of her neighbour the previous night, and her failure to find the girl in the bathroom. She also considered the absence of any light in her neighbours' rooms, and their refusal to respond to her pleas.

Stephanie opened her door and stared into the unlit passageway of the first floor. As usual, the rooms on either side of the hallway were in darkness. So a girl was being beaten in the dark by a man who had searched for her without turning the lights on? This didn't make sense. Or perhaps she was hearing something that wasn't really happening. That made even less sense.

Stephanie moved to the neighbouring door. On the other side she could still hear the thumps and the groans, the whimpers and the horrible plodding of male feet. But she was also aware of something else: a strong odour. A reek of gum disease, beefy bestial sweat revived by fresh perspiration in unwashed clothes, an oily scalp, alcohol breath. A stench instantly recognizable from her second night on the floor above. This was the smell of the man who went to the crying Russian girl and had sex with her, and then stood outside Stephanie's room in a silent vigil.

Stephanie wanted to scream. But she was also tired of

being confused and frightened and rejected and poor and trapped and bullied and . . .

Engulfed by an urge to punch and claw and kick, she gripped her head and shouted 'No!', and before she even had time to question her actions she began pounding the palms of both hands against the door. 'Stop it! Stop! Leave her alone! Leave her alone, you bastard!'

She was astounded by the volume of her voice in the darkness of the corridor, and shocked because she'd done something she'd believed herself incapable of. Just as quickly, Stephanie was seized by an apprehension that hardened under her skin like a film of ice, because the neighbouring room had fallen silent. After apprehension came anticipation, the unpleasant kind, when she knew that a face out of sight, that she didn't want to be noticed by, had just turned in her direction.

They are aware of you.

The nape of her neck and her scalp goosed and she shivered in the cold; a cold she'd plunged into on leaving her room, that had grown so debilitating, as though the house no longer possessed a roof or walls to hold back a freezing absence outside itself, through which *they* came with their footsteps and their cries and their voices and their smells . . . *to show you things.*

Stephanie hurried back inside her room and slammed the door, locked it. But felt as vulnerable as she had been in the corridor, peeled of the sense of physical security a locked door usually provides.

And the cold. It was still cold inside her room. Her feet felt like they were turning blue. Her breath shuddered in and out of her chest.

When you are cold you are not alone.

She swallowed. 'Who?' She looked about the walls, the ceiling, as she inched towards her bed.

They can't hurt you.

'Who are you?' She kept her voice down; even in her shock she was conscious of being overheard. Knacker and Fergal would be asleep two floors above her room, and if they hadn't heard her outburst, or the beating of one of their *tenants*, they probably wouldn't hear her now. She raised her voice. 'Who is there? Tell me. Please. I can't stand it any more . . .' Her voice started to shake. 'I can't . . . I can't get out . . . I can't stand it . . .' Emotion closed her throat.

'I'm cold.'

At the sound of the voice next to Stephanie's ear, she fell upon the bed and shoved herself backwards to the headboard with the balls of her feet, untucking the fitted sheet from the mattress as she moved.

Had she heard a voice?

Yes, she had heard something. But was the voice in the room or inside her head? Was she only doubting the voice because she couldn't see anyone? And if she believed *someone* had spoken, well then . . . she was mad because she was hearing voices. Either that or everything she'd ever accepted as the truth about the natural world and the laws that governed it, had just come up really short.

She reached for the TV remote and switched the muted set off, then nervously eyed the mirrored doors of the wardrobe, but wasn't sure why. Maybe she was operating on some instinctive superstition, or had recalled something fantastical about mirrors that she'd picked up from a book or a film a long time ago. But there was no one reflected in the glass, other than herself, who literally looked like she'd just heard a ghost.

She shuffled under the duvet and drew it under her chin. 'Who are you? Tell me.' Stephanie's voice shook from the cold.

Silence.

She felt wild and mad, almost hysterical and slightly beyond her terror, and in a new mental space she'd not inhabited before; one that was open and unrestrained, receptive and reckless, unthinking. 'Why are you here?' She concentrated her thoughts and feelings into the room; her mind grasped, reached and strained to see, to hear, to know.

The room was taut with tension, like the air of a classroom full of nervous children suddenly exposed under the gaze of a brutish teacher. It was a similar feeling to walking alone at night and hearing footsteps following. The air was somehow thinner, the space quieter, as though the room was holding its breath. It made her feel small, at the verge of something much greater than herself, like an ocean, or a vast night sky. And she felt so sad within it all, and so lonely. The crushing solitude brought a quiver to her jaw and blurred her eyes with tears.

'I'm cold . . .' There it was again, the voice. '. . . me. I'm so cold . . .'

The voice was over by the window. Young, female, distraught. *Lost?*

'I . . . I can hear you,' Stephanie said after a big swallow. 'Who are you?'

Not in answer but seemingly in acknowledgement of

Stephanie's challenge, the girl began to cry from a third location, from over by the wall behind the television set, or even slightly beyond the wall.

'I want to help you,' Stephanie said, but indecision about whether she wanted the contact to continue, on any level, reduced her voice to a whisper.

'Hold me.' This was spoken close to her ear as if someone was now stood beside the bed and leaned towards her.

Stephanie shrieked and backed further into the wall.

Nothing there. No one and nothing in the cold room she could see. But if *they* spoke again she was sure her mind would fizz out like a pinched candle flame, and that would be it for her.

Her skin tingled with pin pricks while she sat still and quiet in a cold silence for five minutes, according to her phone. Her mind became strangely absent, as if it were trying to slip towards, and then permanently maintain, a stunned nothingness.

Eventually, once her astonishment that she was still conscious and breathing, and had survived, slipped into curiosity again, she tried to comprehend what she was experiencing. Something so monumental it made her feel weightless.

Rearranging her position on the bed, she lay down, one side of her body crammed against the wall as if she needed to cling to something physical and tangible. 'Are . . . are you still here?' she asked the room again.

The mattress dipped and the bed softly rustled as the weight of another body lay down beside her.

TWENTY-FIVE

On the cold, wet path outside the house, upon which she stood in bare feet, Stephanie bent double and sucked hard at the night air. Her heart thumped thick inside her ears. She feared she was going to be sick.

Before throwing herself out of her room, and then the house, she'd possessed the presence of mind to pull her coat over her underwear, but had forgotten to force her feet into the unlaced trainers beside the bed.

Clutching her phone in a trembling hand, she worried she might drop the handset and quickly cupped it with both hands.

Rain vigorously speckled her face and bare legs. She stepped back to the front door hoping for cover, but a thick stream of water spattered the concrete and splashed her legs. The guttering high above was holed.

The cold was sobering.

Beyond the small metal gate between the ink-black mass of the encroaching privet hedges, she could see three houses across the road; all of the front windows were unlit. Some of the curtains hadn't been drawn in the upper windows. The houses and those who lived in them suggested disinterest in her plight. The horrible man who lived next door would not be safe to go to.

What could she actually say to anyone about what she had just experienced?

As she'd run through the house to the front door she had told herself she would call the police. But now she was outside, the urgency of the idea shrank inside her. What would she say to them? A ghost had climbed into her bed? People she could not see were coming into her room? A girl in an empty room next door had been beaten? Her landlords intimidated her?

'Shit. Shit, shit, shit, shit.' Her body trembled as her breathing shuddered in and out of her still heaving chest.

She should run right now, go somewhere.

Where?

Some kind of shelter for the homeless? A police cell would be better than that room. Maybe if she told the truth to the police she would be committed and sedated in a hospital. She seriously considered it as an option until the solid tangibility of the street and the great black house behind her, and the physical discomfort of the cold and wet, blunted the spike of her shock and drained the swamping terror that had compelled her to flee the room and stand outside the house like a frightened child stands outside the closed door of its parents' bedroom after a nightmare.

She looked at the time on her phone: two a.m. Three hours until the sky lightened. If she could stay awake that long, and then gather her bags and call one of the girls back home, and call a taxi to New Street Station, then this could all end. Three more hours.

Stephanie wiped the rain off her face, turned around and went back inside the dark house.

DAY FOUR

DAY FOUR

TWENTY-SIX

'Mmm. I just don't like this place. The other people here
. . . And the work is shit. But there's not enough of the shit
to go round, Bekka,' Stephanie said into her phone, and
then continued to gnaw at a fingernail.

'Same all over, bab. If you can't make a go of it down
there, makes you wonder where's any better for the rest of
us, don't it?'

'It would only be for a while. Maybe a week, two at
most. I've . . . I've just had a real setback. Please, Bekka.'

'I'll talk to Pete. It's his place. He's at football. I'll ask
him soon as he gets in. Will call you right away, yeah?'

'Thanks.'

There was pause before Bekka said, 'You OK, pet?'

The sympathetic concern in her friend's voice introduced a tremor to Stephanie's own. She moved the handset
away from her face to swallow and regain control of herself. She wiped her eyes, swallowed. 'Later then, yeah?'

'You wouldn't think about going back . . .'

'Not Ryan.' There were no bones holding her voice
upright. She could barely hear herself and had to clear her
throat again. 'He's seeing someone. Already asked.'

'Yeah, I heard. Didn't know whether you knew. But I
meant, you know . . . Val? Home?'

'Never.'

'Just a thought if it's that bad down there—'

'I can't. It's Val's house. I'm not eighteen any more. I have no rights there. Even if I wanted to go back she wouldn't let me in. We really went at it that last time. Permanent damage.' As Stephanie said this to her friend she wondered if she would soon have to beg her psychotic stepmother to give her shelter.

They said goodbye. Stephanie threw her phone onto the bed behind her. Three down, none to go. Joanie had been her first port of call. She was back with her mum and dad, sleeping in the spare room with twenty grand's worth of debt from student loans. Philippa was three months pregnant – *why hadn't she told Stephanie before?* – and staying with her boyfriend's mum. Besides Bekka and her boyfriend, an Asda cashier and a tyre-fitter respectively, none of her friends or their partners had jobs, despite one degree and over ten good A Levels between them.

We are all, literally, in it together.

She'd also phoned all five temping agencies before they closed to see if they had any work for her. They had all said the same thing in the same voice: *nothing's come in yet.* She'd even asked them to consider her for telesales, but they still offered nothing.

Stephanie grabbed her bag and phone and left the room she could not abide being inside any longer.

TWENTY-SEVEN

'God,' Stephanie said in a kind of nervy exhale, after sharply drawing breath. But the girl in the garden hadn't seen Stephanie behind the staircase window, not even when she had moved into the woman's peripheral vision.

The girl continued to smoke, one hand tucked under an arm, the other arm lazily bent at the elbow. Her cigarette was as long, thin and white as the fingers that held it. Standing beside a stained double mattress that leant against the garden wall, the girl stared into the middle distance, her face half turned from the house to stare at the thickets of wet scrub choking the overladen apple trees.

The girl in the garden also ignored Knacker's dog; this was the first time Stephanie had seen the creature. It was a type of bull terrier with black and brown tiger-like stripes that were smooth and tight around its intimidating musculature. The dog pulled towards the girl's legs, half growling and choking itself at the end of what looked like an anchor chain. Which meant the dog could see the girl too. The dog had also barked when the suggestion of an angry man had run through the house to the Russian girl's room, and during the nights when the corridor outside her room had filled with . . . she didn't know what. So the dog's reaction might not indicate that the girl was actually *there*.

Not for the first time Stephanie was astonished at herself for having such a thought, though it was un-accompanied by a familiar freeze of fear, because it was daylight. *But then* . . .

She had to get to the bank before it closed to withdraw cash with her chequebook and passport, and she carried on down the stairs to the ground floor, wondering if she had just seen the Russian girl – she of the strong perfume and high heels who had ignored her and seemed to exist without electric light, who wept alone in the dark, and who Stephanie had virtually come to believe didn't exist. *The people of the dark.*

But she might now exist. *Oh please let her be real.*

Stephanie stopped and thought harder about her second night in the building; her sighting of the Russian girl had been fleeting as the woman passed into the room. But she had received an impression that her second floor neighbour was tall, blonde and attractive; the girl in the garden was pretty and fitted that description.

If it was the same girl then why was she smoking in the garden when she lived on the second floor? And how did she get into the garden? Probably via the ground floor, though Knacker had said the ground floor was out of bounds. Or maybe she had walked down the side of the house as it was detached.

Excited by the idea that the girl might actually be real, Stephanie turned and jogged back up the stairs to peer through the stairwell window.

The girl had gone; the dog was quiet and had moved out of sight too.

She peered around the garden, from the unappealing, cluttered patio to the high brick walls that ran along both sides of the property and concealed the neighbouring houses. The end of the rear yard was obscured. Brambles at head height erupted through small bushes and surrounded an ancient oak tree in the middle of the area. The sight of the tree made Stephanie feel uncomfortable, though she did not know why. Through the oak tree's lowest branches she could make out the top of a wooden shed, an old structure, lopsided and swallowed by the unruly, inappropriately fecund vegetation. By daylight she could also see blackberry vines, as thick as serpents, red as fresh blood, entwined amongst the dross.

She guessed the end of the garden bordered the rear garden of a house in the next street, parallel to Edgehill Road. Over the far walls peeked the upper floors and roofs of houses.

Between the oak tree and the patio, chipboard and offcuts of timber had been soaked by rain so many times they'd begun to look like cardboard. She could see two entire doors down there and another stained mattress close to where the back door of the house should be. Around the timber, huge chunks of plaster and broken masonry had been dumped in untidy heaps, as if thrown out the back of the house and left to erode in the garden. A great deal of renovation had taken place at number 82, though not recently.

So who would go down there? A hardened smoker? But why, when smoking was clearly allowed indoors?

Stephanie closed her eyes and took a deep breath before resuming her descent of the staircase. She found herself unable to dwell on the girl's vanishing act as much as she ordinarily would have done. Or should do.

On the ground floor, she peered around the banisters and into the unlit corridor that tunnelled towards the rear of the house and the solitary locked door, situated at the end of the hall on the right hand side. Listening intently, she peered back up the stairs but heard nothing.

Curious about what Fergal had been doing outside the door, Stephanie entered the short passage and moved into the shadows. The walls on either side were painted white but had not received any attention in years. The layers of paint on the wallpaper were thick and the colour of vanilla ice cream dropped upon summer pavements. The area was musty with a hint of gas, an underfloor odour she associated with old houses divided into sub-lets, and nothing unusual.

There had once been three doors on the ground floor, but two had been bricked up and painted over many years ago. She could see the outlines of the door frames; they reminded her of empty picture frames in the unused space of an art gallery.

The surviving door that Fergal had been so enthralled by had the vague outline of '1A' between two holes where screws had once held a flat number in place, and a key-hole.

Stephanie put an ear to the surface of the door and listened.

Nothing.

As if in response to her investigation, somewhere, far up inside the building, another door opened.

Stephanie moved out of the corridor quickly and only

paused to check the post: the usual flyers for fried chicken and kebab shops, a minicab card – MILLENNIUM – and a brown window envelope from Birmingham City Council addressed to Mr Bennet. The letter inside was red and the envelope had FINAL WARNING printed across the front.

Bennet?

Stephanie dropped the post and let herself out of the house.

Steely bright light stung the back of her eyes, as though she'd just opened curtains on a new morning, though it was already noon; she'd slept through her alarm that morning and not woken until 11.30 – something she'd thought impossible to achieve in that room after the night's disturbances.

The room's lights had still been on when she'd awoken. Outside her barred window cars had occasionally passed. There was no sign that anyone had been in the bed beside her at any time during the night once she'd returned from the front path.

Once the sphincter-pinching terror that came with the suggestion of a body lying down next to her had become a long period of silent inactivity on the mattress, and long after the cold and drizzle of the night air had calmed her down, exhaustion had chosen its moment to overrun her flattened body and mind. She'd remained unconscious until she'd woken late.

No bad dreams had followed her out of sleep and into daylight either. She'd brushed her teeth and washed in a warm and mercifully silent bathroom, feeling as if she were hyper-real and too large for life; as if she were mimicking a routine that had long become abnormal in the building. But she'd still tiptoed around the parts of the first floor she used, nervous of starting *it* again, of waking *something* up.

At least she was outside now, alive and well. Even pocks of drizzle against her face, that would soon make her hair frizz, were a welcome change to the close air of the house and the smells of neglect and age. Out here, anyone she came across would probably be of flesh and blood too.

Without another person in sight she hurried to the bus stop. And was reminded again how odd she found this pocket of North Birmingham; it lacked pedestrians until you neared the city centre, maintaining a condition of near total silence beyond the main traffic arteries. It was either too tired to stir, asleep, or dead.

She withdrew one hundred pounds with a cheque at the bank, then walked the length of Broad Street, wandering about the cafés and bars of Gas Street Basin to check on her job applications.

After being been told, in the last of ten businesses she'd submitted a CV to, that they were still looking at a waiting list of over 200 applicants, she sat inside a Costa Coffee and treated herself to the cheapest sandwich on offer and a small latte.

Was there nothing left in this city that anyone would pay her to do? Even the assistant managers of KFC and McDonalds had shaken their heads three months earlier, and she expected them to repeat the gesture when she tried again this afternoon. Three days' work last week was starting to feel like a lottery win.

Her desire to not be inside 82 Edgehill Road continued to prickle through her like static, and compelled her to begin a list in her 'Jobs' notebook of those businesses on New Street and Corporation Street where she'd already left a CV, or completed an application form. She intended to check in with them during what was left of the afternoon. She'd do anything to put off a return 'home'.

But as her pen scratched in her notebook, her thoughts wandered off the task and off the page. The world of jobs, shoppers, passing motorists and idling families dwindled in her mind, along with a consideration of her ability to earn enough money to ever do more than scratch out an existence in a rented room.

Thoughts of her access to something far more sinister, and significant, at 82 Edgehill Road reignited flurries of panic in her stomach. If she were honest, a powerful curiosity had come to life too, until she found it near impossible to concentrate on the limited prospects of the minimum-wage, uniformed, service-industry positions she wanted so desperately. And instead of employment opportunities, or employment futilities, it was observations about the house that she was soon listing.

She gave each of her encounters in the house a fresh page in her notebook and was shocked to see how quickly the pages stacked up.

From a sense of three presences in her first room, which she listed as UNDER THE BED/FIREPLACE/THE MOVER, to the RUSSIAN GIRL ON THE 2ND FL, the VOICE IN THE BATHROOM, and FEMALE VOICE, FIRST FLOOR NEIGHBOUR, she progressed to a page titled: THE ONES WHO WANDER. Here she wrote

ANGRY MALE – ALL THREE FLOORS and WOMAN WHO MOVES (who ran into my room from first floor corridor and spoke to me). This final observation was embellished with a footnote: 'Or could this be the same one that sat on bed in second floor room?'

Her lists amounted to multiple encounters with what might be at least seven different *presences*.

A growing suspicion that she was incrementally slipping into some form of psychosis made her wonder how to address the possibility. Maybe at a GP's surgery. Her stepmother's mental illness had been Stephanie's motive for taking A Level psychology, so she knew something about this area. Theories she'd studied about personality disorders suggested mental ill-health was often pre-natal and inherited. An uncle had been schizophrenic, on her mum's side. He'd committed suicide, as had one of his sons who lived in Australia; a cousin she had never met. Perhaps she had that gene too.

Yet the notion of suffering delusions was contradicted by her current surroundings; now that she sat in a well-lit café, surrounded by a thoroughly material and conventional world, her perception within the house seemed anything but balanced or rational. Could mental illness just switch itself off when you went outdoors? Surely it was a near permanent state of being. Which contributed to her doubts that schizophrenia was the cause of her experiences; that condition would give her no rest and she would be hearing voices now.

The world around the café appeared to be a startlingly unimaginative and ordinary place in comparison to the one she returned to each evening in Perry Bar. Gas Street

Basin's boutiques, restaurants and the skyline dominated by the new library symbolized an affront to the grubby and sinister world of Edgehill Road. Outside the house, the world was a place where superstition and considerations of the supernormal remained the preserve of children, of fiction, computer games and films.

At least the trip to the city had shaken her out of what was beginning to feel like a constant delirium. And this was a world she had been fully in step with only a few days before. Her circumstances coerced her to wonder if she now straddled two very different states of existence, one natural and one unnatural.

Making lists of paranormal phenomena in her job-seeking notebook began to feel absurd, and she fought a desire to hide the open pages should anyone at a nearby table glance across. But as belief and disbelief continued to change like governments within her mind, Stephanie returned to her journal. Within each entry she began to add details, pertinent to each experience, like: 'sensitivity to sadness, grief, fear, solitude'.

Her sensitivity to these atmospheres also stayed within the four walls of number 82; her receptivity ceased when the encounters stopped. But if she had some special connection with the dead then surely the dead were everywhere and she would see them everywhere. So what made the house, or her in it, so special?

Maybe a past trauma was locked inside the building and she was picking it up, like a radio received signals. It was an idea or notion she vaguely recalled from a source long forgotten.

And she wasn't alone in her awareness of the inexplicable; Fergal had confirmed as much about the house's other occupants. She suspected Knacker could not accept the idea of them being there, though his recalcitrance did not exclude him from experiencing the same things as her: the camera, the locks on his door?

She added 'ODOURS' to her lists and then defined them. Smells that also dispersed as quickly as they appeared and were pertinent to specific parts of the building, or seemed to be attached to routines conducted within the building.

She noted the 'radical drops in temperature' which had accompanied each and every experience. Again, such changes to the physical world could not have been imagined. *Could they?*

What would experts and officials make of the notebook if she went missing? The morbidity of the idea made her shudder.

A member of the counter staff came and collected her coffee mug, which she intuited as an inducement to leave the café. Stephanie retouched her make-up, packed away her things and left.

A break from the house made her feel like she'd been airlifted from a disaster. The opportunity to organize the debris of her thoughts and recent memories had been vital; she'd even partly regrouped the scattered refugees of her wits and remembered who she had been before she'd moved into Edgehill Road. Time spent in a safe environment to consider her situation also left her with the suspicion that she was not in any physical danger – at least not from what had amassed around her in the house while remaining unseen.

With the exception of the male presence, she couldn't be certain that what she had felt around her in that building amounted to more than fear, loneliness, despair and anger. Or cries for help. And those couldn't harm you.

Could they?

Who were they? What were they? The idea that the suffering had continued for some time, and would always continue in the wretched building, was unbearable for her to ponder. She dared to wonder what she might be able to do for them – the trapped and the crying, the tormented.

TWENTY-EIGHT

Stephanie entered the house as silently as she was able, then crept up the stairs, but only managed two steps across the kitchen lino before she came to a standstill. Her fingers released the plastic supermarket bag and it hit the floor with a thump.

The girl smoking a cigarette by the kitchen sink turned around. Caution flared in the woman's bright green eyes. Surprise was followed by relief, as if Stephanie was not who she'd expected to see.

Stephanie was unable to speak. *Could this . . . Is this . . . Am I seeing a . . . a ghost?*

Greedy for proof she was looking at the living, and without daring to blink in case her eyes opened to find herself alone in the kitchen again, her vision groped about the woman's body: a collarless leather jacket with a bronze zipper, a black polo neck jumper, skinny-fit jeans tucked into the high-heeled boots, three gold rings on her manicured fingers, highlights in her shoulder-length blonde hair, a pretty face with angular bone structure, bronze eye make-up. The woman was detailed, three dimensional, coloured . . . there was perfume too. She recognized it: Miss Dior.

Stephanie snapped herself out of the fugue. To regain

control of her voice she cleared her throat. 'Are you . . . I mean . . .'

The girl eyed Stephanie from head to toe too, and took in the functional white blouse and black trousers she wore to interviews, and her expression developed a haughty disapproval. The woman's eyes were beautiful though, like those of a husky or wolf: green flecked with black, the eyelids offering a hint of the Asiatic. Surely a spirit could not be so vivid.

'I'm sorry,' Stephanie said. 'I'm not sure . . . this might sound crazy . . .'

The woman frowned.

'I didn't expect to see you. You made me jump.'

The woman looked past Stephanie and took in the kitchen with a sweep of her lovely eyes. 'This was not what I expect.' The voice was heavily accented, almost certainly Eastern European. The Russian girl? And possibly the one she had seen outside in the yard that morning, though the hair looked different.

'Are you on the second floor?'

The question confused the woman so Stephanie pointed at the ceiling. 'Upstairs?'

'Upstairs, mmm, yes. You live here?' She seemed to get three syllables into 'here', but Stephanie liked the way she wrestled English words out of her mouth.

'Yes. This floor.'

The girl frowned again and Stephanie identified the first sign of fatigue from communicating with someone for whom English was a second language. Though her relief that the girl was real was far greater. 'Were you outside this morning?'

Her question was greeted with another frown.

Stephanie walked to the sink unit and passed within a force field of hair spray and skin cream. She pointed at the garden with something approaching desperation. 'Down there? Did I see you down there this morning, smoking?'

The girl glanced at the tumult of vegetation and building refuse below, as if she were looking at a dog's excrement on the side of her boots. 'There? Never. Is shit. Whole place, shit.'

'Tell me about it.'

'Hmm?'

'Never mind.'

She recalled Knacker saying something about two girls moving in, about her having company, but had assumed it was another one of his lies. 'You moved here today?'

'Today? Yes, yes. In the morning I come.' The girl took a hard drag on her cigarette.

Now Stephanie stood closer she could see the woman wasn't as young as she'd first appeared. Either the skin around her eyes was aged under so much make-up, or the expression in her eyes appeared too old for the lower part of her face.

Averse to Stephanie's scrutiny, the girl moved away from the dregs of the sooty dusk light hanging around the sink unit. 'You work here?' the girl asked, squinting in the smoke enveloping her head.

'Here? Birmingham, yes. Sometimes. One day here, one day there.'

The girl didn't seem impressed with her answer, though Stephanie couldn't work out why. She already made her feel frumpy, and was now adding worthless to a minor crisis of confidence.

'But work is good here?' the woman asked.

'No. Not really. Same as everywhere.'

'I have good work. Dusseldorf. Vienna. They say it very good here.'

'Depends on what you can do. I'm just starting out.'

The girl frowned and looked slightly offended. Though again Stephanie couldn't understand why.

'I'm Stephanie.' She extended her hand, to break the awkward silence.

The girl took it with her long, cold fingers. 'Svetlana.'

'Where are you from?'

'Lithuania.'

'See you's two met then,' said Knacker McGuire.

At the appearance of the landlord in the kitchen doorway, Stephanie noticed Svetlana's face drop at the precise moment her own spirits plummeted.

Dressed once again in his new jeans and trainers, he was grinning and jaunty on his feet, like a stupid youth who thought he'd done something clever. 'Your room's ready, girl,' he said to Svetlana. 'New bed an' everyfing, like. Put a TV in there too. If I don't say so myself, it's a nice room. Fink you'll be very comfortable in there.'

Svetlana didn't answer. She watched Knacker, her gaze hard, and exhaled a plume of smoke. 'My bags. He bring them?'

'Yeah, yeah. Don't worry about nuffin'. All in hand, like.'

'There is other bathroom, yes?'

'What baffroom?'

Stephanie didn't like the way Knacker had started to squint and jut his chin out. His eyes took a moment to glare at her too, making her feel unwelcome in the room now that another tenant's disappointment in the property was becoming evident. Stephanie turned away and unwrapped her boxed dinner on the counter beside the microwave and feigned disinterest in the exchange.

'This is not what you say. You said *new*. New kitchen, new bathroom. But this? This one is not new. I don't use it. You must be joking.' Svetlana's last line sounded Italian and might have been a figure of speech picked up from another traveller.

'Lick a paint. All's gonna get done up. That's what I said.'

'No, you say *new*. No one can eat here. Is filthy.'

Stephanie was delighted by the girl's resistance, but the slither of fear that was beginning to frost her stomach overruled her shame at preparing food in the dirty kitchen.

'Don't you worry about nuffin'. Other people might not have the same standards as you and me,' he said, as if fingering Stephanie as the source of the dilapidation and dirt. 'But it's all gonna be fixed up. Be like living in a hotel.'

'Hotel?' Svetlana snorted with derisive laughter. 'What kind hotel? Mr Knacker, I tell you I have major problem with this. This is not what you say.' She broke off and said something in her own language.

'You gotta give it time, girl. You know, period of adjustment and all that.'

'When Margaret see this . . . I mean, she will say same as me. You have not told truth. I will speak to Andrei.'

'Settle down. Settle down, yeah!' Knacker was losing his temper.

Stephanie's own nervy bewilderment was beginning to make the two minutes she needed to wait for her bolognaise to finish its first cooking cycle feel like a decade. And the food would also needed stirring, before cooking for another two minutes. She turned to leave the kitchen, her eyes lowered.

'And this girl.' Svetlana nodded at Stephanie and Stephanie really wished she hadn't. 'This girl say the work . . .' Svetlana waved a hand dismissively from side to side '. . . is bad here.'

Knacker turned his head to follow Stephanie out of the room and she caught sight of his pale, angry face haloed by recently pampered curls. He reeked of aftershave. 'You don't want to be listening to anyfing other people say, like. What do they know? And *she* knows how I feel about anyone bad moufing my house. *She* knows it's being fixed up too, cus I told her the same fing as you.'

Stephanie hurried back along the corridor to her room, and caught the end of what had become a confrontation. She admired the girl's courage in the face of Knacker's temper; her own had wilted immediately.

'This is not right. Not acceptable.'

'You don't tell me what's acceptable. That's not how it works. You get me? You's lucky to have a fuckin' roof over your head, considering where you come from. Lifuania! Now I'm a reasonable man, I don't . . .'

Stephanie closed her door and waited in her room until the muffled exchange moved out of the kitchen, went up one floor and passed out of her hearing. Above her head two sets of feet bumped about angrily in what sounded like a wrestling manoeuvre. A door slammed. She flinched.

TWENTY-NINE

Dusk was swallowed by nightfall. The time crept towards ten p.m.

Stephanie remained upon her bed, lying in the same position she had flopped into after Bekka's text message had come in at eight. She'd already packed her bags ready for evacuation, checked her train timetable, and then paced for hours waiting for Bekka to call. But the communication was better disclosed by text than phone call; an easier medium when the news is bad. Bekka's boyfriend 'didn't think it was a good idea for you to crash' and they 'didn't have room anyway'.

The rejection made Stephanie feel ashamed, as if a ridiculous, embarrassing request had been rebuffed. Within her disappointment was also dread, like a doctor had just imparted terrible news. For a while an overwhelming sense of abandonment had made her feel so cold her jaw had trembled.

Straight after her request for charity had been rejected by the last friend she had appealed to, Stephanie briefly considered putting a call in to her stepmother. An idea swiftly killed in infancy when she realized the ashes of a bridge that badly burned might never be reassembled, even on a temporary basis. And it was already late enough for

Val to be drunk, maybe with her boyfriend, Tony, if he had come back since Stephanie had left home. Val would now be half-conscious as white wine swam around antidepressants in an otherwise empty stomach. There was no point trying to communicate with the woman any day after four in the afternoon.

Her demoralized thoughts continued to trickle down, until they became sluggish and vague, at around the same time the girl in the empty room next door began to cry, at eleven p.m.

Stephanie retrieved her carrier bag from the floor beside her bed and removed the packet of earplugs: USED BY FORMULA ONE RACING DRIVERS, or so the packaging claimed. This had been an idea she'd had in town, to cope with the disturbances if she was forced to spend another night here.

She thought about going up one floor and knocking on the door of the room directly above her own, which must now be Svetlana's room, to ask the girl to come down and see if she could hear the crying in the room too. A witness to the disturbance would be the final assurance that she was not suffering from an onset of schizophrenia.

But she decided against paying a visit to the new tenant because the second floor was her least favourite part of the building, was too close to the landlord's flat, and she had a strong suspicion that Knacker would disapprove of any contact between them. Two dissatisfied minds could easily form a conspiracy, or a resistance. And she could not bear the thought of inciting further contact with either of her landlords for the limited time she remained in the building.

At least Svetlana had remained in residence despite the

confrontation with Knacker. She and the new girl were strangers, both disgruntled and wary, but there was safety in numbers. They were witnesses to each other's presence, and the idea of Svetlana upstairs was profoundly reassuring.

Intermittently, through the evening, Stephanie had heard the girl's feet bump through the ceiling while the Lithuanian barked into her phone in her first language. But as with Stephanie's observation of many Europeans, it was hard to tell, by the tone and volume of a voice alone, whether an argument was in progress or if a grievance was being expressed; on a school trip to Rome she had seen people order coffee in a way that made her recoil.

Svetlana's television still murmured, and whoever spoke onscreen sounded as if they were underwater with their mouth full of food. The idea that she may no longer be the primary recipient of Knacker's bullying, or the focus of his shakedown operation, also provided a guilty relief. Svetlana had suggested that another girl's arrival was imminent too – a Margaret, or *Margereet* – who might provide an additional buffer between her and the two cousins.

If she could cope with the *other things,* she promised herself she could get through until Monday. If she was offered work Tuesday to Friday, and if the new female tenants remained, she wondered if staying put for a week, while saving her wages for a new room, was feasible. By next Friday she might even have enough money to legitimately move to a new room. Her bank card would be here too.

Sunday, Monday, Tuesday . . . through 'til Friday meant

six more nights in this building. But the anticipation of just one felt like a penal sentence involving mental torture that was administered arbitrarily.

Eyeing the empty side of her bed nervously, Stephanie slipped the plugs into her ears and let the spongy devices expand until her hearing was engulfed by the thump of her own blood. She placed her phone handset on the mattress between the two pillows. Finally, she slipped the duvet up to her chin and tried to preoccupy her mind with thoughts of what she could do on Sunday, in the city centre, to fill the day away from the building.

THIRTY

The metal of the structure was painted green to match the long grass and clumps of weeds in the overgrown garden. From within the circular mouth of the corrugated iron dome, the old woman did nothing but stare and grin. The elderly figure wore a brown cardigan that was too big for her small shape, over a threadbare tea dress frayed around the hem. Her face was weathered and impossibly old, reminding Stephanie of a small baked apple set inside a white wig.

Stephanie kept looking over her shoulder at the house behind her, while trying to account for the occasional far off crumps and the corresponding shudders beneath her feet. Up in the air a siren wailed with such urgency and despair it made her panic worse.

'Where should I go?' Stephanie pointed at the house. 'Do I go back in there?'

The old woman didn't answer or seem to be anything but amused at her plight in the cold rain beneath the featureless metallic sky.

A little boy dressed in a cowboy costume made from offcuts, hobbled around in front of the old woman. The boy's identity was concealed by a handkerchief over the lower half of his face, which met the brim of the hat covering his eyes. He sang a song that was muffled by the handkerchief. 'All around the Mulberry Bush, The monkey chased the weasel. The monkey stopped to pull up his sock, Pop! goes the weasel. Half a pound of tuppenny rice, Half a pound of treacle. Four maids to open the door, Pop! goes the weasel.'

Come and be his friend, come, come. The woman's gleeful expression succeeded in pressing home this suggestion, while her black eyes glinted with what could have been welcome or mischief; Stephanie didn't know.

A few yards behind the shelter, hanging from the branch of an oak tree by their necks, were the bodies of four women. They wore long grey gowns and their hair was tied up in coils from which stray locks fell across their bloodless faces. All of their wrists were tied together with shoelaces.

You can beat them too. Come, come. They don't mind. Stephanie didn't hear the old woman say this; she heard the message inside her head.

Even from a distance she could see that the eyes of one of the executed women were open. The moment Stephanie realized this, she saw the hanged woman's face in close-up. When their stares met, the woman's expression filled with a frightful intelligence at the horror she swayed through beneath the tree branch.

Stephanie turned and ran to the house, the ground seeming to shudder so violently it added a buoyancy to her progress, like she was on the surface of a trampoline that was gradually settling down after a period of frenzied activity.

Inside the old kitchen with the flagstone floor, someone

she couldn't see said, 'They're inside. They want a word with you.'

The people in the next room she entered had all lifted their arms into the air, as if they had recently been holding hands around the table but now preferred to dangle their fingers in the darkness that filled the spaces between the candle flames.

The eyes of two of the people were closed as their pale features stiffened in concentration. The jowly face of a bald man, his remaining hair oiled flat against his skull, glistened with sweat. The white shirt he wore with a tie and braces was sodden. Beside him a bespectacled woman with set hair and a severe fringe had screwed up her mouth as if in great pain. The third person at the table was female and wore a hat and dark glasses indoors for a reason Stephanie didn't understand but immediately disliked. On the centre of the table was a wooden box with what looked like a curtained door of purple velvet.

Stephanie couldn't see the walls or floor, despite the four candles set beyond the table and arranged in a line along the dark sideboard.

Suspecting that something nearby was moving on the lightless floor, she fought a desire to cringe. She flattened her back against the nearest wall. Sounds of a heavy, thick presence uncoiling continued beneath the table.

The air of the room was cold enough to make Stephanie's teeth chatter; gusts of air whipped her face like slipstreams of energy produced by darting movements in narrow spaces. The sudden flattening and then springing up of the candle light attested to a motion she couldn't see and certainly didn't want to venture her hands into.

Her legs and feet were numb. Not only was she unable to move across the room to where she knew a door to be, she actually began slipping sideways and away from what she yearned for. The movement of her body brought a fresh surge of panic into her unravelling thoughts. An attempt to cry out from a mouth now swollen with what felt like a squash ball wrapped in a handkerchief, was as ineffective as the resistance of her nerveless feet which slid her body sideways along one wall. Her fingernails snatched at the wallpaper at her back.

As she neared the head of the table and slipped behind the seated man, her feet also rose off the floor, and she bent double to try and seize something at ground level before she rose any higher into the cold air.

The moment the three seated people raised their faces to the ceiling and opened their mouths to utter cries of delight, Stephanie understood that her ankles and knees were bound together by a rough string that looked hairy. And her fingers may have been pulling at the twine for long enough for her to have lost several fingernails.

Her inability to breathe around the sopping impediment in her mouth, that felt in danger of sliding over her tongue and blocking her throat, brought a terror of suffocation into the jostle of trauma, panic and horror already overfilling her skull. It was a terror soon eclipsed by the elevation of her body, further up the wall and into thin air, as if gravity no longer had any claim upon her. No hands pulled or pushed her upwards; she was just too insubstantial to remain on the ground.

And it was then she knew the destination of her unwilling journey. She was going up and up and up, and there was nothing to hold onto, because she was being drawn into the black thing upon the ceiling. It was already in position and waiting for her.

DAY FIVE

DAY FIVE

THIRTY-ONE

'No! Not up there! Never!'

Panting like she'd just broken across the finish line of a sprint, Stephanie came awake sitting up, her head thrown back between her shoulders. She stayed that way, staring at the blank ceiling, until her heartbeat slowed.

An avalanche of horrible clips from the nightmare – *another one* – sluiced with jumbled recollections about the house and what had climbed into her bed two nights ago. She rocked forward to clutch her face. Checked the time by peering between two fingers. Midday.

What?

Not possible. The curtains were too thick to provide any sense of the world outside. She scrambled across to the window and tore the drapes apart. Dull light shone through the metal bars and grimy panes of glass.

She'd been asleep for twelve hours. Had not set her alarm because she expected to wake, or be awoken, much earlier. Above her head a distant mobile phone ringtone chanted dance music before being cut short by Svetlana's muffled voice.

What had she been dreaming of? Hanged women . . . that face she could still see, so pale, the lips blue, the eyes alight with life, pleading. She doubted she would ever forget it, ever recover from seeing it so vividly.

A boy in a hat. A woman by a tunnel, or a metal shed; she wasn't sure what it had been. A siren. A dark room. People sat around a table . . . an old hat, braces, grey hair . . . something moving under the table? She'd been choking on something stuffed inside her mouth. Candle light. A box that looked familiar. *Was it?* Her body floating and unable to get back down to the floor, going up and up . . .

Jumbled dark nonsense of dreamtime. The house was driving her crazy.

Stephanie collapsed into the pillows. Thoughts of going out into the wet, inhospitable street, and waiting for a bus in an uncovered shelter with litter about her feet, of tramping around vaguely familiar streets and closed doors, trying not to spend money, filled her with fatigue in advance of even climbing out of bed.

'I can't. I just can't.'

When the panic of the nightmare subsided, the small space created inside her mind buzzed with a new anxiety about money, CVs, application forms, that drove her into a weariness so profound she wondered if she would ever be able to move again.

She took a tissue from her sleeve and dabbed it against her eyes. Then crawled back under her duvet and lay still, in silence, and stared at the watery grey light about the window and allowed it to drift inside her.

She remained immobile for over an hour, until her need for a cup of strong coffee and to pee compelled her to move her legs and swing them over the side of the bed. She would have to go out to buy milk. Perhaps reaching the shop at the end of the road would be manageable.

THIRTY-TWO

As Stephanie stepped off the front path and inside the darkened hallway of the house, the aluminium light of the street shrunk behind her with the closing of the front door. The moment both of her feet were grounded inside the house, she stopped moving, and immediately considered running back outside.

The tall, gangly figure in the dirty puffa jacket that stood at the end of the ground floor passage appeared to have turned its head sharply to greet her entrance with a grimace so aggressive she was sure it had been accompanied by an animal snarl.

Fergal turned his body away from the door, and the fabric of his coat rustled like a serpent in dry grass. Elevating himself to his full height, with his long, bony neck extended in a nasty rebuke, he seemed to tilt the top half of his body towards her. His long arms remained stiff at his sides, the broad white palms confronting her like faces in a gang of bullies. *Come on then!* She knew the posture from outside pubs and nightclubs in Stoke, but was shocked to have it turned in her direction.

Stephanie moved as calmly as she could to the foot of the stairs. Just once, as she passed out of sight, did she glance through the banisters on her way up to the first floor to see that Fergal had returned his attention to the solitary door. He rested his bloodless forehead upon it now, as if with affection.

At the sight of the girl coming out of the bathroom, Stephanie came to a sudden stop on the first floor landing. The girl jumped. Then relaxed her body, and her face into a broad smile accompanied by a giggle.

Stephanie didn't know what to react to first: the fact that another female stranger was indoors and that the figure was living and real, or how the woman was dressed. Those just weren't the kind of shoes you saw anywhere besides nightclubs or strip clubs: white leather platforms with transparent soles and heels; outrageous shoes matched by a tight blue dress that zipped up the front and caught the bathroom's electric light like oil in water. The dress was made of latex.

The woman's raven hair was perfectly groomed into a silky torrent that ended in a straight line at her waist, and her skin was evolving from caramel to orange from a great deal of time spent on a sun bed. The girl looked down her body as if to acknowledge Stephanie's shock. 'I have date already.'

The girl must be Margaret, Svetlana's friend.

At least this was something Knacker hadn't lied about. But the incongruity of two glamorous girls accepting rooms in the wretched house from the ghastly cousins struck her as more surreal than odd. She wished she could accept the house's unpredictable nature; the tension in her neck and limbs warned her that she could not.

Stephanie laughed nervously, but wasn't sure why because she found nothing about the situation amusing. It was Sunday afternoon in North Birmingham, so who went on a date looking like that? Unless they were paid to. Stephanie's blood cooled.

'Margaret?'

The girl cocked her head in surprise.

Stephanie near choked in the aerosol of perfume that clouded off the girl; a scent that may have been pleasant, but became sickly on the grim and dowdy landing. 'Svetlana told me.'

'Oh. Yes. You live too, yes?'

Stephanie frowned in bewilderment.

'Sorry, my English not so good.'

The addendum to Margaret's question enabled Stephanie to understand she was being asked whether she lived in the building and not if she were alive. Though neither question, she decided, was inappropriate at 82 Edgehill Road.

Stephanie looked over her shoulder warily, remembering Fergal wasn't far away or in any kind of mood they would want to engage with.

Margaret said, 'I go,' and started to teeter to the stairs to begin a short ascent, fraught with danger, in the heels. If the girl lived on the second floor she would either be in the room of the crying Russian girl, or in the room Stephanie had occupied during her first night.

Stephanie followed the girl to the stairs, eager to keep the conversation going and to warn her. 'Are you from Lithuania?'

'Albania.'

'You moved in today?'

Margaret spoke over her shoulder, smiling. 'Yes. Yes. Morning.'

'Can we talk later?'

The girl mounted the stairs, her hips and bottom swaying in a manner that could only be provocative in the latex dress. 'Er, yes. We talk. Er, later.'

'After your date?'

'Of course.'

'I have coffee too.'

'You'd probably best drink it yourself. She's gonna be busy for a bit, like.' Knacker stood where the stairs met the second floor.

Stephanie never moved beyond the bend in the staircase. Had he been listening? What had she said? Thank God she'd stopped herself in time. But would he still be angry with her?

'Awright, darling,' he said to Margaret, his eyes dreamy as he leered at the girl from head to foot. He made little attempt to let her pass, forcing her body to brush against his.

The date! Surely not!

Stephanie dipped her head and retreated down the stairs to the first floor. The thought that a pretty girl like Margaret would even contemplate going out with a weasel like Knacker sickened her. Foreign girls could get into desperate situations; she knew they came to England hoping for a better life, to escape poverty, so had Margaret fallen for Knacker's lies about his affluence and professional success and been lured here? But lured here for what?

Not that. Please.

Continuing his admiration of Margaret, Knacker's voice travelled down the stairwell. 'You look beautiful, darling. Stunning, like.'

Stephanie hurried back to her room and threw herself inside before locking the door.

Within minutes she heard other footsteps ascending the staircase – maybe even two sets of feet – accompanied by Knacker's horrible cackle and interspersed with his contributions to a conversation she couldn't make out. Knacker was speaking to another man whose deep voice rumbled in the distance and then passed out of hearing. A voice that seemed too deep to belong to Fergal.

The appearance of strangers in the communal areas of the building should have brought relief, but only succeeded in amplifying her concerns about the nature and purpose of the new tenants.

She left her door open a fraction, so she could see who would eventually come back down the stairs. It hadn't been open long when the cries began above her head.

THIRTY-THREE

Stephanie stared at the ceiling and listened to the sounds of exaggerated female arousal. Rising in crescendos, the cries would stop just short of a scream, while a bed rattled and groaned beneath what sounded like an eager bestial congress. Either Svetlana or Margaret was having sex, but probably Margaret as she'd seemed prepared for it.

The noise originated from above the ceiling of the room next to Stephanie's; she could hear the coupling through the wall against which her bed rested. But was Margaret having sex with Knacker, or Fergal, or the third man who had just been on the stairs?

Punter.

Margaret having sex during her first day inside the house was more shocking than the idea of the participation of either of her landlords. And in the very room where the Russian girl had been crying before she had sex with a smelly male presence that didn't exist.

Stephanie marvelled to the point of shock about how anyone could feel enough desire for that kind of activity inside this building. And yet here was another Eastern European girl, an obvious migrant, and one shaking a bed apart beneath an unknown male presence.

The sounds continued for fifteen minutes, unbroken,

before total silence fell over the house like a black sheet dropped across an old and cruel birdcage. The interior appeared quieter than ever, as if the very bricks and mortar were muted in shock at this carnal display.

As Stephanie breathed normally again, she remained curiously exhausted from the tension the sounds had instilled inside her body. She knew all about sex – *who didn't?* – and she had been active with Ryan, her third lover. But the noises had made her feel like a child who had stumbled across an explicit film and been shocked to her core by what she had seen. Her reaction to the sounds was not dissimilar to her reaction to the violence she'd overheard in the room next door.

Within five minutes of the noisy intimacy ending, there was movement on the staircase again. Stephanie moved to the door of her room and killed the overhead lights. Peered through the gap and heard Knacker's voice on the stairwell. 'Anytime, mate. You just call that number, yeah? Speak wiv me, like.'

When the first floor landing lights clicked on, Stephanie ducked back inside her room, though not before spying a pair of short legs dressed in khaki chinos and brown shoes that descended ahead of Knacker's training shoes. So the man who had gone upstairs with Knacker had definitely not been Fergal. And this visitor had been with one of the girls, most probably Margaret: 'You just call that number.'

Stephanie stood behind her door, paralyzed with bewilderment and disoriented with shock. Outside, a car alarm blipped and a vehicle pulled away from the curb, hurriedly. Upstairs, the toilet flushed. Stephanie glimpsed

Margaret's long, tanned legs, that ended in bare feet, coming down the stairs.

She pushed her door closed, locked it as quietly as she was able. When Margaret came out of the bathroom and returned to the second floor a few minutes later, the girl joined Svetlana in the Lithuanian's room; Stephanie heard the two women talking above her head. She couldn't make out what they were saying. A television came on. Feet bumped about. A mobile phone burst into dance music.

Knacker thumped up and down the stairs three times, and each time added his voice to the conversation in Svetlana's room.

Stephanie sat immobile, in her own silence, looking at the black walls and the white ceiling of her room with fresh eyes, hoping hard enough for it to feel like she was praying, that her new suspicions about the nature of the house were not true.

THIRTY-FOUR

She crept out of her room to use the toilet, and to heat soup in the microwave, but never made it far across the first floor landing because the bathroom light had been left on, the kitchen light too. And like air freshener sprayed into a ruined building, a low lying but invisible mist of perfume struggled to survive a few feet above the worn carpet. More feminine preparations had been underway while she'd cowered in her room. More visitors were expected at 82 Edgehill Road and more visitors had arrived and were now heaving and sweating towards fulfilment on the second floor.

There was no attempt at concealment or discretion. The sounds of sexual congress were muted by layers of brick, wooden floors, wall cavities, carpets and soft furnishings, but the brazen animal noises were determined to be heard in the gloomy squalor of the house, like *they* wanted her to hear. Inside her head she heard Margaret say, 'I have date already.'

Shocked and nauseous, Stephanie also recognized that she'd never felt so excluded and awkward in her entire life. Or so lonely while forced to confront the greatest human intimacy amongst people she didn't know. The sounds of desire frightened her too, but there was also a disgust and horror at herself, for the loosening and warmth inside her own body as it considered arousal, like a disobedient animal, had come to life inside her.

The perfume, the moaning, the grunting, the memory of the Albanian girl's long, tanned legs, Svetlana's eyes, the creak-squeak-creak-squeak-creak-squeak of large beds, the bellow of an ape, all bustled inside her mind's basest and most unruly depths.

The maelstrom she weathered bled into thoughts of livestock mating in wooden pens and metal cages. The house was bestial; it called out to her and a thing she barely recognized tried to respond, like a faint radio signal growing in strength.

She used the toilet quickly, abandoned any ideas about warming soup, and ran back down the passageway to her room, hot with shame every step of the way.

Inside, she hastily locked her door, threw down her bag, clutched her cheeks. Stared at her own mad face in the mirrored wardrobe doors: a face pale and pinched with nerves and disgust.

Who was she now?

Thoughts of herself as a confident girl with friends, qualifications, hopes and dreams, seemed like a consideration of another person; a stranger and a fiction she could not believe had ever existed.

Out there, beyond her door, strange men were moving up and down the stairs; men who had come to release themselves inside the girls above her room.

How did this happen to me? How did I even get here?

There was an awful momentum all around her that she couldn't halt or even slow. Those things she'd heard, but could not see, seemed to be the least of her worries now; the house was no longer safe on any level. She *had* to get out, had always known this. But she'd returned again and again.

Why are you still here?

The question was smothered by a listless fatigue before the query concluded. Because she'd been defeated and had nowhere to go.

After bumping into Margaret, she'd called four youth hostels, but there were no free rooms until Wednesday. She'd reserved one, but today was Sunday. That meant three more nights here, unless she fled for the cheapest hotel she'd found; it charged forty pounds per night.

But after doing some sums, if she spent tonight, Monday and Tuesday in the budget hotel, she'd be broke by Wednesday morning and not have enough for a single night in the hostel. At least ten pounds would have to be used for food too. By Wednesday morning she'd have no money at all and nowhere to sleep . . . besides this room.

She gripped the back of her skull and rocked back and forth on the end of her bed.

The dark walls, the smell of neglect, the wet grey world outside, all seemed to get inside her so quickly now, to weigh her down and bind her in place with a kind of numbness. And more so each day. She worried she had become part of this horrible house. Maybe soon she wouldn't be able to extend her limbs, and even drawing a breath would be an exertion. Could a person be drained of their dwindling resources, of their spirit, by a building? She didn't know, but her belief that she belonged anywhere better was being exhausted.

The dreams.

She was being reduced, digested by the house.

You're a fighter. Don't give up. That's why you're still here. Two more days' work and you can leave. That was the plan. You can't sleep in the fucking street!

But when did courage and strength and stamina and determination become something else, like poor judgement?

She didn't know any more; didn't know anything about anything.

Flat-lined.

'No!' she stood up, her body shaking. She watched her hands as they trembled in front of her face. She dug her fingernails into her scalp to the point of them breaking through the skin. She wanted to hurt herself. Hated herself for being here, for getting herself into this mess. Loathed herself for not leaving and going . . . *where?*

Where can I go?

In the building outside her room, a man jogged down the stairs to the first floor. One of the girls followed him, laughing. They descended to the ground floor and their muffled voices passed under Stephanie's feet.

A few minutes later, the girl returned upstairs with another man. What she could hear of the second man's voice made him sound elderly. 'Yes, well, you don't need to worry about that . . .'

Moments later the other girl descended and then returned, in silence, accompanied by yet another man. Within minutes, both girls were having sex with their visitors. They made a lot of noise. It sounded like the girls were having sex with animals. When she imagined something pig-like, with a red face and black-haired flanks, rutting at a girl, Stephanie stood up and shook her head to forcibly suppress the image. At least it was over quickly.

She was so hungry she felt faint, so tired she felt sick.

She was being tortured. That's what this was: torture. Mental cruelty. The whole world seemed to be in on it.

Nothing, nothing, nothing: you have nothing, you are nothing. Nothing.

Her anger at Ryan turned into a red steam of blame. This situation wasn't his fault, her feelings were irrational, but she still snatched up her phone and bashed out a text message:

IT'S A FUCKING BROTHEL! I'M LIVING IN A FUCKING BROTHEL!

There was a knock at her door. And whoever was outside tried the handle, as though they didn't have to wait for her to say 'come in'.

She thought of the men she had heard tramping up and down the dark stairwell; maybe one of the latest arrivals was confused in the darkness and looking for the bathroom. With the lights clicking off so quickly, it wasn't an impossible scenario. Her scalp iced. 'Who's there?'

'Knacker.'

'What do you want?'

'Need to speak wiv you, yeah?'

I bet you do, you bastard.

His voice sounded suppressed, faux softened, with a thin spine running through it that ended in a wheedling probe; the very last thing she wanted to hear on this earth.

But how often had the pimp been outside her room without her knowledge? Had he heard her call her three friends and ask, in a voice barely a safe distance from sobbing, if she could stay with them? Had he heard about the letdowns? Did he know that even Ryan had no time for her? Was he exulted in the darkness beyond her door, grinning as he revelled at her diminishing choices, the tightening noose, the downward spiral? Had the bastard come into her room and stolen her cash card?

'Not a good time!'

'There's always a time for good news, like. Fink you'll want to hear this.'

'You reckon? I think I've been hearing enough, mate.'

'Come on, Steph, open up. I ain't speaking froo this fuckin' door all night, like. You'll wanna hear what I have to say. Trust me.'

Trust you?

Stephanie unlocked and opened the door, but didn't let him in, even though he tried to move her aside by taking a step forward, right at her. She stood her ground. 'What?'

'All right, be like that. But somefing's come up that you might want to get in on, like. Personal matter. We need some privacy to discuss it.'

'There's nothing I want to discuss with you. I won't be here much longer. Especially now.' She looked up at the ceiling. 'I mean, you are fucking joking, right?'

Knacker feigned confusion. 'Not sure what you mean.'

'Yes you bloody do.'

He stiffened at her tone, his big eyes lidded, the top lip pursed.

'Did you think I'd stay here? With that going on?' She couldn't bring herself to say *it*, to describe *it*.

'That's got nuffin' to do wiv you. What other people do here, yeah, is up to them. Nuffin' wrong wiv people making a livin', like, in the privacy of their own home.'

She took a deep breath and tried to rally her reason through her rage. 'Oh, that's all it is, people making a living? Do you think I'm stupid? That bloody gullible? You're running a criminal enterprise here.'

In response to the word 'criminal' Knacker straightened up like she'd called him something else that began with the letter 'c', and she dearly wished that she could. His face had gone so pale she thought she better shut the door. *But what then?* The windows were barred. And in that moment she worried they were barred to keep people inside rather than out. Fear made a swift return and panic capered behind it like a troupe of clowns. Her fear was stronger than her anger; it had been her natural state of being from the day she'd moved into 82 Edgehill Road.

'You best watch what you say. You don't know nuffin'. Using words like that in my house. My mother's house. Who you fink you are? What's them girls to you? Yeah? What they does is up to them. And they make a better living than you do, girl, if the truth be told. They's not even from this country and they's making hundred quid in five minutes. Tax free. Few months' work and they is on holiday, like, for the rest of the year. South of France. Spain. They have the nice clothes and fings they want. While you're working in some call centre, dressed like a pauper. You's biting your nose to spite your face, woman. Pretty girl like you should be in Dolce and Gabbana—'

'Stop! Fuck's sake. Stop . . . you think I would do *that*?' That's why he had come down with the cheap wine on Friday, to sweeten his offer of her becoming a whore in his stinking, half-derelict house. She was being groomed. *Groomed!* How had that word entered her life?

All I wanted was a fucking room and a fucking job!

Life had become so surreal and grim it was comical. But if she released the mad laugh stuck at the base of her throat, there wouldn't be a trace of levity in the sound that she'd bark into the dismal air. 'Get away from my door or I will scream until the neighbours come running.'

'Who's gonna hear? That old perv next door? He's already tried to book a dirty ride, like. Said he was impressed wiv what he saw.'

She closed her eyes, swallowed. 'You're making me sick.'

Knacker struggled to restrain a laugh. His eyes swilled with mirth. 'No one expects you to go wiv some old bastard like that, girl. We's talkin' high-class gentlemen here. We's got plans, like. Fings are moving very well. And as you got nuffin', out the goodness of my heart, I'm just trying to give you a helping hand, like. All's you got to do is give them a bit a company, yeah? These are solicitors and all that type of fing. Clients of ours.'

'Clients?' She wanted to shriek again with dead laughter. 'Is that who I've been hearing, walking up and down those shitty stairs, clients? Fucking those illegal immigrants in your stinking rooms. Judges, no doubt. Bank managers and barristers. Shall we speak to the police and see if they agree with your pitch?'

Knacker cocked his head at an angle. He rotated his neck. His fists clenched.

Anger and strength drained out of her like cold water and she filled to capacity with indecision and dread once again. She shut the door and locked it. But she didn't move away because Knacker had not moved away from the other side.

'I don't wanna hear nuffin' about what we've discussed getting back to me, yeah? If I hear from the council, or the filth, yeah, anyfing gets back to me about you talking shit about this house, I will be very displeased. You don't know nuffin' about my background, or Fergal's. And we got keys to this door.'

His feet bumped away into the darkness.

When she could no longer hear the footsteps she called Ryan.

He didn't pick up.

THIRTY-FIVE

By nine p.m. another four 'clients' had been entertained by the foreign girls. The volume of anonymous traffic through the house had sustained Stephanie's anxiety and added a tinge of nausea.

Beneath the window her bags were packed, ready for evacuation, to where she did not know. She'd already made the two most desperate phone calls she'd ever made in her life: one to the YWCA and the second to a women's refuge. The latter could only take battered women with a police referral; the former had a long waiting list.

And then she'd made her final decision. She would stay until the morning, pack what she could carry and spend the following two nights at a cheap hotel, keep the last forty quid for train fare and food, and return to Stoke on Wednesday to beg Val to take her in. She'd only ever had a desperate and unappealing selection of options since her first night at 82 Edgehill Road. A demoralized inertia, maybe even hope or delusion, had not helped her cause. But she was all out of choices now. She had to leave in the morning.

Stephanie climbed into bed fully clothed. A pair of trainers were in position on the floor beside the bed, ready. One more night. Just one more night.

She lay in bed for hours while cars slowed and pulled away outside 82 Edgehill Road. Sometimes they stopped and their doors slammed. Footsteps occasionally scraped up and down the cement paving of the front path. In the distance the front door of the house opened and closed. Stairs groaned. Girls laughed. Lights clicked on and off. Mobile phones chanted dance music through the ceiling. Knacker bounded up and down the stairs, shepherding, escorting, blagging, forcing a self-satisfied laugh as everything went his way. A preened and prancing cockerel – she imagined the big lips grinning, the heavily lidded, reptilian eyes counting cash, assessing punters. Where was his cousin? Glaring at a ground floor door?

Thoughts of them filled her with a rage so dark, crimson and hot she worried her grinding teeth might snap. When she was clear of the house she'd cancel the new cash card, then call the police and report the prostitution. It was the only thing she looked forward to: revenge.

The last 'client' arrived just after ten p.m. At eleven, the thing that visited the girl who didn't exist in the room next door began to grunt, and the bed in the neighbouring room groaned against the other side of the wall, like a boat loaded with pestilence had just moored and moved on the swell against the thin hull of her privacy.

Earlier, *he* had been outside her door too.

She'd heard the heavy steps approach from the stairwell. The floor of the corridor directly outside her door had creaked for several minutes as if he were deliberating about which room to enter. When the neighbouring door had clicked open and then slammed shut, Stephanie had felt so grateful she'd breathed hard enough to realize she was panting. But had she opened her door at any point during *his* visitation, she knew that she would have looked out at an empty, unlit corridor filled with the stench of the unclean, or worse.

But that's all it is, a smell, and footsteps. They can't hurt you!

The temperature in her room had since stayed warm, the only blessing she could draw from the disturbance beyond the door of this first floor capsule of light and strained nerves that she occupied and could not escape.

Stephanie slipped the plugs into her ears. Lay on her side facing her lighted room. She thought she'd reached the lowest point in her life a number of times recently, and mostly inside this house. But fathoms of unpleasantness still appeared ready to embrace her. And then there was the renewed contact with Val to come too.

She swore to herself she would not sink any deeper. Dabbed her eyes with a tissue until they closed for sleep.

THIRTY-SIX

In the garden the four women with long skirts sat on the corners of a large patchwork blanket. Their heads were bowed so she couldn't see their faces. On top of their heads their dirty hair was piled into coils. She wondered if they were reading. A small wooden box, with a purple velvet curtain draped over the front, was placed in the middle of the blanket.

Someone had put a wooden ladder against an oak tree and arranged four identical wooden chairs beneath the lowest limb.

Only when she sat on the blanket did Stephanie realize the women were all crying into their thin white hands. How had she not noticed before?

Placed on the blanket in front of each of the women was an old creased chapbook with something written on the cover she couldn't make out.

When one of the women became aware of Stephanie, she removed her hands from her face and revealed what looked like a skull in a wig. The sharp features were tightly papered with a mottled parchment of skin, and the woman's eye sockets were empty. Stephanie tried to scream but had no breath. The woman said, 'What's the matter with my face . . . ?'

Stephanie wasn't in the garden for long before she found herself inside a dark place with wet brick walls, through which the women in the long skirts bustled. When the tunnel became too tight for them to go any further, the women slipped to their hands and knees and rolled sideways into blackened stone cavities near the floor. The holes looked like drains without grates.

'This one is yours,' said a voice behind her.

She looked down at the black space, no more than a little stone alcove at the foot of the wall. 'In there? I can't. I can't. I don't like closed spaces.'

Stephanie looked over her shoulder. There was no one behind her. And even though she was only a little girl, when she tried to squeeze back through the narrow passage, and towards what looked like a door sunken into one side of the shaft, she became wedged.

What she had thought was a doorway was only a cleft in the brick wall. Inside of the cavity something wrapped in polythene was standing upright. 'What is the time?' it asked her.

Stephanie awoke into silence and a cold so fierce it burned her forehead, the only part of her face exposed above the bedcovers. She tugged the plugs out of her ears. There was a delectable moment of cool air filling the ear canals.

A smear of half-remembered images sank into oblivion, until she could not pin down much about the nightmare at all. There had been wet brick walls . . . long skirts . . . a face, a horrid face.

She looked about the walls and ceiling of her room, took in the mirrored wardrobe doors, the little glass table, her bags, the window. She saw nothing move. Sniffed at the chilled air. Detected no trace of the male animal odours.

Thank God.

Silence next door too, and in the rooms of those living above her. But she knew she was not alone on account of the plummet in air temperature.

Pulling the duvet with her she sat up in bed and glanced at her travel clock: three a.m. Her mind scrabbled for ideas of what to do, and for clues about what might be happening, or about to occur.

They can't hurt you was the only reassuring notion that came to her, though she found that very hard to believe.

A girl: it must be one of the female presences inside her room. *Can she see me?*

Stephanie swallowed hard. 'Hello.' Her voice was no more than a whisper. She raised it. 'Hello. I know you're there. I . . . I can feel you.'

Silence.

'It's all right. I promise. *He's* not here. And I won't scream. Are you . . . are you Russian?'

Silence.

Her sense of being watched was acute. And there was a peculiar tension growing inside her eyes and ears, like anticipation. Something was trying to get her attention; not by movement or sound, but through other means.

Another part of her, like some unused sense, seemed to quiver in response to what felt like a change in the air pressure. She might have been close to the edge of an awful drop, or about to cross a road ploughed by fast traffic in the rain. An unpleasant tightness around her belly grew into her chest and made her breathless. As before, her spirits quickly darkened and she felt as sad and lost as a child separated from its parent in a crowd of indifferent adults.

She was stuck in this house and would never be released or found. No one cared enough to come looking for her. This was her end and also her future, because the house was not a true conclusion to existence, only of life.

She had no role to offer the world and had been shuffled into a forgotten and dreary corner to wait quietly until expiration. She belonged amongst dust and dreary colours, age, stone, the plaster that sealed it, the paper that covered it. She amounted to nothing. She had kidded herself that she could function in the world.

A sob broke from her. Stephanie covered her face.

Fingers pressed her forearm.

Stephanie thrust her body back against the wall.

The touch had been freezing. She could still feel the chill indenting her flesh.

'Please . . . don't. Please,' she whimpered.

She clutched her hands over her ears because she was sure a mouth had opened, close by, to speak. She didn't know how she knew this. Maybe she didn't know and this was nothing but her senses spiking with panic, but she could not bear to hear a voice.

The touch of a cold hand became a gentle squeeze around her wrist. And this time she did not cry out, or even breathe. With the exception of the shivers that erupted over her entire covering of skin, Stephanie remained absolutely still.

The lights are on. There is no one there. Can't hurt you, hurt you, hurt you . . .

'Hold me,' a voice said. 'I'm so cold.'

Stephanie closed her eyes tight. Either a young woman had spoken with her mouth a hair's breadth from her ear, or she'd heard the request inside her mind.

Cold, invisible fingers remained attached to her wrist. And whatever was beside her slowly reclined upon the bed. The mattress gently gave to support a weight that could not be, and perhaps her eyes deceived her, or maybe the exposed bed sheet really did move.

'Hold me. I'm so cold.'

Staring at her trembling arm, dumbstruck at her own compliance, Stephanie eased herself down to a freezing mattress that she now shared with something she could not see.

Stephanie struggled to breathe, her facial muscles barely moved. Something covered her face tightly. Opening her eyes fully was impossible. One eyelid was partially stuck shut and the second was completely sealed. The space before her eyes was as black as pitch.

Flurries of panic pricked her stomach. Her immediate and instinctive reaction was to raise her hands and tear off the thing covering her face that smelled of plastic. But her arms were stuck fast against the sides of her body: she was bound from hip to shoulder.

She could wriggle her fingers against her thighs, move her toes, but no other movement was possible. Her legs were also awkwardly and uncomfortably strapped together by bindings she could feel against the sides of her knees and pressing into her ankles and Achilles tendons.

Her skin responded to points of pressure scattered about her body: shoulders stuck against a hard surface; the soles of her bare feet touched what felt like cold bricks without supporting her weight. Whatever had passed under her arms, crossed her chest, and gripped her throat tightly, felt like coarse string. The twine held her in position, held her upright.

Or was she upright? It was so dark and any movement beyond her fingers and toes so restricted, she was no longer sure if she was lying down, lying sideways, or even hanging upside down with her feet pressed against the ceiling.

Hysteria flooded her mind.

Within the secure moorings, the energy of the terror that spread from her core and lit up her muscles only succeeded in producing a frail tremble throughout her body.

The scream she issued through lips clamped around the tube that passed between them, was wholly contained inside her mouth. She tugged at the air with her nose but only drew a short sniff up each nostril. Not much air was coming in through that route.

Powered with all the might of her lungs, her mouth pulled a thin stream of oxygen through the tube. What she managed to draw inside tasted of wood and dust. If she didn't calm down, catch her breath and regulate her breathing, she was going to suffocate while being unable to move anything but her fingers and toes.

When the lack of air made her chest feel as if it were full of cement, any attempt to calm down was engulfed by a panic so total it was mindless. Amongst the flashes of quickly passing memories that crowded the walls of her skull, came a hope that she would die quickly.

*

Stephanie didn't so much sit up in bed as thrust herself upwards and onto her knees. She kicked off the duvet and dropped to the floor, gasping like her head had been held under water.

For a while she was convinced she had been about to die in her sleep. She must have had her head cocked at an unusual angle to restrict her windpipe, or she had sucked the bed coverings inside her mouth or squashed them against her nose. Restricted breathing had then been transformed into a nightmare. The relief that came with finding herself on the floor of her spacious room and able to move her hands through the air and to blink, to see, to breathe, made her eyes blur with tears of joy that ran down her cheeks.

But the room next door was enduring a break-in, or worse.

Her neighbour whimpered and sobbed as her body, and the feet of her assailant, bumped about the floor of the room. The woman was being moved or positioned against her will in a manner that was painful, that made her neighbour sob and cry at the point before her strength failed.

Stephanie ran to the door of her room. Unlocked it and tugged it open, determined to stop the attack, to end the sounds of violence as she had managed to do before, without having a clue why the activity had stopped that first time.

Who can be sure of anything here?

She banged her hands against the door. 'I've called the police. The police, you bastard! You touch her again and you'll be sorry. You fucking pig!'

Her delight that the male presence seemed to comply with her demands was short-lived. Because as soon as the room fell silent, the darkness of the first floor began to fill with other sounds. Or other voices.

About her the cold air muttered with what could have been a radio changing channels. Into the hitherto peaceful room on the right-hand side of the corridor she followed one voice, and seemingly with her whole being, until the voice settled behind the locked door into a low, repetitive intonation of . . .

It sounded like a recitation of scripture.

Stephanie pressed her ear to the door.

The voice on the other side rose and fell, into and out of coherence, to peaks of earnestness before sinking to a muffled, half-sobbed tone of desperation. It was the voice of an older woman she was hearing, a woman speaking quickly.

'To speak evil . . . no brawlers . . . all meekness unto . . . foolish, disobedient, deceived . . . diverse lusts and pleasures . . . malice and envy, hateful . . . hating one another . . . kindness . . . love of God our Saviour . . .'

From the bathroom came the broken utterances of the girl beneath the floor, spilling across the landing at the end of the hallway, as if she too were now raising her voice to get Stephanie's attention.

'Is my name? . . . before here . . . that time. Nowhere . . . to where the other . . . the cold . . . is my name? . . .'

In the room next to her own, the girl who had been attacked had resigned herself to weeping from a misery that seemed bottomless.

'God.' Stephanie placed the back of a hand against her nose and mouth because of the smell; the terrible miasma in the cold air now swelled up the stairwell and billowed across the first floor landing before hitting her full in the face. Into her memory came the image of the tatty brown remains of a pet rabbit wrapped in a blue blanket, that she and her friend, Lucinda, had exhumed from a rockery at the bottom of Lucinda's garden when they were little girls, in a well-intentioned hope of returning the pet to life.

Stephanie turned and fled to her room. Shut and locked herself inside, before sinking to her bottom with her back pressed against the door.

DAY SIX

THIRTY-SEVEN

Her eyes hadn't opened again until ten thirty a.m. and she'd since sat slumped on her bed, wearing the clothes she'd slept in, too tired and too reticent to venture to the bathroom for a shower, or to the kitchen to boil the yellowing plastic jug for a mug of instant coffee. After the previous night's disturbances she'd slept for around three hours that felt like three minutes. The last part of her rest had been as dreamless as a concussion.

Heavy rain struck the window with a violence sufficient to make her shiver in anticipation of entering the cold outside the building's walls, lit dimly by the rise of the sun behind clouds the colour of smoke from an oil fire.

She needed to pee. But would *they* be in the bathroom? Did any of the customers stay overnight, or were they only here briefly? Did *they* use the bathroom? There was one toilet on the second floor but no bathroom. Maybe they came down to the first floor to wash and rinse away the tell-tale smells of perfume and condom rubber. Oh God, it made her feel sick.

Stop it!

Shivery and uncomfortable inside her own skin, she guessed she might now have a chill too. Either that or *something* had chilled her. When she tried to banish the memory of a cold ring of thin fingers about her arm, the sense of the touch persisted.

As with the other arbitrary visits, at least her visitor the night before had not remained in her bed for long. The fingers had lifted almost as soon as Stephanie lay down. The cold had dissipated and taken away the awful tension from the air. But had her bedfellow left something behind, inside her? The dream. A message. *A warning.*

The female presence that had been inside her first floor room thus far also suggested a sense of intelligence on the visitor's behalf; that she was aware of Stephanie. Signs of a sentience Stephanie would rather not consider, because in addition to the repetitive predictability of voices behind floors, walls and closed doors, her torments had moved to a whole new level last night – one that suggested interaction.

Even after tugging her woollen cardigan over her hooded fleece, her nerves still chimed with the discomfort she associated with being cold. Her head ached, consistently pulsing with a vague pain behind one eye and her forehead. Her body was lifeless, her limbs floppy. Even when she finally moved out of bed, a great exertion was required as if her muscles remained asleep. She wouldn't have made it through a day's work even if one had been offered.

You're broken.

Mentally, she set herself the task of making coffee and washing her face. Her bags were already packed. After a coffee she would call the hotel and confirm a room for tonight. And then make her way to the city.

*

Her trip to and from the bathroom was made hastily, and she rushed a wash. But she'd found the bathroom quiet and warm. Instead of putting her at ease, the silence transmitted a nerviness into her and she drew no reassurance from the room's motives for remaining mute. She suspected the house hadn't fully recovered from the previous night. The thickening of silence that came into the house after dark, and the apprehension that accompanied the change of tone, seemed to have lingered deep into Monday morning, as if the demarcation that separated the vaguely sinister atmosphere of day from the tension and expectation of the night, had been removed.

And perhaps the critical mass of the activity on the first floor, during the early hours, had survived the coming of dawn and now everything was just going to get worse. Even worse than it was.

Stop it!

The more she reflected on the previous night, the more she believed she had been witness to a phenomenon both contagious and in full swing; an energy that had developed an awful momentum in the first floor corridor and inside each room branching off it, in turn producing a force of attraction that connected the first floor to something far worse. Something that occupied the ground level, summoning whatever was down there to produce an unmistakable stench of decomposition. Or so it seemed to her now that she was awake.

Not long now and you'll be outside and back in the world. Not your problem. Just get out today. Just get out.

A knock at the door.

Stephanie stayed quiet.

A jolly rap, a little drum roll; someone was in a good mood.

'What?'

It was Knacker. 'Oh, you is up. I been down twice already but got no answer. Fought you might have been at work, but Fergal says you is in, like.'

Twice? That wasn't possible; she would have woken, surely, at any sound nearby, let alone a knock. Or would she? Even though her eyes had only opened half an hour ago, she already wanted to lie back and sink away into a deep, black, indifferent sleep.

Stephanie entertained the idea that she was now too run-down and exhausted to fully wake up until near midday. And Fergal had told Knacker that she was *in*. So she was being watched. Maybe because she knew what they were up to, what their big entrepreneurial plans had amounted to: flogging the bodies of immigrant women to whoever knocked on the front door.

Knacker drew her attention back to the door of her room and the dark house beyond it. 'Wondered if I could ask you a favour, like?'

She pictured his horrible face pressed close to the wood, listening intently, and her entire head shook from the pressure of a clenched jaw. 'I'm not fucking anyone for money, so piss off! You ask me again and I swear on my life, I don't give a shit how hard you think you are, I'll put an end to this bullshit!'

As soon as she finished shouting, she swallowed and stared at herself in the mirror as if trying to reclaim a sense of her real identity. Was she out of her mind?

'Eh! Eh! Steady on, yeah? We've spoken about that,

yeah. And you know my feelings on the matter. This has nuffin' to do wiv that, yeah? The subject is closed. No harm was meant and I hoped none was gonna be taken. But I can see how you might have got the wrong end of the stick, like.'

Was there a right end to his stick?

He knocked again, harder. 'Open the door, yeah? Fought you wanted your deposit back, like.'

'That's not funny.'

'I'm serious.'

She opened the door, then sat on the bed, sullen, wary, and trying to dampen the anger that wanted to spark into hysteria. God knew she was due.

She'd moved the blunt paring knife from under her pillow to the front pocket of her hoodie, and now pawed her jumper and felt the little cylindrical shape hidden deep inside her clothing. She wondered if she could use it on anything beside a vegetable.

Knacker came into her room soundlessly, with a feline tread. She watched her visitor closely. His huge, pale eyes immediately flitted about in their sockets, assessing the room, her packed bags, anything left on the floor, the mobile phone, and all in less than two seconds. His big eyes then lidded and turned on her, their intensity failing to align with the insincere half-smile on his big lips.

She now understood that his eyes had a separate emotional life to the surrounding facial features. And they tried to pin her down again. Make her squirm. Thwart her own thoughts by somehow running interference on her mind and baffling her into a frustrated but wary silence. And there was a great potential in those eyes for their owner to do terrible things. She recognized it all over again.

A slight bounce to his step, he veered towards the metal-framed coffee table. Checked the glass surface for dust as if this was a landlord inspection.

Grinning, he raised his chin, his eyes wide and hungry for signals, facial tics, anything he could use as he stared right at her. Stephanie held his stare with an expressionless face, but suspected he could read her thoughts and feelings anyway, as if they were displayed on a screen. Maybe he had enough on file already to guess the rest.

Insights into his predatory personality had come too late. He'd worked her inside out. If her own thoughts were his prisoners too, then she was entirely incarcerated. By *this*. This *thing*. There was no sign of compassion in those big wolfish eyes. No empathy at all. Only self-interest. How liberating it must be to have no conscience. And if you trained yourself to think like him there would be nothing good left inside of you.

Was there a weakness? Vanity perhaps? Money most definitely. And the two were entwined: his need for power and status, his need to own bragging rights, to be better, to exclude and to look down upon others, because he knew he was also at the bottom. *A rat with the pretensions of a lion, trying to escape humiliation, like the rest of us.*

'You've changed your mind about my deposit. So what do you want in return?'

'Blimey, someone's got out the wrong side of the bed, like.'

'Cut the crap, Knacker. Tell me. Tell me what it is you want. What you can do for me, yeah? Which will amount to me doing something for you. Because nothing else really matters here and we both know it.'

He looked genuinely offended, and ruffled, as if he'd underestimated her and her words had wounded him. Until the mask hardened in a fraction of a second and the grin returned. 'Way I see it you're in no position, girl, to be making the demands for—'

'Then see it another way. That doorway is a line that you don't cross until I leave this building. Unless you are going to give me my deposit, you just leave me the fuck alone on a permanent basis. How's that? I don't really care about what's going on here, or what you thought I might get involved in because I'm skint and young and a girl. But it's not going to happen. Ever.'

He started to laugh while his complexion bleached, and that meant he was heating up with anger. The laugh was just a stalling tactic. Like a bantam weight boxer, he was taking time on the ropes to peer through the sweat that had run into his eyes while he thought about his next move. 'See, I almost like this about you. You's ain't afraid to speak your mind, like.' The smile vanished so quickly she flinched. 'But neither is I, yeah? And there's nuffin' I won't do to protect the financial security of my family. My family home. So if people don't pay their rent, like, I have to take steps. I don't give a fuck who they are.'

'I paid my rent.'

His voice rose to drown her out. 'Same fing if people interfere wiv fings that ain't nuffin' to do wiv them. I will take measures. I fink you know that. I fink you know I won't be treated like a cunt. There's all kinds of people out there who will tell you the same fing. I ain't called Knacker for nuffin'.' Smiling again, he sat on the very edge of the table. She wanted him to sit his bony backside in the middle so he would go through the glass.

He sniffed with satisfaction after his little speech; his putting her in her place as he saw it. 'Why is you always puttin' me in a bad mood, yeah? Every time I see you I have to go and cool off afterwards, like. I always feel like breakin' somefing. And all I was trying to do was help you out.'

Stephanie, literally, held her tongue between her teeth.

'Way I see it, to cut a long story short, at the end of the day, like, you want your deposit so you can go and live in some scrappy hole. That's your business. Ain't my place to tell you you is wastin' your time wiv these call centres and biscuit samples, whatever, yeah? But you is a adult and you is making your choice, like. So I might be able to make that happen, like, sooner than you fink. But I ain't no charity, so you help me out and I'll help you out.'

She couldn't restrain the surge of hope, but stamped on the instinctive feeling of gratitude that tried to sob its pitiful way out. *Wait for the catch.* 'So, what is it?'

'I was coming to that. But this ain't somefing that can be rushed, like. This is business. A misunderstanding wiv the council that I want sorted out, like. And you being an educated girl and all, I fought you might know somefing about how to deal wiv it.'

He hated asking her for a favour; she could see it in the way he tried to sound and look reasonable, like some responsible homeowner in a spot of bother with planners over building an extension. His fingers twitched on his thighs and made little drumming movements. 'I'm a working man, me. Proud of my roots. Bit rough round the edges, like . . .'

Here we go. She wondered if she could swallow another bout of the mythologizing tinged with misty-eyed sentiment.

'. . . and these people down there, on the council, like. They try and jam you up, yeah? Hardworking people are the first to get fucked over, like.'

'What is it? Tell me exactly what you want me to do in exchange for my deposit.'

Knacker tensed up, alert to what he suspected was an attempt to redress the balance of power. His eyes had narrowed to such an extent she could barely see them at all. But she could almost hear his thoughts, like mice scratching behind a skirting board.

'It ain't nuffin' dodgy, like, so don't give me that look, yeah? There's some decent cash in this for you, so I don't want no hassle, yeah? I been bending over backwards for you since you got here. Let's not forget all I've done. New room cus you didn't like the first one. Best room in the house. Bottle a wine thrown in. Cheap rent.'

'I'm not looking at you like anything. I'm trying to understand how I get my deposit back. You still haven't told me what you would like me to do.'

'That's all right then. But there's a tone, like. I can hear it in your voice. I don't like bad atmospheres, me. I'm a laid back guy. Can chill out like the best of them, yeah? We just got a bit behind on bills and stuff. Council tax. Water rates. Few fings on the house, like. We been so busy setting up the business' – he paused to assess her reaction to the word 'business' – 'and all this other stuff, like, wiv doing up the house, yeah? We forgot about a few fings that need taking care of. You follow?'

'So pay them.'

'Ain't that easy when we is so busy here. We got a full day on, and if you ain't doing nuffin', I fought you could go down to the council offices like and sort it out. Write a letter and all that. My solicitor usually does this sort of fing for me, but he's on holiday. Got a place in Ibeefa. I go there sometimes. Very nice it is too. Anyway . . .' Out of the pocket of his silky tracksuit trousers, he produced a small pile of envelopes. 'These been coming.'

'Is that them? Final demands?'

He raised his chin and pursed his mouth. 'Yeah, fought you could look over them. Shed some light on the situation, like, while my solicitor is away.'

Stephanie paused and tried to second guess what it was he was really asking her to do. He wasn't too busy to go to the council offices because there were no renovations at 82 Edgehill Road. The place hadn't seen any attention in years. Knacker and his cousin did nothing but stare at closed doors, smoke cannabis, escort punters into the house, and lurk about like ferrets, so time was not an issue here. But what was?

'This one on the top, yeah? Red one. Is the most serious, I fink. I seen the sums, yeah. The bottom line, like. But them numbers ain't right. Can't be.'

She took the brown envelope and removed the letter. The top of the paper had a red border. She read it quickly. It was addressed to Mr Bennet. She recalled seeing the name before. 'Bennet?'

'Never mind about that. Business partner. Fings were

put in his name while we was down south. Don't worry about that. What's it say?'

It said the water rates hadn't been paid on the house for a year. And then she stiffened with discomfort and looked at Knacker's face: at the frown, at the big eyes full of confusion, while the features attempted to sustain a look of serious concern as though some great matter of national finance were under review. He couldn't read. He was illiterate. Which meant that Fergal was too or he would have read the letters.

'You owe three hundred quid on water rates.'

'Free hundred! For water? They's having a laugh, ain't they? Who's the supplier, Evian?'

'They offer a direct debit payment plan.'

'Fuck that. I do everyfing in cash, me. That's daylight robbery, but free hundred ain't nuffin' to me. They can have that and fuck off. What about this one?'

On the gas and electricity account the address was in arrears close to one thousand pounds. When she told him that was indeed the correct sum, based on an estimate, and that it had to be paid immediately, he turned as white as the ceiling above his curly head.

'And this one?' His tone of voice wasn't so strident now and Stephanie experienced the first spurt of satisfaction in his company since she'd moved in.

'This is from a debt collection agency.'

'Eh? Fuckin' bailiffs!'

'Yes, because like I just told you, you haven't paid the gas or electric for three quarters. The letter says they are coming to take the meter out. It's dated two weeks ago.

You have to phone this number to arrange payment or they can enter the premises at any time.'

And then he lost it. 'I told him, yeah! I told him to take care of fings while we was busy. That cunt's done nuffin'. He's run up all these bills!'

'Who? Bennet?'

Knacker cocked his head back. 'Yeah. But don't you worry about him.' With a smirk on his face, he spoke like he was passing a capital punishment sentence on Bennet, whoever he was. 'And these come froo a few days back too.'

They were nine months old. Warnings from the council that there had been complaints about the state of disrepair in the front and rear gardens of the property. When she told Knacker this he said, 'They's can go fuck theirselves. I might pop round later for a quiet word in their ear, like.'

The last five pieces of correspondence were also from the council and all threatened Mr Bennet with another debt collection agency for unpaid council tax. He was one year in arrears for another twelve hundred pounds, payable immediately.

Knacker looked between his feet. Quietly, to himself, or maybe to her as well, he muttered, 'You trust a person with a fing. Even wiv a simple fing. And you get burned.'

The show of self-pity made Stephanie clench her fists. 'So you give me the money and I'll go and pay off these debts. But I want my deposit upfront.'

Slowly, his head rose. The bloodless face beneath the dyed black hair was a slit-eyed sneer that made the marrow of her bones cool. 'You is wanting your pound of flesh too, eh? Looks like everyone is in on it today.'

A text message chimed its arrival on her phone.

Stephanie looked at the screen, to refrain from having to look at Knacker's horrid face more than through a desire to see who the message was from. But Knacker tensed and fixed his stare on the phone in her hand; his eyes were wide with an expectation, or sense of entitlement, that she should tell him who it was from.

The text was from Ryan:

AM COMING DOWN TOMORROW BEFORE
NIGHT SHIFT. BEKKA CALLED. CAN'T LET
YOU STAY HERE, SORRY. HOPE YOU
UNDERSTAND. BUT AM BRINGING CASH
FOR A DEPOSIT. DON'T TELL ANYONE.
IF IT GETS BACK TO GF THERE'LL BE GRIEF.
82 EDGEHILL, RIGHT?

Stephanie's heart burst. She nearly wept.

She did some quick sums. If she got her deposit back from Knacker today, and another £150 off Ryan tomorrow, that was £310. Add that to the £120 she had from temping and she could find and rent another room in Birmingham for four weeks. And still sleep in the cheap hotel tonight and tomorrow, plus the hostel on Wednesday. That would give her time to find a new room. She would not need to grovel and beg Val to take her in. She became light-headed with a relief that might have been euphoria.

Knacker pushed his chin up, his expression transformed into a mixture of incomprehension and animal suspicion.

'Temping agency. Might be some work.' Stephanie replied quickly.

THANKS. GOING TO HOTEL. TOO DODGY
HERE. DANGEROUS. WILL CALL U LATER
XXX.

She sent the message.

'Hang on. Hang on, yeah? We got an agreement. You gotta sort this business out first. Tell yer agency they can fuck right off. You is busy.'

She looked at him and he did that thing with his face, like Fergal had done: thrust it at her in provocation, daring her to refuse, to disagree, to contradict, to disobey. 'Give it here. I'll do it.' He snatched at her phone. 'They'll soon get the message you ain't available.'

Stephanie clutched the handset to her chest. Her shock and disbelief made him pause; he retracted the hand and shook himself, as if shaking creases out of an expensive two-piece suit. He was a desperate man on the verge of going too far before he'd extracted what he wanted from her, and he needed to compose himself.

Knacker sat back down. 'As I was saying. What we will do, like, is give them somefing. Bit here, bit there. Payment plan you mentioned, yeah? Get them off our backs, like. Wiv letters too, yeah? You been to college. You can write somefing explaining the situation that we been away. House was empty, like. Money wasn't paid. That kind of fing. I shouldn't have to pay nuffin' anyway, if the house was empty.'

'And you'll give me my deposit first?'

'First fings first, like. I wanna make sure you do it right. Properly, like. I'll go down the council wiv you.'

There were so many things she wanted to say. So many

things that wanted to burst from her. So many terrible things she wanted him to feel. Above all else she wanted him to feel like 'nuffin', because that was exactly how he wanted her to feel. But she had to get the deposit back first.

'Yeah, so get that computer fired up and start these letters. I ain't got all day, luv.'

'Computer? The laptop is broken. And you need a printer.' He wasn't only illiterate.

'Pull the other one, love. I is wasting my time 'ere. You wanna earn or sit there moping all day? We got work to do, you and me, to get these leeches off our backs.'

'Our backs? This is your problem. You never paid the bills.'

'Steady on, girl, I'm not in the mood for any of your shit this morning. This has all come as a very great surprise to me. I am very upset by all this.'

'I don't have to do anything for you. But if you give me the one sixty, I'll help you. Cash up front or forget it.'

He was on his feet in less than a second. 'Yeah! Yeah! That right?' He stopped and looked at the ceiling. A bed creaked; footsteps sounded in the room above their heads. He'd disturbed his investment.

Knacker lowered his stare to Stephanie, but his eyes didn't seem to consider the person before him as human. She was merely a thing that irritated him to such a degree he seemed ready to begin smashing it up. The feeling was mutual. He reminded her of her stepmother.

Stephanie stretched out her hand. 'One sixty. The deposit. And I'll help you out. Or I'm pissing off in the next ten minutes and you will never see me again.'

'You're no match for her, Knacker, you pussy. She's got you over a barrel,' Fergal said from the doorway. He followed the statement with his deep, forced laugh.

THIRTY-EIGHT

'Don't worry about him. Just collecting his foughts,' Knacker said on their way out of the house. Fergal had followed them down the stairs to the ground floor, taking up position in the shadows before the white glimmer of the solitary inner door at the end of the hallway.

Knacker coaxed Stephanie out of the house, prodding her in the back, and then steered her by the elbow once they were on the front path. 'We's all got our little quirks, like,' he said, pulling the front door closed.

Outside, Knacker continued to stand too close to her, his face never straying more than a few inches from her own. It was as if he were giving his eyes, his greatest weapons of scrutiny, interrogation and intimidation, an even bigger advantage by pressing them into her physical space until she could barely draw breath without inhaling him. She choked on his aftershave.

And what was that on his head? A knitted Peruvian skiing hat plastered with the Helly Hansen logo, with spidery jaw straps falling beside his sunken cheeks. A wanker hat: she'd never met anyone in one of those hats that wasn't a tool.

When he slipped the Oakley sunglasses on, she realized he was wearing a disguise. Knacker didn't want to be recognized. She'd reached this conclusion too late. Like everything else. He reinforced her suspicion by saying, 'Just stick your head round that hedge. Make sure no one's in the street, yeah? Some people round here I don't want to speak wiv.'

Like the police? 'No one there.'

'All clear, yeah? Nice.' He released her arm. 'Can't stand nosey parkers me, as well you know, girl.'

The open space and cold air of the grey, empty street jerked her back to a fuller awareness of her surroundings, and of herself. Even this close to her own escape, she felt too light on her feet as the adrenaline drained away. Despite everything that had so recently happened in the rooms of Svetlana and Margaret, minutes before she and Knacker left the building, her major share of shock and unease was reserved for Fergal.

At first she feared the effects of heroine, crack cocaine or crystal meth had been responsible for transforming Fergal's face and appearance into something so unkempt. But so quickly? In a matter of days he now looked more haggard and feral than the last and only time she had seen him fully lit up: inside her room on Friday. Barely three days hence but the alteration to Knacker's cousin was ghastly.

As soon as he'd appeared in the doorway to her room, she'd winced at the sight of him, and at the smell that issued from the absurdly tall shape hanging around her door like a large gingery gibbon. He'd grinned his yellow teeth at her and looked homeless, as derelict as the house he'd helped to transform into a brothel. The whites of his eyes were bloodshot, the pupils massive; he was off his head on something. A childish excitement in his expression warned that he was not in control either.

He'd worn the only clothes she'd ever seen him wear: the hooded brown coat with jeans and trainers, but now the sleeves of the coat were blackened with soot or dirt to the elbow, his bony wrists and huge hands protruding from tatty cuffs. The final finger joints and nails of each hand were black. He looked like he'd been scratching around beneath the floorboards or crawling about in the garden. The knees of his jeans were dark with dried stains. Dirty hands, most likely his own, had been wiped across his thighs repeatedly to soil the denim. Stephanie hoped the promised renovations in the house would explain the state of the man, but what renovations had there been?

Everything had changed again, and so swiftly that morning; now she was doing them a favour, her lowly status in the house hovered around an enforced involvement in illegality. The bank notes of her deposit, safely tucked away in her jacket pocket, weighed heavily. They had stolen the money from Svetlana and Margaret.

Just get this done and then take off.

But who were they? And who was this Bennet? All of the correspondence addressed to the house had been directed at someone who was absent, who hadn't paid a bill in a year. Bennet was no silent business partner, because the McGuires were not in business in any reasonable sense; they'd just started running girls, and she was supposed to have been one too. They were broke. They were nothing more than desperate, seedy rodents in a dirty house that might not even belong to them.

She recalled her conversation with the unpleasant

neighbour: someone only referred to as *him* had started the father's business up again. The business was prostitution. The house was known for it; the building had a past. And was *him* Knacker? Had Knacker and Fergal inherited a family house and an organized criminal operation? But then Knacker would have Bennet as a surname, not McGuire. Or were they using alibis? Was this even their house? *My mother's house.* Knacker emphasized that fact at will, but he was a liar who would say anything to support his scams.

Neither of them could even read; Knacker had been genuinely shocked by the knowledge that bailiffs were coming for a great deal of money that was owed to utility companies and the council. But even if you could not read, how could you own a house and be surprised by the news that you hadn't paid any bills? Knacker had seen the figures but did not fully understand they amounted to debts. He was idiotic. His lack of intelligence wasn't suited to responsibility; he belonged to another world where a person made their way through intimidation and rat-like cunning.

What was this place?

I'm so cold. Hold me. Girls behind the walls: crying, repeatedly chattering the same nonsense, one of them being beaten, even raped. Something climbing into her bed for . . . *comfort*. Because that's all that visitor had wanted: comfort. It was a presence so cold and lonely and so filled with despair that the air had turned to ice. No, not *it*; *she* had just wanted to be held. Something terrible had happened in the building, but what? And now new girls, living girls, were being put to work at the same address.

The blonde girl on the stairs and in the garden: *a ghost?* She wondered if women had been killed here in the past. Maybe *they* had killed women here. Residues might have remained. Yet she was mystified as to why she was the focus. Why did she have to know the presences were there?

A horrible carousel spun through her mind and imagination and she recalled Knacker's veiled and unveiled threats, interspersed with the unnatural atmospheres and the sounds of the voices. Nothing was clear, but all was suggesting more than she wanted to acknowledge.

She was still not reacting quickly enough to each new situation, or even anticipating them fully, and she felt like she was stumbling about the street now too, still in shock after what Knacker had gone and done upstairs in the other girls' rooms before they left the house. But she'd be out of this situation permanently within a few hours. Once she'd run these errands and paid off some of their debts, she could grab her stuff, call a cab and clear out. Get Ryan to bring the money to her hotel. She was almost free. Salvation was within reach. She'd decide later tonight about what to tell the police, how to phrase her story. Because after Knacker's performance in the rooms of Svetlana and Margaret, and judging by the state of Fergal, who no longer appeared sane, she wasn't sure that the two prostitutes were safe.

After Knacker had finally accepted her demands, paid her the one sixty in cash, and accepted the fact that her laptop was out of action, she'd been forced to hand-write letters to utility companies, debt collection agencies and the council. She'd used her own refill pad on the kitchen table, because the McGuires didn't have any paper, or even a pen. Knacker had said, 'I will be having these checked later, like, so make sure you get it right.' But checked by who: Albanian and Lithuanian prostitutes?

In the kitchen, she'd taken Knacker's dictation to the City Council, Severn Trent Water and British Gas. And the whole time she was transcribing Knacker's attempt at business English, she wanted to burst out laughing and scream 'imbecile' into his idiotic face. But she had not forgotten that the moment this nonsense was concluded, she could leave.

The deposit that had been returned to her had been paid from the money the girls upstairs had earned. Svetlana and Margaret had been busy for a few days, but clearly not busy enough to clear the three grand Knacker owed on bills he couldn't even read. He'd taken just under twelve hundred pounds off them. The situation was pitiful; Knacker was pitiful.

But not to be underestimated.

Until she was in a hotel room, she would never truly believe she'd escaped Knacker.

And everything inside his house.

On the pavement of Edgehill Road, Knacker appeared smaller, physically diminished, and wary of the light and space like an elderly man being taken on a walk by his carer. He whipped his concealed head about as he spoke quickly and nervously. 'I need to get somefing out the way, like. Difficult conversation to have, but this is a matter of trust, like. Which is pretty thin on the ground right now, yeah? Wiv all that's going on wiv the gas and council, like, and the way you been going off on me, and all that, but I appreciate what you are doing, right? Even though you've stitched me right up on that deposit, if I'm totally frank.'

His voice was hot against her face; he was whispering, wary of being overheard through paranoia or self-importance. 'Fergal too. He might have his ways, like, but don't you worry about him. He's in hand, like. So we've had words and we is gonna cut you some slack cus you is helping us out. So I'm apologizing if fings got a bit heated, like, back there, wiv the girls. But no harm was done, yeah? What you gotta understand, right, is we've been under a lot of stress. Lot at stake here. When you is just a tenant, it's a bit easier.' He laughed at that, laughed at her naivety. 'But we got responsibilities. Don't forget we has been putting a roof over your head. And them girls. You have all been benefitting, like. Sometimes there might be words, but no harm done, yeah?'

She doubted that was true; he'd robbed Margaret and Svetlana. Gone up to their rooms and demanded all of their cash so that his other tenant could pay off bits and pieces of his debts on payment plans at a bank, while he shuffled beside her like a nervous agoraphobic. Knacker was terrified she would run off with the money. That was why he insisted on being beside her now, with one hand clasped around her forearm like a pimp with a recalcitrant street walker.

There had been a terrible row above her head as Knacker whined, wheedled and shouted threats at the two foreign girls. She had been forced to endure the noise coming through her ceiling while Fergal had stood in the doorway of her room, keeping watch, all stooped over and grinning, like someone who should have been sedated and restrained.

Knacker had left both girls hysterical, shouting a combination of 'Bastard!', 'We call Andrei!', 'You bastard!', as he made off with their ill-gotten gains.

In reply he'd shouted, 'You'll get it back, like. Just a loan, yeah? You'll make it back by Friday. Relax, yeah?'

He'd stolen the girls' phones too, so they couldn't call this Andrei, before locking them inside their rooms. He'd come downstairs with a bleeding scratch on one wrist that Fergal had found hilarious. The securing of doors had frightened Stephanie more than anything else to that point in the confrontation. Theft of illegal earnings and private phones was one thing, but the locking of the girls' doors was imprisonment; it had made the very floor feel as if it were moving beneath her feet. The rules of her world had changed again, and so quickly it was hard to second guess future implications.

But the hysteria of the two girls and the banging and kicking they inflicted against their locked doors had excited Fergal, who'd guffawed around a sadistic grin, as if it were all a game. The sound of his mocking laughter was even worse than what Knacker had been doing upstairs. Bookended by a snigger, a delighted Fergal had shouted, 'It's all going off!', before breaking into an oafish ditty that sounded like a chant on a football terrace.

And now she and Knacker were outside, on the cold and silent street, on their way to the bank to pay off fragments of a Mr Bennet's debts.

To get this far and to carry on, she concentrated on the moment when she would have everything she could carry in two hands and strapped onto her back; the very moment when she would be out of 82 Edgehill Road forever.

Nearly there, girl. Hold fast, babe. Do this, then take off.

And she smiled to herself at the thought of the phone call she would make to the West Midlands police that very night. She could almost hear Knacker's wheedling entreaties as the police stepped into the grim hallway of the house.

In the pocket of Knacker's new ski jacket, Svetlana's phone began to chant its dance music ringtone. He whipped it out. 'Yeah? Svetlana, yeah? It's her phone, but she is busy, like. What you want? . . . That's fine . . . Today? Yeah, mate, call later and you can speak wiv her. About four.' He finished the call and grinned.

Stephanie instinctively took a step away from Knacker as he answered the phone. Without even looking at her, or seeming to see her movement, his bony fingers reached out and tugged at her jacket.

THIRTY-NINE

Within seconds of Stephanie and Knacker entering the house, they noticed the solitary door at the end of the ground floor hallway. It was open. Their shock brought them to a standstill.

'The fuck?' Knacker said.

Stephanie panicked, as if the lightless entrance was a symbol that something terrible, something even worse than the current owners, had been set free inside the building.

Fragments of dreams came to life and filled her skull: a sad, pale female face, its blue eyes open and full of horror and despair. A brick tunnel. A little wooden box. A table in a black room. Candles. Polythene . . .

Stephanie took a step back towards the front path.

Knacker's hand found her wrist. The grip was tight. 'Nah, nah, girl. You ain't finished yet, like.' He closed the front door behind them with one foot.

'I'm going once I have my bags.'

'Fuck you is.'

'What? You can't *make* me stay here.'

'We got an agreement, like.' Knacker spoke without looking at her, as if his mostly concealed face couldn't turn away from the sight of the open door at the end of the corridor. 'These bills ain't all done wiv yet.'

'I did what you asked. You have no money left.'

'End of the week we'll be loaded again. You can fuck off once this is sorted proper, like.' A grin spread across his face. The girls were a popular local item already; he'd taken six phone calls during their journey to and from the bank, and he'd arranged bookings for the next three afternoons and evenings. Eighty pounds for thirty minutes with either Svetlana or Margaret: the going rate at 82 Edgehill Road. Some of the callers were returning customers, repeat business.

But an assurance that she could leave once he'd stolen even more of the prostitutes' money to clear the house's debts was another lie, because then something else would be required of her. Knacker thought he owned her now. The realization took the strength from her legs. She wanted to be sick.

She tried to yank her wrist out of Knacker's hand, but his fingers hardened into a bone cuff that became so painful she cried out. His arm merely rose and fell with hers. Then he turned so quickly she squealed.

Knacker crowded Stephanie against the front door. His face moved an inch from hers; his breath stank of the burger he'd stopped to buy in the street and gobbled down like a dog. 'Let's get one fing straight, yeah? About that room you been living in at the cheap rate, yeah? Well your terms have changed. You now owe on the room. Forty quid a week for them fittings and fixtures? You must be having a laugh, girl, if you fink you can rip us off like that. You already owe us on the room. Yeah? Price is hundred a week.'

'What?'

He raised his voice. 'So you already owes me sixty quid for the week you been here. And another . . . let me see, one mumf in advance . . . that's three times another sixty quid . . .'

'You can't!'

'That's one eighty in total on the next three weeks on your first mumf. So you now owe me two forty. Just be fankful I ain't charging you for damages. Fucking dust everywhere in there, like. And here's you taking back that deposit like we owe you. You got a nerve. Fuck's sake, I ought to march you to the cashpoint right this minute and take every penny you owe us. Which is more consideration than these council wankers are giving me, like. So I'll have that one sixty back now, and on the rest, don't make me collect in another way, yeah?' He pulled her to the foot of the stairs. 'Get up in your room. Fucking stay there.'

Without all of her balance, Stephanie stumbled up the stairs with Knacker pressed against her back; one of his arms was around her waist, his other bony hand slapping its way up the railing.

On the first floor he stopped at the sound of a crying woman. A terrible chest-deep sobbing came from the second floor; you couldn't fake anguish like that. It was one of the Eastern European girls.

'Shit,' Knacker said. 'Shit, shit, shit.' His words panicked Stephanie.

'Fergal!' he shouted up the stairwell, his voice so loud it made her jump. 'Fergal!'

There was no answer.

Stephanie made for her room. She took her phone out of her pocket as surreptitiously as she could.

From the landing Knacker shouted at Stephanie, 'Eh, hang on!'

She entered her room regardless, planning to close and lock her door, then call the police. She was now being held here against her will, and something terrible had happened while she had been out; she could just feel it. A woman didn't cry like that for no reason.

Knacker bounced down the corridor after her. He had a key. Shutting the door would undoubtedly provoke an escalation of whatever mass she'd sensed solidifying inside the house since they'd come through the front door, a growing tension she wanted to creep quietly away from.

Too late for that now, girl.

No!

She had to find a moment, *soon*. She shuffled her phone back inside the pocket of her jacket.

Knacker's footsteps paused in the corridor outside her open door. 'Fergal!' he roared into the house.

In response, a fresh surge of woe erupted from the girl upstairs. Stephanie guessed it was Svetlana, because she could now hear the girl's muffled cries through the ceiling of her own room. So where was Margaret?

Ryan. He cannot come here. Police!

She'd risk a quick phone call, keep her voice down. Hurriedly, Stephanie retrieved her phone from her pocket. Her scalp cooled when she realized no one, beside her bank branch, knew she was living here. Not even the temping agencies. She'd planned to move out quickly and so hadn't supplied the address; they all still had the cell in Handsworth on record as her home address. She thought of Svetlana's and Margaret's phones in Knacker's pocket and suddenly felt dizzy from the gravity of personal danger she found herself in.

She punched out 999 as Knacker came through her door, muttering to himself after failing to raise a response from Fergal. 'Fuck is he, like?'

Maybe she should make the call to the police and leave it open with the phone in her hand. They recorded all calls.

Knacker spotted the phone. 'Aye, aye!' He ran at her. Whacked her hand hard. The phone thumped against the floor.

'What the fuck!' she shouted into his face.

Upstairs, a window smashed. Glass tinkled down one side of the house.

'Shit!' Knacker shouted. He scooped Stephanie's phone up at the same time she reached for it. With one hand he shoved her backwards so hard she sat down.

'You fucking prick!' she screamed at him. 'Don't you touch me!'

Knacker was already on his way out of the room.

Svetlana screamed from her broken window upstairs. 'Help! Help me! They kill her!'

Stephanie felt like she'd been electrocuted. Her vision shook. Through the juddering room she saw Knacker bound back at her. His bloodless face thrust against her own. 'Give me your keys!' Spittle flecked her face.

She didn't react or move, beside flinching and instinctively covering her breasts with both arms.

Her head jerked to one side at the same time as she heard the slap of raw meat upon a chopping board. A sensation of having one side of her head underwater engulfed her. One ear became hot. Her hearing sang with tinnitus. A fire alarm had just been activated deep inside her skull. She wasn't sure which direction she now faced.

When her vision settled she was lying on her back and looking at the ceiling. Knacker had thumped her.

A bony, clenched fist was pressed against her face. She thought her nose might snap. Knacker's fingers stank of burned tobacco and tomato sauce. Above the knuckles she could see his big, wild eyes. 'Keys, bitch! Where's your fucking keys?'

Big feet at the end of long strides bounded across the ceiling. Stephanie heard the door above her room being hastily unlocked: Svetlana's room.

Svetlana shouted, 'Bastard!'

Heavy feet boomed deeper inside the room above.

Svetlana screamed. A heavy thump followed her cry.

A horrible silence ensued until the girl became hysterical again. She shouted words in her own language. What could have been a large, fierce animal bellowed in response. The very sound of the roar – inhuman, bestial – made Stephanie whimper. A solid weight crashed through splintering wood. Feet boomed across the floor of the room upstairs as if rushing at the sound of the breakage.

Slap. Slap. Slap.

'Keys!' Knacker bellowed into Stephanie's face.

'Pocket.' Stephanie's voice was a whisper. Her ear still sang like an old wireless; whale songs of trauma whistled from the deeps. The flesh on one side of her face smarted like she'd put her head on an oven hotplate. Inside her skull, blood thumped like a bass drum.

Knacker's fingers went through the pockets of her

jacket and fished out her room keys, her purse and the one sixty in cash. He bolted for the door, slammed it, locked her inside.

Stephanie moved from where she had been lying on her back. On her hands and knees she made for the window. Looked at the bars behind the dirty glass. The window was difficult to open, the frame old and swollen. She needed to break the pane with something so she could start screaming like Svetlana. But stopped looking for a heavy object when she thought of what she'd just heard upstairs. The *thump*. Fergal's shriek of animal rage. A body crashing through wood. The slapping. Fergal must have gotten hold of Svetlana because she had broken her window and screamed into the street to attract attention.

They kill her. That's what Svetlana had said.

Margaret.

Stephanie's stomach turned over and she clenched her teeth and steeled herself to prevent what remained of two cups of coffee coming up.

With a paralyzing clarity, she imagined the girls drumming on their doors, hurling insults the whole time she had been away, threatening Fergal with this 'Andrei' because Knacker had stolen their phones and their money. She remembered Fergal's face: the malice, the savagery, the instability therein. And she believed he could easily have lost his temper while she and Knacker had been at the bank.

Stephanie struggled to her feet, but didn't know what to do.

She looked at the ceiling when she heard another pair of feet upstairs: lighter, swifter, with shorter strides. They bounded down the second floor corridor and moved into the room above her head: Knacker. He began to bellow at Fergal. 'What you done? What you done, you fucking idiot? Where is she? Where the fuck is she?'

Fergal grumbled something she could not make out. But Svetlana heard Fergal's reply because she issued a fresh upwelling of despair, before sobbing through the floor of her room and right into Stephanie's heart.

FORTY

As Stephanie attempted to open the window, as much to air the room of the smell of vomit as to attract attention without making any noise, she inadvertently summoned Knacker. He came through the house and to her quickly.

She'd even switched the television on to run interference over the sound of the old sash window grinding upwards through the wooden runners. But Knacker had heard, perhaps from inside Svetlana's room because the window upstairs was now without glass.

She wasn't going to scream, not after what she'd heard upstairs. Svetlana had briefly stopped sobbing and moaning when the McGuires had dragged her from her room. 'Not in there!' she'd screamed. The desperate fear in the Lithuanian girl's voice had transfixed Stephanie with terror all over again. Unable to swallow or blink, she'd stood immobile and helpless in the middle of her room, her hands clasped to her cheeks while disbelief clashed with the horror that swept round and round her mind in a whirlpool of panic.

In where? Where were they taking Svetlana? To another room? But not the room occupied by Margaret, because Stephanie would have heard their feet through the ceiling on the far side of her bed. There was only one other room on the second floor: the room she had spent her first two nights inside; the room with the fireplace and the hands under the bed and the footsteps. A room facing the back of the building and the junkyard that served as a garden. So she could only assume they had installed Svetlana inside that awful room, or even inside their flat.

Interspersed with the bangs of a hammer in the room above her own, as wood was applied to the upstairs window that Svetlana had smashed, Stephanie had heard faint bursts of a woman crying, somewhere in the distance. She'd assumed it was the Lithuanian girl's grief continuing undiminished, though in this house she could never tell who, *or what*, was crying.

Not in there. Did the girl know something about that room then? After their brief exchange in the kitchen there had been no further opportunity to converse with Svetlana. The idea of prostitution, the prospect of engaging with broken English, and Knacker's clear displeasure about them speaking had deterred Stephanie. She wished she had been bolder. Things might have been different had she and the other two girls discussed the house and the cousins. Regret: the most corrosive horror.

And within the house there was still no sign of Margaret.

They kill her.

Knacker couldn't get inside Stephanie's room fast enough. At the sound of the frantic rattle of a key inside the lock, she slipped one hand inside the front pocket of her hooded top and fingered the paring knife.

The moment she saw the landlord's face come out of the shadows of the corridor and into the doorway of her room, her courage deserted her the same time the strength seemed to evaporate from her arms. She could not stab someone. Could not put a knife into the warm density of a human body. She doubted she could even threaten some-one with a knife. That was not her. And people like her died because they were incapable of doing such things. They waited until it was too late. They screamed and scratched and slapped about. She could picture herself doing exactly that inside this very room. People like her did not fight back, not properly.

Too late.

Knacker closed the door slowly and locked it behind him, turned to Stephanie. His face was pale and his thick lips quivered from the emotion that had taken him over. Maybe it was rage, but she didn't think so. In his expression she intuited what might have been a powerful remorse, or even fear. Yes, he was anxious, so extremely anxious he'd become afraid.

'What is happening? Where's Margaret?'

'He's done one. He's fuckin' done one. I never fought he'd . . .' Knacker spoke quietly, more to himself than to her.

Stephanie's breath caught in her throat. She'd not seen Knacker this shaken or distracted before, and she sensed he needed to tell her something. She suspected he was like that; at the best of times he didn't like silence, liked to obliterate it with the sound of his own voice, to announce and brag and show off. Now trauma was pushing words into his mouth.

He ran his fingers through his curls and momentarily closed his eyes. 'I tell you somefing. Bennet was right.

These fings shouldn't happen. But they do, like.' It was as if he was now speaking to someone else in the room, someone that wasn't her. She wondered if he was mad too, like his cousin.

Knacker looked at the window and became concerned. His usual demeanour returned to the surface of his consciousness; his big eyes glared and swept the room for evidence that he might disapprove of. When he finally looked at Stephanie it was as if he had found her guilty of a great betrayal. Bobbing on his heels, he came further inside the room with his hands out wide from his body, to emphasize his disappointment that she could be so unreasonable. Because she knew that anything she did that was not in his absolute favour was just that to Knacker: unreasonable.

'I . . . I've been sick.' She nodded at the towel on the floor that was covering the wet patch. 'The window,' she added by way of explanation. 'Air. I needed air.'

Knacker peered at the towel. Sniffed. Narrowed his eyes, studied her face, searching for other motives before this potential red herring.

'I want to go.'

Knacker stifled a smile that lived on in his cruel eyes.

'I won't say anything.'

'That right?'

'Yes, I promise.'

'Give me your word, like?'

'Yes, yes. Please.'

'First fings first. We need to clear the rest of these bills, yeah? Don't want bailiffs coming froo the front door at an inconvenient time.'

Her confusion was so great she sensed that her mouth was hanging open in stupefaction. *Bills?* Why was he talking about bills?

'I was finking, cus of the cash flow problem we is having, that you might pay off some more of that council tax, like. We's sorted the gas and electric, but as arranged wiv the council this morning, the council tax still needs sorting. First payment, like. Why wait till Monday? You can do it on the phone, like. I swear on me muvver's life you'll get it back.'

'I don't . . . don't know what . . .'

'You must have a bit tucked away, like. All this perfume and biscuit stuff you been doing, eh? Well the dosh ain't no good to us is it, tucked away in some savings? Time to put it to work and all, considering as you still owe on this room.'

'Room?' She couldn't align her thoughts. A sense of the impossible, of such a great injustice, of this baffling nightmare continuing while also remaining unpredictable, rendered her mute.

'Yeah, this room you puked in. It ain't a forty quid room. I told you earlier. You must have forgotten. Convenient, like.'

She almost had to hold her head still to work out what he was getting at. It was surreal, absurd. 'I did what you asked. I paid—'

'Our agreement was for you to sort fings out and fings ain't sorted, is they? Water's done. Gas, electric. Fanks for that, your help and all that. But council tax is still outstandin' and we need to get them off our backs wiv the first payment. Everyone's got to pitch in, like, in this minor setback. Just as well I been looking after your cash card, cus I fought a time would come when we'd need to put it to work for us, like. All of us. That includes you.'

Her mind cleared sufficiently, or was cleared by a loathing for what stood before her. Even now, at this stage, when a girl had been assaulted in the room above her head, while the other girl had vanished, or been killed, this idiotic man in his designer casual wear, who had tried to run prostitutes from the building, and stolen her cash card, was asking her to pay off his debts with the pittance in her bank account. 'You . . . you came down here to ask me—'

'I ain't askin', I'm tellin', girl. Though you will get it back.'

'You are now trying to steal my money to pay off unpaid council tax. After that . . . that' – she couldn't say his name – 'just assaulted a girl in her room. And Margaret . . .' She paused because Knacker's eyes flitted away from her to evade the horror that showed on her face. 'Where is Margaret?'

'That ain't none of your concern. Little domestic. Fings got out of hand when I weren't here.'

'Out of hand? Are you insane?'

'No he ain't, but I am. Open this fucking door, Knacker, you soft-hearted tosser.' It was Fergal. And he had been listening to the exchange.

Stephanie tried and failed to swallow the icy bolus of terror in her throat.

Knacker's face went taut with fear, his big eyes swivelled to the door. 'All in hand, like. No problem here.'

A hand or a shoe slammed into the door and seemed to

shake the entire building. 'Open. The. Fucking. Door. Knacker.'

Knacker scampered across the room to do Fergal's bidding.

'No,' Stephanie said, or thought she said. In her terror she wasn't sure. But now she felt sick again and her vision wasn't right; the room seemed to be moving around her. Svetlana's cries, 'They kill her', 'Not in there', as well as the sound of the girl's screams reactivated and returned to Stephanie's mind on a spin cycle. Tears welled and blurred the unstable room. 'Don't.' She swallowed. 'No.'

Too late.

Fergal came into the room quickly. Pushed past Knacker. Using one long arm like a yacht's boom, he swept the smaller man off the deck and came for Stephanie in a rustle of dirty Gore-Tex and a flap of soiled denim. Big feet banged the floor until the white, freckled face and bloodshot eyes, the unclean mouth and yellow teeth were suddenly very close, almost touching her face. She coughed in the stench – hormonal, animal harsh, old sweat mingling with new, base scented with something kidneyish and pissy. Her eyelids cramped into an instinctive squint.

A large, bony claw buried itself in the hair at the back of her head. She was broken in half. Snapped double so that when her eyes fluttered open they were staring at the old carpet. Through her shock and the volume of her own breath that panted around a squeal, was an awareness that the fingers gripping her hair would never let go; the grubby digits seemed to have passed inside her skull to hold her thoughts in a permanent freeze of terror.

Outside of her limited understanding of what was happening, this cold recognition of events that clung around her head like a wet rag, she could hear Knacker shouting, 'Leave it! Fergal! Leave it! Fergal! Fink! Fink about it! Leave it!'

And she could also hear Fergal, though she wasn't sure who he was talking to. 'You fink you're so high and mighty. But I been watching you. You fink I don't know what you are? You is wrong. You is very mistaken.' At that point she realized he was talking to her. 'What you still doing here if you ain't gonna earn? You had your chance to fuck off, but you didn't. Cus you is finking about it, eh? I'm right, ain't I? I know these fings. Someone, a little birdy, is telling me all these fings. I fink you know who I am talking about, don't you? An old friend of mine who's got an eye for the ladies. And he's had a good look at you. Very nice it was too, he tells me.'

'Fergal! Fergal! Cut it out!'

Fergal turned to Knacker. 'Cut it out? I'll cut somefing out if you don't watch your mouf. And you is too soft, Knacker. You is a big pussy. This ain't how you get results. Didn't you listen to nuffin' Bennet told us, eh? The only useful fings he ever told us was how to get results. But he could be a real old woman at the best of times, and you're starting to remind me of him. Know what I mean?'

And it was then, when she blinked the tears out of her eyes, that Stephanie saw Knacker's feet, pacing about the carpet, circling Fergal like a nervous boy. And she saw the dried blood on Knacker's green training shoes, dark as creosote and splashed across the toes of both shoes.

'Eh? Eh? I ain't having none of that from you,' he

barked at Fergal. 'Not after what you just gone and fuckin' done. You're the fuckin' problem here.'

'The problem right here, you tosser, is what I am holding in my hand. Your mistake. Who you can't even get in line. You is all mouf, Knacker. What you contributed, eh? Nuffin'. Fuck all is what. All we got I brought here.'

Fergal shook Stephanie's head and she felt some of the roots of her hair tear out of her scalp. Tears dropped from her cheeks and saliva looped from between her lips.

Fergal spat on the carpet. 'This is your contribution and I am afraid it ain't nuffin' but a nuisance. I give you till the weekend to get her up and running and you still ain't produced. Fuckin' around trying to break into her piggy bank, when she should be turning four tricks a day. Cus you don't know your arse from your elbow, Knacker. Cus you is too fucking soft. So I will tell you what I am going to do. I am going to make my point very clear. And if you can do me a favour and watch this, you might end up learning somefing too. Awright?'

And then his stagnant breath was all over Stephanie's face, clouding down from above like a foul mist. 'You listening to me? Oi, you down there. You listening to me?'

Her head was whipped upwards so quickly her feet left the ground for a second, before her entire body crashed back down to the floor. She found her feet but couldn't see the floor because he was making her stare at the ceiling while holding her by the hair like a doll.

A big, dirty foot thumped across the back of her knees as Fergal kicked her legs out from under her. Stephanie sat down hard and gasped from the scatter of pain that shot up from her tailbone when it connected with the floor.

Now she could see herself in the mirror, open-mouthed and glassy-eyed with shock. She had no idea she could even look like that.

She was going to die.

This is it.

In the reflection she watched Fergal dip a long, grubby-fingered hand inside the pocket of his parka. He removed a glass bottle. A small one, the kind that contained medicine. The bottle was unlabelled, the screw-top yellow. 'Hold her,' he ordered Knacker. 'Can you get that right?'

'No! No fucking way. No! I ain't having no part of this. Fergal, no!'

'Pussy. Then watch.' Fergal released Stephanie's hair.

She tried to stand up, but he pushed her onto her painful backside by cupping the entire top of her skull and pressing down. His strength was hideous. She thought her neck might snap and she yelped.

The hand vanished. 'Oi, oi, cry baby. You listen to me, yeah?' He dropped his voice. 'When you is in our house you obey our rules. Simple, yeah? Yeah? Any of this bull-shit, this calling from windows and causing a ruckus and all that and I'll put this on you. I'll fucking burn you without a second's fought, sister. You don't fink I will, then watch this.'

And then she knew what was inside the bottle and she screamed and rolled away from Fergal's feet. Even Knacker cantered back to the mirrored doors of the wardrobe.

'Any little notes, or whispers, or looking out them windows when our backs is turned, anyfing like that at all, and I'll pour this over your fuckin' head. Even fink you can treat me like a cunt and I will know. I will burn you, sister. You get me? This will go right froo your face. I'll fucking blind you wiv this. You hear? We ain't the only ones wiv debts to pay off, yeah?'

A dribble of liquid splashed the carpet and instantly produced white steam. The air of the room swelled with the stink of iron, sulphur, burning toffee and old curtains on fire.

As the room swooped and as little sparking motes of light dropped through her vision, Stephanie closed her eyes on the sight of gangly Fergal carefully recapping the glass bottle. Her stomach walloped over, her throat contracted and she was sick again, right where she sat. Sick onto the floor and onto her hands.

'And I don't want no blubbering. Not a peep out of you, else I'm taking the cap off.'

'Yeah,' Knacker said. 'Yeah, you heard him, like.'

FORTY-ONE

Outside the window of the room she had been locked inside, night fell over the brick entry. Through the solitary window she could see little to either side of the space between 82 Edgehill Road and the wall of the neighbouring property.

The cousins had installed her inside the only room on the right hand side of the first floor corridor. Despite what had happened in her bedroom, and the fact they had crossed the final line by putting their hands upon her, she'd felt relief as she was escorted out of the room where the reek of Fergal's unclean flesh and fouled clothes was replaced by the stink of the acid-burned carpet.

Jesus, God, it could have been your face.

The new room had thus far remained locked and mostly undisturbed during her tenancy, save one evening when she'd heard an old woman's voice reciting scripture. And since she'd been sealed inside the room, Stephanie had successfully suppressed that memory because she could not tolerate another reminder of being swallowed whole and alive by the horror that refused to be sated inside this house.

The window of the room was barred. Before the bars the sash window frame was secured with an old metal fixture that required a key with a square end. It was the kind of lock that suggested the key was long missing.

The grubby glass of the window pane could be broken. But to what end? The McGuires would hear it smash. She'd already imagined her cries for help echoing back at her from inside the narrow stone gap between two detached houses built close together.

The seedy man with a messy front garden lived in the house that neighboured this side, but Stephanie couldn't imagine him running to her aid. And escape from here wasn't possible because the room was a cell. In her misery she wondered if it had been used as one in the past.

Fergal's acid trick had achieved the desired effect; Stephanie shrivelled inside whenever her thoughts returned to the white steam rising from the carpet, the crackle and hiss. Imagining the acid's tearing heat over her face and the pooling of it inside her eye sockets thwarted any urge to shout from the window. To serve as another reminder, the left side of her head was swollen, the ear too painful to touch.

Stephanie knew why she was here and still alive. Why Fergal hadn't killed her like she suspected he had murdered Margaret. Because they were cutting her off and ending her final resistance to their will. Knacker had tried to do this incrementally by selling the idea of prostitution to her, while emphasizing her lack of alternatives, a sales pitch underwritten with suggestions of violence, preceding actual violence, and then extortion. But Fergal had strong-armed and fast-tracked her towards their original goal of selling her body to strangers for profit. It's why Knacker had rented the room to her in the first place. *Girls only.*

Knacker had hoped she was young and desperate enough to be blindsided by his spiel and seduced by the promise of riches, eventually. He must have sensed how compromised she had been that first day, smelled her need like a weasel sniffed out a timorous, hungry vole on a canal bank. But he had missed his recruitment target and Fergal had stepped in with a bottle of acid.

They were a girl down now and she was the replacement.

The sounds of her impending fate were audible through the ceiling. Svetlana had been put back to work. Svetlana was her future.

Above her head, the girl whimpered around the muffled rhythm of a bed thumping a wall as another man threw himself into her body. She had entertained her first 'client' hours before. Had anything remained inside Stephanie's stomach she would have spat it onto the dusty carpet. This was Svetlana's third visitor since Stephanie had been locked inside the new room.

Tonight Svetlana's cries lacked their former enthusiasm, from a time when the tough Lithuanian must have considered herself to be freelance, perhaps one of this 'Andrei's' girls, leasing premises in a building owned by his peers up north. But she was now being forced to have sex after she had been beaten, and had maybe borne witness to, or at least heard, the murder of her friend, a consideration that made Stephanie physically tremble.

This was new territory and within its borders she felt more vulnerable than she had ever felt before in her life; it was a landscape in which all boundaries of restraint, that she had previously taken for granted, had not so much been moved as obliterated and replaced with an arbitrary state of being.

Murder. The very word so close to her actual existence made her feel as if the floor of a lift had just vanished from beneath her feet.

She knew almost nothing about the girls. And the same could be said for everything else at the address: who Bennet was, who the McGuires were, what had happened to those unseen women whose voices and footsteps still lingered inside the dusty, poorly lit rooms. It was ironic that she'd now do anything to go home to her stepmother, to withstand whatever she chose to, literally, throw at her.

How had this happened?

You don't know what happened to Margaret. You don't. You don't. You don't.

She repeated this mantra to the regions of her mind that had already acknowledged the worst, which only responded with some recalcitance by not being convinced.

So fatigued by the day's relentless cycles of fear and anxiety, loathing and hatred, crowned by the devitalizing episodes of outright terror in Fergal's dirty hands, she needed to sit down before she fell over. She was hungry and thirsty and faint, her thoughts becoming vague. She had not stopped feeling nauseous and if she cried any more she feared her eyes would close from the swelling.

Coughing, she batted the fur of grey dust from the pink candlewick bedspread skimming a single bed that looked too small for an adult. She sat down. Turned over the bed-spread and cotton sheet and discovered the grey dust had seeped inside the bed's coverings. A once white sheet was stained by vague brown marks which she immediately covered. The ancient pillow was also watermarked by a former occupant's sleeping head.

A headboard of cushioned white vinyl completed an item of furniture she'd do almost anything to avoid sleeping on. The last bed she had seen of this age and style had been in her gran's spare bedroom when Stephanie had been a child. And this was the smallest room she had yet seen inside the house. It hadn't been cleaned in years, or even aired. The odours of mildew, dust and sour paint refused to normalize into something her nose no longer detected.

Beside the small bed was an empty bedside cabinet made of chipboard and laminated with white plastic. The top surface was fluffy with dust. A grimy mirror was screwed to the back of the door. A solitary light bulb hung inside a plastic shade and made the dim electric light look like it was being shone through a bowl of fruit cocktail, poured from a cheap tin.

It was a room in which an occupant could only feel trapped, hopeless and miserable, which is exactly how Stephanie felt. She zipped her jacket up to her neck until the heating came on, surprised they hadn't shut it off to save money. Perhaps they didn't know how to. And if she was to be left in here all night, she realized she would need to sleep on the floor. The bed was too dirty.

All she had going for her was the knife.

She took it out of the pocket at the front of her hooded top and rolled it between her fingertips. Clenched her teeth until her face pulsed with the heat of her blood. *If one of them came in now . . .*

She didn't know what she would do. The knife was

blunt, the blade short. It couldn't kill, but it might slash, might wound.

And if it went through an—

'Stop, stop, stop,' she whispered to herself.

FORTY-TWO

When the world outside darkened, and as Svetlana's unwilling hospitality extended to her fifth customer, the squeak of a floorboard preceded the rattle of a key inside the lock of her door.

Before the door opened, Stephanie leapt off the bed and then backed against the window. Struggling to swallow the lump in her throat, she slipped a hand inside the pocket of her hooded top. Her fingers squeezed the plastic handle of the knife, but it felt smaller and lighter than it had done before.

Knacker's bony face thrust inside the room, grinning. 'Fought you might like somefing to eat.' He held a yellow polystyrene container, the kind takeaway restaurants used to package kebabs.

Shuffling into the room, he peered about the walls and bed warily, maintaining the grin as if trying to find something positive about the situation he could comment upon.

He placed the carton on the foot of the bed and pulled a can of Carling Black Label out of the pocket of his ski jacket – the coat her deposit must have paid for.

He dropped the can onto the dirty bedclothes. 'This stuff don't come cheap neither. Yous'll have to pay me back tomorrow. Till I can get to a cash machine that is, so you better be quick wiv that pin number, yeah, when I ask for it. Nuffin's free in this world, girl. Don't I know it, like.'

Unable to speak through a blockage of rage, disgust and fear, Stephanie glared at his face. Behind his curly head the light clicked out and plunged the corridor into darkness.

She needed to lose it, needed to get angry and provoke him, and then ignite herself. It was the only way she would be able to use the knife, by losing control in a hot flurry of hate and hysteria. 'What the fuck do you think you're doing? This is kidnap.'

He tried to laugh it off. 'Nah, nah, it's nuffin' like that. You's a bit of a drama queen, ain't ya? Just a little setback, like, that we is fixing. No harm done, yeah.'

'Your cousin threatened to burn my face with acid. He beat Svetlana. Margaret's . . . You punched me. Assaulted me. And now you've locked me in this room. You're in serious trouble. You know that?' She lowered her voice. 'Or, at least, your cousin is.'

Knacker's eyes narrowed. He glanced over his shoulder into the dark corridor, pushed the door to then turned to her. 'Let's get one fing straight, yeah. So pin your ears back, girl, while I is explainin' somefing to you. First fing, you don't know nuffin'. Nuffin' about me or Fergal, our backgrounds. Nuffin'. Second fing is, you better start cooperating, like. I'm doing my best to fight your corner here. But if the truth be told, you ain't helpin' much. Only fing in your favour with Fergal is you helping us out wiv a few small fings. But that ain't enough no more. And I been trying to offer you a way out. I gave you a choice, on a plate, like, but you turned your nose up. Bent over backwards, I have, since you been here, but we ain't got no time for passengers no more. Patience is all used up wiv them that don't do what they are here for.'

'I'm not here for anything. I rented a room. And if you thought I'd be a . . . a whore because I rented a room off you, then you were mistaken. Very much so.'

'None a that, eh? And keep your voice down, yeah? I shouldn't even be talking to you. Decision's been made. Time for discussion is over. You saw what he done to that floor. Be fankful it weren't somefing else, like.'

'You can't make me. I won't. I won't do it.'

'Make you? No one is trying to make you do nuffin'. You knew what the score was, so why didn't you fuck off, like? Like Fergal said, you was tempted. You was finkin' about it. So we is just helping you wiv your choice, like. Bennet . . .' Knacker held back, as though he'd just let slip the first word of a secret while justifying his odious coercion.

Stephanie loosened the knife inside her pocket. 'I wasn't tempted by anything. I don't have any bloody money because you kept my deposit. That is the only reason I am still here. I was trying to get enough money together to get out and you know it. But you thought I was some kind of dumb teenager who'd fall for your bullshit and become a slag. And now you're keeping me prisoner—'

'Prisoner? Hold on a minute—'

'Then what's this? Locking me in this dirty room—'

'Ain't that bad—'

They'd begun to talk over each other in tight, breathless

voices. Why was she bothering? He was a liar, a pimp, he'd assaulted her, and even now he could not stop twisting everything she said. She was never getting out.

Her thoughts sped up; she thought as quickly as she could of motives, horrible eventualities, possibilities, ideas . . . anything she could do to free herself.

The knife.

'You won't get away with it. People know I am here. What do you think is going to happen? Have you thought about that? No good telling yourself you're in control and that it's all going to work out. That your bills will get paid and that I'll become a whore and start earning money for you, so you can buy trainers and skunk weed. I mean, are you fucking stupid?'

Knacker took two steps inside the room, at her.

Stephanie stared at the dried blood on his shoes. 'You come near me again and I'll fucking kill you!'

'That a fact?'

'You bloody hit me. Hit me!'

'Then you should have been quicker wiv them keys, like.'

'You stole my phone. My money. Locked me in here. It's all stacking up against you. But you weren't quick enough. Yeah? Yeah? Because help is on its way, you piece of shit!'

Knacker stepped away from her and seized the door handle. His eyes had lidded and he'd thrown his head back so she could just catch a thin gleam of the reptilian pupils and also see inside his big nostrils. He was shocked because he hadn't expected this from her.

'Margaret's dead, isn't she? That psychopath killed her.'

As she spoke the girl's name, she sensed an immediate increase in his indecision, his torment, the endless mental wrangling beneath the curly hair and behind that bony and big-lipped façade of a face. He was scared of Fergal too, maybe more than he was of getting caught. She could sense it, because Knacker wasn't as far gone as his cousin, hadn't quite left humanity in the same way. And his partner in crime, his muscle, had done something to unsettle the creature before her. She could smell the fear on him, under the aftershave.

'How many? How many has he killed?'

'What you talking about?'

'Here. In this house. I've heard them. Seen them. You know I have. Maybe you have too.'

Knacker looked puzzled. It seemed genuine.

'The girls. The girls in these rooms. They're dead. But they're still here.'

'You is cracked. Fucking cracked. Here's you talking about psychos. Have a look in that mirror, girl. You is making my skin crawl. Saying these fings about my muvver's house. What's a matter wiv you, yeah? I give you a place to live. Try and help you out wiv some quick cash—'

'Shut up. Stop. Stop. You didn't. You did not help me out, or try to help me out. Cut the crap. You wanted me to fuck those creeps for money, you seedy little prick. That's all this was ever about and you know it.'

Stephanie jabbed her hand at the ceiling. 'He's beaten Svetlana and now she is being raped. Raped. You're a criminal. You made this happen. And you will pay for it. It's not going to be all right. It's not a setback or a little problem, you stupid twat!' She dropped her voice to a desperate whisper. 'But maybe it won't be too bad for you if you let me go. If you help me right now. That'll be taken into consideration, won't it? You can save yourself here, Knacker. You know it. Why go down with that nutter?'

Knacker clenched his fists.

'It's gone too far, hasn't it? You didn't want this. But he wrecked it. It's over now. Murder. Kidnap. Acid . . .' Rage and fear had come together to make these words erupt, but now she'd lost her voice. It only took one word to burn the others out of her mouth: *acid*. This might have been the most desperate and important thing she'd ever said in her life, ever needed to say, but she was too emotional to continue.

Though maybe she had struck a blow, because his face was bloodless, but not from anger. He backed into the corridor and recovered sufficiently to glance over his shoulder and into the waiting darkness, in fear of who might be out there.

When he turned and spoke to her, his voice lacked the usual self-importance and arrogant assertiveness. 'Fergal hears you, then I ain't gonna be responsible for what happens. You made your own bed, like. Time to wake up, yeah? Have a good long fink about tomorrow. About what you need to do to make this situation right. To make it better for you, yeah? Cus if you don't then you is no good to him. You can say all the hurtful fings you want to me, like. But I ain't your problem. I fink you know what I'm talkin' about.'

The door clicked shut behind him. Before she could get across the room he'd turned the key inside the lock.

FORTY-THREE

Stephanie awoke on the brittle carpet, shivering. Her discomfort was immediately overshadowed by the sound of a voice above her body.

She'd broken from another bad dream that left her with a vague memory of a discoloured face, whispering from inside a plastic covering, only to emerge into a space where another voice spoke. And the second speaker was either inside the room or situated near the ceiling.

Stephanie didn't sit up, because that would have meant moving her head closer to where the voice originated, *up there*.

Still wrapped inside the aged candlewick bedspread, an item she had shaken vigorously and then turned around to keep herself as warm as possible on the floor, Stephanie tried to orientate herself inside a room as black as pitch.

She strove for a recognition of where the door to the room was in relation to her position on the floor, and also where the window was, the bed, the bedside cabinet.

She remained afraid, though identified more resolve in herself than she'd experienced before at night in the building. She was becoming accustomed to these visitations, or manifestations, or whatever they were, though it was a familiarity that brought no real comfort.

Those that actually *lived* at 82 Edgehill Road, she was reminded with a cruel irony, were now far worse than the muttering but unseen mouths of the building's dingy cavities. She'd still take this situation over being in a room with the McGuires. But as she stared into the freezing darkness, endeavouring to pinpoint the source of the sound, Stephanie still bit into a hand to stop the whimpering that wanted to struggle out of her mouth.

The voice she could hear was brittle with age. And it spoke English. The speaker was a woman, an older woman, and an angry woman. That was apparent, as was Stephanie's belief that it was the worst voice she had yet heard at night inside the building.

As if the speaker had swiftly moved into the distance, the voice became faint within an atmosphere of absolute silence that allowed the words to travel, but not carry far enough for Stephanie to really understand all of what was being said. She caught bursts of speech thrown at her in desperation, fragments repeatedly cut off as if by swipes of a headwind, while the room remained unnaturally still and cold.

'Avoid foolish questions and . . . contentions . . . strivings about . . . they are unprofitable . . . vain . . .'

The voice then muffled as if spoken at the ground, or into a hand held across a mouth, or as if a radio signal had momentarily lost its strength.

When the voice surged back into the room, it moved across where the ceiling should be, and in a manner that made Stephanie cringe into near paralysis.

'A man that is an heretic . . . first and . . . admonition . . . reject . . .'

Struck by the notion that the speaker was crawling across the ceiling and through the darkness above her head, Stephanie cast off her dusty coverings and moved to her hands and knees. Crawled to where she hoped the door would be.

The voice then circled, or perhaps hugged the corners of the ceiling as it moved around Stephanie in an anti-clockwise fashion that gradually increased in speed. 'Knowing that he . . . subverted . . . sinneth . . . being condemned of himself . . .'

Stephanie groped along one side of the bed, the carpet so dry and rough the fabric could have been snow crunching beneath her tender palms and fingertips.

She turned and sat down and then shuffled across the bottom of the bedframe to the wall. When she found the door with the back of her head and shoulders, she made to stand up with the intention of fumbling for the light switch. But at that moment the voice spoke again. And no more than an inch from her face.

'Be diligent to come unto me!'

Stephanie screamed until not a solitary molecule of air remained inside her lungs. She screamed to expel the notion that the invisible speaker now hung upside down from the ceiling so that its mouth was level with her eyes.

When her scream tailed into a gasp, so icy was the room that the skin of her face burned. She had not been dismissed by whatever had gathered about her.

Silence thickened around her like a cold sea blackened by night.

A small voice, and one full of tears, ended the calm by

whispering into both of her ears at the same time, 'For I have determined there to winter.'

She could not understand why her heart did not stop at that moment. Had it done she would have considered cardiac arrest the only mercy she had been shown by the house during her short time beneath its roof. But she managed to stand up on legs she could hardly feel, and to find the switch and return light to the horrible room.

There was nothing on the ceiling and no one inside with her. But the room's dimensions now appeared dirtier and even more forlorn than they had before she fell asleep.

DAY SEVEN

FORTY-FOUR

When Stephanie awoke a figure stood over her body.

Grubby light from the window made her eyes smart. She shielded her face with one arm and waited for a blow.

'Bed not good enough for ya? Can't imagine the floor is much better, like.' This was followed by one of Knacker's rare cackles.

Stephanie sat bolt upright. 'Where . . . You . . . What the fuck are you doing?'

Knacker stepped away. 'Who me? Nuffin', besides giving you a wakeup call. It's gone eleven, girl. Can't have people just lying around on the floor, like, when there's work to be done.'

Stephanie struggled to her feet and lurched for the open door.

'Aye, aye, hold up.' Knacker swiped at her arm.

'Let me go!' She twisted from his grip, leaving him with a handful of her sleeve.

Knacker nearly yanked her off her feet.

She dipped her free hand inside the front pocket of her hooded top. Her fingers found the knife handle. She brought the knife into the room and before his eyes.

'Fuck's sake!' He released her sleeve.

Her heart sped up with a new excitement, one that was

unrecognizable, but it was an excitement that felt welcome and made time accelerate and speed away from her. And she knew she could do it. She could hurt this bastard who had locked her away and who had crept inside her room while she slept, who had hit her – *he hit you!* – and who wanted to force her to have sex with strangers in this stinking, dark, evil house.

'You bastard!' She took one stride towards him. He flinched, his pale eyes bulging from a face stiff with fear. She prepared to swing at him with all of her strength.

Before she could comprehend what was happening, she was unable to move the hand gripping the knife. Her body was tugged backwards. She fell and was dragged across the floor and out of the room.

The doorway, the distant ceiling, the aged wallpaper, the red skirting boards, all rotated about her head. Fingers much longer and stronger than her own peeled her hand open to remove the knife. And when she came to a stop, the ripe and bestial odour that clung around Fergal's bony legs engulfed her face.

The sole of a big, dirty foot found the side of her head and pressed her skull hard into the grubby carpet. Her arm that had wielded the knife was pulled upwards and straight, and so hard she feared it might pop out of its socket.

The bottom of the shoe holding her head secure was gritty and as rough as emery cloth. A downward pressure squashed her cheeks and made saliva dribble from one side of her mouth. She didn't struggle in case the foot pressed down harder and broke her head apart like a cabbage.

'Fuck's sake, Knacker. She nearly gashed you up, mate. If she had I'd a made you clean up your own claret, you useless twat.'

'Nah, nah. Weren't like that. I'd have been there, like. Always am when it counts.'

'Piss off! This silly little slit nearly done you. I knew you was going soft. All that Ganja since you come out the nick has turned you into a right pussy.'

'Fuck off! I won't have it.'

'You won't? You will if I say so! You want to go or something? Eh? Eh? Can't hear you! Yes or no, Knacker? Yes or fucking no? Right here!'

'Nah. Nah. Leave it. I didn't mean it like that.'

'Bet you didn't, you tosser. Fink you is the brains and all that, but you can't get nuffin' right. I hadn't been there she'd be in the street shouting her mouf off by now. You's the weakest link here, Knacker. And we don't have much use for them that don't pull their weight. You're already on a warning. You don't fink I will put you down then you is fooling yourself. I'll put you *in there*, yeah? Right inside wiv *it*. I'll hold the door shut while it has its way wiv you, like it done wiv Bennet.'

'Cut it out. Leave it, yeah? How's I supposed to know she had a blade? Where she get it from? You is just as much to blame. You put her inside here wiv me. Didn't see you doing no strip search.'

'Knacker. Knacker. You start twisting fings . . .' Fergal left that as a warning.

Knacker remained uncharacteristically silent.

Fergal returned his attention to Stephanie. He removed his foot and grinned at her. 'I hear you ain't ready to start

281

sucking cock yet. Well until you is, you got some cleaning to do. If you ain't gonna open your legs, you can get on your hands and knees and do some fucking housework. How's that, eh? And while you're scrubbing, girl, you'll have plenty of time to fink about what comes next if you don't start being a bit more hospitable to our visitors.'

FORTY-FIVE

'Wipe it down. Anyfing they is touched, like. You're a woman, you knows what gets messed wiv in women's rooms and all that, yeah?'

Stephanie knew at once what Knacker was referring to: *evidence*. And there was plenty of *that* inside the room. At a glance from the doorway of the second floor bedroom that Knacker clearly did not want to enter in case he incriminated himself by leaving any trace of his presence, Stephanie could see blood on two walls and speckled across the white material of the bedspread. Margaret's blood.

On one wall the stains had dried black and were flecked in a long arc. Stephanie's imagination offered the image of a woman's head snapping sideways after a bone-crunching blow.

The second spatter had the pattern of a smudge, as if a wet face had been pushed into and then wiped down the wall. Beside the main stain were finger marks: drag lines.

Within the doorframe, Knacker crowded about Stephanie and pointed at the floor. 'And on the carpet. See it? Down there by the bottom of the bed. You need to get it up, like. All of it, yeah?'

Stephanie looked at the shadow beneath the hem of the

duvet at the foot of the bed. Someone had lain still in that spot and bled.

She leant against the doorframe and stifled the urge to cry. The need to break down rippled up from her feet and through her body like a current of electricity that took hold of her jaw. She closed her eyes and tensed all of her muscles to force her face not to crumple.

'Better get started, like. Cus Fergal— We want it done sharpish, like, yeah?'

In one hand Stephanie held the bucket Knacker had given her, containing whatever oddments of cleaning materials he had been able to rummage out from under the kitchen sink. To remove the traces of a foreign sex worker's violent death, Knacker couldn't even organize the right kind of cleaning materials. In the bucket he had given Stephanie there was a rusty bottle of Pledge furniture polish, a near empty spray bottle of Windolene for cleaning glass, a virtually depleted bottle of Best In bleach, and a trickle of Jiff bathroom scourer in a plastic container with a top entirely sealed with crusted fluid. Not the ideal equipment for removing substances that forensic technicians would scour every millimetre of floor space to discover.

Knacker was terrified of going outside the house to fetch new cleaning materials in case he was identified in the street. *You don't know nuffin' about my background.* It was true, but she felt more capable of making informed assumptions now.

Stephanie returned her attention to the room.

Margaret had tried to feminize the space before she died inside it. Silky black wraps and scarves were draped

around the curtain rails and over the white fitted ward-
robes, perhaps to hide a cheap and unappealing background in a space allocated to sexual activity. An impressive
range of perfume bottles and expensive make-up littered
the surface of a dresser fitted with a mirror; the mirror was
angled to reflect the entire bed for whomever was lying
upon it.

The mattress had been dressed with a zebra throw rug
too, and the girl must have brought her own sheets and
pillow cases with her because Stephanie could not imagine 82 Edgehill Road containing anything as fancy
as Margaret's plump, tasselled, satin pillows.

Beside the wardrobe, a stainless steel rail on little
wheels was festooned with gauzy underwear, latex dresses,
clothes made from Lycra, and black dresses. At least
twelve pairs of high-heeled shoes and boots were scattered
beneath the clothing rail.

Yet all of the Albanian girl's paraphernalia could not
disguise the aged and tasteless spectacle of the wallpaper
and carpet. The tropical bamboo pattern that had covered
the walls of Stephanie's first room was replicated here.

At least there were no bars on the windows. Stephanie
wondered if that was why the girls had been installed on
the second floor. Operating from the second floor was
hardly convenient, as customers had to walk through two
storeys inside the dark, scruffy house on their way to see
the girls, with Knacker bantering after them. It would have
been much better to have prostitutes work from the
ground floor, the part of the building that had always been
locked away for renovations, or so Knacker claimed. She
had a sense Svetlana and Margaret had been borrowed, or

leased from this 'Andrei'. But if the girls had been given some choice in coming to work here, window bars would have been an instant cause for alarm. Svetlana had once complained about the bathroom; it now looked like that had been the least of her worries.

Her frantic internal inquiry about Bennet, whom Fergal had referred to as if the man was still in residence, along with the cryptic exchange regarding Fergal's threat to put Knacker 'in there wiv *it*', all derailed once Stephanie entered the room.

Beaten to death. Fists. Kicking feet.

She moved further inside the room. When she saw Margaret's black furry cat – a soft toy on the chair before the dresser, its neck encircled with a red velvet band and heart-shaped locket – a wash of hot tears made her see the room as if through the windscreen of a car in a rainstorm. She dropped her face into her hands and sniffed back the mucus that ran from her nose.

Oh, God. Dad. Dad. Daddy.

They were about the same age. Margaret had been sweet and happy the one time they had met on the stairs. The girl must have had parents, maybe brothers and sisters, people who loved her, and maybe she was just trying to earn money to advance herself with all she had at her disposal: her beautiful body. Margaret had not looked like she was feeding a drug habit.

Something burst inside Stephanie. She fell to her knees. The levee that had held so much fear, regret, anxiety, hope and despair in check, while she had prayed it would all end quickly as she slogged to and from temping jobs, was swept away. And in a fragment of a second she felt the full force of her situation impact and then engulf her. Her body shook like she was going into shock.

She could not be strong any more. She had been punched, had her hair pulled, had been dragged across a dirty floor and shut inside rooms that no living thing should ever enter. And now she had to get down on her hands and knees and wipe away the blood of a young woman who had been beaten to death.

'Why?' she said through her sobs. And she momentarily examined the futility of her recent existence: the endless work and revision for her A Levels so she could escape her stepmother; the soul-destroying jobs that filled her with a boredom that slow-burned inside her stomach and made her want to self-harm; the wretched rooms let by criminal opportunists that she had lived inside because she was poor. *All of it.* 'For this?' To wipe up a victim's blood in a house that had recorded so much loss and confusion and horror she could not begin to process it. Only to then have her body sold for sex when she was finished scrubbing.

Too much. No more now. No more.

'I can't. I can't. Don't make me. I haven't done anything to you. I just wanted a room and a fucking job!' Her cries ended in sobs.

Behind her, Knacker began to fidget. He softened his voice. 'Come on. I don't like to see you like this, Steph. You know that. Aye? Let's just get this done then lock up, yeah? We's all gotta pitch in, like.'

She stopped crying and turned on him. And while she spoke she didn't care whether they killed her or let her live. 'Pitch in? Pitch in! This is blood. A woman's blood. She's dead, I know she is. He killed her.'

'You don't know nuffin'. There was a misunderstanding, yeah? But it's all sorted now, like.' Knacker wasn't even convincing himself. He looked like he wanted to cry, but not for Margaret. Stephanie didn't believe he really understood her death; he was only concerned about self-preservation, his survival.

He slapped a hand to his forehead and winced. 'Fuck. Fuck. Fuck.' And at this display of emotion, this regret that his plans had not followed the script, she probably hated him more than she had ever hated him. And she wanted him dead. He should be dead, not Margaret.

Stephanie looked at the blood. *I'm sorry, Margaret. I'm sorry*, she thought, and swallowed what was left of the emotion in her throat that could have been despair, misery, or even the beginning of madness.

'What will happen to me?'

'Eh?'

'When I have done this. Cleaned her away . . .'

Knacker composed himself with a big sniff up one nostril. Raised his chin. 'You do as I say and you'll be awright. No mouthing off, yeah? I got your back here. You got no other friends in this house, girl.'

Knacker then slipped further inside the room to stand behind her, but not as close as he'd previously favoured since the incident with the knife. 'Now ain't the time, like, for discussing what you mentioned earlier, yeah? About who's responsible and all that, for this, yeah? But strictly between us, yeah, I am concerned by fings as they have turned out. None of this was planned, like. Fuck all to do wiv me, if the truth be told, like. I'm just trying to earn a crust here. So we gotta choose our moment, yeah? Which means you got to play along a bit. You get me? Sake of appearances and all that. You know, bit a cleaning in here. Then maybe we can see about connecting you wiv a client—'

'Fuck off! Just piss off right now!' Even in here, where a woman had recently died, he wouldn't give up.

Having progressed up the corridor without making a sound, a long, thin shape moved across the doorway and the light dimmed; the arms were orangutan like, the shoulders stooped so the horrible head could protrude inside the room.

Stephanie caught her breath. Because for a moment, when she first saw the figure's shape flow across the doorway, she was certain that in the bad light she had glimpsed a black, eyeless oval extend into the room like the head of a large snake, while the end of the protrusion was engaged in a silent snarl that revealed too many stained teeth in a mouth more primate than human.

The bestial head passed into the tarnished light of Margaret's room and became Fergal's face. He grinned at Stephanie and nodded at the foot of the bed. 'You missed a bit.'

FORTY-SIX

It was after Knacker had walked away from where he stood guard at the door of the bedroom, to move down the second floor corridor towards the stairwell to answer Svetlana's phone, that Stephanie first noticed the cold in Margaret's room. Wiping at her nose with the back of a hand that stank of bleach, she stopped scrubbing uselessly at the broad stain at the foot of the bed and rocked back on her heels. Looked about the walls. And then at the window.

But the light had not changed; an iron sky still speckled the dirty panes with spots of drizzle. There was no sun to move behind a cloud because the sky had been grey and grubby with rain for over an hour. This change in temperature was not in her imagination.

The overhead light still shone the dull yellow she associated with long hours in dim warehouses, and the heating had been warming the dusty house for at least half an hour. So there was no reason for Margaret's room to chill, and so much that Stephanie rubbed the outside of her arms.

In the distance she could hear Knacker trying to speak softly to conceal his conversation. 'Yeah. Yeah, but make it eight, like. She's busy, yeah . . . Course she is. This is right proper here, like. All our girls is clean. Tested. Best, like. Nah. Nah. Just the one tonight. Tomorrow, though, we might have another one . . .' He'd dropped his voice even lower.

Stephanie swallowed and looked at the ceiling. 'Can you see me? Can you hear me? I know you're there. One of you. Margaret? Is it you? Margaret, I won't leave you. I won't leave you alone.'

She looked at the doorway. Knacker had gone quiet but she could hear his feet as he paced about by the stairwell. Stephanie turned back to the room. 'I'll find out who you are . . . what they did to you. They won't get away with it. I'll get you help. Somehow. I promise. I promise you all.'

The room stayed chilly and still. Either the cold, or the invasive feelings of sadness and fear, pushed her own spirits down with a mournful gravity. A tremor ran through her voice. 'I know you are afraid . . . and sad. I can feel it. You don't know where you are, do you? You can't remember. You are just there . . . here. Stuck. You frightened me. But you didn't mean to. You just wanted my help. I will help you all. I will get help.'

She realized it was the first time in this situation that she wanted a sign, something, anything, any movement at all, even the slightest indication that she had been heard and understood.

Besides the cold, nothing was forthcoming from whatever had gathered around her, though she suspected the room was listening and that something inside the space was trying to extend and feel its way inside her. She sensed . . . no, she knew, that she was not alone.

And then, as if the room had drawn a breath from shock, the atmosphere altered. She heard nothing but intuited an unseen motion, or an energy, that quickly withdrew from around where she sat by the bucket at the foot of the bed. As if sucked back to the walls, the feelings of grief and loneliness subsided. A pressure lifted from her, upwards and out of her, making her scalp tingle. And something she could not see or hear scattered like a nervous cat around the walls and fled the room.

The temperature of the room dropped even lower. And in place of the departing presence came the odour of sweat and halitosis, as if an unwashed body had just swept inside the room and a dirty mouth had opened and breathed upon her face.

Stephanie gritted her teeth, clenched both fists and raised them into the air. 'You bastard. You can't hurt me.'

A bottle of perfume toppled on the surface of the dresser.

Stephanie screamed.

A black shroud of silk flopped from the curtain rail and pooled soundlessly upon the floor beneath the radiator.

In the stench that intensified enough to make her cough, choke and then gag, as if her head had been forced inside something soft and pulpy with death, she realized there was a hand in her hair. Fingers so cold she believed her scalp was being burned gripped a handful of her hair and shoved her face to the floor. A second hand pulled her hooded sweat top away from her waist line and exposed her back to what felt like a freezing draught.

She struggled onto all fours and batted her hands

behind her body as if to knock off an assailant. 'No! Bastard!' Her hands raked empty air.

In the dim periphery of her hearing and awareness she heard footsteps pound the floor towards the room.

She could see nothing outside of the hair that hung all around her face and stuck to the spittle that looped out of her mouth. And now the painful side of her face was squashed against the floor.

She screamed as a set of cold teeth touched the flesh on her back above her kidney.

Then it stopped. Though her hysteria did not.

Stephanie rolled about the floor, swiping her hands, claws out, at the warming air that surrounded her body. And she kicked out her feet as hard and as quickly as she could at the space above her, at the thin air around her body, because there was no one inside the room any more, and no hand in her hair, or teeth indenting the skin of her back. Not any longer.

On her backside, she shuffled across the floor to the radiator where she sat shaking with shock, panting and wheezing as the adrenaline and cortisone and horror seeped through her body and warmed the crotch of her jeans.

She looked to the doorway and saw Knacker's face cast with an unfamiliar expression. He was so frightened his lips had peeled back from his teeth and his horrified eyes were too large for his thin face, like hard-boiled eggs painted by a disturbed child.

Fergal came and stood beside Knacker. He was delighted. 'That Bennet, he just won't fuck off.' He loped into the room towards Stephanie.

She pulled her legs to her body and clasped her shins. The muscles of her face shook and she could not stop them moving no matter how hard she tried. Across the room in the dresser mirror, she could see that her mouth was open and that she looked imbecilic with terror. She could not speak and her heart refused to slow its banging inside her throat and between her ears.

'Fought you might like to see this.' Grinning, like he was showing a mate a picture of some harmless antic, Fergal crouched beside Stephanie. His long fingers were arranged around a smart phone. 'It's him awright. Fat bastard. He was outside Svetlana's room last night. And I got him. I got him sniffing round her door. They's all getting stronger cus it's all going off. Look.' Fergal turned the handset around and showed Stephanie's unblinking eyes what was displayed onscreen.

Shaking so hard that her vision moved, Stephanie looked at a dark digital image. One that was, at first, unclear. Until the chaos of shadow and pale smudges on the small screen of the phone suggested a fat, eyeless face wearing spectacles, and a head tightly covered in the hood of a raincoat. When she glimpsed what she believed were a row of teeth in a howling mouth she closed her eyes.

Giggling like a chimp, Fergal spoke with enough familiarity to suggest they were sharing a joke. 'It's him, ain't it? It's really him. He come back just like he said he would.'

FORTY-SEVEN

The ringtone of her phone erupted from a pocket in Knacker's jeans.

Fergal whipped his head in Knacker's direction and raised his eyebrows. Knacker fished the phone out of his pocket. 'Someone called Ryan. Fird time he's called today. And twice yesterday. I can't read his texts. She's put a pin number in.'

Fergal's face moved within an inch of Stephanie's nose. 'Who the fuck is that?'

She swallowed but could not speak.

When the distant chime of the doorbell announced itself up the stairwell, quickly followed by the sound of a hand hammering against the front door, Knacker and Fergal exchanged glances.

Knacker became antsy with nerves and started to bob on his toes. 'We ain't expecting no one til five.'

'You expecting someone?' Fergal asked Stephanie, and his breath reminded her of spoiled meat.

'Course she ain't,' Knacker said. 'Like I said, her friends don't wanna know.'

'Shut it!' Fergal shouted at his cousin.

'Awright! Leave it out, will ya?'

Fergal pushed his face into hers. 'What's the pin number?'

Stephanie swallowed and whispered it. Fergal quickly entered it into the phone. He glared at Knacker. 'You should have done this yesterday, twat!' His eyes returned to the phone and he went through her messages. 'She's been texting him. This cunt who's been calling.' He swivelled his head round to confront Stephanie again. 'I asked you a question. Is you expecting a visitor, this Ryan? You given him our address?'

She shook her head. She couldn't manage anything else and was too scared to even sniff at the mucus that had run from her nose. The crotch of her jeans had gone cold and was starting to make her sore.

Through the shock and bewilderment that had not abated since she had been attacked by 'Bennet', and which had only been worsened by Fergal showing her the picture of the dead rapist on his phone screen, Stephanie made a connection between the call from Ryan and the sound of banging on the distant front door. She felt a surge of hope that made her want to cry.

'Get it,' Fergal said to Knacker.

Knacker pointed at her. 'Last night. Yeah, last night. She was making freats, like. Said something about someone knowing she was here, like. Sure she did.'

'I said, get it!' Fergal roared at Knacker, who almost instantly vanished from the doorway in his haste to escape Fergal's wrath.

Fergal returned his attention to Stephanie; the sides of his thin lips were white with spittle, and within his expression the hatred she interpreted made her cringe against the radiator. 'Finks he's hard, does he? Cavalry? Finks he can come here and sort fings out, does he? Well if he wants some then he can have some.'

'No.' Her voice was a whisper and her throat closed again after the faint sound escaped.

Fergal was already on his feet and striding from the room with a purpose that made her feel sick.

'No!' she screamed. 'Don't you touch him!' Stephanie followed Fergal across the room.

He turned in the doorway and glared at her. Nothing else was required to bring her to a flinching stand still. He closed the door nonchalantly. With the key Knacker had left hanging from the lock, the door was secured.

In the far distance, over the sound of Fergal's retreating footsteps, the front door of the house closed, shutting the visitor inside.

FORTY-EIGHT

Stephanie was surprised that she had still not cried. Maybe the tears would come later, if there was a later.

No, there would be no *later*, not after what they had just done in the garden. She had seen it and they knew she had seen it. And what she had seen had made her incapable of anything afterwards, except lying on the bed in a foetal position, staring at the wall, back inside her original first floor room.

Such was her shock she wasn't sure she remembered the events correctly, or even in the right sequence. She could only recall bits of what happened, like clips from a film she'd been watching as she dozed off, and then awoke, and then dozed off again, until she'd finally roused to watch the end credits rolling down a screen. But images from the garden scene would suddenly rush into her mind, and they would be too clear, too loud and too bright, and she would whimper and push the images back into the darkness.

She didn't know how long she had been lying like this in her old room. Hours, surely.

After Ryan had arrived and Fergal had locked her inside Margaret's old room, Stephanie had heard raised voices issuing from deeper inside the building. She'd heard them while pressed against the door. The voices had grown in strength and volume and changed tone. She'd wanted to break the window and scream for help. But fear, *yes fear*, of displeasing the cousins and provoking reprisals she might not awake from, had kept her sobbing and pressed into the door. And fear had become guilt while she repeated a mantra to herself: *Ryan must have told someone he was coming. Ryan must have told someone he was coming. Ryan must have told someone he was coming.*

Guilt had since sunk into regret. Because now, more than anything, she regretted not breaking the window and jumping from the second storey of the building. She was responsible for what had happened to Ryan. Like Knacker had said, she was responsible because she had told Ryan where she was and 'bitched to him, like, about this house. No one likes a grass.'

'Oh, God. No, God, no,' she said to herself as the most memorable scene flashed into her mind once again; a scene from midway through the proceedings, after she had managed to knock Knacker aside and briefly escape the room. A vivid scene which featured Fergal's lanky shape dragging something by a foot through the rubbish sacks and building refuse and long weeds of the patio: a body not really moving beside the clutching motions it made upon its own wet and crimson face.

Ryan.

That was before Knacker ran and caught her in the stairwell. He had grabbed her by the hair just after she had raised a hand to bang the stairwell window. He'd taken the wrist of her raised arm with his other hand, and even he had paused at that stage and said, 'Better not look, eh? When Fergal loses it he don't fuck around, like.'

Her memory revisited an earlier scene: the one when Knacker came to her room a few minutes after the shouting and bellowing had stopped downstairs. Right after Fergal had screamed like an animal and then bellowed, 'You want it! You want it! You want it!' at the visitor, at Ryan.

Knacker's face, when it appeared at the door of the room in which Margaret had died, was bloodless and wet with sweat and he had been wheezing like an asthmatic. He had run up two flights of stairs to check on her, to make sure she 'wasn't trying anything on, like'.

One of Knacker's hands was red and some of the knuckles were already blue-purple. He'd held one hand against his stomach like a claw and kept wincing as he spoke to her. The big toe of one foot had come through one of the new lime green trainers. The shoe looked like a child had blown scarlet paint through a drinking straw across the top.

And then her memory drifted forwards to the sound of Fergal's dirty shoe coming down on Ryan's face on the garden patio, and then stamping onto the side of his head, and then onto his face again, and then onto the back of his head, after Ryan had rolled over and tried to get to his knees.

One of Ryan's arms had been broken and hung limp under his ribs, which was why he had not been able to get up from the dirty ground. They had broken his arm inside the house before they dragged him into the garden. They had disabled him first.

The sounds then issuing from the patio, under Fergal's stamping shoe, had been a *whumf, whumf, whumf*. The following sound, the final noise, had reminded Stephanie of a chamois leather being slapped onto the windscreen of a car. It was the last thing she had heard before Knacker yanked her onto her back and then dragged her up the stairs and marched her down the corridor to her old room.

'I got the bottle. You wanna see it? Eh? Eh? Eh?' Knacker had whispered over Stephanie's shoulder and into her ear. 'God help me I will use it too, sister. On my muvver's life I will frow it in your face, girl. After what you done you is lucky you still got lips round your mouf.'

That is what Knacker had said to her – yes, because he was referring to an earlier scene, when he had first come to her door, panting, with his painful hand and his bony face drained of blood after his exertions with Ryan downstairs. And when she had seen that Knacker was lame – that the hand he'd used against Ryan's handsome face was injured – she had lashed out and punched Knacker. Smashed her knuckles into his big lips and made him squeal. And while his eyes were full of tears, she had knocked him out of the way and had run to the stairwell, screaming Ryan's name into the dim, warm claustrophobia of the house's interior. By the time she'd reached the stairwell window Ryan was past help and past hearing her.

The dog had been barking. She remembered the violence in its bark as it wanted to join its masters and shake the inert meat around the broken patio upon which Ryan had been slaughtered. They had murdered Ryan with their fists and feet, like simple apes whose territory had been infringed by a rogue male.

The noises came back to her. Again and again. *Whump. Whump. Whump. Slap.*

Stephanie turned over on the bed and looked at the window without seeing it.

Not long now.

They'd be coming for her soon. How would they do it? *How will I die?*

She looked at the light fitting and briefly thought about hanging herself. But with what? A belt . . . tights . . .

She didn't know how to tie good knots and knew she wouldn't be able to step off the end of the bed and into thin air. The very thought brought her close to a faint. Part of her mind seemed to be shouting, *I can't believe you are having these thoughts*. But she almost laughed at the sentiment. No, she would carry on breathing until they decided they would stop her heart and end everything that she was: the thoughts, feelings, memories and attachments. Her. *Me.*

Around her, inside the atmosphere of the house, she sensed the continued descent of a heavier gravity. A blackening of the air. A big, old, deep breath had been pulled into dirty stone lungs lined with vulgar wallpaper. It wasn't the same house she had been inside even two days ago. This was another time and place now. Hate and sadism had anointed the air in the same way sex had. The cries and footsteps of long lost women had been the chorus at the beginning of the ritual, a polyphony of misery.

The atmosphere had become enriched and built to a critical mass. Yes, she perceived this now, understood how it worked. A terrible unstable energy had grown inside the space once the right components were in place to trigger a reaction. And she was just more fuel, another sacrifice to something that had been here much longer than she had. She didn't matter, neither did Ryan, or the sobbing girls that were already dead, but were still beaten and raped night after night by something that smelled of human disease. Fergal, Knacker, Bennet: *they* had won.

Once you came within *their* reach in the worlds *they* created, nothing really held them back. Not for long. They changed everything before you noticed, while you were still smiling and trusting and hoping. They had made everything she took for granted redundant, like cooperation and manners and civility and privacy and laws. Silly things that pinged out easily like old light bulbs.

She'd swum through a little bit of the world for a tiny fragment of time until she'd happened across *them*, and now she was going to be put out like a spark pinched between grubby fingers. When she realized this was how her end would look to most people, she seemed to slip over an edge existing somewhere in the middle of herself. And she wasn't sure who or what remained behind.

FORTY-NINE

Fergal stood at the foot of the bed grinning, as if the lanky animal had done something clever.

Knacker peered over Fergal's shoulder like a younger boy admiring booty snatched from a school bag. 'Must have given him the address when they was calling each uvver. Big mistake.'

'Yes, that is a fact, Knacker.' Fergal jutted his chin at Stephanie. 'And I do bet he wished he never come.' He embellished the taunt with a titter.

Knacker smirked approval at the jest.

Fergal pushed his face at her. 'Who else you give the address to?'

Stephanie stared back but never spoke.

Fergal's grin broadened and he showed all of his yellow teeth. 'Knacker. Have you still got somefing that belongs to me? Somefing that keeps tarts in line?'

At that Knacker didn't even smile. 'Upstairs, I fink.'

'Bullshit!'

Knacker jumped backwards, then swallowed.

'I can see it in your pocket, you big pussy. Gotta be the bottle cus your cock ain't even half that size. Give it over.' Fergal snapped two absurdly long fingers in the air, the ends black with grime and Ryan's blood.

Knacker pulled the bottle of acid out of the front pocket of his jeans.

'Tut, tut, tut. Shouldn't keep it by your pecker, Knacker. Don't you know nuffin'? Top might have come off. Your nudger getting burned off won't be no loss to the girls though.'

At that Knacker winced and placed the small medicine bottle in Fergal's outstretched fingers. Knacker's own hands were shaking.

'She don't half make you repeat yourself, don't she?' Fergal began to unscrew the cap of the bottle. 'So who else you told about this place.'

Stephanie pulled her legs further up the bed. She swallowed to find her voice. 'No one. Just him'

'That right?'

They were going to kill her. Curiously, she entertained the thought dispassionately. But even though her imminent death was becoming a fact, she would choose their punching fists and stamping feet over acid thrown into her face. 'He was just bringing me a deposit. For a new room.'

Fergal patted the pocket of his jacket. 'He certainly did. And every little helps.'

The idea of Ryan's money inside Fergal's pocket – hard-earned money he had brought down to Birmingham so that she could escape from the house – stung her more than the thought of them being in possession of a toy she might have treasured as a child. Despite what she had read in the news, or studied in a criminology module of her psychology A Level, or even seen on television, she realized she had never fully understood just how base and cruel people like the McGuires actually were. Nothing in her experience had prepared her for them, not even her step-mother.

'So who else might your boyfriend have told about his little visit?'

'I don't know.'

Fergal unscrewed the bottle cap one full turn. 'Fink harder.'

'He's . . . he's not my boyfriend. Not any more. He lives with another girl now.'

'My heart is breaking.'

'He wouldn't have told her anything.'

'Why not?'

'Because his girlfriend wouldn't want him seeing an ex.' She wished she were lying, but realized she wasn't.

'Not some slag he used to fuck. I can understand that. And your mum can't stand the sight of you. Mine was the same. Your dad snuffed it. We got that in common too. Who else knows you is here?'

'Bank. Temping agency,' she said before thinking it through, and immediately saw that they both believed her lie with a reluctance that caused them great displeasure.

'Yeah,' Knacker said. 'She's been giving out these food samples and all, but ain't had no work for a while.'

Fergal turned his head to Knacker. He was showing all of his teeth and Stephanie was glad he was not showing *that* face to her. 'Anyone ever tell you, Knacker, that you is a useless twat? Eh? That can't get nuffin' right? Not never since I known you? I fink back to that day they put you in wiv me and Bennet, at the Scrubs, and I fink listening to you was the worst mistake I ever made. Now, what are we gonna do about this situation?' The question was intoned rhetorically because Fergal had already arrived at a decision.

It was just as well because Knacker didn't offer an answer; he just stared at Stephanie in silence. And she knew that Knacker wanted Fergal to do something unpleasant, an act Knacker didn't have the stomach for and wouldn't take part in. He didn't care about how it was done, as long as he didn't have to do it.

She was a witness to Margaret and Ryan.

If the two men were caught, she could already hear Knacker's wheedling voice, and see the tears in his big, doleful eyes as he told the police how Fergal had killed Margaret, Ryan, her, no doubt Svetlana too by then, and however many other women Fergal had murdered under this roof: 'Nuffin' to do wiv me, like. I was scared for me own life. Fought it was gonna be me next, yeah? Swear on me muvver's life.'

She felt like she was stuck in some horrible dream in which she was taunted with a vision of the next scene before it happened. She only wished she could live long enough to watch Fergal kill Knacker; she knew there was a distinct possibility of that happening. Taking lives for expediency, or as the consequences of blind rage or insanity, was becoming commonplace, and seemed to have long been normalized at 82 Edgehill Road.

She doubted Fergal had any illusions about his partner's character either. And after his comment about meeting Knacker in what she assumed was a prison cell, in something they called the Scrubs, she now doubted there was even a blood tie between them. A cover story and another lie. She didn't even know their real names.

'Only one fing for it at this stage of the game,' Fergal said.

Knacker raised his eyebrows.

Fergal grinned at Stephanie. 'Black Maggie. Black Maggie's got business wiv her. Bennet's right. Has been all along. So she's going in. Down there. It's where they all end up anyway. And Maggie will want her. Bennet says she never says no to a bit of company.'

FIFTY

Stephanie walked through the dark house between the two men. Fergal led the procession at an eager pace, Knacker following with less enthusiasm and a limp. She could hear him sniffing behind her, as if to clear the situation out of his nose and start over. *No harm done, like.* All she could feel was a relief she knew would be temporary, but at least the cap had stayed on the bottle of acid, and they hadn't repeated their performance on the garden patio. Not yet anyway.

Stephanie could only guess at Bennet's relationship with Knacker and Fergal. But if Bennet had been put *inside* a certain place as punishment, within this building, and if she was going to be put inside the same place so they could remove an inconvenience, then the destination she was being led to was as welcoming as the gallows.

She suspected the unseen occupants of the house had fallen into a hushed and expectant silence, like a crowd of shocked spectators with mouths agape because they knew all about the destination of the condemned. Because that is what Fergal had just done: sentenced and damned her. 'They all end up in there anyway. Down there.' So maybe the other women, the ones she heard at night, had been put inside a special place inside the house. And those that had died there had somehow *survived*.

Hints and subtexts, it was all she had to go on – all she ever had to go on in this house. If things were not clear from the outset in a situation that a person had any doubts about, that person should just start running. Nothing was worth the risk of this. She knew that now. But the penny had dropped too late for her.

Her mind drifted to a memory of Fergal's long silhouette bowed, as if in worship, outside the solitary interior door of the ground floor. Because that was where she was going. To meet whatever occupied the locked rooms in the lowest level of the house; whatever had obsessed Fergal and made him stand alone in the musty darkness, as if he were waiting for a sign, or listening to instructions from *it* or Bennet, from the other side of that door.

We's all got our little quirks, like.

The door had opened the day Margaret was killed; the day there was no going back for anyone.

Black Maggie.

Stephanie kept her face turned away from the stairwell window to avoid a glimpse of the freshly stained garden patio. The innards of the house suggested the structure was more active now too; silent, but humming with an unwelcome energy. Was it her imagination or had the death of youth awoken the site from slumber? She believed she had been trapped inside the house's dreams, but now prayed that she would never have to bear its fully awoken consciousness. She wondered if anyone ever got out of this building alive.

Stephanie stopped on the first floor landing and closed

her eyes until the worst of the feeling of dread and vertigo passed. She would do anything to be back inside her old room there, even with the hole burned through the floor.

You will never leave here.

She would become one of *them*. An unrecorded death. A trace of someone who sobbed through the night and muttered from behind a poorly decorated wall; one of *them* who murmured from the floor, or paced the wretched passages of the house, cold and lonely and looking for companionship.

'Oh, God.'

Fergal stopped and turned to confront her. 'He ain't here no more.' His face was expressionless, but his eyes were alive with what could have been excitement tinged with awe, or even terror.

He eventually smiled in acknowledgement that she must have fully grasped the enormity of what she was about to experience and endure, but would never walk away from, not in any physical sense. Fergal was proud of his role as facilitator. She suspected the cousins might be middle men for something that one of them denied the existence of, and the other didn't fully understand.

Stephanie's face screwed up for tears that never came because she was too frightened to cry. She clutched her hands to her cheeks, then placed one hand on the banister rail before she fell. 'I'm not . . . No . . . I'm not . . . I won't leave.' She wasn't sure who she was even speaking to.

An eternal sorrow. A freezing forever. Perpetually trapped, lost, and only feared if discovered.

It never ends.

'What . . . will I be?'

Would she remember anything, or only bits of things? Would she shiver and repeat herself in the darkness, always wanting to wake while being unable to rouse? Would there be some sense of will and volition in an endless entrapment? Would only her final state of terror transfer into the cold infinity?

Bennet. Bennet the rapist still followed his nature. So who was she? What was she now? She was terror, grief, despair and confusion. *Just like the other women.* Was that to be her sentence? *Forever.*

Stephanie turned around and tried to run back up the stairs to the second floor. Knacker caught her in his arms like a deceitful saviour. Fergal came up quickly from behind and slipped long fingers through Stephanie's hair. His hand became a vice to hold her head steady. His terrible breath puffed about her face. 'You belong to the Maggie, bitch. We're all hers here.'

FIFTY-ONE

From the dim grey light of the long hallway she'd passed into complete darkness. Keeping her back pressed into the wood, Stephanie stood with her palms flat against the wrong side of the door, afraid to leave her access point in case she never found it again. The painted wood moistened with perspiration seeping from her fingertips.

It took several minutes for her to overcome the panic that wanted to become hysteria after they'd locked the door. Her next instinct was to find the nearest light switch. In response, her fingers crawled around the edge of the doorway like insects. A switch should be near the door she had come in through, but no matter how far her hands roamed she could not find one.

She must find a window and break it. From outside the front of the property she'd seen metal bars over closed black curtains on the ground floor windows, so she wouldn't be able to climb out that way, but maybe the rear windows were not barred, or maybe she could scream through shattered glass at the front. Not even the McGuires seemed keen on coming inside here, and she could make a lot of noise before they were forced to silence her.

Or was breaking a window too easy? She doubted they

313

would have shut her inside the place if there was any chance of her attracting attention by smashing glass and calling to people outside the property. *Calling out to that empty, wet, sullen street.*

And she was situated on the garden side of the house. To get to the street-facing end of the building she would need to move some distance to her right, in total darkness.

So what happens now?

Without her eyes she extended her hearing into the void.

Maggie. What was this Maggie? Fergal had called it Black Maggie.

Beyond the door, in the hallway outside, Knacker broke her train of thought when he said, 'Gonna check on Svetlana.'

Fergal never answered. She imagined him leaning into the door, his forehead no more than an inch from the back of her head, while the wood separated two minds and a whole lot of mutual loathing.

'Right then, I'm off,' Knacker added cautiously, as if he were asking to be dismissed. The squeak of his trainers, defined by the limp, passed from the door and along the hallway outside.

'Oi!' Fergal barked. His voice was dulled by wood but still so close to her head that Stephanie wondered if he was talking to her through the door. 'You ain't cleaned up yet.'

Knacker's footsteps ceased. Stephanie knew what Fergal was referring to.

'I fought Svetlana could pitch in, like.'

'You fought wrong cus you is a wanker. Get the rest of

it cleaned up before the first punter arrives. I don't want some perv freaking out if he treads on a toof. I seen one at the bottom of the stairs.'

And Stephanie had too. One of Ryan's teeth had been smashed out of his mouth. She'd seen it for no more than a second before she'd shut her eyes and allowed Knacker to lead her to the door that Fergal had just unlocked and pushed her through.

'Get all that claret up too, in the entry. He was dripping everywhere.'

'He definitely snuffed it?'

'I should hope so. You seen his fucking head?'

'Where is he, like?'

'Under the mattress.'

'What we gonna do wiv him?'

Stephanie clenched her jaw, pulled at her hair. A low keening sound of impotent rage vibrated against her sternum until she cut it off.

'What is *you* gonna do wiv him? Polyfene. In the kitchen. That's what Bennet used. Get him wrapped up nice and snug then start digging behind that tree when it gets dark.'

They were going to bury Ryan in plastic and drop him into an unmarked grave. A sob broke from Stephanie's mouth, which stayed open as if to implore the darkness for mercy. Tears bitter from a mourning still unripe, and from frustration that felt like a cancer, and rage that ulcerated her stomach, made her whole body tremble.

She stifled her torment. In case *something* heard her desolation.

'I got fings to do,' Knacker said from beyond the door

that Stephanie had fused her body into. 'People coming, like.'

Fergal's voice quietened as he moved his head to speak to Knacker. 'You piss me off anymore today and I swear Svetlana will be sweeping up your fucking teef. Yeah? Yeah?'

Knacker hobbled away and she heard the stairs creak under his feet as he returned upstairs to find 'polyfene' and cleaning materials.

Fergal stayed in position at the door. What he was listening for she didn't know, but the idea of him waiting for something to happen in this darkness she had been entombed within was a prospect that came close to turning her stomach inside out.

Only once fright cleared the emotional storm that the reminders of Ryan's murder had created, did she become aware again of how weak she was from hunger and a thirst aggravated by crying. She slid down the door and sat on the floor. She tried to curb her fear enough to think of what to do. And while she waited and prayed that her mind would clear, she listened hard.

Nothing. Not even an ambient sound. Just the distant static of her own hearing inside her skull.

She padded her hands about the floor beside her buttocks. Felt linoleum. She was in a kitchen. She pulled her hands back to her body and then extended them into the darkness again. They met thin air before her face. After gently pushing her hands out from the sides of her body, her left hand touched wood and withdrew as though it had found a live wire.

She felt for the surface again. Wood, possibly laminate. A kitchen cabinet? Maybe.

She wondered if there was a back door inside the room. If she was inside the kitchen at the back of the property then this room should have access to the garden. Maybe the windows were not barred. The door might have a glass panel too that she could smash and crawl through. Her breathing sped up to catch her thoughts.

Down on all flours she placed both hands on the smooth flat plane on her left, then worked them sideways to an edge. With what she assumed was a kitchen cabinet pressed into her left side, Stephanie crawled towards the rear wall of the room. Her nose detected mildew and damp plaster, before an under-sink odour wafted close as if she was near a drain. This was an old space, unused for a long time.

Grit indented her hands. The floor wasn't clean. Small pieces of debris or mouse droppings were collecting on her sticky palms. She swatted them clean. Moved on. Until her fingernails brushed fabric. She explored the thick material with her fingers. Curtains? Must be. *Please don't let it be a long dress.*

Behind the thick fabric she found wood. *A door!* Curtains over a door. The back door.

Stephanie found the door handle and pulled herself upright as though she was dragging herself over the side of a lifeboat.

Locked. She turned the handle again and again, as quietly as she could. Spread her hands wide and padded them over the wood behind the drapes. There were no glass panels.

She lost her balance in the darkness and tottered sideways until the flesh of her hip folded around a hard edge. Another cabinet. Her arms moved quickly, without instruction, to explore the sides and contents of this trap. When she touched a ridged stainless steel surface she understood she had reached a sink area. Leaning forward she searched for a kitchen window. Her fingers touched small glass items that moved and chinked together. A spice rack, or something like that. Then her hands discovered cold plaster: a wall beside a set of small shelves.

She shuffled sideways, away from the door, her fingertips retaining contact with the wall until the painted plaster became wood again. What felt like another sheet of wood. She ran her fingers up and down the edge of the board and found dimples that housed screws.

Below the counter edge that pressed her stomach was the sink. She touched metal taps, knocked a plastic bottle over. 'Shit.'

The noise of the plastic bottle impacting with the bottom of the dry sink unit sounded far louder than it should have done. She was moving her hands too quickly.

Stephanie swallowed and listened to the darkness behind her, around her.

Nothing.

So wooden boards had been screwed over the kitchen windows and the back door.

Why would anyone do that?

Because it is vacant, locked up, closed away.

To stop something getting out that doesn't like light.

Stop! Stop! Stop it!

Her imagination could sink her. It was a liability on a

dangerous voyage into the unknown. Something best left behind by the front door, because her imagination was an entity that would cling to her neck like a horrible chattering monkey, its eyes wide and white with alarm in the darkness.

She had to stay as calm as possible. Rational.

Think. Think.

Keep going.

Just past the sink her hip bumped the edge of another hard surface. It rattled. She pulled her hands into contact with the hard shape set at a right angle to the sink unit. *Metal.* Gas rings. Dials for controlling the gas. Three small buttons indented against the front of one of her thighs.

Light!

Light issued from somewhere in front of her legs: an oven light shining through a door made of glass. The glass was stained with brown grease spatters, but a beery glow still managed to seep into the kitchen.

Stephanie turned around quickly, her breath caught high in her chest.

For a moment she thought the dark towering shapes all around the room were tall people leaning towards her. Until the inert shapes became silhouettes made up of right angles: painted wooden doors, kitchen cabinets.

She felt like a diver inside a sunken wreck. She could see the door she had come in through, and the pine boards over the windows above the sink, a pantry door, other cabinets mounted higher up the wall with frosted glass doors, a tiny table and two quilted chairs. There was a light switch beside a closed door that connected the kitchen to another ground floor room.

Stephanie skittered across the linoleum. Her fingers scrabbled at the light switch. Flipped it down at the same time as she looked up at the strip-light in the middle of a ceiling brown with ancient cooking fumes.

The light didn't flicker. If this was a self-contained flat they could have switched off the lights at the fuse box, or maybe the tube was dead.

From beside the door she looked about the kitchen again. It was old and cheaply fitted. The cooker belonged to a sorry period of time that nostalgia and antiquity had yet to increase the value of. The floor covering was yellow and had a floral pattern, which in turn had been soiled by dirty footprints that were now mostly dusty outlines. The back door had been sealed by floor-length black curtains. Through a chink she could see the wooden boards.

Sealed inside. You are not getting out.

Stop. Think. Kitchen drawers!

Stephanie flitted across the room. There were three drawers above the cupboard doors she had crawled alongside. She eased the cabinet drawers open. Saw string, an old calendar featuring terrier dogs, screws, nuts, rawl plugs, metal hinges, a tape measure, shoe polish, rolls and rolls of brown parcel tape, a screwdriver, a box of candles, a little plastic toy from a cereal box.

She clawed the screwdriver out of the drawer. A Phillips, but she could jab with it. The box of candles felt so light her spirits plummeted. But at least the box was rattling. One white candle remained inside and was unused. She held it in her hand with the screwdriver.

She slowed down; she was making too much noise with her hands, scattering objects inside drawers she could not properly see. The dim light from the oven door was fading, like a torch powered by a dying battery.

In the last drawer her fingers found cutlery and kitchen utensils. She dropped a spatula and fished out the longest knife by the brown wooden handle.

She slipped the screwdriver and candle inside the front pocket of her hooded top. Swiped a strand of hair off her face. Retied her ponytail as quickly as possible with the knife clamped between her teeth.

She made another, more careful appraisal of the kitchen. Saw the box of matches on the stove's hood, above the grill tray. Ran to it.

A centimetre of dust, adhered to grease, coated the top of the oven hood. When she tugged, the match box came away with a ripping sound. Part of the cardboard box remained fossilized on the stove.

She scraped one match out of the box. Struck it against the ignition strip. The head of the match crumbled until she was scraping wood on sandpaper. She tried another match. Same thing. And another. And another. When the fourth match caught fire she nearly wept. She dipped the candle wick into the flame and threw the spent match into the sink.

What was Fergal thinking? She had a knife, light and a screwdriver.

Gripped by a new idea she ran across to the back door and moved the curtains to one side. She moved her fingers around the edge of the wood until she found the first screw hole. *Yes!* Phillips screw-heads. The screwdriver even fitted the first head she tested.

She peered all around the door frame, her fingers

crawling over the wood she could barely see. *One, two, four, another two, one, two, three, four, five, six, shit . . .* At least ten. It would take forever to get them all unscrewed.

The door lock. Could she unscrew the door lock? If she took the handle and plate off, would the door just open? She didn't know.

Her considerations were cut short by a noise in the neighbouring room.

An item of furniture, maybe a chair, had just been scraped across a floor. It was followed by a soft bump reminiscent of a child or animal slipping off a chair. And then came silence.

Stephanie's shoulders started to shake like she was standing in waist-deep, freezing water. She couldn't breathe quickly enough. It was much colder in the kitchen than it had been a moment ago. Her hands were shaking so much she dropped the candle. The flame doused.

She placed everything clutched in her shaking hands on the counter beside the sink unit. Then began to extract another match.

Another bump from the neighbouring room. Then another.

Stephanie swallowed. Struck the match against the side of the box. Not hard enough because she was trying to be silent.

The bumping was soon accompanied by a shuffling sound, as if something was pressed against the other side of the wall and moving slowly. Yes, it sounded like a person or a large animal was low to the floor and gradually moving across the adjacent room towards the kitchen door.

Stephanie hadn't been to the toilet for a long time. Her jeans and underwear were still damp from the last time she'd wet herself in Margaret's room. Her crotch glowed again and the warmth spread down the inside of her thighs. When she finished peeing, the denim on her thighs quickly cooled because the air was close to freezing now.

She struck the match again, but her hands had become too heavy and clumsy for the task and she couldn't even get the match to connect with the box. She whimpered, forced herself to concentrate. She tried again. The match-head flared. She found the candle by her feet and dipped the wick into the flame.

Whatever was on the other side of the wall reached the kitchen door. From beyond the door came a new sound, perhaps the worst one yet. A noise that made her think of hoarse breath being pulled through something wet, like someone was struggling to breathe through a moist cloth draped over their face. This was followed by a groan. Not one of her own; she was too frightened to make any noise.

Another muffled groan. Then the sucking sound again. Or was it wheezing? Whatever was out there sounded like an animal in great difficulty.

She thought her heart might stop. She wanted her heart to stop.

Stephanie made it across the kitchen so quickly she couldn't recall how she arrived on the other side of the room. The candle flame flattened and then wobbled in her trembling fist but stayed lit. She pressed her entire weight against the wood to hold the door closed. Her other hand gripped the knife.

From deeper inside the ground floor rooms came a

fresh commotion from what, she could only imagine, was a new entrant to the room on the other side of the kitchen wall. When a distant door slammed she thought her heart had, in fact, ceased to beat. And whatever had come inside began an immediate casting about.

Walls were bumped. Furniture was thumped. An eager search was in progress, though by whom, and for what, she didn't want to imagine, but she was reminded of the noises of her first floor neighbour and the nocturnal visitor. Yes, this sounded like a search motivated by rage and frustration, and each emotion was out of control.

Whatever was pressed against the other side of the door began to make a new series of sounds: a piteous keening that pierced the wheezing. *Fear.*

The thumps and bangs paused. And then Stephanie received the impression that the second occupant had heard the whimpers and immediately rushed across the room to come to a halt by the kitchen door. There was a muffled squeal that might not have been human, followed by a series of deeper swinish grunts from the aggressor. The sounds of wheezing only lessened when whatever was making the pitiful noise was dragged across the floor and away from the kitchen door, and deeper into the room beyond.

Silence fell in the way that silence always descended in the house: with a totality after these bursts of unseen activity from participants who just seemed to vanish.

In relief that the episode appeared to have concluded, Stephanie's mind cleared enough for her to consider the previous night and the various distances at which she had heard the elderly woman's voice. The unlit bedroom she had been locked inside had seemed to enlarge under the influence of the visitor and then contract after *its* passing. She assumed that if she was to move out of the kitchen, which she would have to at some point soon, she should only move when all was quiet and the air temperature had returned to normal. Only then, maybe, might the dimensions of the building remain recognizable and her path through it logical.

Dragging her fingers down her cheeks she tried again to recall the terrible dreams of which only vestiges had ever remained in her mind. She had seen a horrible bloodless female face, had been a little girl trapped between brick walls, had been on the ceiling, there had been a dark room with candles, some kind of chest or box, curtains . . . most of the rest was a murk that still refused to reanimate into something informative. And yet she now had no doubt that the house, or whatever was inside the building, had been communicating with her through sleep, and using its own idiom: nightmares.

Stephanie took a deep breath, closed her eyes, forcibly cleared her mind of anything but the most immediate practicalities.

In the kitchen drawers she found a stained cloth and wrapped it about her hand now that the hot wax was running down the shaft of the candle. The idea of dropping her main source of light, and of the candle dousing again, was dead-level with her fear of what she might find in the rooms beyond the kitchen. But she surmised it was always better, at least, to see your assailant.

She went back and pressed her body against the only door that would take her out of the kitchen; screwed up her eyes and pushed her hearing into the room beyond, forced it out as far as it would extend.

She heard nothing.

Stephanie sniffed then wiped her nose and eyes on her sleeve.

Just get to a window. Candle. Knife. Screwdriver.

There would be other windows down here and they would be barred and they would be boarded over too. But she needed to get access to a window when the rooms were quiet and not freezing; unblock a window and smash the pane of glass. And then she would need to scream and shout like never before. And whatever tried to stop her must feel the knife.

Don't think. Don't think. Don't think. Do.

She put the knife between her teeth, turned the handle, and opened the kitchen door.

FIFTY-TWO

The impact of the second room's strangeness was worsened by her sense of familiarity inside it. She had seen the place before, what seemed like a long time ago, though her dreams of the room could not have been more than a week old. Time and space, the dimensions and certainties of reality, seemed to command a position as contemptible and forsaken as her own status inside the building.

The walls were painted black and adorned with nothing. The ceiling was black. The floorboards were painted black. Had there ever been a light fitting inside the room, it was long gone. She found it hard to determine where the walls met the ceiling and the floor.

The large round table in the centre of the room was covered in a dusty black cloth with hems that lapped the floor. She would have preferred to have been able to see beneath the table.

Four plain wooden chairs were pushed under the table so the backrests touched the rim of the table top. The only other item of furniture inside the room was a long, black sideboard. Upon the sideboard were two old wooden candlesticks. They gave off an ecclesiastical feel without any of the comfort a residue of Christianity might offer.

The suggestion of a ritual having been conducted inside

ADAM NEVILL

the room made her experience a shrinking sensation inside her skin. A repulsion further embellished by the sight of a wooden box with a purple curtain drawn across its front. The container on the sideboard was no bigger than a small doll's house, though the idea of the tiny curtain suddenly being drawn from the inside made her head tremble upon her shoulders.

The room smelled of dust and damp fabric, it reeked of emptiness and age. But its odours were secondary to its atmosphere. She had never experienced anything akin to that, and wasn't aware that a physical space could even command such a character. Because this space was desolate, and somehow fouled with a corruption she could only guess at. And yet the room was alive too, vibrating with a black energy that pressed her thoughts to a diamond of terror.

This was a tomb, a mausoleum with brick walls painted black, a chamber that both existed in a terrible past and also now. Her assumptions of its nature were instinctive.

A door. An entrance. A way in.

The purpose behind the room's design suggested the obscene, the unholy, the inhumane. Nothing would ever be able to cleanse the space or its blackened walls. So many terrible things had been absorbed into the room, and it could become alive with them at any time. The room was charred by an evil she could not even recognize as human. It had been fashioned by someone, perhaps with the help of *something* from somewhere else.

The flickering of the candle's light inside the sombre room only increased her abhorrence of the place. She

328

didn't want to look at the room, but needed to walk across it, and slowly enough to keep the candle alight too. Stephanie cupped the hand holding the knife around the fragile flame. *When the flame goes out your mind goes out.*

At the far side of the room she noticed a second door, one at first disguised by the absence of variety in the wall's colour scheme. She immediately moved towards it.

Fergal listens. What does he listen for? Bennet?

You heard noises and furniture being scraped inside this room, so who the fuck was in here? Bennet?

A door slammed. You heard a door slam.

This door? So whatever was moving inside here might now be inside the next room you need to go into.

Don't open the door.

You have no choice.

Windows. You have to get to a window. And break it.

As Stephanie made her way to the door, her thoughts chasing each other through her mind like frightened cats, she began to shiver and was forced to pull her arms closer to her torso and to withdraw her head into her body. When the temperature of the room dropped even lower, she froze with panic in anticipation of what intense cold always preceded inside the house.

A noise, accompanying an unseen movement, commenced behind Stephanie's back. Her first notion was of a breeze rifling through loose polythene that covered a solid object; an object close to the door she had just come in through.

The realization that there was no wind, not so much as a draught, and that the room had been empty only a moment ago, brought her to a stop.

The continuing sounds of crinkling plastic now put into her mind the image of something rising from the floor. And a sudden stench of decomposition suggested that something no longer living now shared the space with her.

Stephanie turned around, her mouth and her eyes wide open.

She had come to a standstill between the two doors and beside the table. The light from the solitary candle she held in her shaking hand struggled to illuminate much of the walls and very little of the room's corners, but it did catch features of the room's newest, or perhaps oldest, occupant.

The light was reflected in the parts of the aged polythene not stained or fogged by the inhabitant within the long, plastic sheet. Through the clearer patches in the covering, what she could see of the shape inside appeared dark, like the lustreless brown of aged leather, but mottled black like the skin on the hands of the very old.

The figure shrouded in plastic stood upright but struggled to remain on its feet. Stephanie was unable to look at it for long, but through a brief, appalled gaping she realized the figure had once been female; attested to by what looked like shrunken drinking gourds, tipped with black nipples and pressed into the polythene.

The body was thin, if not shrivelled. A feeble posture suggested it was bow-legged too, though all she could see of one leg was near skeletal. And when it opened what must have been a mouth within a hairless head, she heard a parched voice whisper a single word. She thought it said, 'Time.'

When the second door clicked open, swung wide and

banged against the black wall behind her, Stephanie screamed. And turned to face whatever had just entered the room on the other side. Her vision flickered like the candle's light, and then seemed to judder as if she were drunk.

She struggled to breathe through lungs frozen inside her chest. Gulped at the black air. Staggered backwards until her buttocks struck the table. She'd forgotten she held a knife in her hand, and when she remembered it was there her desire to move her arm and point the knife at the thing on the floor never became action. Because she was too frightened to do anything but whimper out the air she'd managed to swallow.

What entered the room came in on its front. It used bony elbows like hands to pull itself across the floor. The sound of the elbows upon the black floor made a knocking sound like wood upon wood. What she assumed was the head was entirely and tightly bound in brown parcel tape, glinting where the candle light struck it. She recognized the slurps and wet wheezes immediately, and now understood how such an awful noise was created. From where a mouth would have been on an uncovered face, there was a small hole, with a tiny plastic pipe extending through the puncture, through which the thing on the floor tried to breathe.

Once the shape was entirely inside the room, it paused as the blind and blank face moved about, searching for something, groping without sight or hearing. Behind the wrapped-up ball of the head its thin shoulders were draped in a cape of polythene that encased the body in the places where it was still taped down, but had come loose from other parts of its slim, black torso as if from past struggles within the unventilated confines.

Stephanie turned and climbed upon the table so the thing upon the floor could not reach her feet. Even using nothing but two sharp elbows, its movements were uncomfortably quick upon the ground.

At some point, as she drew her second leg up and onto the black table cloth, the candle went out and total darkness returned to the cold and stinking room.

Stephanie screamed again, this time so hard she wondered if her vocal cords would snap like old rubber bands and just flap about inside her throat. Her scream filled her head with flashes of lightning.

The darkness filled with the sound of rustling polythene as the two visitors shuffled and crawled towards the table she knelt upon, as if drawn to her.

When something bumped the table she twisted about and onto her bottom in a defensive flinch.

A dry panting erupted close to one side of her head. At the same time she sensed, as much as heard, a faint woody rapping amidst the rustles of polythene. She could only surmise that a pair of wasted hands were now feeling about the table top near her body. When something as thin and hard as a pencil touched one of her thighs she choked more than screamed.

Beyond her feet she heard the wet exertions of the thing with the taped head, pulling itself up the back of a chair to join her on the table. Both of the visitors were blind but intent on finding her. They were investigating her.

Stephanie shuffled sideways and moved further along

the table top. Between each movement she swiped the kitchen knife in the black air about her. The blade touched nothing.

When she found the head of the table closest to the second door, she fell more than clambered off the table and ran at where she thought the door leading out of this room must be.

And hit a wall, first with a knee and then with her fore-head.

Over by the table, her new position immediately registered with her pursuers, who rustled anew inside their coverings in what suggested a haste to follow her.

Palming herself through the darkness and along the wall, Stephanie found the open doorway. She fell into the next room and pulled the door shut.

FIFTY-THREE

Panting, her back and head flat against the door, Stephanie focused her efforts into stopping the spinning inside her skull; a maelstrom of panic and fear had become her entire consciousness.

They were still in the other room. She could hear one of them staggering like an invalid suddenly released from a wheelchair, scuffling on feet that were mostly bone, while the second one wheezed and scratched at the base of the door she held shut.

The room she had fled into was lightless. The windows would almost certainly be boarded shut, like those of the kitchen. And the boards would be fixed to the wall too, screwed flush with the casement, to prevent even a sliver of daylight from intruding into the hell that was the ground floor of 82 Edgehill Road.

Stephanie raised the shaking hand that clutched the unlit candle. Patting the front of her hooded top she located the pocket and the tiny rattle of the matchbox; not many left. She would have to be careful with each match that could still be ignited.

Only when her heavy exhalations subsided into shallower, tauter breaths, did she become aware of the scent of the room. The place smelled of death.

The space was warm and musty with age, but still acrid with what must have recently been an unbreathable stench of corruption in an unventilated, lightless room. A room she had just shut herself inside.

She coughed to clear her nose, mouth and throat of the smell. Crouched down and slipped the candle between her teeth and removed the box of matches from her pocket. If she could even find a match that was firm and intact enough to light the candle, she knew she would not want to catch so much as a glimpse of whatever was inside here, issuing the miasma of decay. But she could not bear to be in the dark either.

She got lucky, or unlucky; she wasn't sure. The first match she struck against the box fizzed alight. It took her several seconds to hold the candle steadily enough to dip the wick into the flame that left a sunspot in the middle of both eyes. When the candle flame grew large enough to cast a vague, flickering luminance across the room, her initial shock was caused by the sight of the room's walls.

They were pink. The wallpaper was pink striped with mauve, the dry carpet was cherry-pink, the curtains featured a pink cabbage rose pattern, the dressing table was a dark red wood, or lacquered in imitation. It was hideous, but awful in a manner so different to the black room she had just escaped.

Tasteless, aged, another preserved capsule that must have remained intact for decades. How could something so grotesquely feminine and vulgar share a wall with a room so appallingly evil? Because that is what the black room had been: evil.

Only after the sounds from the neighbouring room

ceased did she rise from a crouch and move the candle through the air. The flame's misty yellow glow revealed white fitted wardrobe doors and a second open doorway leading to an ensuite bathroom. And only when she was standing did Stephanie take more notice of the bed: a vast article of furniture covered with a quilted pink eiderdown. And she nearly opened the door and ran back into the darkness when she realized that the bed was occupied. Though whatever lay on top of the coverings did not rouse at the sound of her shock in the stifling darkness.

As immobile as the subject of her appalled scrutiny, Stephanie watched the body without blinking and clenched her fist around the knife handle until it hurt her hand. There was nowhere else to run inside the ground floor flat. If the thing on the bed moved she would have to . . . have to use the knife on it.

But if it's not alive, what use is a knife?

The dark figure remained inert upon the bed. From what she could see from the door, it wore black trousers, inside of which the legs looked short and unappealingly thin. The ankles had collapsed inside patterned socks. A windbreaker was zipped up right under the figure's chin, the head covered by a plastic hood.

Moving around the foot of the bed, close to the wall and the dressing table, Stephanie moved the candle higher to better see the occupant.

A brownish face had sunken into the hood of the anorak. A pair of large spectacles with tortoise-shell frames were still in place upon the mottled skin. What was left of the wide open eyes was magnified through the lenses of the glasses, as was their discolouration and collapse into the eye sockets to now resemble the dried-out bodies of dead snails inside their shells. Long brown teeth, that reminded her of a donkey's mouth, grinned at the ceiling as if the corpse was pleased with itself.

Bennet.

The face on Fergal's phone. *The rapist.* The man who had been put inside the flat before her lay dead on what looked like a grandmother's bed from the 1980s.

Stephanie moved to the curtains. Death had been caught amongst the fetid folds and floral patterns of the drapes and she coughed to clear her airways of the scents of stale decomposition. She clawed them aside to find pine boards screwed into the walls.

Growling with frustration she hammered the side of one fist against the wood, which returned a hollow sound while the board did not even rattle in its secure moorings.

She tied one curtain back to the wall, using the ostentatious gold and tasselled tie that hung from a brass wall hook. When she looked to see how many screws she would have to get out of the sheet of wood to reach the window pane, she noticed the marks in one corner of the board. Someone had tried to get out before her, using what looked like their teeth. Vague black stains surrounded a patch of wood that had been gnawed, and by a person positioned on their knees.

Stephanie stepped away from the windows and closed her eyes for a moment. She wondered why Bennet had been put inside here; how badly he'd offended Fergal to deserve such a fate.

Had they killed him? Those things out there?

Stephanie looked at the bedroom door she had come

through and couldn't recall her legs and arms ever feeling as weak as they did now. *Did they need doors? Or can they just rise?*

As if her thoughts were contagious, she heard a rustle of what sounded like nylon.

Heart thumping the roof of her mouth, she turned quickly. When the candle flame settled, she raised the candle higher above the foot of the bed. The desiccated thing in the anorak still grinned with dirty teeth, and the sightless and collapsed eyes were still fixed upon the ceiling. But had one arm moved? The right arm, the one closest to the window? She couldn't remember whether the withered brownish hand had been in that position before, held so close to the body. The hand was also missing a little finger and the removal had not been neat.

She had imagined the rustling noise. *That is all, that is all, that is all, that is all.*

Stephanie turned to the window, repeatedly glancing at the corpse as she exchanged the knife for the screwdriver. She slipped the screwdriver head into the first screw and used what felt like all of her remaining energy to get the screw to budge. And it did, or she thought it did, about one millimetre. There were at least a dozen screws to be loosened. How would she reach those at the top?

She collapsed against the wood and began hammering a fist against the surface. She called out, 'Help! Help me! Fire! Fire! Fire!' Her hand hurt, but she bit down on the pain and continued to beat the wood because her life depended on being heard.

Beyond the wood a car swished past, moving quickly. No one in a vehicle could possibly hear her and there were never any pedestrians in the street; in fact, she had not seen one during her journeys to and from the house, bus stop and local shop. But there was a neighbour, there were curb crawlers, the punters who came here for sex; one of them might hear her . . .

Stephanie stopped banging the wooden boards. Turned to the bed. Turned to face the awful thing that had just sat up.

FIFTY-FOUR

When Bennet grunted Stephanie screamed.

She ran across the pink room to the doorway. Her hands bumped around the door handle. She was carrying too many things: knife, candle, screwdriver. She could not get purchase on the round door handle.

She dropped the screwdriver, put the knife between her teeth, turned the handle, opened the door. Glanced over her shoulder at the noise of bed springs, but instantly wished she had not. The figure on the bed swung thin legs over one side of the mattress and hissed with excitement.

Stephanie slammed the bedroom door behind herself. The speed of her exit put out the candle.

Turning about, in the absolute darkness of the black room, she felt her body shake, and not just from the sudden freeze and stagnant odour of corruption she had plunged herself back into; terror that threatened to become a seizure had taken hold of her limbs.

With near useless hands she retrieved the box of matches from the front pocket of her hooded top. Slid the box open, withdrew one match. Others dropped and scattered across the floor at her feet. She shut the box.

Against the other side of the door the dead thing in the windbreaker turned the handle and pushed.

'God, God, God,' she muttered at the darkness.

He ain't in here no more.

Stephanie struck the match she held. It flared alight.

She whimpered when she saw all four chairs drawn back from the black table in anticipation of guests.

Nothing was sitting in them, yet. But whatever was inside the little wooden box upon the long sideboard, hidden behind the purple curtain, began to beat out a muffled rhythm. And into her mind flashed an image of small black hands banging a leather-skinned drum.

Old hair . . . black horse's tail . . . wiry hair, doll hair . . . leather skin . . . little black hands beating a drum with a stick.

She dropped the match when it burned her fingers. Back into darkness she sank with the sound of a drum thumping inside her ears.

Using the tatters of her concentration she fished another match out of the box; there were not many left.

The door handle stopped swivelling in the small of her back, and Bennet stopped pushing at the door. But he had not gone because she could still hear the sound of his odious breathing: fast breathing that comes from arousal, from delight. But why had he stopped trying to get out?

As if summoned by the drum, there was a shuffling sound upon the floor of the black room which tore her attention away from Bennet.

Something not wrapped in polythene, something heavy and yet soft, was moving through the darkness that engulfed her. Whatever produced the susurration, this sliding, was concealed by the broad drapery of the

341

black tablecloth. A small mercy and one she was sure would be short lived.

Stephanie suffered the sensation that the darkness about her was filling and expanding with motion. She flinched back tighter to the door, afraid something might be closing in on her face, and struck a match against the box.

No spark, just the sensation of crumbling close to her fingertips.

The next match she tried flared and briefly spat, then sputtered extinct. She dropped it and pulled out what she realized was the second to last match.

This match ignited. Before the flare retracted, she saw movement on the far side of the room, near the head of the table. There was definitely motion, but she could not see what was responsible for stirring the darkness.

Stephanie glanced at the wooden box on the sideboard; the purple curtain was still drawn while the muffled beat thumped inside.

She dipped the candle wick inside the match's flame. Waited for the trembling light to struggle and to grow and to reveal what new and, perhaps, final horror awaited what was left of her mind.

Once the wick caught, Stephanie looked to the door that led into the kitchen as if it offered some hope of salvation.

Gas yourself. Start a fire.

At the furthest reach of the candle's flickering flame, she detected the vague outline of a shape against the far wall, one almost as dark as the paintwork. A silhouette rising from the floor in a gliding motion. From a spasm of renewed terror her head shook, her mouth twitched, her breath condensed about her face. 'Dad. Daddy. Dad,' she muttered, as if he were able to come into the room when called upon to save her.

Up and off the floor the thing moved, as though the lower half were serpentine and the ceiling its intended destination. Stephanie screamed and threw the candle at the movement. It missed and hit the far wall. But as the flame arced across the room she glimpsed what might have been a tatty black head, close to the ceiling, and a pair of shrivelled arms beneath.

Maggie. Black Maggie. Maggie. Black Maggie.

She heard the voices inside her head. Not her own voice, but other voices. Lots of other voices. Voices that now travelled over the ceiling as she fled beneath them and across the room towards her memory of where the kitchen door had been.

Round and round and round the voices went.

Up and up and up the black thing slid to be among the voices calling out its name upon the ceiling.

The drum beat grew louder.

Stephanie batted her hands across the wall, whimpering in her blindness and in her frustration that she could not find the wood of the door, because her hands were now sliding across wet bricks.

The blackness was inside her lungs; she had inhaled too much of it, drawn the darkness inside her chest and through the chambers of her heart like dirty smoke. A taste of water rank with ashes and burned bone filled her mouth.

She turned around and fumbled the match box out of

her pocket and then scraped the last match out of the box. With fingers she could barely feel she struck the match against the wrong side of the box. Then turned the match box over and tried again.

The match flared.

In the air, near the ceiling, a pair of small white eyes, inside a face she was glad she could not see, closed. But when the head slowly moved down and towards her, as if to investigate her presence, it shook what might have been hair with an emotion that resembled joy.

She turned her own face away from the thing above her, glimpsed the kitchen door behind her shoulder. Reached for the door handle. Stepped out of the black room and slammed the kitchen door shut.

FIFTY-FIVE

Inside the darkness hysteria finally came. Madness too. She welcomed madness.

In the surge of a mindlessness born of sustained terror, the violence of her screams took her into a space she had never known before, but had occasionally sensed in the wings of her mind. When she came close to being conscious of this state, she suppressed any flickers of awareness, in case she departed chaos.

Round and round in the darkness of the kitchen she turned and spun and unravelled herself and cut at the nothingness with her knife. Slashed above her head where a face might hang, and down below where something could be crawling towards her legs.

Against cabinets she banged herself but ignored the pain. Over the little table she sprawled only to right her body and to whip the knife through the air, at head height, should anything be closing in.

She picked up a chair and hurled it through the absence; it seemed to travel a long way before smashing the glass out of a cabinet door. She sent the second chair after it.

Drawers were emptied and implements thrown anywhere and everywhere. Some of the things she threw bounced off the walls and struck her body. Cupboards were pawed at. Their contents were released with her screams, to accompany the flight of objects through the lightless place, through the end of the world and through the final reaches of herself.

When she could no longer raise her tired arms, she slumped to her knees and asked the darkness for death.

'Now. Come on. Now. Now.'

There would be some pain and then she wanted black. Nothing mattered any more. She didn't want to think or remember anything. She just wanted to go.

'I want it now. Now. Now. Get it over with, you bitch.'

Her energy, her spirit, her life was spent. She was glad to be rid of it; the struggle for survival was a pain she no longer wanted.

And then she went quiet for a time and wondered if she was already dead, and if a new tenant, some fragrant girl from Bulgaria or Latvia, was lying stiff with fright inside an old bed while listening to Stephanie's cries in the night.

She didn't know. But she didn't think she was dead. Bennet had looked very thin on that pink bed. So perhaps he had starved to death inside here, his last days a relentless torment as visitor after visitor came rustling and sliding about him in the darkness.

And from the moment he'd shoved her inside here, this was what Fergal had been waiting for: the crescendo. He had waited for her cries.

Was he out there now?

Stephanie crawled across the broken things and found the door she had first come through; it felt so long ago, when she had been another person, someone who cared about life. She pushed herself up the door. Struck the surface with both hands. Grimaced at the darkness.

She saw their faces inside her mind, their simian faces, clever and thrusting. She saw again the weasel-quick eyes. Faces fronting minds erased of compassion, of decency, of humanity. She could hear Knacker's voice, which in turn became the memory of a ghost's incapacity and cries.

She inhaled deep from the dead house. Allowed herself to be throttled by her very powerlessness. What did she care now?

Her thoughts leapt on, from face to voice to face to voice, to poor Ryan so limp on the stained concrete patio, to Margaret's sweet smile, to a tooth uprooted from a jawbone, to black blood on faded carpet, to an elderly voice chanting scripture, to a girl sealed beneath a bathroom floor, chattering out her confusion. And something began to glow inside her again, at her very core. Something so hot and unstable it was already black with the carbon of her rage and hatred. She thought of Fergal's bloodless face, and Knacker's equine expressions; she thought of the thing that had been a man called Bennet, and of its speed up and through the house to service its desires on the wretched and the hopeless; she saw the picture of its howling, idiotic face, bestial with violent intent, on a phone screen.

'Can you hear me, you scrawny rat bastards? Can you hear me?'

Stephanie banged her hands against the door. 'They are coming! Yes! And they will take me. But I swear you will not live. You will not leave this house alive. I swear I will come for you. Both of you. You will know me, you bastards! You will know me in this dark. No one gets out alive! No one!'

She turned and flashed her face at the darkness, showed it a mouth full of teeth. And to the darkness she begged, pleaded with the absence of light and hope for a chance to do those things that she would now trade anything, anything at all, for an opportunity to do.

'You think these rats can keep you? You deserve better company. Their blood for my blood.'

And through the cascade and tumult of her blackest thoughts she heard a voice: *I will come unto thee. For I have determined there to winter.*

FIFTY-SIX

She passed from one darkness into another, from exhaustion into sleep, or perhaps she had slipped into extinction. She didn't know, nor did she care much. Her only lingering wish was that the darkness remained still and empty around where she lay, so cold and spent. But inside here and inside her, darkness was the medium through which her visitors and visions travelled. They came and went, came and went. They told her nothing, as if their presence was sufficient.

On either side of her head plastic rustled. She never saw what was inside the coverings, but heard mouths panting wetly against polythene. She knew sightless eyes were close by and that old mouths had opened to mutter notions long obsolete. They only wanted to be close to her and they wanted to be heard. Maybe that was enough; she was an audience for what had been lost and forgotten in the darkness it had been given unto.

In time, the four women wearing long gowns came and stood around her with their heads on one side; they all spoke at the same time like agitated birds in a treeline, though she couldn't understand what they were saying. Perhaps they were praying, because they all held little books that looked like they contained hymns.

At first Stephanie thought they were holding their heads at severe angles so they could better see her lying on the dirty floor. But then she realized their heads were bent because of what was knotted about their throats. Every time the women appeared and she tried to see where the faint phosphorescence bled from, she would find herself moving round in a circle, on the ceiling, and unable to get back inside her body down below. When she tried to work out how far away her body was from the ceiling, she found herself staring down at four people sitting at the black table with their hands raised into the air.

The bald man's face was all loose skin that hung around his jaw; what little of his hair remained was oiled into bootlace strands over his skull. He wore a shirt, tie and braces. Of the two women, the bespectacled woman with permed hair made a crude and horrible gesture by poking her thin tongue out of her wide open mouth. The other woman wore a headscarf and dark glasses. Her face was expressionless. On the centre of the table was the wooden box.

The people all looked past Stephanie at something else that unwound on the ceiling behind her head. It made the sound of oily hands being rubbed together. All of the people's faces were strewn with tears.

When she came to be upon the floor again, and was, perhaps, even awake, a little boy with sunken milky blue eyes, that were probably sightless even though they showed between the scarf over his face and his cowboy hat made from purple felt, skipped around her in the darkness. His knee caps were thick with scabs, his grey shirt was untucked from his shorts and his patterned pullover was dirty and full of holes. Somewhere not far away, old dry hands clapped out a rhythm to which the boy skipped. The boy only ever sang the same thing:

'All around the Mulberry Bush, The monkey chased the weasel. The monkey stopped to pull up his sock, Pop! goes the weasel. Half a pound of tuppenny rice, Half a pound of treacle. Four maids to open the door, Pop! goes the weasel.'

Sometimes there was only darkness around her body, but within it she knew she was tiny. A speck in something cold and blank in every direction that went on forever.

She was so small inside the immensity of nothing she found it difficult to breathe.

DAY EIGHT

FIFTY-SEVEN

'I don't understand why she ain't dead. It offed Bennet pretty quick. And she's trashed the place. Why's she so special? She was wanted in here. That's what they wanted. I don't get it. Why does she get to come out?' It was Fergal's voice that brought her round; it sounded like he was talking to himself.

Stephanie opened her eyes and blinked in a thin, grey light that stung her mind as though she stared directly into the sun. Through a squint she could see smashed crockery, kitchen utensils and shards of broken glass scattered across the kitchen lino.

Perhaps she should have been relieved to see her captors but she felt nothing.

Fergal put his long hands under her arms and pulled her into a sitting position. Her clothes were filthy; they smelled of dust, sweat and urine.

Fergal's long fingers dabbed inside the pocket of her hooded top and patted down her jeans with the swiftness of an expert thief. With one foot he slid the kitchen knife away, then dragged her backwards and across the threshold.

In the dim ground floor hallway, the first thing her

vision settled upon was Knacker's face; it was blanched with fear and twitchy with anxiety. He looked at her like she was a traffic accident.

Fergal carefully pulled the door shut and locked the ground floor rooms. His own expression had remained rigid with concentration, and he hadn't adjusted his focus from the door that led from the kitchen to the black room before he sealed the place. Once the rooms were secure, he rested his forehead and the palms of his hands against the door, his eyes closed. From the rise and fall of his back, Stephanie saw how hard he was breathing.

While she blinked away her grogginess, wincing at the dull band of pain that thumped like a drum behind her eyes, Fergal turned his head from the door and looked down at Stephanie. And she saw an expression she had never seen on his face before: suspicion tinged with caution, even incomprehension. 'It's all gone very quiet in there. Get her upstairs while I fink this froo.'

Knacker hesitated. He didn't want to touch her. When he gingerly reached for her she slapped his hand away. He flinched, stepped back.

Fergal tensed; in the closeness of the hall he smelled dreadful, even worse than she did.

Knacker fumbled the little glass bottle out of the pocket of his ski jacket. 'Yeah?' Showed it to her. 'Yeah?'

Stephanie got to her feet and began walking down the corridor. Both men stared at her without blinking. Knacker shuffled away from her approach.

She turned and climbed the stairs.

Knacker followed warily.

Through the banisters, Fergal watched her every step upwards towards the first floor. 'I'll be right behind that twat so don't even fink about nuffin'.'

FIFTY-EIGHT

'You owe rent on this room. Like I told you, rent's gone up. You's already in arrears, sister. Time you earned your keep, like.'

Knacker looked as skittish as a pony with the scent of a wolf in its nostrils; he was all mouth and front because Fergal had now joined him inside her old first floor room. And Knacker appeared to be rehearsing an old and redundant draft of a script that no one wanted to hear any more. She doubted Knacker would ever surprise her again, no matter how hard he tried. Even though he carried the bottle of acid, since she had been dragged out of the ground floor flat, she was no longer afraid of him.

Today, on this drab and wet morning, in a building that belonged to none of them, she knew that everything had changed: her situation, *her*. The atmosphere of the house had subtly shifted, like the encroach of dusk into an afternoon you couldn't recall passing. She knew she would never be allowed to leave, but she also imagined she had been released from *down there* to do something. A task of some kind. And the urgency to perform this function grew like a slow heat inside her blood. Only she didn't know what the task was; what she *needed* to do.

At least she was indifferent to anything Knacker said

now, and that indifference felt like a great relief from an almost unbearable pressure of rage. She'd completely shut his chunter out of her mind as they ascended the stairs.

Once reinstalled on the first floor, she'd stood beside the window and watched Knacker dump the contents of a black bin bag, what she assumed were Margaret's clothes, onto the bed. A froth of black lace fell out of the bag, entangled in a sticky mass of latex. A dead girl's lingerie.

She was more interested in listening to the women all around her, in case they had a message for her. Through the length and breadth of the house she received the impression that the residents were either talking or weeping, and mostly in the distance and at the edge of her hearing.

When she'd walked up the stairs, even the tall blonde woman had returned to her position outside, beside the garden wall. She smoked a cigarette like she had done that first time. But this time the woman looked up and met Stephanie's eye as she passed behind the stairwell window between the ground floor and first floor. The woman held her stare until Stephanie passed from sight.

Knacker couldn't hear anything within the house. She knew this because of his anxious preoccupation with her neutral state: her uncharacteristic calm and lack of fear in his presence. He didn't like that, and she almost smiled for the first time in what felt like a lifetime.

But Fergal could hear the women of the house. He peered around himself and through the thin daylight that seeped into the building. Agitated, he blinked red-rimmed eyes at the ceiling and walls. In one hand Fergal carried an old vinyl holdall. The bag had been on the first floor landing, awaiting collection. He must have left it there before coming downstairs to release Stephanie. In his other hand he carried the old saucepan she had seen in one of the cupboards under the kitchen sink.

In her room Fergal dropped the holdall at the foot of the bed. Something inside the bag rattled like a chain. He dropped the saucepan next to the bag. Then walked across to Stephanie and craned his long neck forward so his horrible face could command her full attention.

Knacker had moved onto her other side and stood too close, cocky again. He nodded over at the clothes and high-heeled shoes littered across the bed. 'See if they fit. You's got company tonight, so you better look your best. I don't want no lip, else yous'll get another slap. And we'll tie you to the fucking bed, like Svetlana. Wrists and ankles. We'd get extra too if you was tied down. Bareback in the black room with Stephy slut. Might give that old bastard next door a dirty ride, on the house, to get you used to the idea.'

Stephanie turned her head and spat in Knacker's eyes.

Blinking in shock, he raised a fist to strike her. She did not flinch.

Fergal placed a hand on Knacker's chest, his fingers spread wide. Then turned his face away from Stephanie and pushed it close to Knacker's until their noses were touching. 'You fucking stupid as you look or what? That's all over. Finished. And look at her. She'd as soon bite a cock off than suck it. She ain't no good for nuffin'.'

He returned his grimacing face to Stephanie. 'She's changed. Only I can't work out how. So I gotta sort some-fing out downstairs before we finish what we's started.

This ain't right. Fink there has been a misunderstanding down there.' His breath made her choke.

Knacker stepped away and bobbed on his toes, his face white with petulant rage at how he had been spoken to, at how she had spat in his face and not been summarily punished.

'Is they . . . is they askin' you to do fings, like?' Fergal asked Stephanie the question in a voice so quiet it was practically a whisper.

She stared back at him without disclosing anything besides the disgust she could not contain at his breath.

'I ain't happy wiv this, like,' Fergal said to himself. He looked about the ceiling, raised his hands. 'It's all going off in here, but it's all quiet down there. They wanted her. But pushed her out. Don't make no sense.' He thrust a finger at the floor to add emphasis to his point. Then quickly turned to Knacker, who flinched. 'Get her secure with Bennet's pervy tat. Can you get that right?' Fergal clenched his fist around Stephanie's upper arm and made her hiss from the force of his grip. He marched her to the foot of the bed. 'Sit!'

Stephanie complied. Her mind had been broken into and ransacked. She'd come out of that place vandalized. But she had been released, rejected. Was that what Fergal had inferred? She was done with screaming; she'd learned it would do her no good. She had nothing to fight with but patience, because the house was not finished with her; it had allowed a cessation in her torments for its own malign purposes. It was the only reason she was still breathing. What its intended goal was for those that remained alive beneath its roof she did not know, but it had not extinguished her life during the entire period when it had sufficient time to do so. It may have taken most of her wits and her mind and her heart, but it had left her with something, a kind of listlessness coiled around suppressed rage that seemed to be waiting for an opportunity to rise and strike. But even as a wreck, her being alive troubled Fergal.

Fergal nodded at Knacker, who approached her warily, then dropped to his knees and cuffed her left ankle. He extended the chain to the bed frame, raised the mattress and closed the second cuff around a metal strut that ran across the width of the bedframe. Glaring like a sullen child, Knacker removed the tiny keys from the locks on the cuffs and slipped them into his pocket.

'Next time you need a piss,' Fergal said to Stephanie, his face split by a grin, 'piss in that.' He dragged the saucepan by the handle and left it beside her legs. 'I fink we run out of polyfene,' he said through a smile. They must have used up the last roll on Margaret and Ryan. 'I'm gonna go fetch some from that raghead shop.'

'You going out? That wise?'

'You!' Ignoring Knacker's misgivings, Fergal jabbed a grimy index finger at his confederate's face. 'Watch her wiv your life, yeah?'

Fergal stalked from the room. She listened to his footsteps pound away, along the corridor to the staircase, and then heard them boom-creak down a flight of stairs.

Knacker looked at the underwear, clothes and shoes piled on top of the bed, and with such dismay it was like he was surveying the wreckage of a life's work, hopes and dreams after a stock market crash.

Eventually he broke his grim silence. 'I fink you know what he's fetching polyfene for, eh? I fink you know. You could've had it so good too. And Svetlana. And Margaret. I liked her.' He looked wistful at this mention of the late Margaret, and Stephanie wanted him dead with such an urgency she had to grit her teeth to suppress a scream of animal rage.

Knacker strolled across the room, checked the corridor outside to make sure Fergal had gone. He stared into the dim, ugly building until he heard the front door close in the distance. He turned around and sauntered back to the bed, sniffing. He sat down a few feet away from Stephanie, out of her reach, and retrieved the bottle of acid from his jacket pocket and placed it on the bed beside his hip. Played with the lid with one idle finger, his lips pursed. 'Don't got much to say for yourself no more, has you? You know he's gonna do the uvver one too, like. Svetlana. That ain't right. Your fella was askin' for it. That's fair. But the girls. That's bang out of order, like. They was good earners. They never hurt no one.'

Maybe this was a late appeal for her sympathy. While he explained that the murder of Stephanie's innocent boyfriend was justified, perhaps Knacker was trying to come back over to her side by showing his compassion for a girl who had been beaten to death and another who was currently tied to a bed upstairs so she could be raped by strangers. *Even after all that, I still have a heart, like.* Stephanie swallowed at her fury, but it just kept boiling back up her gullet.

'He sleeps wiv his eyes open,' Knacker said, as if the thought had just drifted through his mind.

363

She could see Knacker's face in the mirrored doors of the wardrobe. In this pensive mood he looked older, his face more lined now, and the thick youthful curls both ushered and worsened the effects of age and violence and strife he had held back with his garrulous, disingenuous street attitude and his youthful clothes.

He wasn't aware she was studying his reflection as he reminisced. But a change of aspect to something thoughtful did not soften his hard face; it just made him look pathetic, and troubled. She doubted anything could redeem him. And if he ever appeared rehabilitated, that too would only be an act to get what he wanted. 'You ever seen that? I ain't, not even in the nick, like. His eyes ain't right no more. They's all red and horrible. It's in him. That fing. He needs a doctor.' He grinned. 'But we can't go to the quacks cus we been a bit naughty, like.'

'He's mad. And he hates you.' It was the first time Stephanie had spoken since they had removed her from the ground floor flat.

Knacker started at the sound of her voice, like he'd been slapped across the back of the head. He gathered himself, slipped off the bed and walked across the room to the window. He clasped his hands upon his cheeks. 'Fuck's sake,' he muttered. Without turning around he then asked her, 'What is it, like? That fing down there? You been in there, you tell me.'

'You'll find out. Soon enough.'

Knacker flinched more than turned towards her. 'Eh? What you on, yeah?'

Stephanie enjoyed the spread of the smile across her face. 'You think the *polyfene* is just for me?'

'You watch your mouf. I ain't telling you twice.'

'Tell me what you know about it. And I'll tell you what I know.'

His face visibly quivered with rage. 'There ain't no deals. None of this, you tell me somefink and I'll tell you summat. Who you fink you is dealing wiv?'

'A dead man. So fuck off. Go on and fuck off out of here. You think I want to look at your ugly face, you prick. I'm already gone. I'm still down there, with them, with *her*. I don't give a shit. But when I go, I don't want your stink anywhere near me.'

What little colour and animation had remained in Knacker's face, vanished.

Stephanie shrugged. 'You think I am afraid of death? It's what comes after that's worse. But I'm prepared. You're not. He can't do anything to me that's worse than what happened to me down there. What I have seen. What comes next. But you . . . you won't even be half ready. It'll be bad, Knacker. Really bad for you. I only wish I could watch. Maybe I will.'

Knacker swallowed. He'd started to look at her in the same way he regarded Fergal, whenever his partner in crime mentioned the ground floor flat, or alluded to what was inside it. 'Piss off.' It came out of his mouth without any edge or force; the tone of a scared and beaten man. He paced across to the door in a hurry, as if he were about to pitch himself through it, but paused in the doorway, afraid of disobeying Fergal. And maybe he had nowhere else to run.

'You're a prisoner too, Knacker. You're going nowhere.

Not after what's happened here. Not after what you've done.'

'I ain't done nuffin'.'

'Oh you have. You've stood by and let him kill. You've supplied him with victims, aided him, abetted him. No one will see your role as any different to the one who laid the final punch.' She thought of Ryan and nearly lost her voice. The sudden pang of heartbreak surprised her so much she lost her train of thought.

Knacker stopped pacing and filled the silence, desperate to release the pressure in his tormented and frantic mind. It was as if he now needed to make himself understand the impossible. 'He's always had a screw loose, but this place . . . fuck's sake. What's down there . . . it made him worse. That fing Bennet told us about.'

'The Maggie. Where'd it come from, Knacker?'

'His mum and dad had it wiv them since he was a kid. I reckon they was all at it. All of 'em. Whole family was perverts. His Dad put girls in there . . . in there wiv it, like.' He came towards her. 'Where you was, what did you see? You see it? That horrible fing. It's been trying to get inside my head. In dreams, like. Nasty fucker. It's turned me own against me. Fergal is in wiv it. They're togever now. They fink they can cut me out!'

He was coming apart. All the tight flesh on his narrow, bony face seemed to be alive with jitters, like there was something twitching beneath the skin. One of his eyelids went into a spasm around a big open eyeball, exposed by fear. And then, as if they were friends, he tried to smile at Stephanie. 'You're a smart girl, so you tell me. Tell me what's here, like. You been in there, where we put Bennet. What is it? You tell me, yeah?'

She shook her head. 'You tell me about Bennet first.'

Knacker clenched his fists and paced about by the window like he was eager to be on the other side of the bars. 'Smelly cunt. It's all his fault. He let us come in here, yeah. What, did he fink we would believe them porkies he was telling in the Scrubs? It's all fucked up. Cus of *it*, like. Cus of *it*. I hate that fing. Fergal's gone the same way as Bennet. He don't wash his clothes no more. And he ain't never took his coat off once, like, not since he was let out. I know it. The unclean are pure, he kept saying that when I told him he was riffy. Bennet used to say the same fing, in the Scrubs, like. They couldn't get a comb froo his hair. They shaved it off. He was crawling with lice. Assaulted a guard when they hosed him down.' Knacker's shudder was almost a convulsion. 'Bennet was a dirty bastard. He always was. But not Fergal. He had pride, like. What makes them like this?'

'This is Bennet's house?'

'Yeah, too right. And everyfing in it. Ain't got fuck all to do wiv me, like. And I will tell them, like. Yes I will. You don't need to worry about that. They'll know who done what in here.'

'Why did Bennet's family bring it here?'

Knacker shuddered and scratched at his arms, under his sleeves. 'Was already in here, like. When his mum and dad bought the house. Somefing "bad" had been in the house for a long time. Bennet used to say that. This ain't my house, he'd say. Weren't my mum and dad's house neither. Don't matter whose name is on the deeds, or who inherited what, he always said this place belonged to the Maggie. Has done since before his lot come here. And he would say *she* likes fings done her way, like.'

'But you came. You stayed.'

Knacker clenched his fists again and partially spat out his evident regret. 'We fought Bennet was mad. Easy mark when he told us about running girls here, like his dad had done. Christ, the money they was making. The money we could have made. Hurts to even fink about it. Wasted. All of it, wasted. It's criminal. But he was really onto somefing, yeah, with the girls. Bennet. His dad and him had a nice little business going that we was gonna take over when Bennet snuffed it, like. But he was nuts. His whole family was fuckin' nuts to have that fing in their house . . . It was their religion. You believe that? Their religion.

'Bennet used to say, never ever go froo that door downstairs. Cus no one can live in there, like. His dad went mad in there, yeah. He was down there wiv it for years, like. His mum fucked off. It's why the social took Bennet off his dad when he was a kid. His dad was fucked in the head.

'And they made it worse wiv giving it girls, like. Anyone you give to it don't last long, he said. It's big, he kept saying. It's got so big now it'll put you out after it's played wiv you. We fought he was crazy, cus of them drugs he was on. Morphine. But there was somefing in there. This fing that Fergal started hearing.'

'Why did you put Bennet inside?'

'Cancer. He hadn't got long and he was getting on our tits. Fucking whining. Coughing like a cunt all the time. We couldn't sleep in the flat. That's when he starts going on about down there and all. All the time, like. I fought it was the morphine they give him at the hospital, that made him say fings, hear fings. Said he could hear all the girls he'd done. The ones his dad done too. And the ones that was done by others before his family come here. And then we get here and he keeps saying he don't know if he wants to stay in the house no more. Fought it was a mistake coming here, back home. He'd come here to die. Said he had somefing planned. Arrangement wiv that fing down there. He was let out the Scrubs early, cus of the cancer. But then he weren't sure he wanted to go froo wiv it any-more, this arrangement he had wiv down there. He started saying he wanted to die in the hospice instead. We said fuck off, like, cus he had to help us set up the girls. Teach us how and all that.

'Mumbo jumbo, I fought. I didn't know what he was talking about. But Fergal did. Cus *it* was already telling him fings too. Told him it wanted Bennet, like. In there wiv it. That they had a deal for when Bennet come out the nick. This house don't forget nuffin'. And when we was pissed up one night, fings got out a hand, like.'

'And you put him down there. A terminally ill man. You wanted him dead. And you thought you had killed him by putting him inside.'

'Fought? He was dead. Fergal checked. He didn't last the night. And no one screams like that and comes out standing. No way. 'Cept for you.'

Stephanie smiled as cryptically as she could.

'It's wiv you now, ain't it? That's what he's afraid of, eh? Fergal is shitting himself cus it's speaking to you. I'm right. I know I am. It went from Bennet's dad to Bennet, then from Bennet to Fergal. Then from Fergal to you. I fucking know it. You can't trust no one. Can't trust nuffin'. What's it want now? You tell me? Yeah? Yeah? What's it want?'

'Let me go. Let me out. I'll say you helped me. That you were a prisoner too. Two against one. You were afraid for your life, and rightly so. Because when Fergal's done me, Knacker—'

'Fuck off! You don't know nuffin'.'

'And when he's done Svetlana—'

'Fuck off! We go way back. Me and him been in all sorts of scrapes.'

'It'll be your turn.'

'Fuck off, I said.'

'And you know it.'

'Fuck, fuck, fucking hell.' Knacker dragged his fingers down his face and shook his head. He was out of his league. He turned and ran to the bed, snatched up the bottle of acid. 'You tell me, yeah? You tell me what it's asking for? More girls? That's what it wants, eh? More girls? That what I gotta do to keep it away from me, yeah?'

'It wants company, Knacker. What it always wants,' Fergal said from the doorway, before he walked into the room and slowly shut the door behind himself.

FIFTY-NINE

Hours had passed; it was dark outside. Stephanie could feel her humanity trying to return.

During the previous night, trauma had flattened any sense of who she used to be, and it had only reinforced its grip of numbness after the fresh violence of the morning. But now the part of herself that registered fear and grief and hope was incrementally expanding and trying to remind her of who she was, and how she should respond to the things she experienced. A part of her psyche had run into the road and was screaming before Stephanie's windshield, flagging her down with crazed hands, trying to slap and claw its way back into her life. But she didn't want to feel normal again, not yet, because when the end came she would only feel worse.

What she had witnessed after Fergal had crept up the stairs and entered the room had left her feeling sick and physically weak for hours; the violence he had inflicted upon Knacker was a statement and a reminder that she was not like them. Not of them, nor this house.

Fergal had not left to get *polyfene*. He had pretended to leave to test Knacker because he suspected betrayal. This was a place in which the worst things happened and the worst people flourished. Maybe something had told

371

Fergal as much: a serpent that might be whispering to him again.

It takes one to know one.

And now Stephanie began to shake again, to tremble and to desperately want the relief that could not come, because she was cornered and trapped and chained to a bed and forced to remember. In here, fixed to a metal bed-frame and looking at the empty wardrobe, with the mirrored doors smashed out, she was left with nothing meaningful to occupy her mind. And again, in her memory, she could hear Knacker shouting, 'Leave it out! Leave it! Fergal! Leave it!'

After the first punch had landed on his forehead, Knacker had started that chant as his wits scrambled to get airborne so he could begin blagging his psychopathic *mate* into another course of action. But Fergal wasn't having any of it. Fergal enjoyed it. Loved it. Any reason, any excuse; violence made him come alive in a way that nothing else could, not even alcohol or drugs. Stephanie understood this now.

And her memory was misfiring as it had done after Ryan had been kicked to death. Most of what had happened in the room that morning she managed to suppress, save for key images, scenes in Technicolor that stabbed quickly into her thoughts and then repeated their highlights in a slow motion cycle, before vanishing again and returning her to the present, sickened afresh and weak in body.

And then she would hear Knacker's voice again. How high-pitched it had become, squealing as the younger man, his *friend*, beat him. And the cycle of reluctant remembrance would begin anew.

Fergal's neck and face had bloomed bright red, and then shadowed to a purple-black that was too awful to look upon, but too compelling to not see. His expression was all yellow teeth and flared nostrils, slit eyes inside screwed up skin; he'd actually snarled like an animal. Saliva had spat from his mouth like he was a barking dog with a disease. He had been transformed, totally, by rage.

'It was her! It was her! Tried to get me to grass to the filth!' But Knacker's attempt to save himself and transfer the violence onto Stephanie had only incensed Fergal even further. And the blow he'd then wielded into Knacker's bleached face had made the sound of a coconut thumped by a cricket bat. Skull echoes and jaw judders.

Stephanie was sure Knacker's neck had snapped or his skull had shattered like a ceramic vase. 'Fuzzzzz sake, like,' Knacker had mumbled, and his arms had gone limp as he tried to hold Fergal back, or shove him away; by that point the intentions behind the gesture were as unclear as Knacker's drunken eyes.

Knacker had then tried to turn around and stagger away from the attack, which only produced the same re-action as petrol thrown onto a garden fire. 'Don't you turn your back on me!' Fergal had roared this over and over again, like he was creating a rhythm for the flurry of bone-deep punches while spraying the air with spit.

Not being able to gain easy access to his friend's face had simply enraged Fergal to such an extent that he had clutched a handful of Knacker's hair on the very top of his skull, and pulled his head down so that he could hammer a fist into the smaller man's face. And even though Stephanie had turned her head away, a sound followed her, a noise similar to a large metal spoon repeatedly striking an open crate of eggs until they were all smashed to liquid.

A part of her she had only known inside the kitchen of the ground floor rooms, feelings she still tried to condemn in retrospect, emotions she believed had no place inside of her, had suddenly surged at that point with a blind and maddening excitement. And only afterwards did she detest herself for the overwhelming presence of this new desire. But at the time of Knacker's destruction she had wanted to chant 'Kill him! Kill him! Kill him!' as Fergal punched and punched and punched something that had gone silent on the floor. Then she had thought of Margaret, young, beautiful Margaret, and she had groaned and felt her stomach desperately trying to retch its emptiness into a room that felt small and insubstantial around the frenzy of violence she was convinced had created another dead body at 82 Edgehill Road.

But even the punching and the kicking that smashed Knacker's body half under the bed, where he choked for air through the blood that was inside his broken mouth, was not sufficient punishment or satiation for Fergal's rage. Because he then pulled Knacker out from under the bed by his curly hair, dragged him like a child across the floor, raised him from the ground and pitched his floppy body into the mirrored doors of the wardrobe.

Only the silvery crash following the explosion of a human body through two broad glass doors snapped Fergal out of his violent trance. And for a while he seemed disorientated, and just stood still, sniffing and looking at the cut knuckles on one hand. Eventually he gazed at Knacker and nonchalantly said, 'Cunt.'

Holding one arm stiffly, supporting the wrist with his other hand, Fergal wandered out of the room, sniffing as he went.

And his exit broke Stephanie from her torpor and she scrabbled as far as the remit of her chain would allow, to locate, seize and retrieve a long sliver of mirrored glass from the carpet, before returning to her former position at the foot of the bed.

She slipped the piece of broken glass behind her bottom and beneath the bed. And then sat back against the mattress, panting and almost weeping with relief that the violence had stopped.

Incredibly, and impossibly, Knacker wasn't dead. Though he didn't move from where he was positioned half inside the wardrobe cavity, he had coughed and muttered something to himself before falling silent again.

Fergal had come back into the room grinning, one hand wrapped in sodden toilet paper. He'd smiled sheepishly at Stephanie as if nothing significant had occurred in the room, said, 'Oh dear.' This was followed by the deep, forced 'Ho Ho Ho' imitation of a laugh. 'Fink he's gonna have headache. What you fink? He he he.' He prodded Knacker's still and silent form with the toe of a dirty training shoe. 'You's been asking for a shoeing, Knacker, longer than I can honestly remember.'

The next laugh that came more readily sounded devious. He followed the laughter by spitting a long slug of phlegm and saliva onto Knacker's back, before he dragged his mate by one leg across the broken glass and into the corridor outside.

Fergal only returned to the room to side-foot the larger pieces of broken glass to the foot of the wardrobe and away from Stephanie. And as he kicked the glass she'd shrunk at the thought of him searching under the bed and finding the shard she had retrieved.

He'll kick you to death where you sit.

But Fergal never came near the bed. And before he left the room he grinned at her. 'Oh, do you know if that shop by the pub sells polyfene? Afraid you is going up the garden behind that tree wiv your boyfriend. You can keep him company.'

DAY NINE

SIXTY

Feeling damp and uncomfortable, Stephanie awoke some-time in early morning, lying in a foetal position, huddled into her herself on the floor at the foot of the bed. She shivered, uncomfortable inside her own skin, and realized she had come on as she slept.

There had been a dream but she couldn't remember much of it besides the fading and ill-recollected notion of someone standing alone within a wide, flat field of small green crops. And she had come awake saying, 'No, no, no, no I did not . . .' But another vague and surreal dream was the last of her worries now.

She quickly became aware of how weak she felt from hunger, her stomach burning and cramping; all she had eaten in three days was half of a sloppy burger Knacker had brought her. At least Fergal had given her water after he'd returned to the house following a sortie to find *poly-fene*. Whether he was successful or not she had no idea. But he didn't kill her when he returned, so maybe his pursuit of a roll of plastic in which to encase her body had failed. Instead of delivering a violent death he had brought her water. Tap water collected in a dusty plastic measuring jug he must have rooted out of the kitchen cupboards.

Stephanie drank all of the water within minutes of

379

Fergal's departure from the room, about a pint's worth, and she had urinated into the saucepan sometime later, not long before she fell asleep while curled around the shard of broken, mirrored glass. A waft of her own waste hung around the foot of the bed as she fell away from the world and into an exhausted, wretched sleep.

After waking, during the hours she'd had to sit alone and reflect, she had fashioned a knife handle out of a single stocking that had once belonged to Margaret, and which she had been able to reach in the centre of the bed. She made the handle by repeatedly wrapping the flimsy hosiery, from toe to rubbery hold-up top, around the shard so that she wouldn't cut her hand on the edges of the long fragment of glass when she found an opportunity to stab Fergal.

She had thought of using the glass spike on Fergal when he brought the water, but he had stayed clear of her and not lingered. Just put the jug on the floor and said, 'Yum, yum.' Then checked the cuff around the strut of the bedframe and left the room without another word. She had needed him closer.

Next time he came inside she would have to cut him, and before she fell asleep she had made considerable efforts to recall what she had been taught during her GCSEs, about where the major arteries were inside a human body. She needed to find one under his pasty flesh where it was exposed at throat or wrist. She doubted she could wield a fatal blow with a piece of mirror, and it would probably snap within the resistance of his dirty brown parka if she missed his flesh, but she wanted him hurt before he killed her. That idea was not only a source of comfort but now her sole purpose. The idea, uncomfortably, functioned as a source of excitement, as if the new aspect to her character that she'd discovered downstairs, and while Knacker was kicked around the floor, was trying to take hold of her again.

After his beating there had been no further sighting of Knacker, or even any sound of him on the first floor. A small mercy. She imagined him writhing around broken bones in a bed at the top of the house. Or perhaps Fergal had finished him off and buried him in the garden. No matter the length of their shared criminal history, she could not imagine them repairing their bond after such an attack. The duration and ferocity of the violence would have been a deal breaker between even the most devoted brothers. And the most awful aspect of all, lingering from the confrontation, was Fergal spitting onto his insensible mate as Knacker lay semi-conscious, half inside the ruined wardrobe. They were worse than rabid animals.

Perhaps Knacker had even been left bleeding on the kitchen floor of the ground floor flat, something she would only wish upon her worst enemy. So in her cold and discomfort she hoped that Knacker was in there, *down there*, and being investigated right now by the occupants before he joined them in a darkness that would never end for him. But then, if she were forced to endure an eternity inside this house after her murder, as a semi-aware presence, she realized her suffering would be greater if Knacker was inside the blackness with her; he might be able to torment her as Bennet still made his victims suffer.

She clenched her eyes and her fists and her mind to shut out any recall of the previous night, and what death inside this building seemed to suggest as a continuance of self, or a part of self.

Stop it, stop it, stop it . . .

She held the shard of glass tighter and did not return to sleep. Instead she sat alone in the darkness and listened to the other women of the house. Her neighbour sobbed against the wall for hours. A door on the first floor opened and closed several times; what she assumed was the bathroom door. Feet moved up and down the corridor outside. Steps of the distant stairwell creaked.

Around the curtains she watched dawn arrive incrementally in a variety of colours: indigo, blue, silver, white, before settling for grey. Rain pattered against the window to wake the world. With a trickling sound the radiator came on and warmed the room. This usually happened around six.

So was this to be her last day? She seemed to have been living on borrowed time for days, before her end came in this wet city, inside a half derelict house upon a mostly forgotten street.

It's how so many must die.

When thirst and hunger made her moan, she decided she'd had enough. It was time. *That time.* Time to speed things up, to force a resolution, a conclusion. To get this over with.

I will not spend another night inside this house.

I will not spend another night inside this house.

I will not spend another night inside this house.

She moved the shard of broken mirror and held it close to the small of her back. Moved the glass about in her fingers to gain the best purchase for a thrust.

Aim for an eye.

That was asking a lot for someone who had never stabbed anything before. Maybe the bigger target of a cheek would be better. The glass would snap on impact but the point was sharp and should leave a mark that would be permanent. A scar on the awful face of a demented killer would be her final act and her legacy. But it was better than just dying in this evil place.

Maybe that's what death mostly was: misery, exhaustion, despair, and just getting used to the idea through a series of steps towards the inevitable end. Who had the luxury of going at home in bed, surrounded by loved ones, satisfied their life had been fulfilling and had fulfilled some purpose? Since when did death have any regard for personal development or time? Maybe there was no such thing as time anyway.

Her thoughts seem to grow too vast for her skull and they made her feel tired, sluggish.

You can sleep when you're dead.

Or can you?

A brief notion of taking her own life from the wrist made her shudder and she shut the thought out. No, she didn't think suicide would be possible. Not yet. But after another couple of days of this she might be more comfortable with the idea.

I'm not going out like that.

Dispassionately and uncharacteristically, as if some dark and insidious reptile was coiled inside her mind and hissing advice, she decided it was better to be killed after inflicting a terrible wound on her murderer. And if she died angry and vengeful, perhaps she would remain as such, and not as a victim who lingered between these horrid walls forever.

Not long now.

The first visitor to enter her room was a surprise.

SIXTY-ONE

Stephanie heard two sets of footsteps slowly make their way to the door. One of them had to drag itself down the corridor. The second set of footsteps followed patiently and in silence.

When the door was unlocked, she heard someone breathing heavily from the exertion of turning the key and the door handle.

The door opened slightly, but no one came through. Not for a while anyway. Voices entered instead.

'I want it done by the time I come down, yeah?' It was Fergal, but whoever he spoke to did not answer, which angered him. 'Yeah? You fucking deaf as well as stupid?'

'Awright, awright,' Knacker said in reply, and in a voice that suggested a speech impediment.

'She's the reason you got fucked up, so deal wiv it or I will deal wiv you.'

'I said awright, yeah?'

'She ain't done by the time I'm done with the other slit, then you can start cutting your own polyfene to size. You got it? Five minutes, tops.'

'Yeah,' Knacker said quietly.

'Show me.'

A whisking of a Gore-Tex coat.

'And what about the other fing?'

In the corridor outside, Stephanie heard a rustle of plastic.

'All right,' Fergal said. 'I find you is lying about doing this, I'll kick the last few teef out your face. Don't you unlock her till she's cold neither.' At that, Fergal walked back to the stairwell, presumably to attend to his own business with Svetlana.

The subtext of the conversation, and the fact that they didn't care what she heard, brought Stephanie close to a faint. Momentarily, she could not feel her legs or her arms, and was so frightened she could no longer see straight.

And then Knacker shuffled into the room to kill her.

SIXTY-TWO

'We best get this done quick, like.'

Knacker couldn't look at her as he spoke, nor as he winced and limped inside. As if for a reassurance of privacy for what he was about to do, he shut the door behind himself. 'You know this is coming, so let's have no fuss. None of that, yeah?'

Her mouth hung open and she panted from something that felt like heartburn. She must have looked like she was going into shock. Maybe she was. Then she felt sick but managed to tighten her fingers around the mirror-knife. *Can I even lift it?*

Knacker's face was so horribly disfigured it helped to shock her out of the wilt of terror. One of his eyes was sealed shut, the eyelid purple, blue and black, and grotesquely distended like a plum was attached to the front of his face. His nose was twice its former size, and split horizontally across the bridge. A thick band of black blood indicated where the skin had been broken over the cartilage beneath. The second eye was defined by its red discolouration about the blue iris. His bottom lip resembled a dirigible.

He struggled to bend his right leg and she could see the evidence of a swollen knee through his jeans. He appeared to have lost the use of an arm too, which hung limp at his side. Either that or his ribs were broken and he was cradling them. In the hand attached to the slack arm was the bottle of acid.

He saw her looking at it. 'Didn't fink it would come to this, like. Sorry about that and all, yeah? But fings is set in motion, like. You know how it is.'

He raised his other hand. The fingers gripped a blue plastic bag; she recognized the variety from the Sikh grocer's that was close to the end of Edgehill Road. Knacker swallowed, licked his top lip. 'You know the score, girl.'

For a few seconds she didn't understand what the bag was for, and then she realized he intended to suffocate her by putting it over her head and holding it tight about her throat.

'Yeah? You know?' he said, as the comprehension in her eyes must have given away her sudden understanding of how she was to go.

He held the bag out front and shook it to make sure he had her full attention. 'Better be quick, like. Not that others here appreciate it, but I'll get the job done, yeah? And quicker if you help me out wiv this fing. You won't feel nuffin'. Promise.' A slither of the old bull-shitter, the wheedler had reappeared to convince her that she should surrender herself to murder and die without any fuss.

'Better if you put it on, yeah? It's just like going to sleep.' He said this as if he'd performed the act on himself a hundred times. But under the bruises, his face paled and became more colourless than she'd ever seen a human face go before. He bent double. Spat some blood onto the carpet and then vomited. 'Ah fuck. Ah fuck. Ah fuck,' he said to himself, then straightened his back. 'Fuck's sake.' He sniffed and looked at her again with that one red eye.

Stephanie glanced at the door and wondered if the lanky baboon was outside, listening; Fergal could move discreetly when he wanted to. So she kept her voice down and spoke quickly. 'Acid. Throw the acid in his face. I will tell the police you were a prisoner too. I swear. You won't get in trouble. I promise. I promise.'

Knacker swallowed. 'Nah. Ain't gonna work, Steph.'

'Let me go. There's two of us. We can do it. He'll kill you too. You know it.'

She was tempted to produce the mirror knife and say, 'I have this', `but another more implacable instinct made her keep that hand concealed.

Knacker shook his head. 'We gotta do it this way, like I explained. Or I'll have to use the bottle.'

With a wince he partially raised the hand holding the acid. 'Clock's ticking. Put this over your face, like. You know, like a hood. Or I gotta burn you, girl. If I was you, I know which I'd rather have.'

Stephanie swallowed. Gripped the shard of mirror in her hand. 'OK. Do it now. Before he comes back. I'm ready.'

Knacker looked surprised, but was so eager to get the job done in case Fergal came back and kicked his teeth out, that he shuffled to her side without further delay. Then extended the arm holding the bag. 'Here. Just put it over your 'ead, like. Then I'll hold the back tight. Be done in no time. No holes you can breave froo. I checked. You won't suffer, like. Swear on me muvver's life.'

If it goes over your face you won't be able to see where you stab. Do it when he's close.

She took the bag.

Knacker's red eye watched her take it from his fingers, but he stayed back, out of reach; he was hurting enough and didn't want to risk any more pain.

She shook the bag open with a hand that felt like someone else's, and tentatively placed it on the top of her head so it perched like a paper hat from a Christmas cracker.

'All the way over, like. Don't work otherwise. Right down to your chin,' he added in a business-like fashion, as if he were instructing someone how to wear a motorcycle helmet. 'Use both hands, like.'

She had no choice; she had to put it over her head, because he was only going to come closer to tighten the bag around her throat to suffocate her. And when he was that close she would have to strike.

She pulled the plastic down to her forehead using one hand. If she used both hands, she would need to put the shard of mirror down and might not find the makeshift knife once the bag was on her head.

Maybe he's going to use the acid anyway, but doesn't want to look you in the eye when he pours it over your head.

But there was no other way to lure him closer. She had a go at the bag with one hand, then slipped the knife around her buttocks and held it under her thigh so he wouldn't see the spike.

Nervously, she pulled the bag further down her face, and then at the back of her head. The bag rustled over her eyes and she was engulfed with the stench of plastic. She looked down and could see the floor and her body through the top of the bag that opened around her neck.

And then Knacker was behind real quick, breathing hard.

He was impatient. Aware of the time and Fergal's threat, he must have rushed in to smother her. The bag tightened around her throat. The light went out.

Too late!

Knacker's knees thumped into her back. He was sat on the bed behind her to keep the bag tight at the nape of her neck.

Stephanie sucked in her breath and the plastic bag crumpled around her face. She breathed out and the bag partially inflated. There wasn't enough air inside the bag to take more than a shallow intake.

She panicked, got to her knees, her spine a bow with his knees trying to hold her in place. But it was his eagerness that lit her up like a match had been dropped upon a trail of gunpowder; a trail that started in her stomach and rose to her brain. She flashed red and hot and burned black all over and inside too. And she surrendered to the hateful, vengeful chaos that heated her blood. She thrust a hand backwards. Slapped his face.

'Eh, eh. None of that, like. You's too fond of having a go, ain't ya? You fink I've forgotten how you give me a slap? Eh? Fucking gob on me, bitch, and this is what you get.' His tone of voice had changed; the resignation and bedside manner of the reluctant executioner had gone. Another act.

Stephanie leaned her shoulders and head backwards

like a gymnast and drew her fingertips down his face as he pulled his head back.

'Fuck off,' he whispered.

She slipped her fingers inside his open mouth and felt his tongue like a nervous sea creature recoiling at an intrusion inside its shell. And before he could spit her fingers out of his mouth, or bite them, she clenched her fist as hard as she could with her thumb positioned under his jaw.

Her nails were long and sharp. And they went through his tongue like the prongs of a large fork through a thick slice of ham.

Knacker gargled around a scream.

She held his jaw tight, her thumb deep under his chin and pressing his pronounced Adam's apple. And she yanked his head down at the same time she twisted her body about to face him.

The bag had come loose around her throat; he had let go of it to claw at her hand inside his mouth. And to her satisfaction she realized that Knacker couldn't bite her fingers because she was holding him by the lower jaw. Elation leapt inside her; she'd bridled the pig with her fist and had to grit her teeth to stop herself screaming from the joy of having this thing in her hands.

Knacker stood up fast and pulled her upright with him. The leg chain rattled taut. But she did not let go of his jaw, even though his mouth was leaking spit and blood all over her knuckles. He made a choking sound that refused to become the word he tried to shout. It sounded like: 'Ergoo, Ergoo, Ergoo.' *Fergal.*

A timely reminder of how fast she needed to work.

No messing. Kill him.

It could have been someone else's voice inside her head. She did not recognize it and was briefly shocked by the sound and the sentiment that the voice expressed. Though she was compelled to agree with the instruction.

She brought the hand with the mirror shard up from her side. Using the thumb of that hand, she hooked the hot plastic bag entirely off her head. Then peered down at Knacker's red and gasping face which she moved closer, just above her waist-level. She noted he was trying to get the lid off the bottle of acid, but was struggling because he only had one eye to see with and only one arm that was much use. So the limp arm was probably broken. Fergal should have controlled himself; he should never have disabled his ally.

Stephanie shook Knacker's head about like she was playing with a dog that had its jaws clamped on a rubber toy.

Knacker gargled, sputtered, dripped.

Quickly, she brought the glass shard up and punched it through the thin skin of his throat, between his Adam's apple and the tendon at the side of his bony neck. Only after the glass went in deep, and until her knuckles brushed the stubble on his jawline, did she realize that she was smiling with all of her teeth.

Hot blood jetted over the back of her hand. Something that felt like warm water from a garden sprinkler speckled her face. She dipped her head, blinked her eyes clear.

Knacker dropped the bottle of acid at his feet and brought both hands up to a throat that ran bright red right inside the collar of his jacket.

She held him tight by the jaw and lowered his head to the floor. He went down and sputtered like he was choking on a bone. She had no idea a human mouth could produce so much saliva.

He took one hand away from his wet throat and briefly flailed it at her face.

Keys. He put the keys to the cuffs in his pocket.

One thing at a time.

Bleed him. Bleed his strength away.

She kicked him hard between the legs and forced his head against the floor. She raised her uncuffed foot and pressed the sole of her trainer against the side of his head. He kicked out his legs like a farm animal in a slaughterhouse. His feet shot under the bed and he could not pull them back out. Knacker's strength was ebbing and his visible red eye started to turn up inside his skull.

Stephanie was standing in a puddle. 'Do you want to know *somefing*, you bastard?' she said. 'You're bleeding out, like a pig. It's what you deserve.' She knelt down beside him and looked at the door. It was still closed but would not be for long. *Keys.*

She let go of the mirror shard and used that hand to go through one of Knacker's jacket pockets with her free hand. She fished out her phone, her purse. Threw them on to the bed. Slipped her hand around his stomach and into the other pocket of his jacket and pulled out a tobacco tin, Ryan's engraved Zippo lighter, a condom, the keys to the door and another set of smaller steel keys that looked like toy keys. *Handcuffs.*

Confident she could now take her hand out of

Knacker's mouth, she released his jaw and withdrew her sopping fingers.

Knacker began to rasp, loudly, so she kept his head still with one foot. His legs still kicked about under the bed, though the actions better resembled spasms. A final surge. His last.

Using both hands, Stephanie slipped the small key inside the steel cuff about her ankle and unlocked it with one smooth turn. The cuff opened and she kicked it off her foot. Breathing hard, she took her other foot off Knacker's head.

As she uncuffed herself, Knacker managed to pull the mirror shard out of his throat with one twitching hand. But to put up a struggle at this stage he'd probably need most of the blood that was soaking into the carpet to still be inside his body.

Stephanie picked up the medicine bottle filled with acid. 'Gonna use this on me, yeah?' Her voice was quiet and calm now. She tried to unscrew the bottle cap but it swivelled around and made the clicking sound of a child-proofed lid. She pressed the lid down and gingerly removed the cap. The stench that came out of the bottle made her whip her head back.

She took a step away from the shuddering, jerking thing on the floor that gulped at the air. She leant over and carefully poured half the bottle's contents onto Knacker's crotch. And then stamped on his face. His nose cracked and slid sideways like a snail's shell under the sole of her foot.

She stepped away and surveyed his suffering with

disgust, but also with a surge of satisfaction and pleasure that was near sexual.

Recapping the bottle quickly, she made sure not to tighten the lid; she'd need to get that off quickly when the time came to throw the rest of the acid into Fergal's face.

Svetlana. Get up there now. Might not be too late.

Stephanie snatched up the blue plastic grocery bag and hooded Knacker's head to muffle his gurgled shrieks. 'I'm free and I've burned your cock off. And now I'm going to open that skinny prick . . .' She picked the piece of mirror from the floor while Knacker choked through the sizzle and the steam of his death, that had just gotten so much worse than he ever could have imagined. '. . . with this,' she said, and rewrapped the blood-drenched stocking around the base of the mirror shard. The end of the glass spike was chipped, the chip somewhere inside Knacker's throat.

With the acid bottle in one hand and ready for launch, Stephanie opened the door and checked the corridor. The dismal passage was empty.

She locked the door behind herself with her old set of room keys. And walked away from the gargling sounds that choked under the door as if a large fish were trying to breathe on land.

She tapped 999 into her phone keypad.

There were preliminaries when you called 999.

Which service?

What's your number?

What's your full name and address?

Can you calm down and tell us where you are?

After Stephanie issued the address in hushed tones, her

calm, or her shock, broke down and into, 'They're trying to kill me . . . They're killing another girl now. Have killed others. They killed Ryan. His body is in the garden. The house is full of dead people. Bennet killed them. They killed them . . .' The information was coming out too fast and she was angry at herself because she was worried that she wasn't making sense. But something in her voice must have informed the operator that she wasn't faking. The phone made some clicks and the operator's voice lost its softness. Stephanie was told to stay on the line and that a car was on its way.

'Come quick. Please. Fergal has gone upstairs to kill Svetlana.'

The operator told her to calm down. Then asked her to leave the house.

She could. *Oh, God.* She could bolt down those stairs, run along the ground floor corridor, open the front door and run into the street. Her legs were soaked in blood. A car might stop in the street.

Svetlana.

She might still be alive.

Not now. He'd have done her by now. Get out. Run.

'Stephanie, are you still on the line? It is very important that you stay on the line. Do you need a doctor? Are you injured?'

She didn't answer the operator. Instead she was mostly listening to the house. The house was quiet. And she remembered her fear in that room, while chained to the bed, when Knacker had come inside to choke out her life inside a plastic bag. She looked down at the bottle of acid in her fist and ran for the stairs. She panted as much as spoke into the phone handset. 'Leaving phone on. Gotta help Svetlana. He's killing her.'

She slipped the phone handset inside the pocket at the front of her soiled hooded top and began an ascent of the stairs to the second floor.

SIXTY-THREE

Struggling to breathe easily, Stephanie stopped twice on the stairwell; the second time she stopped she hovered on the verge of passing out. Her vision shrank behind what looked like black smoke speckled with diamonds and she was convinced the walls were moving. She clutched the banister. The strength and resolve to get this far was deserting her fast.

Rounding the staircase slowly she looked up at the gloom of the second floor, and at where she had started at 82 Edgehill Road. Where it had all started. Pushing on with soft feet, up one side of the stairs to minimize the sounds of her ascent, she forced herself to regulate her breathing or she would be good for nothing.

She was soon looking at three closed doors of painted red wood. All of the rooms appeared to be occupied. On the right hand side, where she first heard the Russian girl, and where Margaret must have died, she could hear muffled sounds of grief: a chest-shuddering sound of a young woman wracked with misery.

One of them.

To her knowledge, the door of the room at the corridor's conclusion had always been locked. A distant series of bumps now issued from inside, through the door, and into the fusty air of the old passageway, as if someone had fallen to their knees heavily. Only the suggestion repeated itself again and again as if they were always falling, standing up, falling.

One of them.

She shivered. The cold registered through her clothes and around her face as she edged along the wall to the first door: the one to her old room. Readying the bottle of acid in her hand by uncapping it, Stephanie listened outside and dropped the white plastic cap at her feet.

Thump. Slap. Thump. Interspersed with moans, female moans, as though someone was having sex. Was Fergal raping Svetlana before he killed her? The fact the idea no longer shocked her was the only thing that did shock Stephanie. And without another thought, she turned the handle and shoved the door open. It banged against the foot of the bedframe.

Stephanie walked into the room. Fergal turned his head to look at her. His face was tense with concentration and what looked like annoyance. He was standing near the head of the bed and leaning over the mattress. He held a pillow over Svetlana's face; his other hand was raised to deliver a punch. He was beating the woman to death, with his second choice of hand, while trying to suffocate her at the same time. The fact that Fergal had damaged his right hand on Knacker the day before was the only reason Svetlana was still alive.

The room swam. Stephanie took in the sight of the naked female body, the head obscured by a pillow, the arms and legs pulled out from the body in a star shape and secured with thick leather cuffs at the four points of the old bedframe. *Her old bed.* She swallowed and tried to quell the urge to be sick.

From the fireplace came the monologue of a distant female voice.

Under the bed, unseen hands tore at plastic, as if on behalf of the helpless girl above who could move nothing but her fingers and toes.

Behind her head, by the windows and small table, nervous feet padded back and forth, back and forth. And whoever moved with agitation was whimpering. She threw a glance behind herself; there was no one there.

The skin of Fergal's face smoothed out with surprise as he took in Stephanie's bloodied jeans, mired hoodie, and what had flecked and speckled her face in the struggle downstairs and had now dried. He didn't speak. Just squinted as if trying to fathom out how she had come to be standing beside the bed with a jar of acid raised in one fist and a shard of red glass in the other.

'That tosser can't get nuffin' right,' he eventually said, with a slow shake of his head.

His reaction to whatever had bustled into his mind next so surprised Stephanie that she hesitated. Fergal's face screwed up and he began to cry, 'You ain't havin' her! You ain't havin' her! She's mine!'

His voice was thick with tears and his cheeks became wet and shiny in seconds. And in his distress and grief Stephanie saw a much younger, boyish face, and one so contorted by anguish she thought her heart might break. She wondered what kind of life this man had endured until this point in time. And she sensed, the permanent damage of not being wanted. For this man, who had also once been a small boy, perhaps rejection had been comprehensive from his first breath.

She swallowed. Forced herself to remember how dangerous he was. Made herself look again at the woman he was murdering. 'Get away from her!'

Fergal released the pillow and stood up to his full and unnatural height: a dirty scarecrow man of bones, in filthy Gore-Tex and blackened denim, who wept like a ten-year-old boy in a world so hopeless and loveless that the very consideration of this world was unbearable. And Stephanie knew in a heartbeat what the Black Maggie had done to the man. She'd finished what life started.

'You ain't havin' her! You ain't!' He took a step towards Stephanie.

She showed him the bottle. 'I'll use this, you bastard!'

Fergal snarled and threw himself across the room at her.

Instinctively, she stepped backwards and cringed.

One huge dirty hand swiped through the air and grabbed her shoulder so hard she nearly fell over. When his head was no more than three feet from her own, she jerked the bottle at his big, mad face.

The liquid came out in a silvery string, striking Fergal beneath one eye and spattering across his nose, cheek and forehead. He'd stepped into the stream and its near instant sting brought a sudden halt to the forward momentum of his long body. Stephanie jumped backwards to avoid the liquid ricochet.

Her second jab with the bottle didn't produce much liquid and what came out disappeared between Fergal's knees to soak into the carpet.

She was never entirely sure what happened next. Something that felt like a brick struck one side of her head, turned her body around completely and sent her crashing into the fireplace. She moved to her hands and knees with her hair in her eyes from where it had come loose from her pony tail. Inside her ears was the sound of a distant kettle whistling above deep water. Which only cleared to fill her head with the sound of an animal's roar. An ape in terrible pain.

She turned and saw Fergal, snapping from the waist and lowering his head to his knees, then throwing his head backwards at the ceiling before breaking himself in half again at the waist, trying to throw something appalling from his face. His long-fingered hands covered his features and extended over his head and into his hair, a mask of spidery white bone gripping his head. He sounded like he was trying to breathe and shout through a snorkel as he fell about the room. He glanced off the bed and then dropped through the doorway.

When he wrenched his hands off a face that Stephanie could not bear to look upon, he screamed, 'You ain't havin' her!' before scrabbling to the stairs.

Stephanie's hands were sticky and when she looked at them she saw deep cuts on the palm of the hand that had been holding the glass shard. Her skin looked like uncooked pastry sliced on top of a pie. The mirror-knife had broken inside her hand as she fell. Fergal must have swiped her off her feet with a punch.

Outside, Fergal grunted and banged his way down the stairwell.

Stephanie looked at the bed. The girl's bare breasts were rising and falling.

On her knees and then her feet, Stephanie staggered to the bed.

A tiny voice was talking somewhere inside the room. From where? Close by. It took her several seconds to realize it was the police operator still speaking on the phone inside her pocket, imparting instructions.

Stephanie pulled the pillow off Svetlana's face. 'I'm here. I'm here now. Alright. I'm here . . .' She only stopped jabbering when she saw the damage below.

Stephanie crawled around the bed and uncuffed the woman's ankles and wrists. They were beautifully pedicured and manicured she thought, uselessly.

Once freed, Svetlana didn't make any attempt to remove her limbs from the open bonds. Stephanie climbed onto the bed and slipped her arms underneath the semiconscious woman and pulled her up and onto her own chest.

Stephanie flopped back against the wall and slipped a hand under Svetlana's chin. Gently moved her head backwards so that Svetlana would not choke on her tongue.

A distant police siren came into Edgehill Road.

Something was hissing into the carpet. It smelled of a chemical burn.

With a shaking hand, Stephanie fished the phone handset out of her pocket and said, 'Ambulance. She's hurt. She's really hurt. Please . . . please hurry.'

NINE DAYS IN HELL

'And if the roses of your garden sang a weird song,
you would go mad.'

Arthur Machen, *The White People*

SIXTY-FOUR

THREE YEARS LATER

Home.

My name is Amber Hare. My name is Amber Hare. My name is Amber Hare.

The bed Amber awoke upon was like a vast winged armchair. Emperor sized and upholstered in leather and chenille: comfortable, protective and nurturing. The mattress was handmade, and constructed out of fifteen hundred pocketed springs. In collusion with sheets and linen crafted from the softest cotton and layered flannel, the bed produced a comfort as close to a mother's arms as anything manmade. She was never in a hurry to leave the bed's embrace and warmth each morning, had forgotten how deep, restful and unbroken sleep could be. Because it had not been any of those things for the last three years.

By the end of her first week in the farmhouse, and her first week back in England for ten months, having spent fifteen thousand pounds on the bed and its accessories was bothering her less than it had at the beginning of the week.

Do people actually live like this?

Six days in residence, six whole days and nights without going any further than the garden and the fragrant interior still surprised her each morning. Right from the moment she rose from the bed, an array of scents wafting through the expanse of open space and misting over every pristine surface seemed to rush forth like eager servants to welcome her into the new day: recent paintwork, fresh plaster and the astringent traces of cut timber mingled with the pollen of new fabric released by the waffle-cream curtains and thick rugs.

Can this be mine?

If she chose to sit for a while in the living room or the dining room to admire her new home, the Aspen leather furniture that moulded her body released little welcoming puffs of exclusivity. And moving through the building put her within reach of an ostentatious tang of polish that dispersed from the hand-scraped, tobacco oak floors in the hall and ground floor rooms.

She never opened the windows of the new house, all recently triple-glazed and fitted with the best Saxon locks. She kept them closed and locked and told herself that she would not countenance the idea of airing the house because these aromas should be preserved. She also knew this was not the sole reason for keeping every point of access secure.

Amidst the scents of the discreetly luxurious she continued to observe the same ritual: wake naturally, make coffee in the kitchen, and then leisurely tour the freshly renovated farmhouse, finishing in the study. From the study she would walk to the new bathroom. Shed her briefs and t-shirt and step into the granite-tiled wet room. To shower for so long her whole body steamed until it was time to be swallowed by a white towelling robe.

After nearly a week, the various floors within the farm-house began to issue a reassuring sense of permanence beneath her tanned feet; a stability combined with the novelty of being in a new place, particularly comforting when she feared she had become addicted to transience.

On this, her sixth morning in residence, with a mug of hot coffee in one hand, she moved again, carefully and patiently like a discharged patient returning home after a long illness, drifting through the four bedrooms on the first floor. Virgin carpets, as thick as bear fur, engulfed her feet to the ankle bone.

The floors of the house were too precious for shoes. There would be a rule about shoes. She wanted nothing from *out there* getting inside. Not that she was planning on entertaining anytime soon. But only on this day of her occupation did she realize that the interior felt less like a show home and more like the best room in a top hotel that she had spent a week inside. Soon it might even feel like a home.

Amber promised herself she would never take the house for granted; she would always notice and appreciate everything inside of it. She had never lived anywhere like this before, nor had she ever expected to.

When she passed through the doorway of the room selected to be the study, air sharpened by the scent of the new leather chair stung the top of her nose. As usual, she made herself look at the view, while toying with the idea of what came next: what she needed to revisit inside the room.

Through the broad double windows she watched the wind ruffle the lawn and move through the trees bordering the garden, gently swaying the tips of the branches. A seagull hovered and trembled high above, as if temporarily trapped against an invisible force-field, until it followed the current of air in the opposite direction to glide away. Before the bird sank from view its large beak opened, but Amber heard no cry.

Inside her home, the atmosphere would remain still, cool and silent in any weather. Not a single draught had prickled her skin in any part of the house.

Sealed.

Even the loudest sounds generated by the outside world seemed unable to penetrate the pristine walls, new doors, or the reglazed windows in their deep casements. Yesterday, from the kitchen windows, with her freshly pedicured feet spread on the flagstone while she made an espresso from her new Grigia coffee machine, she'd watched a helicopter pass over the house. She had strained her ears to catch the faintest whop-whop or buzzy grind of the rotors, but heard nothing.

Opening the doors of the house was like leaving a cinema to return to the grip of a briefly forgotten air temperature, and an immersion in the hectic energy of the street – what people called the real world.

Looking out across the gentle contours of the maize fields beyond the foot of her property, she wiped her eyes. She felt safe.

She would stay here.

This is mine.

Home.

SIXTY-FIVE

By the time Amber had carried all of the treasury boxes into the study and distributed the files through the brushed steel cabinets, and after she had finished attaching all of the selected clippings, pictures and notes to the cork boards mounted on the walls, the view outside her windows had dissolved into darkness and turned the panes of reinforced glass into mirrors.

There was no light pollution from neighbouring properties, because there were no neighbours. There were no primary road routes for three miles either and the closest lane was unlit. The nearest town, Shaldon, could not be seen from anywhere on her property. Even if someone stood in the lane connected to the front drive, the house would not be visible to them.

The original brick walls of the farm yard, further reinforced by an inner ring of mountain ash trees, planted years before, entirely concealed the house from the north-facing front and the building's two sides.

The occupants of the nearest houses had been investigated by a security consultant on her behalf. There were three farming families, and sundry locals comfortably retired. A sparse population that had failed to raise a single criminal record, and not one of them knew who she was. There would be no house warming either. She was entirely alone.

A relocation agency had found the property through a search arranged by her solicitor. The agency had met her requests for total privacy with an exactitude that startled Amber the first time she visited the farmhouse.

Almost one year ago, when the first of her three ocean cruises ended, she'd been driven to the house from Southampton docks by a chauffeured car service to approve the agency's find. After five hours of deliberation and a consultation with an architect, Amber decided this was indeed the place that would become her first home: a building close to the settings of some of the happiest periods of her life, defined by holidays with mum and dad in Goodrington and Torquay, way back when she was eleven, before her mum died, and probably the last time in her life she had been truly happy.

Even after all that had happened during the last three years, the very idea that she could now make bespoke requests to discreet professional firms, established to serve a wealthy clientele, still retained the novelty to swamp her with diffidence and feelings of unworthiness. Though of late she was less surprised by such things. After years of making do and never having much money, she was quickly becoming accustomed to what money concealed and altered beyond recognition. She was even starting to feel less guilty.

Only after the work on her new home was complete and the security system operational, did Amber finally return to the house to find it transformed beyond recognition. Six days ago.

Nine months of the house's new life had been spent under the auspices of master builders and interior designers, who partially rebuilt, and then completely renovated the building's interior to her taste. For the entire time that others searched for her future home, and then remade the farmhouse, she had been at sea, though Amber had not left land to forget. While sailing around the Mediterranean, the West Indies, the Florida Keys, and the Eastern Seaboard of America, she had sought and found distance. And then she'd returned to land to resume the search.

For him.

For it.

For them.

Amber turned in her chair and faced her reflection in the window. A pale face amidst short, blue-black hair peered back at her. She'd never be blonde again.

Out there, beyond her reflection, beyond the boundary of her property, she'd found that she could happily watch the land undulate towards the coast of Torbay for hours, a book open upon her lap and a pot of tea beside her. Three miles of fields used for maize, flanked by pasture for grazing sheep, that she surveyed in the same way she'd so recently surveyed the great tumult of heaving oceans.

On the first day, when she walked in the garden, the nervous bleat of a ewe had carried to her from the distance. She'd seen birds in the trees and on her lawn, but no animals inside the walls. Nothing much bigger than a fox could get inside the grounds without her knowing.

The security system had been installed by a firm endorsed by members of the royal family and a myriad celebrity clients. Any form the size and weight of a small child upwards would activate the halogen security lights and a series of motion sensors connected to alarms that would get a local security company on the phone in seconds, and to her door in twenty minutes guaranteed, if she wished.

The front gate of the grounds could only be opened from inside the house, or with a key fob if she was on foot, or sat inside her Lexus RX 450 on the lane outside. Every point of access could also be locked automatically by Amber from inside the building. On security she had placed no limits on budget.

She reclined her seat before the desk in the study. Sipping at a chilled glass of spiced rum and Coke Zero, she attempted to wipe her mind clear of the emotions and thoughts and memories that had amassed during the day, while she reopened the files and fixed key visual materials to the walls. Alcohol always helped.

When she was ready, she took a long look at the faces tacked on the wall above her desk. Faces she had refused herself more than a glance at through the day, and only to establish their placement on the walls, as if she had merely been hanging framed watercolours to enliven the room. Now she looked right into their eyes.

'I came back. I said I would.'

During the long investigation, the inquest and the writing of her account that had absorbed the first year after her escape, the strangers in the photographs had begun to feel like a group of friends. A strange sense of kinship had occurred between the dead and living victims of the house. By the time she was released into the world and began work on the first of two films she executive-produced, she knew she would never be able to leave the dead people behind; they were not to be ignored or forgotten in the way they had been for so many years.

Besides the only two people she had known – the sole male victim, Ryan Martin, who had once been a boyfriend in her other life, and the girl who had briefly been a house-mate, Margaret Tolka, whom she'd only known in passing – Amber had learned all that she could about the murdered strangers, the other victims: the fifteen.

Amber arranged fifteen tea lights in the long, horizontal pewter holder at the rear of her desk. Carefully, using one of the cook's matches that she kept inside her study, she lit a single candle for each of the victims, including the two who had yet to be identified because they were found without any teeth in their skulls.

Thirteen victims were matched by photographs. For each of the two unidentified women an inclusion on the wall was signified by the picture of a white and pink rose respectively. She called them 'Top Girl Walker' and 'Bedfellow'.

If the first four victims of the house – Lottie Reddie, Virginia Anley, Eudora Fry and Florence Stockton – all murdered ninety years before Amber set foot inside 82 Edgehill Road, had ever been photographed individually, their pictures had not survived or been discovered. An investigative reporter, Peter St John, had found the only photograph that included images of the four: a formal group portrait of a spiritualist society called The Friends of Light. The picture was taken in 1919 on a Bank Holi-day weekend, with the members of the society arranged before the bandstand of Handsworth Park in Birmingham.

This was also the biggest of the photographs attached to the wall because Amber had enlarged her copy so that the relevant faces could be seen more clearly. The faces of the four victims were neatly circled in black ink.

Virginia Anley had a face Amber would never forget, a face she had once dreamed of: the eyes open, the body hanged beneath a tree branch.

Two of the first four victims, Lottie Reddie and Virginia Anley, were found buried in the foundations of the house. Post-mortem, it was determined that their bodies had been cemented into a pair of bespoke soil cavities, dug into the foundations, and laid side by side.

The other two victims from the early twentieth century, Eudora Fry and Florence Stockton, were entombed within fireplaces in the building. Eudora was bricked inside the original fireplace of the second floor bedroom that Amber initially occupied; Eudora had been the first presence to speak at the address, during Amber's first night inside the house.

The fourth woman, Florence Stockton, was the oldest of the four: a widow, who was found behind a walled-up fireplace in the first floor room that Amber had been imprisoned inside for one night, before Fergal had introduced her to the rooms of the ground floor. And it had been Florence Stockton that Amber must have heard on the ceiling of the room, reciting scripture. Verse, she'd since discovered, to be from chapter three of Titus in the *King James Bible*.

The rope used in the executions of all of the first four

victims was once popular for hanging washing in turn-of-the-century Birmingham yards.

The four women had been murdered around 1920 and then buried with the ligature still knotted about their necks. It was proven by the damage to the bones in their spinal columns, and through the way the twine had been cut while suspending a heavy weight, that all of the victims had been hanged first.

Any evidence of what had been presumed to be a sexual motive in the first murders had long been erased by decomposition. But each set of remains was found missing a finger.

This was the second significant connection between each murder at 82 Edgehill Road: the evidence of a missing body part – ears, fingers or teeth, and missing hair in Margaret Tolka's case. The first connection across every era of murder at 82 Edgehill Road was the cause of death: strangulation by ligature.

Peter St John, who became Amber's researcher and co-author in the year after her escape, did discover some information about The Friends of Light, and their spiritual leader, Clarence Putnam, though it was scant. At its peak, the organization had boasted a treasurer, chairman, secretary, and established international links with several churches and spiritualist colleges. Clarence Putnam had been the first owner of 82 Edgehill Road when it was a new build, and also the founder of The Friends of Light. With key members of his congregation, he'd moved from the country to the city before the Great War. He was originally a pastor from Monmouthshire, and a respected authority on pre-Roman British history, who'd become a zealous devotee of spiritualism. Many believed he was gifted with second sight. Any remaining records of his time on earth suggested he had lived an honourable life and he was now buried in St Mary's Church in Handsworth, amongst the fathers of the industrial revolution.

Peter had also connected women reported missing in the Midlands at the time, to the first four victims who were featured in the photograph of The Friends of Light, all of whom possessed a connection to 82 Edgehill Road, which had been used by the group as a spiritualist meeting house. Peter had even beaten the police to the information and broken the Friends of Light story, and it had been Peter St John's feature in *The Sunday Times* that had compelled Amber to make contact with him through her barrister.

All four victims had been declared missing by their families between 1920 and 1924. Although initially treated as suspicious by local police, no one had ever been suspected of their murder, nor held responsible for their disappearances.

The membership of the group was unremarkable: a collection of grieving Christian souls, many of whom had lost sons and husbands and fathers at the front in the Great War.

Peter and Amber hadn't provided much information about the first four murders in their co-authored book, *No One Gets Out Alive*, because they'd discovered little evidence, material or anecdotal, about the disappearances. Someone known to all four of the women, and probably a member of The Friends of Light, perhaps Clarence Putnam himself as it was his house, had murdered them and hidden their bodies at 82 Edgehill Road. And as Peter had said to Amber on numerous occasions: 'This part will go all Jack the Ripper, but no one will ever really know who killed the first four, or why.'

Following the demise of The Friends of Light sometime around 1926, the house was left mostly vacant for twenty-five years until it was bought at auction by plasterer Harold Bennet in 1952. The house had remained the property of the local church to whom Clarence Putnam bequeathed it, and was subsequently occupied and quickly vacated at least five times between 1926 and 1952. No explanation was ever discovered for why the building could not keep its tenants.

Only one other interesting fact about the earlier life of the address had been uncovered by Peter St John: during the Second World War, a local council report claimed that gypsy émigrés had occupied the building: an elderly woman and her blind grandson. They had been evicted, judged insane, and rehoused in a Somerset asylum during the Blitz.

Amber finished her drink. She'd known for a long time that the nine days she'd spent at 82 Edgehill Road, three wearying years ago, needed to take a backseat; there was little more she could ever learn about that period of time. *Her time.* Despite Peter St John's dead ends, the new search must concern the preceding one hundred years; a story that occurred long before she crossed the threshold of *that place*.

The last time they'd spoken on the phone, Peter had claimed he had something for her. Not much, but it was the *something* that was now burning a hole through her mind.

SIXTY-SIX

PIMP MURDERED AT BIRMINGHAM BROTHEL.

That had been the first headline. And it was the first cutting Amber considered the evening she resumed the search.

Memory swiftly brought nausea.

The opening story broke the afternoon that she and Svetlana were found at the house by two police officers and a paramedic, who had been first on the scene. Amber had heard a news report on a radio at the police station. For a few moments she had not realized the story was about her and Svetlana. No names were mentioned at that stage; she wished it had stayed that way.

The news of the 'murder' initially only made headlines in Midlands' newspapers and media. But further revelations from 82 Edgehill Road were blaring from national news broadcasters by ten p.m. Within weeks, hundreds of hours of coverage about the case were screened in Great Britain, following the gruesome reports of what had been found in a scrappy back yard in North Birmingham. Once it had been widely established that the case was unique, most major European news services and broadcasters were also following the minutiae of the criminal investigation too. From Europe the story quickly found a global audience.

POLICE SEARCH GARDEN AT 82 EDGEHILL ROAD.

One entire wall, from desk top to eye level, contained only the highlights: the triggers to help Amber organize her memories. Her recollections would inform the wider research she now needed to embark upon. Because this story was a long way from finished.

SEX WORKER TURNED KILLER.

The cuttings had a pertinent subtext. A second, more personal story was being told on the wall, about the world's endlessly changing perception of her former self, Stephanie Booth: victim, perpetrator, collaborator, martyr, victim.

Amber guessed she could paper the entire first floor interior of the farmhouse with stories about her old identity, and with stories solely from the British media.

PIMP CASTRATED AND BURNED WITH ACID: WHAT A SEX WORKER DID TO SURVIVE.

Only now, sat in her study, and looking at the patchwork mosaic of newsprint, photocopied pages from online sites, and photographs secured during the research for her book, could she better comprehend what the world's perspective of Stephanie Booth had been, and also of the victims and their killers. And she remembered very quickly that she'd never cared for much of it, and still didn't.

SECOND KILLER STILL AT LARGE.

Even with the horrors of the house still fresh in her mind, the media had shown no quarter. They had made her absorb a peculiar brand of vindictive persecution to accompany the black horror she had literally crawled through, stained by blood and urine.

POLICE TEAR DOWN WALLS.

It was the media that had driven her into what two doctors had called 'emotional breakdowns', not the house. The house had left scars, had stolen things from her she could not replace, but she had beaten the house and escaped whatever occupied it. The world, however, could not be defeated, and its media was incalculably different. Her best defence had been the screaming of her own story straight into the maelstrom of competing voices; the opinionated and ill-informed voices that always knew better. So she'd screamed and then disappeared.

My name is Amber Hare.

But she would never forgive the world for what it had done, nor trust it again. Because of how it had *interpreted* her without restraint or remorse, for the purposes of its own entertainment.

CASTRATRIX GETS DOZENS OF MARRIAGE PROPOSALS EVERY WEEK.

The words and images on the wall jerked awake a flurry of dormant feelings that simultaneously made her panic, want to laugh hysterically, and also made her feel as though her heart was bursting. After one year at sea, gazing into a distance so old and dark, an immensity she'd hoped would scour her mind in the way salt water cleaned all traces of former occupation from shells upon the shore, Amber had feared these very cuttings. It had taken a long time to rediscover the courage, and the will, to return to this time in her life. She had never underestimated the past, but had also never anticipated the force with which memory could return. Memory might even be insanity.

In a clinch of terror, accompanied by what she sensed was a plummet in her blood's temperature, she was briefly convinced that she must never leave her sanctuary.

Just in case.

Stop!

Only three people in the world – a solicitor, her agent, and a private security consultant – knew she was here, why she was here, and who she was.

STEPHANIE GOES INTO HIDING.

Amber was under no illusion as to why she now sat in the largest room upstairs in her new home, why she had made herself sit inside a space dedicated to one of the worst cases of serial murder, abduction, torture and sexual depravity that Great Britain had known. She was sitting here, as she had known she would during those months at sea, for the same reason she had stopped the course of anti-depressants during the first year following her release from the house. And even though she had observed the recommended course of counselling for victims of violence and sufferers of post-traumatic shock, and gracefully submitted to numerous psychological and physical tests, she had resisted most opportunities to forget, to forgive, or to ameliorate her experience.

She wanted to remember. And even when she took her mother's maiden name, Hare, and transformed herself into Amber Hare, anonymous lottery winner, her need for the truth endured as her mind endured.

She may have survived, but she would not fool herself

that she was free, or ever would be free. What happened inside 82 Edgehill Road would, and should, distinguish the rest of her life, and define her, and no one could persuade her otherwise. It would take a long time to put back that which had been taken from her.

But more than anything else, what had occurred at 82 Edgehill Road had not finished, not even when she was stretchered out of the building, because *he* was still missing.

Fergal.

And what *he* took from the bowels of the abomination that had masqueraded as an ordinary rundown residential address in North Birmingham, had never been recovered either.

It.

Black Maggie.

The details of the coroner's long inquest and the theories of criminologists, the Serious Crimes Analysis, Behavioural Profiling, Geographical Profiling and Physical Evidence teams, the essays by forensic psychiatrists, the arguments of lawyers and journalists – all of these records, filed inside the steel cabinets that surrounded her desk, were only part of the story: the acceptable surface and the last known chapter, but not much more.

Now was the time to go back in. It was an acknowledgement that brought her no joy, but a recognition of a duty; a duty supported by a desire for resolution. Nor was the plunge she was about to take into *that place* a descent to be taken solely for herself. This was for her friends up there on the wall.

Amber swallowed the last of her drink. Then went and retrieved the bottle of Sailor Jerry rum from the kitchen.

She returned to the study and refilled her glass. The measure was larger and she didn't add Coke.

SIXTY-SEVEN

MAN KILLED WITH BRICK. WOMAN STRANGLED.

Until the police took her back to the house to move the investigation into the second stage, Amber had never been in the garden of 82 Edgehill Road; she had only ever seen the rear of the property from the kitchen and stairwell windows, and she had only ever known that part of the address as a patch of neglected, unpleasant, and yet incongruously fecund land that encroached upon the refuse-strewn patio. The patio appeared in her mind now as a polluted shoreline, between the house and the explosion of wild vines, hanging fruit and weeds that reached near head height to the rear fence of the garden.

But for a long time, the police did not believe her encounters with the garden had been so slight. The press certainly didn't believe this was the case, and as a consequence the general public were also convinced of her deeper involvement in the murders.

Only a self-prescribed treatment of work had sufficed as an effective escape: telling her own story, the true story, that most had refused to believe, with the help of Peter St John. And then telling the story again with a documentary film-maker, Kyle Freeman, in the film *Closer by Darkness than Light*. Before she added weight to the feature film

426

adaptation of her book, *Nine Days in Hell*, by taking the role of executive-producer. *Nine Days in Hell* was still being seen by a great many people around the world, and the movie was already three months into a theatrical run in the UK. *Nine Days* was only an *interpretation* of her story, but Amber acknowledged that the feature film had achieved a greater rehabilitation of her image than her release from police custody and the verdict of the coroner's inquest.

The film recast her as an innocent victim, a role that had finally begun to stick, to the disappointment of so many for whom fifteen murders and an incalculable number of rapes was not sufficient sensation. They wanted a living scapegoat into which to pour their bile, and in some cases, their desire. But Amber's newly returned status of victim-survivor would never be universally shared or observed; she only had to look online to understand this.

Revisiting the exacting detail of her experiences, and all that was discovered about 82 Edgehill Road, may have been painful and exhausting enough to leave her close to collapse twice, but the process was just and ultimately rewarding. For Amber, the book and films were not entertainment; they were testimony. And the truth had subsequently made her very rich.

Amber closed her eyes and recalled her first breathless, jumbled accounts at Perry Barr Police Station; how she had wept with relief, horror, sorrow and despair, when trying to speak, to communicate so much, and all at once.

She clenched her eyes shut and moved on.

There had been treatment for her injuries, and her clothes bearing three blood types were taken away and put inside evidence bags. Within hours of her arrest for Knacker's murder, she had told the solicitor appointed to her and the detectives that first interviewed her that she believed Ryan Martin and a prostitute from Albania, known as Margaret, were buried in the garden, and probably inside polythene and probably behind the oak tree.

She had been correct on both accounts.

Two of the house's last three fatalities had suffered massive head traumas. Ryan Martin had been kicked unconscious and then finished off with a house brick. He had to be identified by a distinctive birthmark on his left ankle.

The girl she had known as Margaret had also suffered a massive head trauma, but had been killed by strangulation with ligature; her killer had left the garden twine in place and within her plastic shroud. The spool of twine the garrotte had been cut from was discovered in the kitchen of the disused ground floor flat.

What the press never knew at the time was that, unlike all of the other victims, whose spindly and disarticulated remains would soon be discovered and brought back into the world from various unconsecrated tombs scattered about the property, only Margaret and Ryan were buried fully dressed. The only other distinguishing feature of their murders was missing hair and teeth.

Once her week-old remains were recovered from a shallow grave, a large section of Margaret's hair was found to have been removed post-mortem. Ryan had lost six teeth, two from his upper jaw, four from the bottom. Only four of these teeth were ever recovered by forensic detectives.

For most of the life of the investigation, this was not seen as significant when considering everything else that would soon, literally, be unearthed at the address. The inquest only served to record the known facts of the case and the details of her own gruelling experience. What few were able to accept was the greater and older mystery that she alluded to, and that remained unsolved. The role of the stolen teeth and hair in the story would never be understood until Fergal Donegal was apprehended; or, as Amber hoped, his own tatty remains were uncovered in a place as lonely and miserable as the one where he had interred his victims.

Amber closed her eyes and clenched her hands until her fingernails hurt her palms. Reliving this was going to be the hardest part of being alone in the house. The pain in her hands returned her to the present. She opened her moist eyes and stared at the next headline.

SIXTY-EIGHT

GARDEN OF EVIL: TWO MORE BODIES.

Amber rose from her chair to touch the pictures of Simona Doubrava and Olena Kovalik, pinned side by side beneath the tabloid headline that took the investigation and media interest to a whole new level: the game-changers.

One week after the discovery of Ryan and Margaret, the rear grounds of the entire property were excavated on her insistence that there were more bodies. And five feet from the poorly interred bodies of Margaret Tolka and Ryan Martin, two other sets of human remains were discovered on the first day of the excavation.

She had never subsequently considered one girl without thinking of the other; they were even found buried in the garden like occupants of a family plot. The horrible and painful way in which they were extinguished at the hands of Arthur Bennet, and embraced by the arms of death, was something the two girls also shared.

Halfway through her third or fourth glass of rum, Amber felt a surge of bitterness that became a cinnamon-tinged reflux. This point in the investigation signalled the first indication of police unease. And the distrust in her statements lingered until she was finally released without charge, one year after being stretchered out of the house covered in Svetlana and Knacker McGuire's blood.

Six feet from the oak tree, Olena Kovalik had been found in the overgrown garden; she was lying face down beneath three foot of black, stony soil and refuse-strewn weeds. Naked and wrapped in an opaque polythene sheet, Kovalik's remains had been reduced over time to a foul soup of hair, decomposed tissue and bodily organs, through which mottled bones had protruded like dead tree branches from a marsh.

Forensic analysis of the position of Kovalik's leg bones, and the position of the ligature, created a belief that her ankles had once been tied to her throat by garden twine. This had been the cause of death: the twine had slowly and fatally strangled the twenty-four-year-old woman, but only after she had been buried alive beneath the cold earth.

Olena Kovalik's grave had been dug into the uneven ground ten feet before the garden shed, itself situated close to the rear fence and a row of fir trees screening 82 Edgehill Road from the adjoining properties in the next street.

Simona's remains were found three feet away from Olena's in much the same condition, face down again. But it was believed that although Doubrava's wrists and ankles had been tied, and she had been strangled, the girl had additionally been buried with her pelvis and buttocks raised over a crude cairn of broken house bricks, as if in provocation. In death as in life she had been denied dignity.

Olena Kovalik was Ukrainian; Simona Doubrava was Czech. They were known to have worked as prostitutes at

82 Edgehill Road between 1999 and 2001. They were identified by their dental records and gold fillings. Their teeth were intact. Determining missing hair was not possible, but each girl had a toe missing. Murdered by strangulation and then mutilated. Murders attributed to the life-long sex offender Arthur Bennet, deceased; the last owner of what would soon become the most notorious house in Britain.

Amber sniffed and wiped the tears from her cheeks.

Only one of the girls had ever been reported missing: Simona Doubrava.

Olena Kovalik's family had not notified the authorities of her disappearance, a fact that Amber realized was still capable of making her cry whenever she saw the girl's photograph. The same fate of contemptuous neglect would probably have been her own had she died with her face wrapped inside Knacker's cheap plastic bag.

When Amber first saw pictures of Olena, photographs mostly from various European police departments who had arrested the girl for soliciting and minor drugs offences in Belgium and Germany, Stephanie immediately knew where she had seen the girl before: standing in the garden beside an abandoned and soiled mattress, smoking a cigarette.

Olena Kovalik had turned tricks to feed a drug habit that an old boyfriend and petty criminal had introduced her to in 1996. How she came to Britain was not known, but she had probably begun working for Bennet voluntarily, though the full facts of their arrangement were not known and probably never would be; few records were kept in the criminal underworld.

More was known about Simona Doubrava. She had left home and crossed the borders of her country without realizing her visa was fraudulent; she had thought she was going to work as a PA to a managing director of a software company in Munich, but soon discovered she had been duped by an organized criminal gang and was put to work in various brothels across Europe, initially in Odessa where she was forced to pleasure long-distance freight drivers.

By the time Simona Doubrava was shipped to England, prostitution was all she had known. Effectively, she had been a sex slave from the age of seventeen. She was acquired by Bennet through someone he'd met in prison, while serving time for attempted rape in 1997.

Several customers of 82 Edgehill Road around the time of Simona Doubrava's death were traced; two had even come forward to assist the police investigation. Both men recognized the petite, raven-haired girl who bore a distinct resemblance to a young Jane Seymour. They said she had spoken good but heavily accented English.

To widespread horror, it was believed that Simona had probably never actually been outside 82 Edgehill Road once she'd first entered the building; two witnesses admitted she had been secured to the bed while 'entertaining' them. One was certain he had met Simona Doubrava on many occasions in a first floor room – the very room, Amber realized, that was next to her own at the address.

When the same witness, who'd been a regular customer at the house, was told by Arthur Bennet that Simona was no longer working from number 82, and that the girl had returned home to Poland, the witness had become suspicious but had felt unable to share his concerns. At the time he had been married with three children, but the witness had known Simona was Czech and not Polish because they had often spoken about Prague.

The witness, or her 'boyfriend' as he referred to himself, had been upset by the girl's sudden departure and admitted to having fallen in love with her. He'd always wondered what had become of her, and even claimed that he and Simona Doubrava had discussed her escape from Bennet, whom she loathed. It is possible that such a scheme for Simona Doubrava's liberation had hastened her death. As Amber knew, the house had an uncanny way of learning everything about a person.

Against the advice of her solicitor, Amber had insisted on telling the detectives that she had never been sure, at the start of her residency, whether the other girls that she had seen or heard inside the house were even alive. She assured the police that she had seen Olena Kovalik in the garden on two occasions; and possibly once more too, ascending the stairs and then entering a room on the second floor.

Enough evidence of Olena Kovalik's hair was discovered to attest to the fact that she had indeed once occupied the improperly cleaned second floor room.

Amber also speculated that it had been the Ukrainian, Simona Doubrava, who had wept nightly in the room next to her own on the first floor. An exhaustive forensic sweep of that room also confirmed Amber's hunch, with the discovery of just enough DNA belonging to Doubrava.

Neither the police, nor the judiciary, nor the press believed in ghosts, which disinclined them to believe

Amber, despite the uncanny accuracy of her testimony. The investigators surmised that Amber had been told by her captors, 'the McGuires', which rooms had once belonged to the murdered women, and that they must have received the same information from the girls' killer, Arthur Bennet, before he died of pneumonia caused by exposure in the bedroom of the ground floor flat. Which was exactly what her solicitor advised Amber would happen if she ever claimed to have seen or heard Doubrava and Kovalik at the address, because the girls had been murdered over a decade before she ever set foot in Birmingham. And, as everyone knows, the dead don't speak, or move.

Amber insisted she had *experienced* their apparitions, and the supernatural direction of her testimony contributed to the success of her book, the popularity of the Kyle Freeman documentary, and the record-breaking success of the Hollywood film. But the paranormal angle that Amber championed accounted for officialdom's distaste for both her and her testimony, as well as the total condemnation by the other victims' surviving families. And that had been the hardest thing of all to endure.

You saying that my daughter is not at peace? That she is still in hell? That he is still raping them . . . You are wicked, wicked . . . as wicked as he was. How could you? My Kelly. My girl. My little girl . . .

Amber would never forget the day of the inquest when the elderly mother of Kelly Hughes, whose remains were found beneath the first floor bathroom, broke down and had to be removed from the room. And as Amber thought of the scene again, her eyes thickened afresh with tears.

'I am not a liar'. Amber had stated that simple fact

435

over and over again to police officers and lawyers and psychiatrists and counsellors and horrified parents for one entire year.

Her own father had never lied and she had followed the example of the kindest man she had ever known. And in the darkest places only kindness matters.

SIXTY-NINE

HELL HOUSE: GIRL BURIED UNDER BATH.

There she was, young and blue-eyed and blonde and happy. Kelly Hughes. A musician, a devout Christian, unquestionably a virgin, who had taken a place at the Birmingham Conservatoire to study violin but disappeared one week before term started, presumably abducted from a bus stop in West Bromwich in 1979. Never to be seen again until her bones and their parchment flesh, the colour of age-spotted papyrus, were brought lipless and grimacing from beneath a cheap bath on the first floor of 82 Edgehill Road.

Strangled and wrapped in polythene. But not murdered and hidden by Fergal or Knacker, because Hughes had died twenty-seven years before the McGuires' reign as the kings of ruin and depravity at number 82; nor had Kelly Hughes died in the grubby clutches of the convicted sex offender Arthur Bennet.

It was soon determined by the age of Kelly's remains that Arthur Bennet had been a mere apprentice to a master. And the master was Harold Bennet, his own father; a man who had murdered seven women inside the building.

Amber closed her eyes. The darkness juddered behind

her eyelids. She stood up before the judder became a swoop, went for a window to gulp fresh air. Then paused and decided against opening the study window. She closed the blinds instead.

Too much. Too much rum. Too many memories, too much horror. Too much all at once.

Amber left the study and closed the door on it all.

Number 82 had pulled her back inside itself; yanked her out of comfort and back between the dim brownish walls, close to the relics the house had reluctantly given up after her escape.

The house had been demolished; every trace of the building to its black foundations had been removed and covered with cement, poured deep and wide. There was no number 82 any more. Between numbers 80 and 84 there was a smooth concrete surface that Birmingham City Council swept twice a week. And in the middle of the concrete plane stood a simple memorial, upon which fresh flowers were still thrown over floral tributes that had withered and blackened.

But the house had maintained a second life inside her mind for three years; in a quiet back street of her memories, 82 Edgehill Road had been rebuilt, brick by brick. And Amber had just called again upon a house that was still full of voices and footsteps and the cries of women and fierce white faces contorted into snarls that spat and shouted . . .

. . . and they rose inside their plastic shrouds . . .

. . . and round the table in the black room they still peered at the ceiling in ecstasy . . .

. . . around their hidden feet she *uncoiled heavily and . . .*

. . . opened white eyes.

'No!'

Amber wanted to slip her fingers inside her mind and pluck out, from the moist black roots, the returned images of the slim female bones, browned by age and carelessly abandoned inside silty polythene wrappers. And she wanted to scrape out the photographed faces with their freckles and smiles and braces and mousy hair faded by time and the sunlight's bleach. Because they were all inside her mind again and jostling for attention. Pleading for release and for salvation. Like they had when she'd lain shivering in the old beds of those strange rooms.

But Amber had told them they must stay on the walls and outside of her heart; that was the deal. And not pour through her mind like screaming children released from the iron doors of some terrible school, every time she looked at their faces.

As she moved away from the study on unsteady legs, the spiteful words and hurtful looks of those who'd investigated and interviewed her also flickered alive, and loudly broadcast their voices from her mind's memory tracks, all on repeat with no fade. They were interspersed with looped flashes of interview rooms, courtrooms, ante chambers, and so many other municipal rooms that she had lost count of; plain rooms she had sat inside, on plastic chairs, to repeat her story, and repeat her story, and repeat her story . . .

You mutilated him. You burned the genitals off his body with acid.

You cut his tongue in half with your dirty fingernails.

439

You cut his throat with broken glass.
You stamped on his face while he was in agony.
You threw acid in a man's face.
*Disproportionate response . . . disproportionate response
. . . what were you thinking? . . . You expect us to believe
that you saw ghosts?*

'No! No! Piss off! I am not a liar!'

Inside her own mind she could return to *that house* at
any time, just like she had done every day for the first year
in custody.

The police had tried to grind the truth out of her with
their raised voices in their plain rooms; the very same
truth that she had uttered within three hours of being carried out of *that place* on a stretcher.

Too much. Too hasty.

One thing at a time. She had been careless. Was drunk.
Hadn't paid attention to how many of those spicy rums
had been slipping down her throat so easily, unlocking
inner doors like gatecrashing oafs at a house party; doors
that should only be opened one by one, day by day, week
by week, and not too many at once. Time could rewind
quicker than she could think.

In the corridor outside her study, Amber stopped
moving until her vision and balance were partially, but not
wholly, restored. Applying more effort than dignity was
ever comfortable with, she carefully moved to her bedroom.

She turned on all of the first floor lights as she made
uneasy progress through the farmhouse, including all of
the lights in her room, before she undressed and climbed
into her bed.

SEVENTY

They were patting their hands against the walls of the house.

Outside the building in the total darkness of a rural night, the thumps of poorly coordinated arms, that sought and eventually found the windows and doors, carried up to where she lay in bed.

Amidst the bumps and scrapings there came whispers from voices either dreary and muffled with sleep, or sharpened at the foothills of a private panic.

'What is my name? . . . before here . . . that time . . . nowhere . . . to where the other . . . the cold . . . is my name? . . .'

Amber shivered in the cold and tried to remember where she was. She could not understand why the room around her was so dark. Instinctively, she knew it should not be like this.

Someone below the window was talking. Maybe not to her, though she could not be sure. 'And then you said . . . I said . . . I wouldn't . . . unreasonable . . . but who was I . . . you, you told me . . . you swore . . . it was . . . meant something . . . a sign . . . frightened, the more I . . . and now I know . . .'

The first one to get inside the building began to speak

from the hall downstairs. '. . . involved . . . you are . . . you said . . . not that simple . . . must understand . . .'

Bare feet scuffled upon the stairs, supported by further evidence of movement: a fumbling out there in the darkness, as if someone aged and blind was determined to find her. The tone of the voice from the stairs was stiff with accusation. 'Not going . . . refuse. I said it. I said it . . . wouldn't stop . . . and look . . . what happened . . . the lights . . . even listening?'

The first visitor to rise from the foot of Amber's bed came off the floor quickly. She could not see who it was, but she heard the trespasser sigh as it reached full height. Thick polythene crinkled as the limbs flexed within their coverings.

'What is the time?'

But it was not terror or shock that knocked Amber out of sleep. The smell of an old, dirty house from a past life, and the scent of those who had walked its corridors and cried out from behind so many walls and doors, gathered like a heavy black smoke and sank down to where she lay. And it was the stench of these things that choked her awake.

SEVENTY-ONE

Amber sat in the kitchen and watched the sun rise over the trees at the end of the garden.

She had been drunk. A half empty bottle of rum, dehydration and a feeling of seasickness was sufficient evidence of excess. And she had immersed herself too quickly and too deeply in the faces and the stories that were shut inside the study. So many familiar eyes, smiling out of the old photographs beside yellowing headlines, all but forgotten in the world beyond her doors, had made the recollections materialize beyond the reach of her control.

That is all it was.

No one who came close to understanding what she had suffered, and what she knew, would hold her to account over a nightmare endured at any time for the remainder of her life. And since post-production on the feature film had finished, she had not examined the story of 82 Edgehill Road, and her leading role within it, in any way similar to last night's scrutiny. Post-production was a year distant. So the cause of her recent relapse was obvious. And when you are alone, as she knew so well, it just takes longer to calm down.

She turned on the radio, tuned it to a local station. She half listened to a joyous report of fecundity in parts of

South Devon: the size of the soft fruits, tomatoes, potatoes, wheat, the market gardens in bloom like never before, the best harvest in decades. She watched the same headlines every night on the local television. The cheery news made her feel better. This was a good time, this was a good sign. She was in a place of beauty, of growth; she would be healed by nature, by the sea air, the sun . . .

But how could she lay to rest this uneasy suggestion, the one she'd failed to dispel, that the nightmare she had suffered was distinctly different to those she had experienced during the first two years that followed her escape from *that place*? And, in both intensity and clarity, the nightmare was an exception to the dreams she'd endured while at sea. Those dreams had been nonsensical, old fragments reviving and blending with current situations: Knacker capering around the ship's decks, dressed like a teenager and trying to sell drugs to wealthy octogenarians; Fergal captaining a ship in dress whites, his gingery face grinning from beneath a peaked cap; The Friends of Light holding a séance at an adjoining table in a restaurant.

The scars of her experience had manifested in curious ways. The ruffle and rustle of plastic would never be mere background noise again; polythene had lost its utilitarian innocence three years ago. She would be unable to live anywhere within view of a late Victorian house; the very design of certain houses made her shudder inwardly when passing them in the street. She had run from rooms to prove her aversion to the smell of Paco Rabanne aftershave, which brought on anxiety attacks. Her first sighting of cut hair on the tiled floor of a hairdresser's salon, where she had her own long hair cut off and the remainder dyed black, had made her nauseous. Dust was something she could not abide on the floor of any room she crossed. She would never again sleep in a room that contained a fireplace; they had all been removed and the chimney flues filled before she took possession of the farmhouse.

Most of her more recent dreams she only half remembered after she'd awoken, their traces mere lingering discomforts that ceased unsettling her when their obvious absurdity was consciously confronted in daylight. Some dreams still made her call out and cry in her sleep, but there were fewer and fewer of those now. The shock of the surreal scenarios had lessened as time flowed behind the new course she had set in her life; as greater distances moved her away from *that place*.

The dream last night had been different. It had possessed textures that dreams should not emit: scents, temperatures, sounds and voices too loud and clear to be produced from the muddle of an unconscious mind.

She had been inside the farmhouse, she was sure of that, but it was transformed into another building, and one she had also once dreamed inside and in just such a vivid way; she had experienced things inside that other place that were also impossible, as doctors and therapists and counsellors had told her patiently, in reasonable voices, and in so many soothing rooms.

The dream had come too easily, as if provoked by the mere act of thinking about the house and the dead girls, by letting her heart reach out.

What did I do?

Amber watched the clock on the microwave. As soon as it was fully light she would go out and . . . *do something* ... drive. Drive anywhere. Maybe visit a nearby town or seafront, go to an aquarium, a zoo, ride on a steam train, idle along a beach, eat a cream tea, because she no longer wanted to be alone in her new home.

The motivation to leave the house made her angry.

Already?

She felt tricked by the farmhouse, as if it had retaught her contentment, but used the promise of happiness as bait.

Intent on a shower and change of clothes, she paused at the foot of the staircase and looked up at the smooth walls and rosewood banisters. Her stomach clenched on coffee and residues of rum. Her neck and shoulders tensed. She was apprehensive about climbing these stairs and walking deeper inside her beautiful home. Up there, inside the study, were the mementoes that would make her dream of terrible things, over and over again, in a place she wanted to be at peace.

It'll never end because you won't let it end.

Burn the fucking lot!

Fingers spread wide on her cheeks, she closed her eyes. At least one year had passed since she had felt like this; since she had felt this bad. She'd almost forgotten how bad it could be.

Was you finking you could just walk away, girl? That we wouldn't find you, yeah? You is taking the piss, girl.

Yeah. Yeah. You owe us three years' rent on that room. Ho, ho, ho.

Was you finking you could take McGuires for cunts?

Stop! Stop!

She opened her eyes.

Don't let them back in. Not their voices. *Never again.* Because when she heard the squeaking of the rats that she'd put down in that shit-tip of a house, she would see the two cruel and bony faces in her mind again. She would open a dialogue, a discourse she had endured most every day for a year after she'd escaped them, as they chattered and cajoled and manipulated and twisted her mind. It had taken one year of cognitive behavioural therapy to silence their voices.

Amber climbed the stairs.

Halfway up she saw the dust: a large tuft of sooty dross lying insolently on a middle step.

SEVENTY-TWO

A memory of her driving instructor saying, 'Who are you signalling to?' irritated Amber and she switched the indicator off.

She'd passed her driving test two months before embarking on the first ocean cruise and now instinctively indicated every time she turned the Lexus, irrespective of whether there were any cars on the road. But anything that made you a bit safer was good; you could never have enough safety in your life.

She applied the handbrake and reached for the key fob on the key ring that hung from the ignition. As soon as she depressed the button in the middle of the fob, a shiver passed through the metal bars of the gate at the top of the drive. The locks disengaged and the barrier began to open.

Back to the compound: home.

At the beginning, and now at the end of her first week she'd seen the same white car on the lane outside her home. She knew it belonged to the nearest neighbour, so was nothing to be afraid of. She'd never seen any other cars pass the house. Few motorists used the road anyway, which was fortunate because the tarmac was barely wide enough for one vehicle.

Glancing into the rear seat, she surveyed the results of

her successful shopping trip that had concluded one hour before sunset. She'd spent a day moving between Totnes and Torquay and had set off back to the house at seven p.m. because of her aversion to driving at night. In the rear of the vehicle bags of fresh fruit and organic vegetables, bought at a farmers' market, were neatly packed inside fabric bags-for-life; she kept the bags in the car to remove the possibility of ever having her shopping packed in plastic. Two ornamental stone owls destined for the patio of the rear garden continued in their ability to amuse her, as did the bedding plants, grow bags and stone pots she had bought impulsively, when suddenly overcome by the idea that she should make the house more her own.

Magazines and a good haul of books from Waterstones, plus a dozen DVDs and two HBO box sets of series she had missed while at sea, would account for a few weeks' worth of relaxing evenings. Anything else she'd forgotten to buy at the start of the week rolled about inside the shoulder bag that had fallen into the footwell of the passenger seat.

The gate finished its shuddering arc and was now open. Amber released the handbrake. Out of another ingrained instinct, she took a glance into the rear view mirror.

The lane behind her was clear of traffic, but who was that standing at the side of the road, at the corner before the hedgerow curved out of sight?

Amber flinched and removed her foot from the clutch pedal. Was thrown forward in her seat. The car was still in gear. The engine stalled. A light flashed and something beeped in alarm on the dashboard, the sound adding an impetus to the shriek inside her mind. Her hand scrabbled for the ignition key to restart the car quickly.

The Lexus rumbled alive. She turned her head and peered through the rear windshield.

The lane behind her vehicle was empty.

'No you don't.'

She hit the switch for the electric windows on her arm rest. The windows rose with a whir. She reversed onto the road to face the direction in which she'd seen the figure in the lane, then squeezed the key fob to close the gate.

One hand on the steering wheel, the other thrusting the gear stick up to third, Amber revved the engine and drove up the lane to the curve in the road.

There were no inlets to the fields opposite her property; the hedgerow was too thick to climb through and there was no footpath, just a narrow drainage ditch, a thin grassy verge, and then tarmac. When she'd first seen the lanes around her home she was reminded of bobsleigh chutes. If someone was standing in the lane, just before it bent out of view, they should still be on the road and visible the moment she rounded the bend.

Would the man, because it had been a man, a very tall man, even have had the time to move out of sight while she turned the engine over and reversed? Maybe, but he would have had to move fast to remove himself from sight. Even on such long legs it would have been a stretch. Perhaps he had dropped down into the ditch to hide himself. Maybe a man could lie flat and be invisible from the road. But on closer inspection, in a surveillance sharpened by anxiety and fear, she could see that the grassy drainage trench was not deep; not even a rabbit would escape her view into the depression.

Amber slowed down and put the Lexus into second gear to take the bend. She held her breath as her car nosed around the curve in the road.

She was presented with a view of a long empty incline that rose to the top of the hill she had so recently descended. There was no one in the road.

But she had seen the figure of a man. A man standing on the grass verge looking directly at her vehicle. He had been watching her, there was no doubt in her mind; such a figure was not something she could have merely imagined.

Or was it?

Amber continued to the first section of road wide enough to turn her car around. The manoeuvre became a ten point turn, her judgement and control of the vehicle spoiled by her state of mind. She stalled the Lexus again before she managed to move the car back in the direction of her home.

During her slow return journey to the farmhouse, she scrutinized the hedgerow on either side of the road again, looked for a break in the foliage through which a gangly figure might have slipped into the surrounding fields, where it might then crouch down and grin, pleased with itself, after having intentionally shown itself to her.

Because he *has found you.*

The dream. A sign.

Such was her desire to get back onto the front drive, and to shut herself inside the walls of her property, that Amber shot the Lexus through the open gates as soon as the metal bars clanked and wobbled three parts open, nearly scraping one glossy black door on a gatepost. From here on, the motion sensors would trip the alarms if anyone clambered over the walls or the front gate.

Amber parked close to the front door of the farmhouse. Abandoned her shopping and scrambled out of the Lexus to get to the porch. Eyes flitting in her sockets to take in the front garden, trees, and the top of the walls, she let herself into the house. Then closed the front door.

In the hall, which she had never been so pleased to see, she realized that in her panic she had left her handbag in the car. Which meant the pepper spray was back inside the Lexus. She remembered the spares in her bedside cabinet, close to a bed she had, until recently, slept so peacefully inside.

Mobile phone clutched in one hand, the fingers of her other pawing at the panic button set inside the silver locket that she kept around her neck on a chain, Amber ran for the stairs. And nearly fell at the top.

The sight of a mouse with a long black tail would not have surprised her as much as the sight of the dust on the top step: grey, furred, and no bigger than a golf ball, trailing tendrils of what appeared to be black hair.

He's inside.

Amber depressed the panic button. Then stood still as the alarms began to scream in the hallways, both upstairs and downstairs.

Fumbling down one wall, her balance shot by fear, she moved towards her bedroom and realized that in the din of the alarms she'd be unable to hear the sounds of an intruder.

Get to the bedroom. Get it out. Get it out. Get it out.

452

It took a reckless, unthinking impulse to get across the threshold of her bedroom; she worried *he* might be standing behind the door, or lying on the floor at the side of her bed. She would have to get mirrors positioned in every room of the house, like road safety mirrors, so she could make sure that each room in the house was empty before she entered.

There was no one inside her room.

Nonetheless, she could not get to the bedside cabinet fast enough to unlock her armoury. On the ring that contained the keys for the house and car, her frantic fingers located the key for the locked safety deposit box.

She unlocked the box, flipped the lid. Then tore the black Beretta out of its grey spongy moulding; an illegal handgun she had acquired online, after working out what to ask for on a website forum.

Safety catch off, the gun gripped in one hand, she scooped up the can of pepper spray from the drawer and tucked it into the back pocket of her jeans, then ran to the door to lock herself inside the bedroom. The shriek of the alarms muted.

Her phone was vibrating; she hadn't heard the ringtone because of the alarms. She answered the call. It was the security firm.

'Sorry, I am not the home owner,' she said to the operator who'd barely had time to recount his minimalist spiel. But what she had said was enough: the code for a rapid response.

'Can you give me your location at the property?'

'Master bedroom.'

'Please lock yourself inside.'

'Have done.'

'Is the intruder inside or outside the premises?'

'Not sure.'

'Is the intruder still on the premises.'

'Don't know.'

'A team will be with you shortly. Please stay on the line.'

It was dark by the time the two men from Pretorian Security finished their search and drove away.

From inside the kitchen, Amber had watched their torches in the fields beyond the rear wall of the garden, the lights jogging up and down as the two men were forced to run behind their dogs while searching for any sign of an intrusion.

The security men, or 'operatives', had eventually returned to the house to report that there had been no intrusion; none of the alarms had been tripped on the perimeter, which meant no one had climbed over the gates, or the walls that circled the grounds.

The two men were convinced, and convincing, when they told her that a swift manoeuvre through the side of a hedgerow that impenetrably thick, 'to keep even panicking livestock off the road', was 'highly unlikely'. Though they did concede that whoever she had seen may have been able to vault the hedgerow from the road, and that 'the foliage had been sufficiently elastic to resume its previous shape'.

The operatives were very professional and took her claim seriously. She was a good judge of what people thought of her, and she was sure that both of the men recognized a very frightened girl when they met one. The alarms and motion sensors were tested and deemed in perfect working order, and two patrols would now inspect the outside of her property that night. There was nothing more they could do.

But *he* had been outside, and there had been an intrusion inside the property.

This.

Amber had arranged the second offending ball of dust on a piece of newspaper on the kitchen counter. One she could accept as an anomaly; two signified an unnatural occurrence.

She stared at the second dust ball accusingly, and then at its neighbour which she had not long fished out of the kitchen bin. Using a laminated chopstick from the Chinese culinary set, a housewarming present from her agent, she poked the balls of dust. Thick and grey, the dust had collected around and encrusted upon what appeared to be several long black hairs that formed a circular scaffolding inside the dross.

After the builders and designers had left the farmhouse, the entire building had been professionally cleaned. Since her arrival she had not found a speck of dust on any surface. Dust was something she never overlooked on her travels. She guessed this was the kind of dust that gathered in old buildings, poorly insulated buildings with gaps between the skirting boards and floors, dust that wafted across rooms beset by the infinitesimal debris of ages.

Her underflooring and floor had been newly laid; she had admired the workmanship on her arrival. There were no gaps around the sides of any of the rooms to allow dust like this to puff up and into her shining new world, and in a mere seven days too.

Perhaps the dust had come up and around the steps of the stairs. The wood of the stairs was newly varnished, though the steps were still original to the farmhouse.

Amber's mobile phone vibrated and she started, then swept up the handset to see who was calling; few people had the number.

Josh.

The sudden rush of relief at the very sight of his name on her phone screen made Amber dizzy. 'Thank God.'

'I was driving when you called,' he said. 'Motorway. Pulled over soon as I could.'

Amber heard him, but his explanation didn't register. She didn't recognize her own voice when she said, 'He's here. I saw him. Outside. In the road—'

'Slow down. He? Fergal?'

'I saw him less than an hour ago.'

SEVENTY-THREE

'Are you sure? Did you get a good look at him?'

'Yes. No. But how many men are that tall? It was him.'

'What was he wearing? I'll get a description to the police right away.'

Amber tried to recall what she had actually seen, and for what must have been no more than a second before her car stalled. 'Don't know. Because the sun was setting behind him. I only saw a silhouette.' But it was the outline of a man she wouldn't forget in a hurry.

She rubbed the outside of her arms; they goosed at the remembered suggestion of the figure's height, and the direction the long bony head had been turned in.

'How could he possibly know you are there?' Josh was trying his best to maintain a sympathetic tone of voice, but she knew that he didn't believe her. He'd always maintained mostly unshared reservations about her testimony, about her sanity. She couldn't blame him. They all did; everyone she had employed. Everyone thought the same things about her: that exhaustion and depression and anxiety had taken such a toll on her that she had begun hallucinating inside 82 Edgehill Road from the first day of her residency. That she was hyper manic, as one doctor had suggested, and that she had become acutely paranoid

457

because of what *they* had done to her and threatened to do to her. Trauma did that. Shock did that. Sustained terror and an unrelenting fear of your own death did that. The prolonged anticipation of torture and rape did that. Loss of control and imprisonment did that.

Her instability had hampered the inquest from the start; that's what she had been told politely and impolitely on numerous occasions. But she was paying Josh and he had to take her seriously. Josh had always acknowledged that her fear was genuine – that was never his grievance – but he could not believe what she said about the *other things*.

Amber's eyes burned with tears. Her distress remained silent until she sniffed.

'I'm on my way. Give me three hours. I'm in Worcester.'

Amber cleared her throat, heeled both eye sockets with a hand. 'The dust, and him . . . I had a dream. A new one. Inside here. They were in here. They got inside, Josh. They were in my room . . .' Her voice failed.

'OK, OK, I'm setting off now. I'm going to assume you have your "little friend"?' Josh's voice was strained with disapproval at her possession of the weapon while she employed him. He had not asked her the question to verify that she was ready to defend herself; he was afraid that she might use the handgun on herself, or on one of the neighbours who might foolishly walk their dog across the top of her drive.

Amber sniffed. 'I'm ready. Ready for that prick. I almost want him to show up. You know, that's the crazy thing. Part of me is even excited by the idea of finishing this thing. Of finishing him.'

She had come down from fear to light up with rage. Even her hands trembled. It felt good too, if good was the right word. It felt natural and necessary and vital and unstoppable; she couldn't prevent this kind of rage even if she chose to. *They* had gifted the rage to her the night they locked her in the ground floor flat. Where *she* had been.

In the background, beyond the border of her thoughts that were lit up red, and that made her teeth grind until they felt like they were made of clay and oozing together, she could hear Josh's voice. A stern voice that was gradually rising in volume: 'OK, Amber. Amber! Listen to me. Amber, now I need you to calm down. To think this through. Amber, are you listening to me?'

But she wasn't heeding him. This was her home, her sanctuary; she had suffered for this and she had earned this and she had paid for it with more than money. And that rat-faced prick was not coming back to frighten and threaten her.

To break her.

'I will not let him! I will not! Where is he? Josh! Where the fuck is he?' And she only realized she was screaming a few seconds after she'd begun. 'Three years! Three years and he's still out there. He's got her. Her! Why can't you find them? Why? Why, Josh? Because he took *her* from the house. That's why. They never found *her* . . .' And then, to the shocked silence at the other end of the phone, she whispered, '*She* hid him. Hid him, Josh. That's the only way Fergal got away. *She* knows how to hide. *She* hid in that building for a hundred years. Why will none of you believe me?'

Josh stayed quiet. Not even he knew what to say. He'd

been in Iraq and Afghanistan; he'd been in wars and Amber believed he had killed men. He was now a bodyguard for the wealthy and their children because Josh knew how to spot danger and anything that might seem suspicious or risky; he was a risk manager. He knew how to hide and he knew how to hide people from their enemies. But not even a man like Josh was in *her* league.

Her.

Maggie.

Black Maggie.

The words thumped deep and low, rhythmically, like a little drum in a wooden box, beaten by unseen hands in a black room that opened doors onto another place you could not see the end of.

'In about an hour I'll pull over and check in.' Josh was doing his best to remain calm and professional after she had screamed at him and practically accused him of failing her. 'Then I'll call you as I am approaching the house. It'll be late. But do your best to stay calm until I get there.'

Amber sniffed. 'Is there any news? Anything that you can tell me?'

'Sorry. No.' And she knew that as he said this, Josh was also struggling to comprehend how a sub-literate career criminal, well over six foot tall, with limited resources, with filthy clothes and hands covered in blood, with no known friends in the West Midlands, with half his face burned away by concentrated sulphuric acid, could have stayed hidden for three years and left no trace of his whereabouts. Aside from the body of the Accident and Emergency nurse he had followed home and forced to treat his injuries, before he throttled her to death with her own tights, the day after his flight from *that place*.

Amber placed a tea towel over the dust on the newspaper, and then uncapped the bottle of Sailor Jerry.

SEVENTY-FOUR

There were people were in the garden. Men in white suits with elasticated cuffs and rubber boots. Some of them were moving. Their faces were obscured by masks and hoods. The men moved around the holes they had dug in the black earth. On thin paths made out of slats, they carried blue crates as they walked between the holes.

One of the insertions into the soil had been covered by a white tent. Through the entrance she could see a figure bent over and scraping at something they held close to their face.

Green canvas screens had been erected across the back of the property so people couldn't see inside the garden, and the maize in the fields, an ocean of waxy leaves swept by the wind all the way down to where the sea splashed and frothed upon the stony shore, was hidden from her view. But she could hear the crop and the sea out there, the old and eternal sea, hissing.

Underneath the longest limb of the oak tree that grew in the middle of the lawn, four women hung by their necks, their heads cocked like pensive birds. They watched the movement below their booted feet, as the men in white suits collected more of the brown things that looked like sticks from inside the holes. They put the sticks inside clear bags and then gently placed the sealed bags inside the blue plastic crates.

A machine juddered and sucked water out of a hole dug close to the house. A woman stood by the machine and smoked a cigarette. Amber wouldn't meet her eye but knew the woman was looking at her.

Lights in the sky made parts of the garden white and left other sections in darkness. It was hard for Amber to tell what was shadow and what was a person slipping about in the mud, made worse by the rain. Amber peered at the night sky. She could see four big lights, but no stars. Sometimes the lights moved over the house, sometimes they just hovered. The sounds of the rotors made her nervous because she knew she was being watched and filmed.

In the field at the side of her property, through the tree branches, she could see the candle flames of the vigil. She could hear the singing of the women's group that had been camped in the field for days.

Downstairs, inside the building, a crowd of people chattered. All of them were talking at the same time as each other.

From behind her back a voice called her name. A man's voice she recognized and her eyes filled with tears at the thought of Ryan being so near. But there was something wrong with his voice and when he called to her again, 'Stephanie', it sounded as if his mouth was crammed with food.

She turned from the window and looked at the red door of the bedroom, now open and resting against the foot of the bed. From where she was standing the figure inside the bed distracted her from Ryan; she could only see the top half of a dark body with arms thrown out sideways. The face was covered. The occupant of the bed wasn't moving.

'Stephanie,' Ryan repeated, the word moist, lisping and more slurred than before, as though he was struggling to move his jaw around an oversized tongue. He turned his face away, dipped his head. 'Got ver deposssit.' When he said this she was sure he must have been dribbling, because he made a sucking sound as if to draw something back inside his mouth.

'I don't want to be late for work,' she told him. 'Can I stay at your place?' she asked, afraid of the building around her. She didn't want to stay another night inside the farmhouse.

The light in the corridor outside winked out and put the already dim passageway into darkness. The lights were on timers. She could no longer see Ryan's legs in the doorway.

She ran into the corridor on the second floor of the house. This was not where she lived; she lived one floor down, in the room with black walls and mirrors.

She heard Ryan on the stairs, going down. Lights from the garden flashed against the window of the stairwell, but Ryan would not look at her and kept his face turned away as he descended.

When Amber arrived downstairs she couldn't find Ryan. She kept calling his name.

Down here, it was hard to hear herself think. She wasn't sure whether the sounds of rustling plastic were coming from the doors that opened onto unlit rooms, or whether the voices were coming from the walls.

*

The ringing of her phone woke Amber. She sat bolt upright and said, 'Ryan. I can't find—'

And then she realized many things all at once: she was lying on the sofa in the lounge of the farmhouse with the curtains closed; her phone was vibrating across the coffee table; the television was still switched on, and the film must have finished because she could see the DVD menu on the big screen mounted on the wall. She had fallen asleep and had had a bad dream.

Thank God.

But all of this information about her situation and her surroundings confused her. Because someone was running up the stairs outside the room, and she had caught the last of their shadow leaving the living room as she sat up.

Amber looked at the ceiling.

Footsteps bumped heavily across the floor upstairs, and then stopped.

She reached for her phone and tried to work out which room was directly above the living room.

Your bedroom.

She picked up the phone and answered the call from Josh.

'Amber. It's me. I'm—'

She cut him off, her voice so tense she squealed, 'He's here.'

SEVENTY-FIVE

'Just you and me, Amber. There's no one else inside this house.'

Even though the space at the top of the house was little more than a crawlspace, Josh had gone inside the loft with his Maglite. He'd walked through the entire building swiftly and silently while Amber waited in the kitchen, holding her breath and anticipating the sound of a struggle from upstairs. But she'd only heard Josh once, opening the doors of the walk-in wardrobe. He was the third man in a single day to search the premises for an intruder.

Josh slumped into an easy chair in the living room and the leather upholstery wheezed around his shoulders. He was relieved to know his client was safe, she knew that. Josh made her feel safe and she didn't have the courage yet to ask him how long he could stay with her at the farm-house. She knew he was in demand, mostly protecting the children of the super-rich from kidnap. For the first two years after her emancipation from Knacker and Fergal, she had been constantly surrounded by people. In her third year, she had wanted to be left alone and had begun to believe the advice of the police that Fergal was long dead. But she now found herself reconsidering her decision to not employ a permanent bodyguard in Devon.

When she'd first met Josh, two years ago, after the publication advance and newspaper serial fee had come
through and she was able to privately hire someone to
look for Fergal, to augment the unsuccessful police man-
hunt, Amber had struggled to believe that Josh had ever
been in the military, let alone the special forces. He wasn't
tall and didn't look athletic; his body was firm, but bulky,
like the old-school English cricket players that her dad had
idolized. His hair had gone and he invariably wore an
innocuous Gore-Tex coat over loose-fitting black trousers,
hiking boots on his feet. But one consultation covering her
personal safety, changing her identity, and how he had
tracked criminals and their kidnap victims, had dispelled
all of her doubts about his expertise.

'The only room I haven't checked is the locked one.'

'Study.'

'The study. But there is no one in your room. I even
looked under the bed, but there is no under-your-bed. It's
like a solid plinth.'

'For good reason. And before you get comfortable, can
I see for myself? Or I'll never sleep.'

'Of course.' He stood up. 'Follow me.' And paused to
eye the gun on the black marble kitchen counter. 'Either
put that away or give it to me. Just knowing it's here is the
end of my career. You know that. I'm going to need to get
rid of it soon, Amber.'

When you find him. That's what they'd agreed as a
compromise.

Now the danger had passed, though perhaps there had
been no danger, Amber was reluctant to touch the gun.
Her genuine reticence about firearms seemed to be the sole

factor reassuring Josh about her possession of the weapon; he was happy to pocket the gun and would replace it for her inside the case. 'Just show me where you keep it.'

'I'm sorry, Josh.'

'For what?'

'Wasting your time.'

'Your personal safety and peace of mind is not a waste of my time. I was in Worcester on your account anyway, but I'll be billing you for the digression.'

'A lead?'

'Thought it might have been. But alas no. I received information about an assault. The attacker's description was not dissimilar to our man. Tall. Transient. Facial disfigurement. Even ginger. Police got him. But not our boy. This chap once had his cheeks sliced back to his ears with a Stanley knife by football hooligans in Cardiff. They were old scars.'

'Jesus Christ.'

'I sometimes wish he'd stop by and say enough is enough, people.'

'I never know where Jesus fits into all this.'

Josh stayed silent and led the way up through the house.

'God, Jesus, whatever,' she said, reticent but unwilling to change the subject. 'I mean, I believe now. You know?' It was awkward for her to talk like this, and Josh was never going to be the ideal participant in a discussion of this nature. But it had been a long time since she'd had a conversation with anyone, and maybe that was why she needed him to listen. 'I know that there is something else, after this life. But I'm not sure what.'

'Let's hope your brush with the other side is not all there is, eh?'

Josh had always been an understanding ally; he had two daughters, the eldest was Amber's age. He knew about her experiences in great detail and sometimes she sensed the profound effect they had upon him. Once, Amber had even seen him wipe an eye clear of tears with a thumb, while they went through the evidence about what had happened to the other victims of 82 Edgehill Road. Back then, Amber pretended she hadn't noticed Josh's distress, but his tearful reaction had endeared him to her, and his involvement had remained personal. *Fathers with daughters. My own would have been the same.*

'Beats looking after the brats of the rich every day, eh?' he'd said when he finally accepted her custom. Across two weeks he'd deliberated the idea and potential consequences of taking her on as a client; the delay on his decision was due to his reservations about the *other things* that she had claimed about her time in the house in Birmingham. A familiar anxiety now bustled anew inside Amber: that if she kept pushing at that side of her experience, one of the few people she could trust might abandon her.

They arrived on the first floor of the farmhouse and began searching the rooms again. After they'd completed a search of the second bedroom, including a check of every window lock, Josh spoke without looking at her. 'I know you think you saw things, unnatural things, in that place, Amber. Saw them and heard them as clearly as you can see and hear me now. And I don't know how you came to learn certain things about that house that happened years before you were ever there. But none of that helps me.'

He was almost telling her off; she had wrenched him out of Worcester, had screamed at him on the phone, had doubted him.

'I'm sorry I lost my temper, Josh. I never meant anything by it. I was just so certain that he was here. I was frightened. I don't doubt you, you know that. It means a great deal to me that you came.'

Josh checked behind the curtains of the second spare room, and nodded in acknowledgement.

Amber worked her fingers into knots, squeezed them tight, and was unaffected by the pain. 'I once thought that I was seeing things that weren't there, and also hearing things that weren't possible. And I am not an irrational person. I was not irrational then. Everyone thinks I was, but I was not. The fact that I rationalized everything and didn't trust my instincts put me in hell in the first place. My instincts are all I have left, Josh. And I was so sure that I saw him today.'

Josh turned to look at her. 'He's not here, Amber. He could not be here. Or even in Devon. I know you are here, and my knowledge of your whereabouts has not been compromised. Your barrister knows you are here, but she would not divulge these details either. Your agent knows you are here, but wouldn't dare jeopardize her cash cow. Peter St John, does he now know that you are here?'

'Not yet. But I have to tell him. He's coming to see me next weekend.'

'He still chasing a new book?'

Amber nodded. 'But we're only catching up on loose ends.'

'I see. Something I should know about?'

Amber shook her head. 'I still want the parts of the story that are incomplete. About the first victims.'

'Which is why you've carted all those files into your study.'

Amber nodded, but smarted at Josh's clear disapproval of her continuing research into the history of 82 Edgehill Road.

Josh sighed and shook his head. 'What I am alluding to is the improbability of your being discovered. The low risk. It is possible that one of us who knows you live here has been hacked, but I doubt Fergal Donegal would have the wherewithal to do that, or know anyone who might do something like that on his behalf.

'Remember, he only ever had tenuous links with organized criminals from England, Kosovo and Albania, at a peripheral franchise level. He was small time and only ever on probation for Andrei Makarov. We know he was done a big favour with the loan of the two girls. A favour to be paid back once he'd recruited local talent. Fergal failed as soon as he began. Because he was a psychopath. The kind that ends up in prison, over and over again, who never thinks about the consequences of his violent, impulsive actions. He is not the kind of psycho who ends up in a boardroom running an international company.

'So Fergal finding you down here, by calling upon investigative criminal resources, is an unlikely scenario. Nor was his arsehole in crime, Knacker, top rank. He was an even smaller potato. If anyone discovered your new identity, and where you are, it would most probably be a journalist. Not Fergal Donegal. And if the press have rumbled this rather tasteful set-up you have down here at the seaside, why have they not gone public?' Josh stopped talking and came to a standstill outside the study.

Amber nodded. 'I know. It doesn't make sense. Not in a logical way. But . . .'

Josh raised his eyebrows. 'Can I see the incident room?'

Amber unlocked the door. 'You're probably going to need a drink afterwards.'

'My thoughts exactly. What have you got in?'

SEVENTY-SIX

'Not bad, this,' Josh said, swirling the amber liquid around the bottom of his highball glass.

'As long as you don't overdo it.' Amber had switched to black coffee and her elegant cup now steamed on the table.

She and Josh sat at right angles to each other: Josh on the chair, Amber on the sofa with her feet pulled off the floor and a cushion clasped to her stomach. She felt as if the cushion was pinioning her to the seat to prevent her from a frantic pacing about the room.

Josh raised an eyebrow. 'The same can be said for other things.'

'I felt it was time to go through it again.'

'I can see that. You think I will find him?'

'Who else have I got?'

'The police were thorough.'

'For as long as time and resources allowed.'

'I've mostly followed the same leads and lines of inquiry they did. The routes are finite.'

'I think he is alive.'

Josh pursed his lips and considered his response. 'I don't. And neither do the police. Andrei Makarov and his associates have a deep reach inside the British Isles. It's not unlikely that they rubbed Fergal out. He'd damaged their merchandise. Two of Makarov's top girls were in that house with you. If Fergal put in a call for assistance to Andrei, which he may have been forced to do after you'd finished with him, Makarov's cronies would have whacked him as soon as the news of Margaret Tolka's murder broke. Not to mention the fact that he put Svetlana in hospital for a month. And he'd stolen their money too, which was Andrei Makarov's money, in Makarov's mind. Reprisals against Fergal would have been severe. Conclusive. Evidence dissolved with the same concoction you threw in his face. Because that's where Fergal got the acid from: Andrei Makarov's gang.

'But let's just say, for argument's sake, that Fergal hid somewhere. An abandoned building, the house of a mentally disabled person, or a pensioner that he used as a hostage for a while. Such things have been known to happen. But it's now been three years. Do you think a man that unstable and sadistically violent would have managed to maintain his cover? With that temper? If all that you said about him was true, I don't think he could have contained himself for twenty-four hours.

'Even with some medical assistance from the nurse he killed, he wouldn't have gotten far. You probably blinded him in one eye, at least. He must have gone mad from the agony of the burns. And he had nowhere to go to ground. Who could Fergal have called for help in the West Midlands? I am certain he had no connection to the area besides Arthur Bennet, who was a loner, like his father. The Bennets were never connected to any gangs in Birmingham. So how can you be sure that he's still alive?'

'You know that I don't know. But everything I said to the police is true.'

'I know.'

'Josh, can I ask you something?'

'Not if it's what I think you're going to ask me.'

'If . . . you find him. If he is alive. I don't want there being any chance of him escaping again.'

'Hold up.'

'No chance of him coming here.'

'If he is found, he'd do life.'

'That's not even fifteen years.'

'In a psychiatric hospital on a very secure wing. I shouldn't imagine he'd ever get out in your lifetime for three murders.'

'They could put him in Broadmoor. That's near here. I don't want there being any chance of him ever getting to me.'

'I am not an assassin, Amber.'

Neither of them spoke for a long time.

Josh eventually checked his watch. 'You'll have to show me to the servants' quarters soon, kiddo. I've got an early start. I need to be in Surrey by noon tomorrow. The children of a man who owns one of the Arab Emirates want to go to Chessington World of Adventures.'

The disappointment on her face was obvious.

Josh sighed. 'There's some serious protection strung around this place. Anyone scales a wall and the boys will be on their way. They're a good outfit; you can rely on them. It's why I picked them. Not to mention the arsenal in your bedside cabinet. And you sleep in a locked room. You're safer than the Duchess of Cambridge, and you don't do public engagements.' He smiled, but Amber struggled to acknowledge his attempt to reassure her.

'But . . .'

'What?'

Amber turned her head in the direction of the kitchen.

Josh tried to smother his smile. 'House dust.'

'How did it get in here? Those aren't a few specks. But clumps of dust and black hair. And I know where I saw them last.'

'Your hair is black.'

'But not that long. And the dreams. The horrible dreams. Two, that came at the same time as the dust. Nightmares like I used to have. I would have dealt with the dreams and the dust, but what I saw outside . . . It's like . . . It was a sign.'

'I can't help you with those kinds of signs, Amber. Other than to make an educated guess that after you cracked the seal on those files yesterday, and got them all out for a thorough going over, while shit-faced, I'd have been very surprised if you'd not had a nightmare. Not to mention seeing people peeping over the garden gate. Baby steps, love. Baby steps.'

'That's what I told myself. But here we are.'

Josh looked at his hands. The glimmer of mirth in his eyes had gone. He looked older, his features subtly subsiding, his eyes sadder, less focused. 'We both know there are things you will never forget, Amber. Ghosts, if you like, that those of us who have been in certain situations have to live with. Stuff we need to lock down.'

He gathered himself and looked around the room, released another weary breath. 'Look at this bloody place.

It's not half bad, kiddo. So why bring all of that in here?
You're asking for trouble. Let this journo, Peter, take care
of things. Meet him on neutral ground when he has something useful to tell you. But until he does, just give yourself
a break and enjoy this. Get that crap out of your study.
Put a treadmill inside there, a rowing machine. It'll do you
more good.'

He leant forward in his chair. 'Just how many girls
your age have their own farmhouse by the sea, and all to
themselves? Especially girls who had nothing not so long
ago and who are very lucky to be alive.'

Amber looked around her living room. 'I refuse to feel
guilty about this place.'

'No one is asking you to. But there are no more warehouses, call centres, or latte promotions in the mall for
you, kid. The service industry is here to serve you now.
Don't let old shadows spoil what is a very nice view.
Because you'll cripple yourself with it. You won. They lost.
Now enjoy yourself. You're young, you're not bad looking, you're loaded. If you start living a normal life again,
you'll meet someone.'

Amber threw her head back and laughed derisively.
'Josh, people believed I was a prostitute in that house. And
after what I did to those bastards . . . Men will always
think I am a monster. They're afraid of me. And the men
who are too interested in that side of things in my past, I
don't want to meet. I can't have my history being part of a
future relationship. But I would have to tell someone who
I was close to. I don't think it could work. Not yet. Not
for a long while.'

She finished by offering Josh a tired smile, hoping it

would suffice as a message: *believe me, I have my reasons for being a celibate recluse.*

The famous picture of her appeared in her mind: the one in which she was wearing a hooded top, her face without make-up, eyes darkened by insomnia. A photograph shown on the enormously popular online Puff Post site every day for a week, accompanied by garish headlines: CATCH A GLIMPSE OF STEPHANIE BOOTH: SAINT OR MONSTER?

The photograph was taken on one of the many occasions that she was taken back to the address to assist the police search of the house. A newspaper had been tipped-off by a police officer and informed of her movements. A photographer disguised himself as a forensic detective to rip a slit in the plastic screens surrounding the crime scene so he could take a picture of her being led into the house; it was the first picture of Stephanie Booth the world saw after she was found.

By the time of the inquest, three other police officers had been suspended for selling information about her to the press. Her mobile phone was bugged twice.

The picture of her with hair tied back and wearing a tailored black suit, complemented by court shoes and flesh-toned tights, as she entered court with her barrister, was the picture that really began the frenzy.

STEPHY, THE BLACK WIDOW, CHARGED £80 TO WALK ON VICTIMS.

That second picture and the fabricated stories began the marriage proposals; they came in thick and fast from all over the world. For months after the second picture appeared, she had even been known in the tabloids, and in social media, as the 'Castratrix'. Apparently she had performed 'inhumane acts of sadistic revenge' against her pimps in a dispute over money, while wearing high heels and provocative clothing.

She became an object of curious fascination to men almost as soon as the original stories broke about the murders in a brothel; for a long while, it seemed male fantasies had refashioned her experience to their own tastes.

Amber doubted Josh would ever be ready for her apocryphal tales of courtship. Like the one about the portly man who repeatedly photographed himself naked save for a rubber pig mask, and sent Amber the images through her agent and lawyers: photographs with an emphasis on his shrivelled genitalia. The man had always addressed Amber as 'Mistress' and requested she burn off his 'sissy prick' before slaughtering him at her leisure. He wanted to pay her fifty thousand pounds for the honour. His only stipulation was that she wear patent black high heels and paint her toe nails blood-red as she ended his miserable existence. The police discovered he was a hedge fund manager and the correspondence ended.

Besides the more radical feminist activists, and until Kyle Freeman made *Closer by Darkness Than Light*, the only sympathetic and unnervingly accurate portrait of her experience appeared in the form of an installation, made by a British artist, who recreated a miniature replica of 82 Edgehill Road out of animal bones. He then papered the inside walls with pictures of female murder victims and their killers. He called the sculpture 'The Edge of Where?'.

Amber had found photographs of the installation too

difficult to look at for long, but of everything that was interpreted about her, the installation was the best depiction of the place she had survived. The sculpture sold for two million pounds.

Everybody loves a survivor.

Her experiences were only now kept alive by the success of *Nine Days in Hell*, and the genital torture films that were emerging in Eastern Europe on small budgets: a sub-genre of torture porn that always featured a kidnapped woman in a haunted house; a young blonde woman resembling her old self, who became possessed and resorted to a torture that involved the genital mutilation of her captors.

She had just been a minimum wage temp, who couldn't afford to go to university, and only owned three pairs of shoes. There was nothing extraordinary about her, never had been; nor was there anything special about most victims of killers. People were reluctant to accept she was just a girl who had rented a dusty room in a dismal house in North Birmingham. And yet she had spawned an industry of exploitation that she had never fully understood.

She'd felt better for as long as Josh was talking, and for a few moments afterwards, but no longer. 'I wonder if I should have come back. To this country.'

'You had your reasons. And what was the alternative? Staying at sea for the rest of your life?'

'Maybe, if it came to it. I felt I was . . .'

'Getting better?'

Amber gave him the evil eye. 'Recovering. I think I might even have been happy on a ship for the rest of my life.'

'You had to stop and find a home eventually. And wherever we may go, or find ourselves, I believe we remain the same people. I don't think we can change, not in any meaningful sense. New places don't change us. Not really. Because no one travels light. We just have to learn to take less baggage with us and to pack our cases more carefully, and then make a fist of it. But if you ever need someone to watch your back on the *Queen Mary*, I'm up for it.'

Amber opened her hands and looked at them; they'd finally stopped trembling. 'I came back to find them, Josh. Because it's not finished. I didn't come back to be found. And that's how I feel now, found.'

'It's in your head, kid.'

'You wouldn't understand, mate. But I can sense a connection. Always have done. I think he was there today, outside. Maybe not physically. But there all the same. I think they know . . .'

'Know what?'

'Where I am, and where I was, all this time. They were just waiting.'

'Like I said, kid, that's the past. It's always waiting, always. Simple things, anything at all really, can bring it up. Up inside us. It doesn't go away. We just have to learn to stop the past in its tracks when first we feel its reach. That's what I was told.'

'Did it work?'

'Sometimes. But you have to try. Or you're stuck back then. Stuck on a loop that goes round and round in tighter circles until you snap.'

Amber twisted her fingers, eyed the bottle of rum. 'I'm not the same, Josh. They took something out of me. In that house. Something small, subtle, but significant, that's hard to pin down, because I don't know if I can remember what it was that has gone. But I know . . . I am sure that something is gone. Gone from me. I thought . . . I want it to be over. For him . . . For him and her to be found. Then maybe everything can rest. In me. In the others. Because I am not sure anything is at rest.'

She still had a sense of her old self, though the older she became the more distant that girl seemed to be. But she still struggled to discover any enthusiasm for anything. Only her work on the book and film had engaged her. But her concentration was in tatters again. She was too quick to rage.

'It's hard to explain. It's . . . The food on the ships, it was wonderful, but I couldn't get excited by it. The new countries I saw. Same thing. I know things are good but I can't . . . unclench. My mind is like a closed hand. I can't open myself.' She waved her hand in the air and growled to swallow the lump that had blocked her throat. 'Clothes, a car, all of the beautiful shit in this house, everything I ever dreamed of having, I have it now. But I can't appreciate it. I can't. I try. I was doing OK this week. But I'm blocked. Again. It seems irrelevant, superficial, this . . .' Amber looked around the room. 'These things can't touch me, inside. Not this part of me that is talking to you now. That's the same. It's what was underneath that.'

Josh looked sad and couldn't meet her eye. In silence he recognized what she had said, Amber could tell. He knew what she had lost. Because he too had lost things, lost important things to the darkness.

'But this place. In here. My first week. I was feeling . . .

No One Gets Out Alive

content, at least. Even safe. I thought it was because I knew that I had finally found a home. That I was where I was happiest as a child. It was like I was called back here for some reason. Something important, from my child-hood, made me come here. But now, after today, I don't know . . . Maybe I only feel like I've been welcomed here. That something was pleased that I came here, so I wasn't happy at all for myself. Not really. I've felt relief. But maybe not my own relief.'

'Then why don't you go back to sea. Take another three months, or six, a year.'

'I can't. I can't run any more. I want to be who I was again. Something has to be buried or burned so that I can be who I was again. I need what they call closure. That's what it feels like. If I hadn't come back now, then I would have done later. Why later and not now?'

Time doesn't matter to her.

Amber eschewed the coffee and poured herself a gener-ous measure of rum. They sat in silence for a while and sipped their drinks.

Eventually Josh stood up and yawned.

Amber climbed off the sofa. She reached out, nervously, and touched his arm. The contact nearly made her cry. 'Thanks, mate.'

Josh made a growling sound and gave her a quick, tight hug. 'You're going to be all right, kid,' he whispered into the side of her head, then broke from the bear hug and made his way to the stairs.

'Shout if you need anything. Extra pillow, you know, stuff like that.'

'I've stayed in good hotels, Amber. But I already prefer

your place. I'll be fine. And you make sure you shout if you hear anything, OK? If I can isolate one loose floorboard and put your mind at rest, I won't be annoyed if you wake me up. Agreed?'

Amber nodded, and then followed Josh up the stairs. Despite all of his reassurance and explanations and wisdom and logic, she didn't want to be downstairs on her own.

Josh looked over his shoulder from the top of the stairs. 'And if you hear a chainsaw, it won't be you-know-who coming through the front door. It'll be me snoring over in the east wing.'

SEVENTY-SEVEN

Once the light beneath Josh's door was out, Amber pulled the door of her study closed, as quietly as she was able. For a while she sat at her desk with her face in her hands. Number 82 was no more. The building had been erased from the earth it once contaminated. The remains of the victims had been laid to rest. So how could all of *that* come back? And here too, where almost no one knew where she was?

They had not been on board the ships, or in the hotels, or in the secure accommodation the police and her legal team had found for her, for the two years after she was carried from Knacker and Fergal's appropriated domain. But she had definitely seen a shadow outside the living room, that very afternoon, and what had cast the shadow had walked through her home: she had heard the intruder's footsteps. Fergal had stood in the lane outside her property, and he had wanted Amber to see him.

The dust on the stairs was not ordinary household dust, but a variety of dust she'd seen before, gathering under the beds and in the corners of rooms in another place. But a place that now seemed intent on reforming inside her dreaming mind; what had been buried within its walls and under its floors was exhuming itself inside her nightmares. And such things might not stay within sleep.

How?

She thought about what she could remember of the two recent dreams. An excavation of the garden to exhume human remains had been underway when she dozed that afternoon. And though the farmhouse was very much transformed in her nightmare last night, the dead had entered her home. Each episode had been populated by the ghastly victims of Edgehill Road. The overwhelming advice from her instincts suggested the episodes had been shown to her, in effect transmitted to her.

But how?

She had learned that hauntings in Britain were mostly regarded as having an attachment to places and past events, not to specific individuals in a variety of locations. The farmhouse had no earthly connection to the house in North Birmingham.

So how could they have found you here?

Maybe through the deep, ephemeral and instinctive connection she had always been aware of at the back and sides of her mind. Fergal – if he was truly in Devon, in some form – then had he carried this desolate host to her? If such horror still clung to him and orbited her, then he had to be found, and destroyed.

She would sleep with her gun beneath her pillow.

Amber took down her 'Bennet' files from the second steel cabinet, now more intent than ever to resume her familiarization of the case history, and the next part of the story; the part responsible for the majority of the human remains found in the Birmingham house and garden.

As she moved the files onto her desk, she wondered again if she had restarted something by engaging with this material so intensely. And by looking hard again she might make it worse. If that was the case then she carried a connection to the past like a taint in the blood or an anomaly in her genes. If she were a conduit for the Maggie, and the congregation of victims from Birmingham, then reacquaintance might occur anytime, anywhere.

She reopened the Bennet files and began spreading the documents and cuttings about her desk top. Whatever tied a former occupant, or occupants, who had murdered four women around 1919, to the Bennet family, and then connected the Bennets to Fergal Donegal, was at the very root of what occupied the house. And the answer to the question of what cast such a baleful and sinister influence over the various households, from the very beginnings of the building's life, would require a great leap of imagination; a leap that no one was willing to take on her behalf. So here she was, again.

The Bennets were Peter St John's almost exclusive obsession, but to her they were the least palatable part of the story.

With the exception of the vast store of Arthur Bennet's pornographic paraphernalia, and what Fergal had once referred to as 'Bennet's pervy tat', the Bennets had kept no records. They were both dead. Their motivations went to the grave. Others had been assigned the unpleasant task of sifting through the grotesque relics and vulgar artefacts surviving the Bennets' respective careers as abusers, rapists and murderers.

Harold Bennet had died of a massive stroke in Winson

Green Prison in 1985. The house had passed to his son after Arthur was released from his first stint in prison for attempted rape in a local park. Little was known about their relationship when the men shared the house. But Amber was sure the father had not tutored the son; that had been the role of something else that cohabited with them. An idea Peter St John, and near anyone else she had spoken to, refused to even entertain.

Arthur Bennet's various attempts to create brothels at 82 Edgehill Road were all non-starters too, which is why he'd killed fewer women than his father; he'd always traded on the local reputation of Bennet senior's more successful former operations. Arthur's most lucrative and arrest-free period ended when he killed both of his girls, Olena Kovalik and Simona Doubrava, sometime in 2001 and 2002 respectively. His criminal entrepreneurialism was also repeatedly disturbed by the amount of time he'd spent behind bars: imprisoned four times for attempted rape, indecent assault, common assault and theft, and cautioned for public exposure on Perry Common Playing Fields, as well as for stealing washing in Handsworth.

Numerous other fines were levied against him for non-payment of bills and handling stolen goods, but nothing that shed any meaningful light on why he and his father emulated, in an increasingly degenerate form, the ritualistic murders of the first four women at the same address when George V sat on the throne of England.

Harold Bennet had left nothing behind in an attic cache to incriminate himself. Nothing personal of the father had survived his son's long infestation of the house. It was also deemed unlikely that Bennet senior would have kept a diary; the only books found at the address were Haines Manuals for a Ford Sierra, Ford Cortina and Austin Metro, and two old editions of *The Guinness Book of Records*.

To Amber, what was most significant about Harold's legacy was that at the time of her own residence, all of the furniture, the fixtures and fittings, had belonged to Harold Bennet and his wife, Mary. Arthur Bennet had made no alterations or additions to the property he'd inherited. He'd either lived alone amongst his parents' relics or shared the property with others to whom he'd sporadically rented rooms, mostly from 1989 to 2003.

To Amber, the preservation of the parental home did not appear to be a testament to one man's laziness and poverty, as it had seemed to the investigation; she saw the conservation of the father's sick realm as a deliberate enshrining of the past, and a testament to *what* had been served there.

Everything else she flicked through about the Bennets seemed innocuous. Harold Bennet had been a plasterer, a working-class man with a history of drunkenness and violence towards his wife, Mary; a wife beater who eventually murdered his spouse.

Mary had been Harold's first victim, killed sometime in the mid-1960s. After throttling Mary, he'd wrapped her body in polythene and concealed her remains inside a ground floor fireplace; the fireplace in the same room in which Amber had stumbled across Arthur Bennet's corpse. Arthur Bennet had died mere feet and one layer of bricks away from his own mother. He may never have known.

His father had told Arthur that his mother had 'run away with a tinker'.

Freed of a marital incumbent, Harold had gone on to kill another six women at the address, while his young son, Arthur, who became his teenage son, lived in the same house. Did young Arthur Bennet know of the murders? Had he ever witnessed one? No one would ever truly know, but it was widely assumed Arthur not only knew, but probably assisted during some form of apprenticeship to his father, before embarking on his own less prolific career as a killer after his father died.

When the police identified the remains of the woman they had disinterred from the ground floor fireplace as belonging to Mary Bennet, Amber also realized that Mary had been the *presence* that repeatedly asked her for the time. And given the evidence of her recent dreams, it seemed that Mary Bennet's yearning for the time may not have abated, despite an official burial.

Harold Bennet's other victims were procured from various sources. He had always provided rooms for known prostitutes, a category to which the victim Angie Hay belonged, who was found under the floor of the street-facing second floor bedroom that Amber had never seen inside.

Harold had also taken in vulnerable women as lodgers and then coerced them into prostitution, as in the case of Ginny MacPherson, who was discovered under the flooring directly beneath the bed that Amber had slept in during her first night in the house.

Both sets of remains had been bound inside polythene.

A factory worker missing since 1967, Susan Hopwood

was found with her head mummified in parcel tape beneath the ground floor bedroom, only feet away from Mary Bennet in the fireplace. Hopwood had been on the run from domestic violence. Though it was never established whether Hopwood was buried alive, Amber had cultivated her own thoughts on that subject.

Harold Bennet abducted at least one girl too, Kelly Hughes, whose remains had been discovered beneath floorboards on the first floor, on top of which a bath tub had been mounted when Harold turned a box room into a bathroom, presumably during the year of her death.

All of Harold's known victims had been reported missing between the years of 1965 and 1981.

Besides those whose identities had been established, the toothless bodies of two nineteen-year-old girls were also discovered within a second floor wall cavity that had once contained an airing cupboard; it was believed that they had been killed by Harold Bennet within days of each other. They were also assumed to have been foreign nationals – perhaps exchange students, tourists, or even hitchhikers.

Amber had referred, in her old notebook, to a presence as 'the woman who moves'. At the time of the discovery of these two unidentified corpses, she began to believe that the mobile presence she had encountered may have been two separate entities: the presence that climbed into her bed, and the presence that rummaged inside her bags. Though the presence that became a chilling bedfellow had spoken English and had not been foreign.

There was still much to learn, and Peter St John's obsession with the father and son act also moved attention away from the victims. This seemed grossly unfair, because at 82 Edgehill Road the killing had always been easier than the dying.

Neither Bennet had been religious. They had no connection to anything of a spiritual or an occult nature, or none Peter St John or the police had ever established. As far as the police and media were concerned, the sins of a violent, abusive, alcoholic father were passed on to a son with learning difficulties, who developed his dad's predatory and aggressive sexuality. But this was an inadequate explanation of why the house's next generation of violent pimps and killers had adopted the house's repellent traditions. Amber had always considered the Bennets and Fergal as mere tools, homicidal tools, susceptible vessels for something that found them useful, a presence that compelled others to kill on its behalf: 'for company', as Fergal Donegal had once told Knacker in Amber's presence. But was *company* the whole story? Perhaps death increased the power and reach of what had been served in that building. Death became *her*. If so, was Amber to become a tool or a victim? The enormity of that thought made her breath catch. 'Jesus Christ.'

Every woman killed at the house was murdered by strangulation, suggesting a ritualistic aspect to the murders. Official conclusions at the inquest had settled for 'copycat behaviour' in the matter of the close connection between Harold Bennet's modus operandi and that of whoever had killed the first four women in the 1920s, who were all strangled with a washing line.

Harold Bennet had used garden twine to strangle his victims, before burying their remains in fireplaces, wall cavities and under floorboards. Arthur Bennet had merely deposited his two victims in the garden, in shallow graves, but had strangled each of them with the same garden twine his father had used on all of his known victims. Fergal had used the same twine as Harold and Arthur Bennet to kill his sole female victim, Margaret Tolka. Several spools of the twine were discovered by police in the ground floor flat.

The significant links between the murder of each woman across one hundred years, the use of a ligature and the taking of a trophy, demonstrated to Amber that an entire facet of the bloody history still remained unexplained. The killers changed; the methods and intent remained the same.

So she must have directed them: Black Maggie.

But how can she be here?

Amber left the study and went to her room. Undressed and sat in bed, propped up by goose-feather pillows, her body warmed by the finest cotton sheets and a duvet covered in Mulberry silk. Trinkets of a lifestyle designed to entirely relocate and redesign her away from poverty, its dust and dross, the cheap sub-lets and slum lords, the criminal low-life, the indignity, the hopelessness of being at the bottom and having less than nothing. And yet here she was, inside her very own palace, feeling that she was still within the grip of history's dirty hand.

The clock said two forty-five a.m. She had hardly slept the night before and the day had been full of driving and shopping and panic and strange men in her home, searching the rooms for what she had escaped from three years before. Thinking about the Bennets had reduced her to a headachy and nervy state. She was also frightened, but her fear was tinged by the beginnings of a loose and hot anger; a volatile and vengeful anger she could feel inside her teeth.

Amber slid her body under the covers. She was not far from a coma of exhaustion, the kind of marrow-deep fatigue that follows the turning of a tide of terror.

She chose to end her inner debate by revisiting Josh's logic: *Fergal cannot know that you are here . . . it is virtually impossible . . . he is probably dead . . . no trace for three years . . . he disappeared because he was disappeared by other criminals . . . they're all sociopaths and they don't trust each other . . . rats and weasels . . . you opened the case files when you were drunk and had a relapse . . . that's all . . . too much of a coincidence to be anything else . . . the files, the dreams . . . just dust . . . an old house . . . that's all . . .*

She was not abandoning her new home. Not to the past. Not to *them*. Never.

Just try and get through the night.

Don't go inside the study, not for a while. Pace yourself.

Take a few days off. Go to Cornwall. Look at the sea. Read some books. Eat, drink, walk. Spend time outdoors . . .

Stay away until the weekend. Peter's coming. He'll stay for the weekend . . . you won't be alone . . .

Either feeling marginally more secure, or just too tired to think any more, Amber fell asleep in her brightly lit bedroom.

*

'Not bad. But I seen better. You should have seen the place I done up in Ibeefa.'

Amber tried to answer Knacker as he cockily strutted about the black room and inspected the walls. His big pale eyes were wide with an eagerness she knew well; eyes lit up with an intent to undermine and wound, to criticize and torment.

She was desperate to spit her anger into his bony face. But she couldn't speak and her legs and arms were numb. There was something jammed inside her mouth that tasted of rubber. Saliva dripped off her chin. Her head was filling with the smell of empty hot water bottles, of diving masks pulled over a dry face.

Knacker paced around her, backwards and forwards. 'I fink I will be very happy here. Fink I'll take this room.' A new pair of red training shoes on his strutting feet trailed laces and paper price tags.

The room was pitch black. The walls and floor were thick with layers of oily emulsion. Light from the four candles glimmered against the paint like moonlight on the ocean at night. A smell of dried damp, dust, and the stale woody air that collects under floorboards interfered with Amber's thoughts, made her forget things, and seemed to increase her helplessness like an anaesthetizing gas.

'We got a deal. An agreement. You fink we'd forget about that? Was you finking we is the kind of wankers that might overlook promises you made?'

She tried to scream 'No!' in defiance, but her mouth was blocked. All of her strength and will was exhausted by trying to remain on the floor. Her body was so insubstantial and weak, her feet had drifted a few inches above the ground.

And there was something above her, on the ceiling, drawing her upwards with an overpowering magnetism. The urgent desire to have her up there made her struggles and her rage dissolve into despair. She was no longer sure what produced the strongest and most paralyzing bondage: the tough green string that tied her legs together at the ankle and knee, and secured her arms to her torso, or the burning frustration at being unable to cry for help.

This reaction pleased whatever it was that drew her up and up and steadily upwards, off the floor. Her consciousness was open and being rifled like a handbag stolen in a crowd. She sensed an amused satisfaction, and an intimate awareness of her feelings. It wasn't enough that she was helpless and bound; they were all inside her head too, whispering like horrible children she had been shut inside a wardrobe with.

'And if you is finking you is staying here, then you better start producing the readies, like. You's got all them bills to pay off too. Council's on my back. Gas, 'lectric, water. These fings don't come cheap, neither. So you's best start earning what you owe on all this, yeah?'

'Yeah. You heard him,' Fergal said from the doorway. 'And you can make a start wiv our visitor. He's quite partial to you, and you know you want it.'

The scents of Knacker's aftershave and Fergal's rancid clothes gave way to a smothering cloud of bad breath from behind her head. She tried to turn to see who had pressed themselves into her buttocks and was now panting over her scalp. But the little pudgy fingers inside her hair made sure she stared straight ahead. A bristly chin scraped the nape of her neck. A small, fat hand began to untuck the shirt from the waistband of her jeans.

'And he wants to watch, like,' Fergal said from the doorway, and grinned at what he carried in his dirty fingers.

Held by the wet hair on top of his head, Ryan's face was offered up for her inspection. His forehead looked to have been painted red and only one of his eyes was visible; the other eye had been covered by a blue bulb of flesh the size of a potato. His lower jaw jutted out at an angle and something flopped out one side of his mouth.

Amber closed her eyes to avoid the sight of the figure drooping from Fergal's stained paw. And silently, desperately, with what little mobility she retained, she struggled within the embrace of the stinking thing that now rubbed itself against her back. This only diverted her efforts to stay near the ground, to add substance to her growing weightlessness as she began to rise up through the darkness with the oily, fat man clinging to her body. He was breathing quickly now, nasally, almost asthmatic with excitement. He wrapped his small legs around her waist. Holding the hair on the top of her head, he yanked her head back to show her the thing that clung to the ceiling.

Amber refused to look at it, but whatever was up there slipped inside her mind.

I will come unto thee. For I have determined there to winter.

Now she was writhing on the linoleum floor of an old kitchen, amidst broken glass, wood and crockery. Mindless, she chanted at the swallowing darkness on a cold floor: 'Their blood for my blood. You think these rats can keep you? You deserve better company.'

Amber came up from the mattress and out of the bed-clothes with the duvet gripped between two clenched fists. The animal sound she made from deep inside her stomach vibrated against the bones of her face.

'No. No. I didn't. I never did . . .' She spoke and panted at the same time, until the real world reformed around her. Her eyes opened upon her bedroom: cream carpets, Selva furniture, long linen drapes, Zenza Filisky light fittings, a walk-in wardrobe lined with the shelves she had filled with designer shoes – Zanotti, Westwood, Geiger, Choo – none of which could walk her away from this.

They had gathered inside her head: Knacker, Fergal, Bennet; she remembered that much. They had come into her head and her house and taken it over and changed it and made her a captive and a prostitute. Amber sobbed. And whatever had been slowly moving around the ceiling had directed them like puppets.

Amber clutched her face and rocked backwards and forwards and pushed at the lingering images of those faces that remained in her mind: spittle-flecked mouths, thin lips, broken noses, ferrety eyes alert to opportunity, devious reptile minds concocting their next ploys, subterfuge, disingenuous offers, entrapping demands, accusations.

She breathed deeply of the air inside her room. And she was pleased to discover that her bedroom still brandished the aromas of elegance and new luxury. The stink of the black room and its occupants had cleared. She took another deep breath to entirely rid her sinuses of the miasma from the past, powerful enough to bring her out of sleep. And her nose detected another scent, one unique to the night but instantly familiar. A fragrance to awake and pour remembrance through her; memories thick with a sadness so great her heart broke.

She was smelling Lynx deodorant and tea tree shower gel, and the jasmine fabric detergent she had used in the old washing machine when she and Ryan had lived together. And beneath those perfumes, she could smell the deep masculine scent of his shirts that had never been unpleasant; an intimate fragrance she had once happily lain in the midst of, after they had made love in the bed with the broken leg and cracked slats at their terrible flat in Stoke.

The scent of Ryan bloomed thickly about her bed, for no more than a few moments, before it vanished.

Amber clambered out from under the duvet, her nose probing the air as she chased a trace.

Not a vestige remained. Ryan had gone.

But there was someone outside her bedroom.

A body shuffled away the other side of the door, as if retreating after being caught listening to her. Muffled footsteps bumped along the first floor corridor – an uneven tread of feet, a hobble, as if the walker was lame.

Josh? She might have woken him. Maybe she had been shouting in her sleep, screaming, thrashing to break herself out of the nightmare. But why would Josh have difficulty moving?

Outside in the corridor a door closed.

Maybe the bathroom door? Josh might have risen to use the toilet and listened at her door to make sure that she was safe. He might be half asleep and uncoordinated, unsteady on his feet.

Amber needed to tell him about who had just been close to her bed. Because no one was going to persuade her right now that Ryan had not been inside this house. He had come back to her. And she needed to tell Josh about the dream that had sickened and terrified her awake. Amber ran to her bedroom door and unlocked it. She opened the door onto an unlit corridor.

She looked right and left, the light from her bedroom illuminating the passage: the woven carpet, cream coloured skirting boards and silver light fittings, closed doors, their antique brass handles glimmering in peripheral light. The door to Josh's room was closed. The bathroom door was shut and the room beyond was unlit. But she had definitely heard a door closing out here. Yet there were no draughts – the house was too well insulated – and none of the windows were open. Maybe Josh had opened a window and created a slipstream of air?

To her right the footsteps continued. The sound of a descent was clear: there was someone on the staircase. She mustn't jump to conclusions; it was probably only Josh going below for a glass of water, or planning an early start. Maybe he had come out of the bathroom and closed the door before making his way down. Knowing he was in the house gave Amber the confidence to venture through the corridor to the summit of the staircase. She slapped on the stairwell lights.

The staircase was empty.

Antique wood still shone from the recent treatment and polish, a professionally evoked shimmer that made the presence of the new clumps of dust incongruous and unwelcome. Thick clusters of hair and dust, the shape of cumulus clouds, now idled with an unpleasant suggestion of being small furred mammals. From the top of the stairs she could see each dust ball at rest on its respective step, and they issued the impression and the impact of dirty trespassing footprints in her beautiful new home.

'Josh,' Amber called out quietly. 'Josh? You up?'

Silence.

Why would Josh walk through the dark? No doubt he could – he'd be good at it; trained to move without the guidance of light. Maybe he hadn't heard her. 'Josh?' Amber started down the stairs. 'Josh?'

No answer came from the unlit ground floor. But the silence down there was broken by the sound of feet; distant feet scuffing across the tiles of the kitchen, maybe no more than three careless steps. Maybe it wasn't Josh. *Ryan?*

Amber went down to the hall, tiptoeing around the dust so it did not touch her naked toes. At the foot of the stairs she turned on the hallway light and moved to the kitchen. The door was open and the room beyond concealed by darkness. She paused and shivered from the cold of deep night and the contact of the chilly wood beneath her feet. 'Josh,' she repeated loudly.

A door closed inside the kitchen. She covered her mouth with a hand to shush her sudden intake of breath. That must have been the door that led to the adjoining garage. But there was nothing for Josh inside the garage; no reason for him to be in there.

The security lights had not come on in the garden. If a

person moved near the house the garden would be plunged into relative daylight. And she would have seen the sun-bright security lights shining through the kitchen windows. So no one had broken in.

Her reason stiffened into a resolve to pursue the noise, to know who was inside her home. Because now she was angry. She would not have this; would not have strange smells and footsteps inside her home. They had no right to be here, to come inside and wake her and frighten her.

Momentarily she paused in fear that her experiences at 82 Edgehill Road had opened an aperture in her mind that would force her to perceive the hidden life in any building, especially at night, as if she were now tainted at some undetectable cerebral level. If that were true she would never find peace in any place where a life had passed, where a spirit had returned. *There must be so many of them.*

Breath sealed inside her lungs and ready to break into a scream, she stepped up to the threshold of the kitchen and reached inside the darkness for the light switch on the wall. Flicked it down. Solid oak cabinets, Arhaus stools, Sub-Zero & Wolf double cooker, the rolled steel hood, the integrated refrigerator, slate-tiled floors, steel spotlights. But empty of life.

Amber's eyes found the door that led into the garage. It was closed. There should be nothing inside the garage besides her Lexus, an empty freezer cabinet she had yet to fill with supplies to get her through the coming winter. There was a new mop and bucket too, some cleaning materials with unbroken seals, unused gardening tools, nothing else.

The garage extension was the newest addition to the house and had been purpose-built. Whoever had just walked into it would not be able to get out unless they opened the garage door by using the control panel beside the metal roller door. And she would hear the motor from inside the kitchen if the automatic door was activated.

Amber inched inside the kitchen and watched the door that led into the garage. Listened.

Heard nothing.

For a while.

Until someone spoke beyond the door. People. At least two people were talking in hushed voices inside the garage. Their words were too muffled to be intelligible. But this was not Josh in her garage. This had nothing to do with Josh. And there had been no break-in. This was something else entirely.

The room bloomed with perfume: Anais Anais.

Sorry, my English not so good.

Amber twisted around on the spot, her vision in desperate search of the source of the scent. In her mind she could see Margaret's beautiful face, the lips outlined with a pencil, the lipstick glistening, the torrent of hair sweeping over white shoulders and a backless latex dress.

You look beautiful. Stunning, like.

There was no one in the kitchen with her. So how could Margaret and Ryan be here? And such became her rage, her despair, her wishful thinking that this could not be happening all over again, *here*, that Amber wrenched open the door separating the kitchen from the garage.

And stared into a cold darkness. A void not penetrated

by the kitchen lights. A space impossibly lightless, though not silent or still.

The garage should have been a small space, big enough for a car and freezer and not much else. But now she wondered at the size of the darkness beyond the open door.

The air was cold and the air pressure all wrong for an enclosed space; it was like coming up on the deck of a ship at night, and venturing out from the dimensions of a small cabin to see a vast sky above an ocean. One unspeckled by stars, or lit by moonlight; an eternal night that she could not see through. And into her mind came a new consideration that she might be nothing more than a speck of matter, stood inside a tiny yellow rectangle of light within an immense darkness; a lightless space so vast she feared she didn't know which direction was up and which down. Vertigo iced her thoughts and prickled the nape of her neck, before she was overwhelmed by the feeling of being watched from inside this darkness.

An intangibility out there had managed form without shape. She suffered a notion of a growing heaviness; solidity with a slow and almost fluid length that now moved towards the light and, perhaps, extended a head forward.

The presence in the nothingness beyond the doorway made her skin shiver and her lips move without speaking. Her mind was impacted by shock, and a fear so great it felt like a concussive blow against her skull.

A thing unseen was now sliding from out of the black room. A heavy wave approached her feet as if she stood upon wet sand: a surge and then a seeping of an invisible presence that drowned her shock with confusion; a bafflement and an incomprehension of the *black* that now swept through her mind. And within the cold current her myriad thoughts seemed to be no more than impulses on magnetic tape, quickly rewound and seemingly erased as memories flashed and vanished in moments too short to measure . . .

. . . she was terrified by the size of a sunlit ocean . . . and recalled an urge to jump from the side of a ship into depths, so swirling, green, blue . . . alive with bubbles rising and becoming a layer of foam . . .

. . . a night sky seen from an observation deck . . . a canopy of darkness so vast and scattered with lighted debris . . . and here was her imagination extending its feeble grasp of what existed beyond the earth's atmosphere . . . the inquiry dissolving before her mind was pinched out like a candle flame . . .

. . . and now here was a hospital bed . . . her sat behind a table in a white room . . . new clothes laid out on a hostel bed, the blouse pinned against a cardboard sheet inside plastic . . . 'I don't like these' . . . 'You'll have to wear them because you don't got no money' . . .

. . . being helped up the path to a house by a police-woman in plain clothes . . . green plastic screens arranged around the front of the house . . . her bloodless face photo-graphed through a tear . . .

. . . 'he's in there, on the bed. The room is pink' . . .

. . . a cup of watery tea that looked like chicken soup . . . 'they're not even making an effort' . . . her barrister shouting at a detective, her elegant hand with painted fin-gernails striking a laminate surface . . .

. . . the strip lights above her work station in a ware-house where she swooned with the flu . . .

. . . her dad in sunlight beside a caravan, wearing his

shorts and laughing at the sight of his white legs because she was laughing at them too . . .

. . . a toy fox with a dirty muzzle she treasured as a child but had not thought about until now . . . a girl at school in a pink dress holding up a paintbrush, the bristles tulip-shaped with grey paste . . . small milk bottles in a plastic crate, the silver foil tops seeping yellow cream . . .

. . . an abandoned car seat in a field that smelled of cat piss . . . a paddling pool swamped with the cut grass that had collected on small feet in a garden divided by a creosoted fence . . . homemade sausage rolls in a Quality Street tin . . .

. . . her mother wearing a wig, her face showing the skull beneath, skin thin as rice paper, eyes distant, the eyes of a stranger . . .

. . . four people sat round a table, tears on their faces, throwing their arms into the air . . .

. . . dust on uncarpeted wood beneath an old bed . . . polythene stained black on the inside . . . bricks, soil, plaster, timber planks spotted with house paint . . . raised carpet that smelled of garages . . . rusty nails . . . a tree heavy with cooking apples . . . coils of black dust . . . wild flowers, jungle weeds . . . what looked like old newspaper in a floor cavity that soon showed itself to be a dead girl's hand . . . black and white photographs of faces, smiling . . . Margaret's tanned legs walking upstairs . . . blonde girl with a cigarette . . . a dog's wet mouth . . . black hands . . . leather drum . . . tooth on a stair, dribbling its root . . . parchment eyes behind thick spectacle lenses . . . a pink bedspread . . . a tube in a masking-taped face . . .

Amber bent double, nauseated by the sudden gush of

memory and colour, by the very speed of the carousel, the swoop and swill of her mind, backwards and forwards and round and round. Her stomach turned inside out. Emptied itself like an upended plastic bag, pinched at the bottom corners and shaken. She heard the vomit splash against the kitchen floor but saw nothing through the myriad sparks dying in the black, circular void where her vision should have been.

She sat down, then slumped on the cold flagstones of the kitchen floor. The black oval, the blind spot, and its terrible depth, shrank and vanished from her vision.

Unable to tell whether the bombardment of her mind had come from within or without, and too sick to care and just relieved it was over, she lay upon the cold tiles and spat the bitterness from her mouth.

Black Maggie had riffled her like worn pages in an old paperback, then tossed her aside.

Why? You want to know me, bitch? 'Bitch. You bitch.'

But the scrutiny that had knocked the breath out of her was gone. Had lifted. Was no longer trained upon her.

She was so tired she didn't think she could stand up; she felt like she'd just completed one hundred sit-ups on a varnished gymnasium floor.

Amber peered down her body and between her feet and saw the rear wing of her black Lexus inside the garage, one edge of the freezer cabinet, the new red bricks of the garage's inner wall, a copper pipe in fabric cladding. She smelled cement, plaster and oil.

She wiped her mouth with the back of one hand and closed her eyes.

SEVENTY-EIGHT

'What's all this then? You going somewhere?' Josh spoke from just outside the kitchen. He'd seen her bags in the hall stacked neatly beside the front door. When he stepped inside the kitchen Amber avoided looking him in the eye. She prodded the poached eggs with a fork. 'Just for a few days. Two eggs enough?'

'Plenty. Smells good.'

She suppressed a tremor in her voice. 'All local. Bacon and sausage too. Even the bread. There's coffee in the jug. Just made it.'

'Cheers.'

In her peripheral vision she watched Josh approach the kitchen bin and drop a grey lump inside. More dust that he didn't want her to see. He took a stool at the breakfast bar. 'You're up early?'

'I often am.' She left it at that, but could feel Josh watching her, and she assumed with a familiar expression of mystification at her habits and a concern for her mental health.

'Thought I'd take off to Cornwall for a few days.'

'Good. I'm pleased to hear that.'

Amber brought two steaming plates to the table top.

'Sauces and stuff are all there.' She nodded at the condiments.

'Mmm.' Josh nodded at the plate with approval, his mouth already full. 'Did you even go to bed?'

'Too much on my mind.'

'You'll drop, kid, if you're not careful. I'm guessing you never slept the night before either? You OK to drive?'

'You'd be surprised at what I can endure.'

Josh was taken aback by her retort and tone. He didn't pursue his curiosity any further as to why she was leaving her house after just one week; a place on which nine months of modifications had just concluded, with a three hundred thousand pound price tag on security and renovations alone.

They ate in silence.

'Give me a call when you get back here. Just check in,' he eventually said before draining his coffee cup. 'I better hit the road. And it's just as well you're up to open the gate.' He dabbed his mouth with a napkin. 'That was lovely. Thanks for breakfast.'

Just before the front door he paused. 'I want you to take some more of my infernal advice, Amber. Don't live here on your own. Take it from someone who made the same mistake. Discussion of full details not possible. But do not live alone with all that up there.' Josh pointed at the ceiling, towards the study. 'And with what is up here.' He tapped the side of his head. 'And I am not talking about getting a cat. Is there a friend who might like a long holiday in Devon?'

A friend: the idea made her laugh unpleasantly. The closest she had to friends were the people she paid to look after her interests: Josh, her barrister, Victoria, her agent, Penelope, her researcher, Peter. Her old friends from Stoke, Bekka, Joanie and Philippa, had all sold stories to papers when the story broke through the news stratosphere and when the world developed a large rubber neck. Her relatively ordinary adolescence, troubled by an insane step-parent and the death of her father, augmented by a few flirtations with soft drugs and a couple of idiotic boyfriends, had been sifted through in as much forensic detail by the tabloids as the black stony soil of 82 Edgehill Road had been analyzed by murder squad detectives on their hands and knees; and all because of her *friends*.

She'd relegated her 'friends' to the part of her personal history she had no inclination to revisit. The fact that not one of her old friends had offered her help when she'd needed a friend most, was something she would never get past. Only Ryan had stepped up.

And look what happened to him.

Amber swallowed the lump in her throat brought on by the memory of her dead ex-boyfriend. The vivid strangeness of his presence in her dreams, and inside her home, produced a quick ripple of panic.

'Like who?'

Josh shrugged; he could see that he needed to distract her again. 'Don't they call them companions, for you ladies of leisure? So get a companion. A maid. No butler because you can't trust them around the lingerie. A housekeeper. I mean, what with all this bloody dust everywhere, don't you need someone to keep it clean?'

She started to laugh at the preposterous suggestion. 'A maid. I'm not sure I even believe in such a thing.'

'A PA, if it makes you feel better. Find someone who can live in. Light duties. Bit of company. Situation immediately vacant for right candidate. There are agencies for this sort of thing. If you do find someone, I'll check them out. I'm serious. You do not want to sleep in this house alone. Because you won't sleep in this house. If you had your way I'd still be here at Christmas in the same clothes.'

'I'd buy you an entire wardrobe.'

'You could afford it too. I've seen the posters for your film all over the sides of the 38 bus in the West End. But I'm not house trained. Too many bad habits, and I don't like sitting on my arse all day. Last night is all I will inflict on you.'

Amber felt like a child again, watching her mum walk away from the school gates. Her smile failed as soon as the front gate shuddered closed and Josh's car disappeared from view. She went back inside the farmhouse, and distracted herself by attending to the dishes and wiping away the cooking oil spattered on the kitchen surfaces. While she worked in the kitchen she left the door connecting the kitchen to the garage open, so she could keep an eye on the car and the room around it, to make sure that all remained in place and as it should be, until she left the house that morning.

During the night, once she'd gathered her wits and pulled herself off the kitchen floor, just after three a.m., she'd showered, dressed and packed. Standing in the wet room and allowing the force of the water to drown out the sound of her crying in case she woke Josh, she'd realized her experience before the mouth of the garage had been

similar to a psychotic reaction, or a hallucination produced by powerful drugs; conditions she had read about
while researching her book with Peter St John.

But there were no drugs in her life. She constantly
questioned her sanity and knew she was teeming with
paranoia, insecurity, phobias, aversions, and a persecution
complex that medication and therapy might one day successfully soothe, if she chose that route. And maybe her
psychological trauma was still so catastrophic she was
generating her own ghosts inside the farmhouse. Two
psychiatrists had already told her as much, and that she
may never fully recover from those nine days at 82 Edgehill Road, and should maintain a programme of structured
therapy until a physician deemed it prudent to stop.
Advice she had decided against taking once the investigation and the inquest concluded. Maybe that was another
unwise decision. For a long time she had longed for a
doctor or psychiatrist to categorically tell her that she was
mentally ill and had imagined everything.

But she was not going to fool herself that the impossible had not returned to her life. Not now. And her
connection to 82 Edgehill Road would no longer be
shared with Josh or Peter St John, because neither of them
would entertain her ravings.

Maybe the kind of person who claimed a special relationship with the dead – a medium or spiritualist – would
engage with her. She'd just spent hours considering the
option of inviting such a 'gifted' individual to her home,
while also worrying that a medium might try and shake
her down for a small fortune. Going that route also made
her feel she was introducing the inauthentic to an experi-

ence she had never embellished with spiritual beliefs or superstition.

But what troubled her most since she had struggled up and off the kitchen tiles in the early hours of the morning were her thoughts of Ryan. If her impressions of the night had been correct, Ryan was not at rest, and nor were any of the victims of number 82. But not even dear Ryan, who had unwittingly sacrificed his life in an attempt to save her, was welcome here.

Ryan had been with her last night, and inside her room, at least *in spirit*. A presence of Ryan. Or perhaps an illusion of her ex-boyfriend that *something* had introduced into her home to taunt her and drive her mad. In the middle of the night, as she'd thrown clothes and toiletries into her Samsonite cases, Amber had even considered that Ryan was trying to warn her. And maybe Margaret Tolka had performed this function too, by filling the kitchen with the fragrance of perfume. Revenants that acted as sensory warnings. Beside Bennet, it was possible that was all the dead had ever tried to do at 82 Edgehill Road: warn her.

She had come across such things in her study of hauntings, but she wasn't convinced; they hadn't warned her last night, they had guided her downstairs. And now her confounding ignorance of why *this* had come back into her life had begun to feel terminal.

SEVENTY-NINE

Amber jogged upstairs to fetch her portable hard drive from the study and her laptop from the bedroom; all of her electronic files were saved to both devices.

She unlocked the study and flicked the lights on. Picked up the back-up hard drive from her desk, keeping her eyes averted from the faces and headlines plastered to the wall. The room looked like the secret chamber of an obsessive, a spy, or a stalker. And she acknowledged with discomfort that she may be all three of those things about her own history.

Amber drew the blinds to see the vista outside. Her vision swept the garden and the rolling green mounds of maize beyond the foot of the rear fence, and took in the copses of trees dotted about the land where hedgerows met at the corner of the hilly fields. The giant swelling of the ocean beyond the hills glinted in a thin line of white gold on the horizon. And within the gentle sway of row upon row of long, supple maize leaves, she picked out the presence of what she thought was a leafless tree, withered black by age or even scorched spindly by a lightning strike.

She had gazed out over these fields each morning for a week and recalled that no tree stood in the centre of this field, particularly one that suggested a direct line from itself to the rear gate of her garden.

Amber screwed up her eyes.

The thump of her heart became too noticeable and irregular between her ears. Her scalp prickled.

This was no tree.

The figure was the only black in the green sea of crops, and seemed to draw in the shadow of a passing cloud to stain dark the wide open space that circled the silhouette's lonely vigil. This was a man. A tall man standing with his head bowed.

Amber hoped hard enough for it to feel like a prayer that this was a farm worker, or an unusual rambler studying a map. Because the indistinct head was lowered or bent over something that it seemed to be studying: an object held close to the chest and cradled like a baby. The thin, uneven silhouette of the head soon revealed itself to be close-cropped and bony by raising itself so that far off eyes could peer back at her.

Amber dropped the hard drive and only held onto her laptop by her fingertips.

She staggered away from the window to evade the piercing scrutiny of a face obscured by distance, the features seemingly blackened by soil or soot, though the figure was too far away to reveal what discoloured the flesh. The idea of the thin and unsightly sentinel being aware of her introduced a stutter to her breathing. She ducked down from the level of the window sill, backed out of the study in a crouch, and fled for her room and for what was locked inside a small aluminium case within her bedside drawer.

Amber stopped short of the bedside cabinet, pulled up hard by a better idea: *take a picture.*

She wrenched at her iPhone in the top pocket of her denim jacket. Ran back to the study and willed herself through the door and across the room and up to the wide window frame. Focused the camera on the field of maize, shining with sunlight and no longer concealed by passing clouds. A field now empty of anything but the crop.

EIGHTY

'I've some more anecdotal stuff on Bennet senior from the children of former neighbours, and some council records of complaints about number eighty-two. But nothing earth shattering on that front.' Peter St John turned his laptop round so Amber could see the screen. 'I have the hard copies at home, but scanned these for you. You can take the memory stick. It's all on there.'

Amber collected their lunch plates and stacked them on the room service trolley so they would have more space to work. Prompted to do the same, Peter arranged the coffee things. 'Coffee? Or you staying on the wine?'

Peter's sandy hair and thin features looked good with the new tan; his green eyes glittered like a warm sea. He'd been in Spain. A white cotton shirt and cream linen jacket further defined the impression of a well-heeled and comfortable man. A marked difference from the pale, chain-smoking journalist, pathologically anxious about money, that she'd met three years before. They may have done each other a world of good financially, but Amber now envied Peter's effortless self-assurance, his aura of serenity.

'Wine, thanks.'

For privacy they'd eaten in her room at the Duke. Peter

had arrived in Plymouth at noon. On Monday Amber called him and mentioned problems with the farmhouse and Peter assumed the building project was unfinished.

Though their book had included as much detail about the history of 82 Edgehill Road as was available at the time of publication, as well as material uncovered during the first year of the police investigation, Peter had spent the next two years researching the building and its occupants in more detail, discovering and poring over applications for planning permission, censuses, local history, any rental agreements, tracing individuals known to have lived at the address across one hundred years. He'd even undertaken a foray into genealogy.

Peter's fastidiousness, Amber knew, had not been down to his ingrained investigative thoroughness alone, nor was it taken to satisfy Amber's desire for alternative theories about the house and its previous occupants. The case had become the making of Peter St John, the uniqueness of the story a vertical accelerant for his career. Four generations of murderers had lived and been active at the same address in North Birmingham, and not one of them had been brought to justice. Peter had written the definitive book about the murders and made the story his life's work; he was the first person to be summoned by the international media, as a talking head, for any feature about, or similar to, the case. In their entire careers most journalists would never encounter such a sensational story, not to mention his exclusive access to one of two surviving cast members; the second survivor, Svetlana Lanka, spoke poor English and had long ago returned to her home country. Her official testimony about the presence of anything unnatural in the house had never been substantial. She and Margaret had not resided at the house for long either, but had both heard voices and noises in unoccupied rooms, and even become frightened of the second floor room that Amber had spent her first two nights inside.

'So what's that?' Amber asked, while peering at the official-looking form, loaded onto the laptop screen; the first document Peter wanted her to see.

'This is one of three official complaints by neighbours in Edgehill Road about flies and a bad smell that they all cite rising from number eighty-two. The complaints match one of Harold Bennet's frequent periods of renovation.' Peter didn't elaborate.

'And these,' he said, as he opened a new folder on the screen, 'are new scans of court records, some Crown, of the Bennets' respective prosecutions under The Sexual Offences Act of 1956. I've found others for kerb crawling, keeping a brothel, disorderly conduct at or very near the address. All new material.'

'Supplementing what we already know.'

'Yes, but it focuses the picture. Reveals more of the legacy. The pattern of repeat behaviour that was never perceived as being part of a bigger picture. Of something much worse. Even when some of the victims' last known addresses were number eighty-two, connections were never made by the authorities.'

It was nothing Amber wanted to read, and a further sign they were moving in different directions. Here Peter was again, collating even more actual and anecdotal evidence of violence and dysfunction, anti-social behaviour, disturbing stories of sexual offences against women; more interminable and unpleasant accounts of what awful human beings Harold and Arthur Bennet had been. Their ghastliness explained little about what dwelled inside the building before they took up residence.

'I do have something on Knacker too. Stories and so forth, from people who ran with him for a while.'

'Keep 'em.' Her retort came out sharper than she'd intended.

'Knacker McGuire', as he'd called himself, was someone for whom Amber would have considered a programme of electric shock treatment to entirely erase him from her memory.

While carrying out his fourth sentence at Her Majesty's Pleasure for an assault on a Russian prostitute in Bayswater in 2004, when he had been 'on a bender' in London, Arthur Bennet had briefly shared a prison cell in Wormwood Scrubs Prison with the house's next generation of pimps and killers: Fergal Donegal and Nigel Newman; the latter being the real name of the habitual liar 'Knacker McGuire'.

After their own releases Fergal and Knacker had travelled to Birmingham. The purpose of their trip was to divest the ageing and terminally ill misfit, Arthur Bennet, of what he had boasted was a profitable brothel in North Birmingham; a 'family business' from whose complement of young girls he had taken his pick as lovers.

Amber hadn't read the book about the Bennets, *Deadly Inheritance*, but she had read the book about Knacker and Fergal, *The Devil's Entrepreneurs*, a fairly sensational red and black jacketed, true crime offering aimed at the airside market of airports. The author had acquired information on the killers before Peter: morbidly predictable histories of petty crime and violence, burglary and drug dealing; careers founded in broken homes, suspensions and expulsions from secondary schools, and time endured under the fists of violent fathers.

Interestingly to Amber, what *The Devil's Entrepreneurs* revealed was that neither Fergal nor Knacker had any previous convictions for violence against women; those appetites only appeared to have manifested in Edgehill Road.

More urgently than ever, Amber needed Peter to target his research solely upon the spiritualist activity at the house between 1912 and 1926, with particular emphasis on anything connected to the name 'Black Maggie.' She'd been pushing him to do this for over a year. But maybe not hard enough.

She'd paid for all of his expenses and for his time researching the house's past since the completion of their first book. If there was a second book, she had promised Peter an endorsing preface and assured him the jacket could carry her name. The sizeable publishing advance for *No One Gets Out Alive* had gone to her and she had paid Peter a ghost writer's fee, as well as sharing the not inconsiderable royalties with him; the book had been translated into thirty-five languages and been involved in seven publishing auctions. Even then, Peter still needed to work; the proceeds from each film had been Amber's alone, and that had made her fortune. Peter had done well but he still needed to earn.

In the hotel room, Amber struggled to smother her impatience. 'Peter, the Bennets are conquered ground.

There's not much more I can stand to read about them. Don't you have anything about The Friends of Light? And Clarence Putnam? We know he was their first leader. How could he have not known about the first four murders?'

Peter looked surprised and then hurt at Amber's outburst. But unless he discovered something soon about the pre-Bennet era, she'd really have no choice but to seek a desperate *alternative* form of investigation into what had followed her to Devon.

Peter fidgeted in his own disappointment. 'Amber, you just never know what will join dots to something else further back in time, a clue about the past. This whole case has shown a connectivity from the start. I still feel it necessary to examine every piece of material evidence and anecdotal detail, even hearsay. You just have to understand that the further back we go, the less there is to examine. I can't work any faster than I am.'

'I don't doubt your principles or your amazing ability to uncover all of this, Peter, but I want to know about the first victims. And The Friends of Light. I know there is something there.'

Peter gave her a look she recognized from Josh: one of pity and sadness, familiar in the eyes of anyone who recognized her determination to investigate a mystical origin to the crimes. To Peter, the first era was ancient history; he doubted the murderer of the first four victims had a relationship with either of the Bennets beyond copycat behaviour. Harold Bennet had relaid the ground floor of the house sometime in the early 1960s, and may have discovered the remains of two of the first victims. And if Harold Bennet had unearthed the bones of Lottie Reddie and Virginia Anley, he had reburied them without report-ing the grim find. It was also possible Harold Bennet had been inspired by what could be done within the privacy of one's own home, using the very bricks and mortar that his new family seat was constructed from. It was the most logical theory, which officialdom, the media and the public had mostly since accepted.

The inability to explain her need for the missing information began to stoke the fire of Amber's panic. Unchecked, she knew how quickly such feelings turned to anger. She already felt like breaking something in the hotel room.

Of those involved in the investigation, or on her behalf, only the director Kyle Freeman believed links existed between The Friends of Light, the Bennets and her captors, *the Devil's Entrepreneurs*: Knacker and Fergal. Kyle had accepted Amber's story at face value, and so easily she had even questioned his readiness to believe her. But within a week of moving into the farmhouse, Amber now knew it no longer mattered who believed her, or whether her ideas were suitable for Peter's new book.

She covered her face with her hands and groaned quietly with frustration and what was swiftly becoming despair; an emotion she had prayed she would never feel again in relation to *that place*. But here it came, as leaden as it had been three years ago.

'Hey, come on,' Peter said. 'It's not that bad. And anyway, forget the court reports. In fact, forget the Ben-nets. I did find something else.'

Amber's hands were off her face. 'What?'

Peter grinned. 'Or rather a friend of mine did. George

Ritchie. He teaches history at Birmingham University and specializes in folklore. He's been on the case of the Black Maggie for a year. But . . .'

'What, what?'

'I wouldn't get too excited.'

'Why?'

'It's a tad bizarre, I'm afraid. I was in two minds whether I should even show you. Afraid it all seems a bit tenuous to me. But I put it on the memory stick. The folder is called "Black Maggie." Here it is.'

EIGHTY-ONE

Peter could not stop grinning as if embarrassed by what he was telling Amber. 'It's pretty silly. But the first thing George sent me were song lyrics. From a call and answer folk song used by Warwickshire, Herefordshire and Worcestershire field workers up until enclosure. And it's quite a salacious ditty. But George thinks the origins of the folk song are pre-Roman.

'The version of the song we have words for includes remnants of an old fertility rite from deep midwinter. Performed to usher out the cold and darkness and bless the coming crops, that kind of thing. Apparently, a version of this rite was performed for centuries in various incarnations.

'George's notes are at the bottom. Here you go: "In the song, four maidens, probably low-born virgins, we can only assume, were restrained and deflowered in honour of a pagan deity, known as *Black Maggie* in Tudor times. Though the practice probably never survived the fifteenth century, a song about the rite was still sung until the 1800s in some counties."

'George can't find any evidence of the song past the First World War. Someone wrote the lyrics down in 1908 for posterity. A priest called Mason, from out Hereford way, who bemoaned the end of rural life, blah, blah, blah, and the industrial revolution. He tried to record all the local folk songs before they were lost forever. Mason didn't have much luck because this is all obscure stuff that George dug up.

'But at least it's local.' Peter smiled and relaxed back into his chair to drink a second cup of coffee. 'All the Black Maggie stuff I have for you is on there. You want me to try and sing the song?'

Amber's attempt at a conciliatory smile failed. She read what Peter had pulled onto the screen.

When four bonny lasses are laid upon the green grass
When four bonny, bonny lasses are laid upon the green
    grass
And tied fore and aft, the black lamb will dance a jig
When four bonny lasses are laid upon the green grass
When four bonny, bonny lasses are laid upon the green
    grass
Old black mag will lift her skirts and dance a jig
When four bonny lasses are laid upon the green grass
When four bonny, bonny lasses are laid upon the green
    grass
Black oxen will draw her wagon hither, far Queen
    Black Mag
When four bonny lasses are laid upon the green grass
When four bonny, bonny lasses are laid upon the green
    grass
Thine honour, these maidens, thine honour, the corn
    doth rise like grass

Amber scrolled onto the next page of the file.

Peter leant forward to guide her through the notes. 'George says there are vestiges of an older idea inside this verse. Fragments of a similar theme were found on some Roman-British ruins in Wales, that were used for storing grain around 400 AD. Wasn't old Clarence Putnam from Wales? I seem to recall he was, but the link is so thin it's barely there. There's a wall mosaic. Here it is.'

Peter highlighted some text and a black and white photograph of chipped stone fragments on a square card. 'George thinks the connection to the folk song can be found through the images of four maidens on the tiles of the ruined grain store. The fertility rite stuff is there too. And George says that these ideas always travel and change over time. But the interpretation of the painting, most widely accepted by historians, is of four maidens being laid *beneath* the grass. Suggesting death. Probably sacrifice. Here you go . . .'

Peter scrolled down the screen and pointed his index finger at the brief footnotes. He read them aloud:

'"Though the maidens on the mosaic are depicted with torcs, or neck rings, in serpent form, de vermis, possibly to represent a Goddess that we have no name for."'

'George thinks the mosaic and the folk song developed out of an even older Northern-European-wide practice, between 100 BC and about 500 AD, in which people were tied down and throttled in peat bogs. Started back in the bronze age, continued through the iron age. It's in his notes. See here: "Often young women or common criminals were used, to ensure the end of winter and a good harvest come spring."'

'Eerily coincidental, but I don't think we need go back that far for the Bennets, do you? Or The Friends of Light. I mean, they were devout Christians. It'll get our book stocked in the New Age section of Waterstones.' Peter found this incredibly funny; Amber was nearly sick into her lap.

'But this is all I can dredge up about your Black Maggie. You all right? You look a bit peaky.'

EIGHTY-TWO

Three days later, Amber opened the front door of the farmhouse and turned off the alarms.

The first thing she noticed on the hall floor and connecting staircase was the dust. Small mounds the size of mice and rats exploring the clean, new spaces, as if poised to clamber further up the polished steps to the bedrooms.

The second thing she noticed was the smell. Competing with the fragrance of the new furniture, floors and walls, was a pungent undercurrent of damp wood, sour emulsion, tangy loft spaces and stale underfloor cavities. The stench of 82 Edgehill Road.

Such was the dross on the floor of the living room, she might have been inside a tomb; one recently opened and excavated by explorers. Only she had not just walked inside a cave in the Valley of the Kings, or ducked inside a Saxon barrow, she had entered her own home. A place so newly renovated it should have retained its pristine condition after only being occupied by a single person for a mere seven days. Yet the interior now looked to have been shuttered and derelict for decades.

With hands she could barely feel, Amber drew the curtains and allowed more of the sun's illumination to fill the wide space of the living room and adjoining dining room.

Bales and rolls of sooty dust, amidst disintegrating clumps and lumps, reared up the skirting and seemed in the process of crossing the wooden floors from one side of the room to the other.

Bands of morning light pierced the clean glass of the patio doors to reveal myriad diaphanous motes wafting on air currents. The harder she looked, the more the very air became a perpetual shower of dust particles, forever falling, constantly stirred, moving, relocating, glittering, gathering, growing.

She peered at the sole of one bare foot; it was blackened by the filth spread around the floor. Same thing in the kitchen. Her fingertip came away black, time after time, on every flat surface the kitchen boasted. The surfaces, the pots and pans hanging above the central work station, the breakfast bar, the oven, microwave and sink, were all filmed with dust, a multitude of specks accumulating and spread finely to fade the room to grey. Twenty thousand pounds to build, but now as dirty as a long-abandoned squat.

Amber opened the patio doors and stepped outside. She sat on the first of the three steps that led to the grassy pasture of the rear lawn and began to cry. Could not stop crying; the tears of bitterness, rage, frustration and outright despair would not end. Tears of the helpless. Her body trembled, her hands twitched as if cold.

The late summer sun was warm and bright, and only the most talented fine artist could have adequately captured the quiet and gentle beauty of the Devonshire morning: a most English idyll, with a subtle, intense power. Maize shivered in a faint cooling sea breeze;

momentarily the heads of the nearest plants swayed sideways in the capricious air currents, and then nodded
towards her. The crop beyond her garden gate might have
become an audience to her wretchedness, raising thou-
sands of hands to the air to wave above a vast crowd that
whispered and rustled in anticipation of what came next.

*Thine honour, these maidens, thine honour, the corn
doth rise like grass.*

'My God, my God,' she said to herself, and to the earth
and trees and sky, to whatever bore witness to her misery.

*You took her back, you took her back to the green
grass . . . the harvest, to the country. Took her from the
city. From out of the darkness. And you carried her back
here. You are a carrier.*

'No.'

Or did she take you back?

*Black Mag let you run, you stupid bitch. She let you
run here. She found you here. She went through your
mind. She found your memories of the seaside. Of Dad,
Mum. She made you come here. She wanted it for herself.
Because she's inside you.*

Used. Used like the others.

*You took an oath. You promised to keep her. You
would have said anything to get out of that place . . . did
you?*

'I didn't, I didn't, I didn't!'

You did.

'I can't remember. Oh Jesus, I can't remember.'

She couldn't fully recall her night on the kitchen floor
of the ground floor flat, surrounded by broken glass and
crockery and splintered wood; the night she had truly lost

her mind through sustained terror. A time in which she had become convinced that she was no longer inside the house, or even part of a recognizable world; a time in which she seemed to have existed on the border between one world and another.

And in such places, didn't she know only too well, that the precision of a person's recall could not be relied upon. Memory developed a second life, and the imagination cultivated the visuals of memory and embellished them over time. Isn't that what the therapist had said: that her memory and imagination had combined within that house, and continued to do so after she escaped it? Because in hindsight she remembered herself looking down at her body on the kitchen linoleum, and not lying amongst the wreckage and peering up and into the black, so it was never a true memory, or she would have recalled the room from the floor?

Like so much of that time in her life, she seemed to have walked within a perpetual nightmare that began the very moment the front door of *that place* closed behind her. And what she had experienced in the rooms of the ground floor flat had made her want to die, and quickly. That she had not forgotten. She had desired the void. Total extinction. An end to consciousness. Had prayed for it. Because she had seen things no mind was built to withstand.

So maybe the building had been a prison, a place of exile for something older than the house, even the city? The house was a place *it* had scrabbled back into, when called. A temple. Perhaps called upon innocently and inadvertently by those idiots of 'Light'. Had they invited something back to twist the minds of the simpletons that occupied its tomb? Or had Clarence Putnam brought it to the big city from Wales? He had been an amateur historian. But whose will drove his purpose? She would never know. Those fools may have continued a degenerate rite once practised freely. An ancient honour. And what if they were answered when they called out to the darkness?

Nonsense. Nonsense. It was nonsense.

The song. Maidens beneath the grass . . . the nursery rhyme of the gypsy boy in the dream she had a thin recollection of. He had been at the house during the Second World War with his grandmother. They had been committed to an asylum. *Four maids.* Had he sung something about four maids? *To open a door.*

Women hanged by washing line. Buried in soil. Cemented into foetal positions like the unborn. Walled up, the crouching bones.

Amber suspected she was going to throw up. She was breathing too quickly and her heartbeat was accelerating her panic to a place where she worried she might need an injection to calm down. She was mad; these were the thoughts of the damaged, the deranged, the impaired.

Amber stood up and turned upon the house. 'Who are you? Where are you!'

Her shaking vision raked the window panes for the sight of an unwelcome face; one that might peer out at her, gleeful, triumphant, sated, with little white eyes open. A thing that had followed her here.

There had been no nightmares, no intrusions, no trespassers, no darkness beyond the doors of her hotel suite in Plymouth. Whatever she had fled from, whatever she had encountered in her first week in this new house, had followed her here, to this building. So would *it* follow her anywhere and eventually appear wherever she settled? At sea she had been moving. In sheltered accommodation she had never been alone.

For I have determined there to winter.

What did that mean?

Me? Winter in me?

Oh, God no. Please, no.

Have you been biding your time?

Amber turned and stumbled onto the lawn, lost her footing while she clutched her skull to still the spin and the flash of the images and the ideas that gushed like condemning evidence into the courtroom of her mind, testifying to her collusion and collaboration with something no one believed in. Something that could not exist. And at the edge of her vision, the maize plants continued to flow and wave, like so many small green banners rejoicing at the return of a queen.

All around her property the crops grew to record heights and highs. The local television news said so. She recalled a police constable in Edgehill Road, who had been shushed and glared at by the detectives that first took her back to the address, after he had remarked that 'those cookers are a good size'; the constable had been referring to the abundance of massive cooking apples rotting brown in the grass of number 82, or pulling down the supple branches of the trees that encroached upon the roof of the ancient, sagging shed.

The blue sky now blinded her eyes into a squint. The vastness of the earth's cold soil suddenly became apparent: deep layers of turf and root and spindly tendril, sucking at nutrients in the dark, beyond the eyes of the living who occupied some thin, ephemeral film of breathable gas, below the suffocating extinction of the black void above and around, all around.

Was this thin coating of oxygen around such dense earth all there was to life, to existence? How could it be all there was? The idea was ludicrous. The unacknowledged irrelevance of humanity was the notion's only defence.

We have never been alone.

Amber felt faint, staggered and then fell to the cool, soft grass that embraced her weight. She wiped her nose with her forearm.

'No.' She shook her head. It could not be true. The idea was so crazy you'd have to be crazy to even entertain it. This bounty had nothing to do with her. The harvest in South Devon had bloomed to its record-breaking surplus before she had even set foot on English soil at Southampton. The agriculture, the weather, could not have any connection to her.

Not everything is about you. Isn't that what her stepmother used to shout at her? Was she so egocentric and solipsistic to assume that she had become the focus of the unworldly? Singled out to carry a message or perform a special divine task? Schizophrenic delusions. Wasn't she hearing voices again?

'I won't accept this. No. Won't. No. No. No. This is not happening. Not really. None of this. They fucked you up. They fucked you up. You were already fucked up, but they fucked you up even more.'

Inside her jacket her phone began to tinkle and vibrate.

She stared at the screen. Number unknown.

EIGHTY-THREE

'Hello, I'm outside. In the lane. Outside the gate. I must say you're well hidden. I been past your house three times already!' A happy, excitable voice, satisfaction or relief that the obscure destination had been found, human warmth generating from the other end of the call; it took a long time to pierce Amber's preoccupation with such unworldly matters.

'Hello? Hello?' the voice continued, the enthusiasm ebbing to confusion.

Amber swallowed. 'Yes.' Her voice was a hoarse whisper, her larynx thick with tears.

'Amber? Ms Hare?'

That was her new name, yes, the name of the lonely, pale, rich girl prone to tears, but it seemed an odd signifier, one strangely detached from who she was right now, right here, hunched over in the garden of a defiled dream house, her face wet with tears, her heart so laden with dread she wondered if she would ever have the strength to move her feet again.

'Sorry, Ms Hare? Can you hear me?' Confusion was turning to concern at the other end of the call.

Amber recognized the woman's voice. This was Carol, the prospective live-in housekeeper and companion she had interviewed by phone on Thursday, just two days ago, the day after she'd met Peter in her Plymouth hotel. She'd conducted four interviews by phone with applicants recommended by the home help agencies for the residential opening at her farmhouse.

How could she allow anyone else to enter this place that had gone so bad so quickly? A place contaminated, toxic with nightmares, infested with the dead, soiled by dust and rank with the stench of killers. What kind of house was this to keep? And what kind of person would seek a companion to share hell with them?

During the interview Carol's warmth and her sweetness, through the sound of her voice alone, had immediately attracted Amber, reminding her of those surviving sensations of her mother that she still held dear. Carol had quickly become a shortlist of one.

She'd arranged for Carol to visit the farmhouse this morning, Saturday, to meet more informally, to see what she thought of the house. Amber almost laughed at that now; a woman to keep this dirty shrine to old magic, murder, the restless dead, and the tomb of a still-living mad woman. It would be inhumane to expect another to cohabit a place so unstable. In her desperation, what had she been thinking?

Amber sniffed, wiped at her nose again. 'Yes, Carol. I can hear you now.'

'Oh good. I was saying I am outside.'

'Fine.' She had to turn her away. But the woman had driven all the way from Tavistock for the appointment. Carol had been looking forward to the trip; that's what she had said on the phone. Carol was a widow and her daughter had recently emigrated to Australia with her husband, taking Carol's sole grandchild away to the other side of the planet. Carol had confided all of this to Amber during the phone interview. She'd spoken directly, candidly.

Carol had once supervised the canteen of a stately home open to the public, had nursed her sick mother to the end of a life blighted with cancer, nursed her husband to the end of the horror of Alzheimer's, then cared for her granddaughter five days a week, while her parents worked to save for their future, in Australia.

Carol had cared for the young and the old, the sick, the confused, the dying. Amber had sensed compassion, patience, a bedrock of kindness, an innate understanding of the troubled heart, a soft and nurturing presence that sought to share a rare goodness with another, a stranger like her.

'I can't let you in.' Amber walked to the side of the house and glanced through the patio doors. *The dust.* 'It's a bit of a mess.' The statement was absurd; she wished she had said nothing.

'Don't worry.'

'I'm sorry. I've been away.' Amber couldn't think of anything else to say, and her dread and fear swiftly warmed into a heat of mortification. If Carol saw the dust and the dross she would think badly of her; think she was a dirty girl. Irrelevant to even think this way. Why did she even care? Her own innate nature was a banality that didn't cease in the face of black miracles. And there was no job now, not here.

'A bit of mess don't frighten me. Maybe this is something I can help you with.' Carol's words bounced along melodically, given flight by an eagerness to help, to please.

Amber moved past the garage extension and stood on the front drive, stared at the electric gate. 'It's not safe.'

'Pardon,' Carol said.

Amber swallowed. 'Sorry. It's . . . it's not safe here. In here. Not safe.'

'I don't understand.'

'I can't let you in. Can't let anyone in. I'll pay for your time. I will. Your petrol. But I can't let anyone in here. Not now. I'm not really who you think I am, Carol. I want to be who you think I am, but I can't be. *They* won't let me. Because it's getting worse. And I'm so tired. So tired by it all . . . And it's happening again. Quickly. Soon it will get worse, like it did before. Right here. Something followed me. It waited. But it's inside here now.'

Carol ended the call, and never called Amber again.

EIGHTY-FOUR

Her face was in her hands. She sat in the dirty living room. Every place would be dirty that she made home. Dirty and murdered. It was hopeless. Coming back to England, to Devon, had been futile. Telling the truth and trying to hold the meanness and savagery and cruelty of the world back had been in vain. Because here she was again: a young, frightened woman, alone and waiting for something much greater than herself to destroy her.

Stepmothers, jobs, landlords, murderers, the police, journalists, the crazies – they'd all had a go. She'd stood tall for a long time, she had resisted them all. But could do so no longer. She was drowning again in cold black water with no sandy bottom beneath her raking toes; maybe it was better to sink now, get it over with.

She thought again of the warm voice of the woman outside her gates. And yearned for it so much she felt pain.

No matter how much she now craved an end to her solitude, she'd only occupied a world of silence aboard the cruise ships, rarely indulging in fraternization, beside small talk with the other passengers; always guarded about her past, while forever pausing to consider what she should say about her new identity. And this charade had contin-ued for so long, she'd found herself absurdly excited at the mere prospect of a stranger's company. Pathetic. She realized now just how greedy she had been for the warmth of another.

But she had not run for the nearest sea port, despite gazing longingly at the docks for a week in Plymouth. Nor would she check into the hotel nearest the farmhouse tonight, accompanied by nothing but an overnight bag, even if she suspected that an anonymous room was the safest environment and possibly all she would ever be able to call home again. Instead, she had come back and she would stay in the place she had wanted to call her own.

Amidst the exhausting push and tug of confusion, fear and rage, she recognized a new purpose to resist, and also a morbid curiosity that comes from acceptance. Defiance was hardening inside her; resistance stiffened from an unstable current of vengeful anger. It felt like a heat behind her face. She would not be moved from here. She would not abandon her new home, or the person she wanted to be.

Resigned but frightened, and even appalled by her decision, she had returned to where *they* were. All of them. The Black Maggie and her constituency of the lost, the desolate, and possibly their killers too. So perhaps she was acknowledging she could run no more. Her sense that the experience was destined to repeat itself, no matter how far she ran, would not desist.

Because you have determined here to winter.

What was here must be found, drawn out, confronted. And she had to do it alone. *The box! The little box. Where was it?*

So maybe it was all about her when on land – an idea

Amber had toyed with until the weight of it began to feel unbearable, and she could only imagine herself as a silent and haunted figure, elderly, friendless, childless, whispered about, and sitting alone on the deck of a ship in the middle of a vast ocean, her legs wrapped in a blanket.

But would that be so bad compared to . . .

For how long could she hold out here before fleeing back to the sea? How much time did she have to summon priests, and those with second sight, and commit to other desperate measures to diagnose what had returned and now moved around and through her like an unidentified virus?

What will it take?

It did communicate. Amber thought of Fergal's bony and soiled length, pressed against the innocuous ground floor door of 82 Edgehill Road, his face committed to some horrid transmission emitted from deep inside those abandoned but still occupied rooms. He'd once said it was Bennet that told him things, but maybe Bennet was only a go between for something older and far worse.

'When will you speak to me? What do you want?'

There was a physical dimension too: dust and odours were conjured, sounds, then freezing hands that had once stretched across a tingling space to touch her flesh at night. Once the seal was broken it happened quickly. Once the Maggie was awoken, once she found you, she didn't waste time: nine days in Birmingham . . . *and the ninth should have been your last.*

She hadn't slept for days, not properly, and could barely keep her eyes open. The last of her energy was burned off in the garden. She made her way upstairs to her room.

Amber unlocked the drawer beside her bed and took out her weapons.

She called Josh. Received his answering service.

'Mate. I'm back. Here. They're *all* here too.' She started to cry and ended the call.

Apprehension throttled her like a ligature; anxiety paralyzed her limbs. What new strategy would be employed against her tonight to drive her out of her mind?

She called Josh again. 'I used to hope that I was sick, mate, so then I would know it wasn't real. But I had tests. Scans for tumours and strokes, vascular problems, dementia, abnormal brain function. I had to. After what I came out of that place claiming, I didn't have any choice. But nothing unusual was found by the doctors. Only Cyclothymia. It's a bipolar disorder. Depression. I had it two years. I was manic, then depressed, manic, depressed.

'I know what you think, but I had clinical interviews with psychiatrists too. I saw a therapist who helped me through the shock. The depression surprised no one after what I had been through. They expected it.'

The time allotted for a message ended with an insolent bleep.

Amber called Josh again; was glad he never picked up. 'Josh, I think I was already on my way into depression by the time I moved away from Stoke, because of Dad, and Val, being unemployed, money, all kinds of crap. This isn't about depression. Or hypomania and hallucinations. I always knew it was something else. I knew it was and it still is. It's more than all that. It's here. I think it's inside me. It got inside.' She ended the call.

She would soon be all out of fear; her reservoir was close to exhausted. She told herself that she must use all of her strength, the inner resources that had gotten her so far away from that dismal hell in North Birmingham, and these resources must now divert or quell the terrible rip currents of panic when *it* started again.

They were here. There was no mystery now. No doubt left in her mind. Wishful thinking had finally been put to the sword; doubt had been beheaded. At least that was something: the first step to self-preservation and the wall you leant your back against when you made a stand.

What did it want, this Maggie, this God? The ghosts of its victims were lost, cold, lonely, but somehow still entrapped by what they had been slain to honour; those pitifully repulsive remains, mottled dark and moist, twisted, crouching, tethered and collared inside soil or plaster, nailed under the stained planks, but still grinning through their polythene shrouds. She wanted to free them, the slaves that were awoken and sent to harrow her. Or maybe they were here to prepare her for the presence of a God? She didn't know. 'Are you here for revenge?' she called out from where she lay. 'Or do you think I owe you?'

The sound of her own voice seemed brazen in the air of her bedroom. But her words also possessed a hard outer case of triumphant defiance that felt accidental or unintended. She wondered if she were so morbidly desperate she was now trying to goad whatever stalked her. Did she really want this thing out in the open, this squatter that sat upon and suppressed her reason with heavy black coils?

But when next *it* swelled around her, with the sounds

and movements and smells and the words in the darkness, Amber knew her only chance of survival would require the shutting down of her own instinct to scream and run. She must rediscover and then tear open the part of herself that had once cut a throat, castrated a man, and then walked up a flight of stairs to burn the face off a murderer.

She needed to enter the mad red place that killers inhabited; inside there she might see her enemy's face. And when Amber reached the outer limits of her reason, only then might the Maggie reveal where she was hiding.

And if she is hiding inside me . . . then there was only one thing to do. Amber clenched her hand around the gun on the bedclothes beside her hip.

The idea took her breath away.

Only grace or rage had any hope against such horrors as walked with her, and she had always struggled with grace.

Her thoughts drifted and she reminisced of her 'slaughter' of Knacker McGuire, as the press had described her actions, and how she'd 'disfigured' Fergal; she had always told herself that she had just cause, that the extremity of her situation had compelled her to act in a way that she had never acted before. But what she had done to those men was judged, by nearly everyone else, as evidence of insanity. She had come out of that house with her arms bloodied to the elbow and her teeth bared like an ape menaced by leopards.

So perhaps an ability to destroy had been bequeathed to her, and with it the desire to damage and maim her enemies had been a gift too: such suspicions often made her suspect that she had been tainted. Corrupted like the others, altered when visited inside her own madness by the greater darkness that surrounded us all, and always had done. Wasn't consciousness raised and opened wide to admit spirits and accept the blessings of gods? Was chaos not a path to the most total darkness? Perhaps the worst of her was truly determined by *other things* she could only imagine and not perceive.

'Do you think I will kill for you?'

Josh, Peter, Victoria, Penelope: all of her managers, representatives, biographers and guardians, were uncomfortable with this facet of her story. Perhaps even more uneasy with her violence than they were with her claims that something old and powerful and unnatural had filled the stinking air of *that place*; a place where something *other* had created an environment for cruelty, sadism and sacrifice. And it wanted her for itself, for its purposes.

She called Josh again. Left another message. Whatever happened here next, she wanted him to know how she felt before the end.

'She's old, Josh. Very old. Peter's shown me. The information is on the red pen drive in my study. I don't know what I can do. I'm trying to work that out. How do I fucking fight her? What if she's inside me? Oh God . . .'

Old tastes and habits had been sated at number 82, where *she* had determined to winter.

'It's in a folk song, Josh, and on some broken pots from a long time ago. It's all Peter can find. All we know. But she's old. Black Mag is very old.' The message time came to an end with another long bleep.

Perhaps it was not hard for old, unseen *others* to detect this propensity for the bestial in a species of animal that claimed Amber among its multitudes; the potential was everywhere, smouldering black and red behind every face. Easy to find in the Bennets, in Fergal. Maybe she was a challenge, and a greater reward.

From wars and holocausts to seedy murders in suburban houses, and ordinary wives smashed in banal kitchens, there always appeared to be so many takers for the darkness, the clever and patient darkness. And for those that strangled and buried its maids and maidens there were rewards: vast, bountiful, fertile, whispering rewards.

A terrible gravity of inhumanity now oppressed Amber's thoughts as she lay upon the bed, as if some barely defined but incalculably vast history of burnings and torture and murder and war and violence, of despair and hopelessness, had gathered around the bed to expose itself; to extinguish any momentary and futile urge to resist the great momentum of indifferent darkness.

The one we will all reach in death.

She called Josh a fifth time. He didn't pick up. 'What's the point, to anything? The darkness was always there anyway. Was there first. It will always be there. We love but those we love die, like Mum, Dad . . .

'I've seen such beauty in the world, mate. From the decks of the grandest ships. But it didn't care about me. Beauty doesn't care about any of us. Only darkness wants us.'

Exhausted by her bleakest thoughts, Amber looked at the window. She could almost hear the distant rustling of the maize.

Her tired eyes closed.

EIGHTY-FIVE

The figure walked through the dark crop. Head bowed purposefully to watch the progress of its feet, obscured by the fronds and shadows of the furrows that ran between the long, restless rows of broad leaves.

The plants grew to the height of the figure's knees. And the careful progress suggested the visitor did not want to lose its footing between the drooping leaves or drop the precious cargo that was clutched to its chest: a small thing that suggested it was not without significance, but obscured by the dirty folds of a coat and by blackened hands. Something no bigger than a cat, wrapped in white cloth and cradled by grubby fingers, held close and tight, in the manner of a nervous but joyous father in an operating theatre; this swaddled newborn was safe within protective arms.

A smoky sky streaked with the amber of a breaking dawn created enough light for the visitor's silhouette, and for some scant detail of the traveller's apparel and cargo. But the dim orange light, like that of a candle held behind a bottle of brandy, did not reveal the traveller's identity, no matter how much Amber's eyes implored the spectre for some sign that it was not what she most feared.

The lone figure strode on, lanky, stooped, tired, ragged,

and yet indistinct like a scarecrow with a face shadowed by the brim of an old hat, though this head was not covered, but seemingly shorn and issuing the dull gleam of old leather.

The gate in the garden fence was open to beckon the weary stranger into the garden; to tarry no longer, out there in the rustling and whispering green leaves that caressed the thin legs that strode endlessly and inexorably and inevitably towards her.

All around her bed, the thin women stood up and came closer.

Amber awoke, her body stiff with cold, as if night air had been flowing into her room for hours, to settle and lower the air temperature to near freezing. She had fallen asleep fully dressed but uncovered by the bedclothes.

Four thirty a.m.

She had not expected to sleep so long; had expected to rouse long before the pitch black of a moonless country night had fallen. But she was tired, so tired now, by it all, by everything, and she had slept deeply . . . and then dreamed of the stranger's approach to the house. The very same figure she had seen out there twice before, as if it were guarding the front and rear of a new territory, its chosen habitat; preventing an exit but yearning for an entrance. And it had been bringing something to her. Something that wanted her.

Amber remembered the images that closed the dream, that fell away when her mind hauled itself awake. But the final frames remained, as did her distress at how uncomfortably close the women's faces had come to her own, peering, determined and bloodless, beneath coils of black hair. One of them had been wearing a hat and had raised unpleasantly thin arms into the air of the black room, exulted or excited by what had been found: *her*.

The wrists of the woman in the hat had been bony and pale, the extremities of the fingers pointed as the figure reared backwards in its obscene joy. The other three had jostled about the bed and then leant over her body too. Long teeth, bad teeth, discoloured teeth in receding gums inside the ovals of narrow mouths, nostrils black in pinched noses, eyes bright, their expressions sharp, perhaps gleeful: Amber held that much in her mind, after one of the faces had veered too close to her own, as if to embrace her, and she had roused quickly to utter a small shriek as she sat up. Her chest heaved, either from panic or from holding her breath, and she peered around her bed, eager to establish her whereabouts.

Inside her bedroom. Yes, she was inside her room and sitting up in bed. She was alone. But the rigidity of her limbs and the nervous anticipation that churned in her stomach attested to the nature of a dream vivid enough to be a sign. Another sign. Reluctantly accepted but a clear indication of intent.

She turned her head and looked towards the window. Her eyes were greeted with the vision of the same sky that had covered the world in her dreaming mind: sooty and angry with clouds concealing the last few stars; a vaulted carapace of black cumulus, rippled with the distant furnace of a rising sun.

Another sign.

Are you here now?

She lowered her legs from the mattress and stood up. Approached the place upon the floor where she had stood in the dream, before the open window. At the corner of her mind flickers of terror attempted to catch and spread. Nothing about her breathing was easy. But she still approached the window.

He was closer to the house now. In a garden half revealed by the dim dawn, he was down on his knees, with those long, dirty fingers that she had once felt around her skull, stretched towards the sky. And when she appeared at the window the figure raised a murky face to look upon the house. What she could see of the face glistened, as if wet with tears, or with the trails left by the plump bodies of insects.

Amber stepped back and covered her deceitful eyes. Felt the trembling begin in her ankles and spread to her knees and onwards, until her fingers shook with a slight palsy against the flesh of her face.

No.

She would not, she could not give in to the screams that would smash the thin glass of her composure and then rebound and echo off these tranquil walls.

Remember, remember, what use are screams and tears?

Amber uncovered her eyes. She picked up the handgun and returned to the window on poorly coordinated legs; her teeth were so tightly clenched she feared they would soon snap. And she looked down at an empty lawn.

Barely revealed by the struggling sun of the new day, the grass was still dark. But nothing was lowered to its knees on the lawn; nothing implored the sunless sky with long, thin arms; no wet and blackened face was trying to reveal itself to her. Not any more. Nothing so filthy and horrid was out there now. And nor was whatever it had transported here: that dark lump covered in what could have been white lace, clinging to the front of the intruder like a babe at the teat.

Outside the door to her room, muffled, uneven footsteps moved away and down the first floor corridor, unhurried, but eager to be followed.

Amber wiped a sleeve across her eyes. *Let them come.*

Let them all come to speak their minds, with what little memory and instinct and sense they still possessed in the lightless cold that they could not understand, and had always struggled to know since *she*, old Black Mag, had harvested them from the pits in which they had been bound and throttled.

How many were there? Why did some stalk her, muttering for her attention, while others remained silent?

It was a small mercy, but she was sure she had never made Harold Bennet's acquaintance. He had died in prison, been incinerated municipally and not interred *on site*. But was the son, Arthur, here in Devon? He had died in the house of his criminally insane father and murdered mother, and been active in the dismal apertures of the family home. So where was the rapist?

Fergal was here, impossibly, but he had not died or been interred at number 82. Or maybe he was not dead? Was he really outside? Amber tightened her grip on the weapon.

And where was that bony-faced wretch, the prince of weasels, Knacker? Why had he not reintroduced his reptilian intent into this building? He had appeared solely in dream. After all, he had ended his days in that place too, like Bennet Junior. How could Fergal be here and not Knacker or Bennet?

She wondered again if she now carried the Maggie like a parasite that had nestled into the very flesh and blood of her body. *She* must travel with her constituency. She'd never know the thing's motivations or purpose. Why it had let her go free from its temple in the roots of the house. Perhaps Fergal had stolen the thing he served, against its wishes, and it had wanted her to destroy its disciples with glass and acid. Or had it let her go for some other, even more hideous role that she was required to play elsewhere? There were no books on the subject; nothing had been found beside a few old songs and some broken masonry. All she had ever had were her wits, her guesses, her instincts. But the rules to the Black Maggie's ritual were not clear, not yet. And what would she have to do, where would she need to journey, to understand these rules and find their limits? But whatever happened, she must never add herself, or allow herself to be added, to the growing congregation of the lost and confused. Victims remained victims; tormentors remained tormentors. If that wasn't hell she didn't know what was.

She could not be a victim.

She looked at the gun in her hand. 'I'll do it before you have me! You hear?'

Maybe suicide after a long and wretched period of depression, enriched by unbearable visions, was the plan for Amber: her fate, wherever she fled. *They caught up with you. Found you here.* So maybe suicide was no escape either.

The next maiden laid down.

'Is that what you want, bitch? Another dead girl? That what you came for?'

Holding the handgun at her side, Amber used her thumb to disengage the safety catch. She doubted a bullet would have any effect on what now moved through this building, but the gun made her feel stronger. And if Fergal was still alive, if somehow, by some impossible byway, he had found her here, and that truly had been him down there upon the lawn, then she would finish the task she should have completed three years ago. The idea of executing him, of holding the barrel against his unseemly face and squeezing the trigger, gave her a pulse of excitement that made her breath catch.

'Are you inside me?' she shouted as she opened the door to her room. 'Or are you out here, bitch?'

She could hear the slow and careful tread of something ahead of her, descending the stairs now, and she was reminded, uncomfortably, of the time she had been led down to the kitchen and the garage door, only one week ago.

So was this poor Ryan again, in her home? Was this her blood-spattered knight, broken and then smashed dead by a house brick? She needed to know if he was suffering. *Still suffering.* And if Ryan was tormented then it was her duty to end his pain.

This was not only about her; if *this* was happening, right now, right here, then *this* concerned all of the poor souls that had followed her from their wretched graves in Edgehill Road. She'd always promised that she wouldn't forget them. 'How do I set you free? Tell me! One of you! Tell me what the fuck to do!'

Ryan had lost teeth. The forensic detectives had gone through *that place* in North Birmingham on their hands and knees, and picked up every hair that remained on its rotten floors. Ryan's two missing teeth had not been overlooked, kicked aside, or trodden into the freshly turned soil of the yard. Of that, Amber was sure. So the missing teeth had been gathered, *collected*.

Margaret Tolka had lost hair. She had been in the kitchen here too; she had filled the air with a residue of her attempt at sophistication: Anais Anais perfume. Other victims had been found with missing teeth, fingers, toes, perhaps more hair, though it was not possible to be sure of what had been extracted from those that had been buried the deepest for longest. Bennet had lost a finger. All of the Maggie's victims had been interred incomplete.

Amber's heart sped up at the notion that gradually grew and formed; one that suddenly seemed less macabrely fanciful and more logical, as she took step after step to the summit of the staircase. Without a physical emissary, without jailors and assassins, could Old Mag do anything but harrow her and drive her crazy? She wondered if she could live with the dreams, and if she could learn to live with ghosts, until she found an answer and a way out. And was this how old Black Mag carried her companions, through gathered remains, *trophies*? Which implied she must be right here in some physical sense, but how was that possible? Had she been cradled outside in Fergal's arms, and carried for three years?

There was no one on the stairs. Though as before,

Amber heard feet scuffle along an old track, like an invisible path or routine was now forming on the new floors as a fresh infestation of the dead took hold. These presences had always been known to repeat themselves.

Distracted, clutching at logic, even at such a time as this, she searched her mind for a solution to how the grisly artefacts, these trophies of a devil, were transported here? Fergal. He had to be alive. And he must have carried the relics of a foul God here. 'How? How? How can you be here?' She shouted to squash her panic.

A door opened inside the kitchen.

Amber stopped moving. She remembered too vividly what had assaulted her down there; what had opened her mind and flicked through her memories like they were playing cards, shuffled quickly between unseen hands and read by the presence of something unnatural, a thing that had nearly put out her life like an irrelevant ember fallen from a hearth.

She was wanted by the void. Nothingness, endless darkness desired her. The eternal cold, the end of self, the repeated stuttering of final words awaited her inside this very house. She was needed. Someone had come to the house to take her across, over to the other side. It had been kneeling on the lawn like some dreadful blackened ferryman. Was that *its* purpose: unfinished business?

'Fergal! You bastard! You want me? I'm here!'

She chased another idea and its surreal consequences, because if she were to die and her estate was given to the charity for battered women that she had been so generous towards, and as instructed by her will . . . *my God, the will* . . . that bequeathed the house to women who were denied homes where they could be safe . . . if she died here would she one day mutter to them herself? Was it her destiny to be dead here, but present and unseen? Would she plague the shattered and nervous female refugees who came to this farmhouse for shelter in years to come? Would she climb into their beds to seek warmth and companionship? Would she harrow them with her own vague memories and her stammering, her blindness and her confusion?

What is the time?

Amber swallowed and wished she could rinse away the dreadful enormity of the thoughts that swelled inside her skull. She would have to change her will, and insist that the property was pulled down, destroyed, the very earth around its foundations sown with salt, then sealed flat with concrete.

Her attention was seized by the open kitchen door.

She had reached the foot of the stairs, and through the kitchen doorway she could see that the door into the garage was open on the far side of the room. The dawn light that fell from the kitchen windows glinted off the paintwork and windows of her car. And there was the edge of the freezer cabinet too. At least the interior of the garage had not dissolved into an impenetrable but seething darkness.

Amber raised her arm and pointed the gun at the mouth of the garage. 'I know you are in there.'

Can't hurt you, can't hurt you, can't hurt you . . .

She tucked herself inside the kitchen door, but leant her back against the wall so she could see the whole room. And it was then that she became aware of the smell. The air of the room was now fragranced with Ryan's scent: his deodorant and soap, the fabric conditioner, his perspiration. And the sense of him in here blurred her eyes with tears. 'Ryan?' Her voice was no more than a whisper, but the word invoked a response from the unlit garage.

An ungainly mouth, one perhaps filled with saliva or liquid, tried to speak within the far darkness to which it had retreated. The wet muttering was unintelligible. But she could hear the speaker moving, the distant thumps of a clumsy body against the garage door. A shuffle as if from a foot scuffing cement or being dragged behind a cumbersome shape.

'Ryan.' She swallowed to clear her throat of emotion. 'Ryan?'

'Ba . . . a . . . ee.' *Baby*: that's what he used to call her.

'Stefff.' *Steph*.

There was now a terrible sniffing, and a wheezy inhalation, as if the speaker was afflicted with infected sinuses that filled his airways with liquid. It sounded as if someone in her garage was not only struggling to speak, but to breathe.

Blood. Drowning in blood.

'Stefff . . .'

What followed the attempt to pronounce her old name sounded like 'Here', or even 'Come here', but Amber couldn't be sure, so insufficient, or mangled, was the mouth that uttered these horrid but pathetic sounds.

Amber took four steps across the kitchen towards the doorway. 'Ryan?'

The presence was close to the floor, in a far corner, struggling to move around the bonnet of the car.

She stopped and told herself that she could not be sure that it was Ryan inside there, fumbling in the darkness. This could be a ruse: a scent, a pitiful whimpering of her name created as a lure, a trap, to get her inside that dark, cramped space. A place that might swiftly change and suddenly have no walls, no floor, no up or down, like the ground floor of number 82. *She* made doors. There were doors around *her* that opened into other places.

When you die you fall through the doors.

Amber clenched her jaw at the thought of the savagery and indignity and pain that had been inflicted upon the young man, the only person who had cared enough to try and free her with what little money he possessed. *They* had broken Ryan's arm in the house, then dragged him outside and stamped on him, crushed his sweet head with a brick. Her heart broke again. How many times could a heart break? It could break in two over and over again until it withered the soul; she was discovering this the hard way.

'No!' She shook her head like a wounded horse, leant against a kitchen counter. 'No!' she shouted, and wanted to shoot something, and then keep shooting it in the face. 'You bitch. You bitch. You bitch. You bitch!'

Amber walked to the gaping doorway. 'Baby. I'm coming. I won't let them have you.'

She looked into the garage. Could she see him? 'Ryan?'

She sensed as much as saw a vague silhouette against the grey metal door of the garage, the top of a head with an uneven outline above the black roof of the car.

There was a light in the room too, faint but unaccountable: a bluish ambient light before the doors of the garage that faced the front driveway. Amber screwed up her eyes and stared right at the shape that began to harden within the thin illumination. An indistinct and pale oval seemed to be in the process of slowly moving, or edging, from the closed door towards her, until it appeared to reset its trajectory back to the garage doors, before slipping out again, but no more than a few feet each time.

The pale smudge in the air by the door made a sound. And the very moment Amber heard the liquescent noise she received a new and wholly unwelcome perspective on the phenomenon: if this was a head, a head and an indistinct white face, then it was leaning into the garage before being rewound to its starting position, to then move inside the room again, like a film stuck in a projector. Either that, or a body cloaked by darkness was taking a step, over and over again, and some vague ambient light was catching a suggestion of its face.

The noise was repeated, wet and thick; a sucking mouth in the darkness.

Amber swallowed the lump in her throat.

The visitor's attempt to communicate, if that was what it was, was hampered, as if what serviced for a mouth was badly obstructed or could no longer function as it had once done. Sibilant, almost drooling, she thought another attempt had just been made at her name. '*Shhtefff.*'

'Ryan.' Her own voice was at the edge of breaking, eroded by fear and shock and disbelief.

'*Pozzzzit . . .*' What followed was unintelligible, but repeated three times, until she interpreted 'We can go now' from something resembling '*Ick an go nowsh*', or whatever the salival mess tried to pronounce.

Amber wondered if she was hearing the voice inside her own mind. 'Ryan? I'm not there any more,' she said to the flickering that was now dimming. 'Ryan, Ryan, I'm not there any more. Not there. Why are you here? Why are you . . .'

She lost sight of the dim smudge of light, which became a greenish, degraded phosphorescence beyond the bonnet of her car. It began to resemble the motion of a silhouette superimposed over a dark background, was X-ray vague, a blurred film negative, until it vanished from the air.

Amber stepped into the garage. The cement was instantly chilly against her feet. She could smell oil, the silent respirations of a new car at rest, fresh bricks, new concrete. Dust balls gathered around her feet like she'd stepped inside a large pen filled with grey rabbits. 'Ryan?' she whispered. 'Ryan?'

She turned and raked the wall for the light switch, clicked on the overhead light. Shadows instantly shrunk, the murk cleared, the white plaster ceiling gleamed. She walked along one side of her car to the garage doors, all the time afraid that something might reach out from beneath the vehicle and seize her bare ankle.

There was no one down there. Nothing but dust.

But there had been someone there. *Hadn't there?*

'Ho, ho, ho.'

Amber screamed.

The laughter that issued from directly outside the garage doors was deep and forced, mirthless and mocking, and she knew where she had heard such a derisory sound before.

EIGHTY-SIX

The air of the garage bloomed with the fragrance of stagnant toilets, stale tobacco smoke, fusty carpet worn white to the weave, underfloor exhalations: dusty, mouse-tainted, nitrate-sharpened, pissed upon, scented, and pissed upon again.

Amber began to hyperventilate.

She fell more than stumbled back to the kitchen.

Outside the kitchen windows, the security lights clicked on.

'What is my name?'

The voice in the hallway outside the kitchen either changed quickly, or was replaced by a more nervous speaker, as if these familiar words had been uttered by a young woman who stood near the front door. But the urgency with which the second woman spoke transmitted an even greater panic into Amber. 'Before here . . . that time . . . Nowhere . . . to where the other . . . the cold . . . is my name? . . .'

A third voice announced itself and sounded as if the speaker was halfway up the staircase. And whatever now spoke sounded exhausted. 'And then you said . . . I said . . . I wouldn't . . . unreasonable . . . but who was I . . . you, you told me . . . you swore . . . it was . . . meant

562

something . . . a sign . . . frightened, the more I . . . and now I know . . .'

Amber stepped into the hallway. There was no one there, and no one on the staircase.

'Involved . . . you are . . . you said . . . not that simple . . . must understand . . . Not going . . . refuse. I said it. I said it . . . wouldn't stop . . . and look . . . what happened . . . the lights . . . even listening.' This was the voice from a distant fireplace. The words swilled through the air, accompanied by a gust of dilapidation that came out of the kitchen.

Amber backed towards the doorway of the living room. Slapped on the overhead lights.

Another voice rose from the kitchen she had just fled; that of a teenager, a frightened and confused girl, once buried beneath the floorboards of hell. 'I . . . don't . . . can you find . . . where . . . where . . . this . . . am I?'

A spark of blue across the ceiling of the living room and hallway, a sound of thin glass imploding, and the house went dark.

Amber screamed.

From the garden a yellow glow hit the house and sought cracks to seep through. It took Amber a few seconds to realize the halogen security lights on the rear exterior walls of the farmhouse had come on. *Intruder.*

She wanted to be sick. Her mouth managed nothing but a whinny while her thoughts fell apart inside black chaos. Losing her balance, she stumbled then righted herself, only to thump her face against the wall at the bottom of the stairs.

Get out, get out, get out! The front door; she had to get

to the front door and get out of the building. Behind her, close to her back, the quiet, tremulous voice of a young girl whispered, 'I'm cold . . . I'm so cold . . . Hold me.'

Amber turned to see who was now standing at the foot of the stairs.

No one there.

Footsteps thumped around her in the hall to get ahead of her and to the front door. A slipstream of cool air prickled about her throat like ephemeral hands. There was a snigger, 'Ho, ho, ho!', from across the darkened living room.

From another unseen mouth, inside the garage, came the voice of an older, brittle, aggressive woman, that slowed the flow of blood inside Amber's seemingly weightless body to what felt like a sluggish trickle: 'To speak evil . . . no brawlers . . . all meekness unto . . . Foolish, disobedient, deceived . . .' The voice flowed through the unlit air of the ground floor, to hit the ceiling and slap the walls, to fill the entire space of the hallway that Amber had stopped moving within. 'Diverse lusts and pleasures . . . Malice and envy, hateful . . . hating one another . . . Kindness . . . love of God our Saviour . . .'

Amber crouched down and covered her ears. The sound of the voice was too horrid, was maddening. Every word from the woman's mouth chipped away another fragment of her restraint. Behind the restraint was something red and black and thoughtless; she sensed its wild, addictive furnace of energy. *Pushing.*

'A man that is an heretic . . . first and . . . admonition . . . reject . . . Knowing that he . . . subverted . . . sinneth . . . being condemned of himself . . .'

Shoot yourself.

'Stop it!

In the mouth.

'No!'

They're filling you, filling you up with black things, with dead things.

Something began a tapping at the patio windows, on the far side of the lounge.

The rear garden remained flooded with an orange glow from the security lights. The light seeped across the lounge and into the hall. Through the living room doorway, Amber could see fresh clumps of dust spread about the floor. Could make out the black trees and dark grass of the garden, highlighted by an orange tint of what looked like premature, or fake daylight. Someone was standing on the patio, looking in.

She inhaled so quickly she issued a little shriek and nearly fell. So severe was her fright, her mind felt disembodied from a sense of where her physical form had been moments before. She stared at the long, blackened shape, at its head bowed and its filthy body withered and hunched over what it held tight to its chest.

'I see you,' she whispered, or thought she whispered, but was so beside herself with shock she may have thought she had spoken without actually speaking. She pointed the gun at the figure. What stood before her eyes was no illusion.

So dramatic was the switching off of the security lights, and the sudden return of the darkness outside, Amber thought she heard a click.

She fired the gun. Her hand rocked. A flare flashed. The window splintered.

The house had long returned to silence. Amber remained still, listening hard, waiting for her eyes to accustom themselves to the darkness inside. Across the living room, the gradual seeping of dawn revealed a spider-webbed glass door and an empty patio.

Her phone vibrated against her buttocks in the back pocket of her jeans.

It was Josh and he didn't waste his breath on preliminaries. He had always been direct, if not abrupt, but his tone startled her. 'Amber. Where are you?'

'Here—'

'Where's here?'

'Home. The farmhouse.'

'OK. Listen to me. I do not want you to be alarmed. This is a precaution. Think of it as a fire alarm at school. A drill. Take it seriously, but it's almost certainly nothing to worry about. Can you get to your car?'

'Of course.'

'I need to see you right away. Now, where is your car?'

'The garage.'

'Good.'

'Josh?'

'No time. Listen up. I need you to get into your car with your *little friend* and pepper spray. And I need you to make sure your car is locked and that your windows are sealed before you leave the garage.'

She could tell Josh was speeding and that he was speaking on his phone at the same time as driving, something she had not known him do before. 'Josh. My messages—'

'Forget them. Just listen. Open the garage door. Then open the gate from inside your car. I'm coming towards you. Meet me at Pit Wood.'

Pit Wood was not far from the farmhouse: by the crossroads, about two miles from her. 'What? What is it? I'm not going anywhere until you tell me what this is about.'

There was pause as Josh chose his words. '*He's* here. Devon. Has been all along. You were right. Now bloody move, please. Get out of that house.'

EIGHTY-SEVEN

Josh nodded his head towards the caravan. 'He's been living in there.'

His grip tightened on Amber's upper arm when she felt her knees sag. Within her vision, the grass, stone walls, a distant copse of trees in the field's corners, and the blue, cloudless sky all shifted around her, swooped slightly, and then settled. She clutched Josh's arms until the strength returned to her legs. 'Here? You sure?' Her voice was little more than a whisper.

Josh nodded.

They stood side by side in a sloping field used for grazing sheep. A cold wind crawled over the northern wall, picked up and batted Amber's hair about. Towards the southern edge of the pasture a collection of grubby sheep chewed the thick, dark grass that grew close to the stone wall separating the bottom of the field from another beyond. The herd was aware of their presence but not alarmed.

Partially covered by an unruly hedgerow, in the northwestern corner of the field, a small, heavily discoloured, orange and white caravan slouched into a corner. From a distance, Amber could see that the edges of the visible panels were water damaged and part sprung from the frame. The exterior surface of every panel was long rusted, green with mildew and stained brown at the corners.

As they approached she saw that one tyre was flat and the short drawbar that projected from the chassis flaked rust. Three dirty windows at the front of the caravan were visible, and another two at the side. Around each window condensation obscured most of the shadowy interior, and the black rubber seals around the glass panes were crumbling. Through two of the windows at the front, purple bedding had been squashed against the filthy glass, as if stuffed there to block out the light or prevent anyone from seeing inside.

Amber had met Josh at Pit Wood and followed his car to the field; the caravan was within two miles of her farmhouse. She and Josh had embraced swiftly in greeting, and Josh had cupped the back of her head to whisper, 'Sorry, kid. I'm so sorry. You were right.'

She had never wanted to be right, and said, 'Don't be. Please.' Though Amber had stopped short of explaining that Fergal had been outside her house, stood on the patio and staring into the living room the night before, because she had begun to believe that Fergal had not been present on her property in any form or manner that Josh would ever accept or understand. But how could he be alive? She'd shot through the window at where he had been standing. And he had also moved with an impossible rapidity from the lawn in the night. She had seen him below, and then he had vanished.

'Come on. I'll explain when we get there,' Josh had said, as he released Amber from the bear hug. 'The police will have to be notified soon. And before the news breaks we'll need to get you stowed somewhere safe. If I am right about this, it'll make headlines. Not the kind you'll want on your bloody doorstep either.'

They'd parked their cars, bumper to bumper, in the inlet by the road-facing gate of the field containing the caravan. Before they left the cars, Josh asked Amber to give him the gun. He let her keep the pepper spray and winked as he said, 'He's not here, so you won't need that. But if you do, remember to point it towards the enemy.' Josh helped Amber climb over the gate, and led her inside the northern wall and across the grass to the stained and derelict caravan. Only part of its roof was visible from the lane that bordered the field, and only then if you were looking hard for something; otherwise, the vehicle was invisible unless its spectators were inside the field. A good place to hide. A good place to wait.

Josh sighed. 'Caravan belongs to the farmer. Seasonal labourers once used it, but not for a few years. Our man stayed there for a while until the farmer realized he had a squatter. He thinks Fergal broke in sometime during the winter.'

Amber turned to Josh in surprise and confusion. Josh rolled his eyes and nodded. 'I have no idea how he knew you were coming here either. But he knew you were coming to Devon, and near Grammarcombe Wood specifically, so he installed himself in this old caravan months before you came back to settle down. To await your arrival.'

Josh blinked rapidly, clearly perturbed by the implications of his discovery. 'I just don't get it. How could he have known? The master builder, the head designer, the architect – they didn't recognize you. Your appearance had changed too much when you met them. And that was what, nearly a year ago? Nine months, right? But even if one of the contractors recognized you, then how did Fergal Donegal hear about it? I just don't understand. How did one of the contractors get the information to Fergal? Not to mention *why* they would tell him. A third party? A go between? Maybe. It's unlikely the information was passed on in any other way. Unless . . .'

Amber touched his hand. 'Josh.'

'Your barrister, your agent, I need to talk to them both. See if they've been hacked. Though who would Fergal Donegal know who could do that?'

'Josh . . . Josh.'

He broke from his reverie and looked at her.

'That's not how he found me.'

Josh sighed, then opened his mouth to cut her off before she mentioned what he feared.

'Please, Josh. Listen. He didn't need to be told I was coming here. *She* knew.'

'She? Amber, I'd rather you didn't go there—'

'I saw *them*. Last night.'

Josh looked at her as if she was a stranger that had come up to him in a crowd.

'He's been outside the house for days. Fergal. Getting closer. He wanted to show himself to me. Torment me. Drive me out of my mind with fear. That's how they controlled us at number eighty-two. And he was carrying her last night so that he could show her to me.' *Introduce me*, she nearly said, but the thought of actual contact was too hideous to contemplate. She dropped her voice and said to herself, 'He was her black oxen. That drew her wagon hither.'

Josh frowned. For a few seconds he was unable to speak. 'You saw him. *Him*. Fergal. Last night. You never—'

'It probably wouldn't have made any bloody difference who I called. I don't think anyone would have seen him. No one but me.'

'Amber, now look—'

'Josh. He was there, standing on the patio, and as real as you are right now. It was no illusion. And he was holding her. *Her*. His Black Maggie. I fired at him. Broke the window. But there was no one outside.'

Josh swallowed. In his eyes she could see bafflement and the usual concern, a belief that she was delusional, perhaps insane. But mixed in with his shock was an anxiety that she might even be right.

'Come on. Let me show you inside,' Josh said, to break the silence that settled thickly between them.

Amber didn't follow.

Josh paused. 'You're safe. It's OK. He's long gone.'

Now it was her turn to have doubts. 'How can you be sure he was here?'

Josh sighed and looked at the sky. 'After we met, last time, well, I came back. And stuck around while you were in Plymouth. You seemed pretty convinced he was here. I couldn't see how that was possible, but you were so bloody frightened. And I felt I owed you some peace of mind. So I came back and made a few enquiries. Random ones, really. And a few things turned up . . .' Josh paused to squint and stare into the distance.

'What? For fuck's sake, what turned up?'

'Break-ins, three bloody breaks-in. At your farmhouse. When it was still a building project. The builders should have reported it to you, but never did, because nothing was taken.'

'I don't understand.'

'Someone broke into the building – your farmhouse – when it was a construction site. So I checked with the local fuzz about any similar cases round here. And there were a few. Maybe not connected, but all occurring at the same time. Food. Someone had been stealing food. Sheets had been pinched from washing lines. Nothing valuable. Some stuff from sheds. No money, no white goods. Basic stuff from gardens, from the back of shops. Milk off doorsteps. Like someone was scratching out an existence round here. Nothing major, nothing too obvious, nothing serious to attract much attention. So I made some calls and visited a few of the people who'd reported the thefts. And I found an eye witness. Someone saw Fergal. The guy who owns this field saw the bastard, which led me down here. I caught up with the farmer a few fields that way' – Josh nodded to the west – 'as he started work this morning. So I checked the caravan out and called you.'

'Saw him? He actually saw him?'

'His description matched. He disturbed Fergal right here, one evening after Christmas. And he watched the bugger run away from this,' Josh stabbed a forefinger at the caravan. 'Didn't go after him because he said there was something not right about the guy. Said he was black with dirt, filthy. Worse than any tramp he'd ever seen. Reminded him of a coal miner, or some escaped convict from a film. Couldn't believe his eyes when this lanky figure just streaked out of the caravan and legged it. But he did see his face, or what was left of it on one side.' Josh shook his head in disbelief. 'Same height, nearly seven foot. Gangly, face all messed up.' He paused to wince. 'Was pretty sure he only had one eye too. But he was alive, Amber. The prick was still alive and down here around the same time you signed the contract on that farmhouse.'

Josh nodded at the caravan. 'The farmer showed me inside this morning. Lucky for us, he hadn't got round to clearing the place out. Couldn't face it. He just padlocked it after Fergal took off. Keeps meaning to have it hauled away as scrap. Fergal never came back once he'd been rumbled. He's pretty sure about that. Come on.' Josh walked quickly to the caravan. 'It's still unlocked. I told the farmer I'd call him when we were done. But I didn't tell him a murderer on the run had been kipping in his field last winter.'

Amber felt as if a slow-acting drug was taking effect on her body and mind as Josh explained how he'd made the connection between Fergal and the caravan. Now she felt breathless and almost too weak to follow her protector through the long dewy grass. 'God. Oh, God,' was all she could manage by way of a response, as she walked in a daze up to the dented and stained door.

In her vague and formless thoughts, some kind of resolution, some answer, was trying to suggest itself to her, but her notions and ideas and guesses still made no sense. If *he* had been here, then maybe he was alive, and still hiding out locally, close to her home. But that didn't explain why she had been unable to see him that morning after she discharged the weapon. Or the couple of times she had seen him outside, at the back of the house. It was like he'd just disappeared on each occassion. 'I don't understand,' she said to herself more than Josh.

'Makes two of us,' he said over his shoulder, and then opened the caravan door.

'Careful, Josh, don't,' Amber said, when he poked his head and shoulders inside the murk. Josh's hands supported his weight on the outside of the door, and he used the strength in his arms to haul his head away moments later, one forearm immediately under his nose.

Amber shrieked. 'What? Josh, what?'

'The smell. Not the kind you get used to. We can't go inside anyway. It's evidence, or will be very soon. But you can see enough from the doorway. You can see how that pig lived in there.'

'I . . . I don't want to.' She felt sick, and was sure she could smell the sebaceous, oily stench of Fergal's clothes around her in the field, like a malevolent spirit released from its tomb; the same bestial spoor she had withered before in the dim sinuses of Edgehill Road.

'Been treating his face with something. Couldn't have healed properly. Those bandages look nasty. Milk's gone off too. Toilet's backed up. He literally lived in garbage. It's all over the floor. Knee deep. Bet the bastard never opened a window either . . .' Josh's commentary on what he could see inside the dismal pall of the caravan's interior, muffled by the arm across his mouth, increased Amber's nausea.

Josh turned away from the door, wincing. 'Police will have to go through it. Poor sods.'

'Is there . . . is there a box? A wooden box?'

'Box?'

'Like a cabinet. Can you see? With a curtain across the front? Can you see?'

Josh shook his head. 'Just rubbish. Rot. Stained bedding. Like a landfill. I'll tell the police to look for it. This is the box from number eighty-two?'

Amber nodded. *She* liked them dirty. Like Bennet. Like Fergal. Hadn't Knacker said that? Deranged and subservient, depraved and sadistic, filthy; their flesh as corrupt as their minds, as spoiled as *she* was. Black Maggie.

Amber cast her eyes around the field, at the very grass, looking for disturbed earth. 'Has anyone gone missing, Josh?'

'Missing? Here?'

'Girls.'

His eyes saddened as he fully understood the question. 'No. Nothing like that.'

'Not yet. We have to find *her* and the bastard that carried her down here.'

Josh frowned, unsure how to react. Amber didn't care what he thought of her or her crazy ideas. She'd taken her lead from Josh for too long, as well as the police, legal firms, representatives of traditional authority and order, purveyors of reason. And they had failed; failed to protect and hide her. Because they had failed to *see*, and to understand what she had been telling them for years. And Fergal had been here, and he had brought the Black Maggie to Amber's door, to resume the cycle of terror and torture and rape in service of the thing that once inhabited a house in Birmingham.

She had believed herself tainted three years before on

the dirty linoleum of an abandoned kitchen; the connection between her and old Black Mag must have been exploited by some invisible, intangible, remote means that made no sense to anyone but her. It had known she had come to Devon, or maybe known she would come to Devon. And then her actual presence, when she had arrived to buy the house, had drawn it to a specific location. Maybe those old Friends of Light and the Bennets had also understood how such an influence upon the living was possible, before it was too late for them too. Amber Hare-was-Stephanie Booth was the foothold in new territory. Death became Black Mag; murder, *sacrifice*. And how high the corn would grow when maidens were laid beneath the green, green grass . . . But if Fergal had been near her home, with the box, all along . . . then maybe the resumption of *her* activity, her purpose, was largely dependent upon her physical presence. The Maggie had to be brought here, transported, carried to Devon. Which would make her range limited. Maybe she could sense Amber when close, could invade her senses, her mind, her sleep, at a psychic level undetectable to others. Maybe . . .

Amber lost her footing, her balance, and took several steps backwards to stay on her feet. 'Jesus. Oh, Jesus Christ!' She clutched her head from the impact of a sudden terrible idea inside her mind.

'What? What is it?' Josh moved across to her, held her elbows. 'What is it, kid?'

Amber closed her eyes. Worried she might faint from the abrupt and horrible arrival of her most recent revelation, she drew one deep breath after another to steady herself. 'I'm OK, Josh. I'm all right. Cars. Back to the cars. Now!'

'Of course. Let me lock up.'

Josh walked off to seal the outlaw's den with a padlock. Amber ran for her car, wiping at the tears on her pale cheeks.

Josh caught up with her by the gate. 'I know this is hard . . .'

'You got some more time for me, mate? Today?'

He nodded. 'What did you have in mind?'

Amber inhaled deeply to ease the constriction squeezing her chest. 'I think I know where they are.'

EIGHTY-EIGHT

'Here. *He's* here. They are under here.' Amber stood in the middle of the garage and pointed at the smooth, shining concrete floor beneath the soles of her Converse. She wasn't cold, she wore a fleece and jeans, but her whole body was shaking and adding a slight warble to her voice.

Josh stood in the mouth of the garage as if unwilling to enter the space. He looked hard at where Amber was pointing, at the floor, and slowly moved his eyes up to her face. 'I don't understand.'

'Fuck.' Amber looked at the ceiling, hands over her mouth, trying to think quickly enough to find the words to explain, to express what she wanted to say, what she needed Josh to accept. It felt hopeless before she'd even begun. 'At night, Josh. After the dreams—'

'Amber. You know what I think about—'

'Please, please, please, listen to me. Please.'

Josh sighed. 'OK. But I need to call the police very soon about that caravan.'

'The police won't find him alive. You will never find him alive. He's dead, Josh. Dead. You were right.'

Josh never spoke, but could not suppress the usual mixture of embarrassment and pity he felt for her.

'He was dead before I came back to Devon to live here.

Before this place was finished. Don't you see? That's how I can see him. It's why I can see him and why I can hear the others, even if they're not there, like we are here. They're ghosts. But the dead, the victims from number eighty-two are here. All of them. Or bits of them. Fergal brought them here. The *trophies*.'

'Amber, please.'

'Think. Think about it. Think like me for one second, yeah? Be a crazy girl, yeah? Margaret was missing hair. Ryan teeth. They're here, those things Fergal took from his two victims. The other women, the girls, they were all missing body parts. Fingers. Toes. Maybe hair, but it wasn't always easy to tell. Some of them had been buried for a long time. But think about the missing parts that were never found. *They*, the people, the presences, the ghosts, were all stuck inside eighty-two Edgehill Road because their remains were there. *She* kept them, kept them all close. That's how it kept going, for a century. It's what she needed to keep them with her. So that they stayed with her and couldn't get away; even if the bodies were removed she had other mementoes.' Amber peered about her feet, not even wanting the soles of her trainers to touch the floor.

Josh was frowning because he did not know how to react. 'Bennet and his dad must have had a stash off-site where they kept their . . . their trophies. They died and left no records. If it was anywhere, the stash would still be in Birmingham.'

'No it's not. That's almost like what we were meant to think. Because it's all here. *She* has them. They, some-how . . . are a part of her. It's how she keeps them close.

580

Captive. Even though they are dead, they're not free. She kept parts of the dead. The ones I have seen and heard. She makes me see them.' Amber began to tear up. She thought of Ryan and sobbed, but quickly forced herself to stop. 'And Fergal was alive, barely I'd say, but still alive when he brought her here, with her fucking entourage of the murdered, whose torments never, ever stop. I know it. This makes sense. To me, Josh. Please, for me, do this for me. Help me with this.'

She had worn herself down trying to figure out the final part of the puzzle, but it had finally revealed itself to her at the caravan: Fergal had been here all along, at the farmhouse, ever since the renovations, waiting inside the building, where she determined *to winter*. And he had been with *her*, the Black Maggie; he had always been in Amber's home, *with her*, physically and otherwise, even after death. At the caravan he was just waiting for a chance to transport himself and his keeper into her new home.

Temple.

Josh had stepped towards Amber when she became too upset to continue. He tried to keep an instinctive smile from spreading across his face. 'In here. They're all in here, the murder victims from Birmingham, or bits of them? And this Maggie thing, that you claim Fergal worshipped, and Arthur and his old man too. Fergal brought it here from Birmingham? Amber. Amber, please.'

Amber wanted to scream. Her fists clenched so hard her cuticles began to hurt. 'Yes!'

'Look, kid, a man wants you dead. A murderer. He is in Devon and knows you live here. That is a fact and that is very serious. And now we need to notify the police and have them search for him and pick him up. That is the plan. That is what we are going to do right now.'

'Waste. Of. Fucking. Time.' The shaking was getting worse. She was wasting time; the man she paid to protect her was wasting time. 'Hammer. Sledgehammer. Drill. One of those things that smashes floors. One of them. I need to get one. Torquay. There must be a shop in Torquay—'

'Whoa. Hold your horses. You are not going to smash up your house, Amber.' Josh looked around himself, aghast at her, his face paler than she had ever seen it; she worried he might soon try to restrain her. 'This place? Think. Think about how much money you spent on this house. The time that was spent making this beautiful. Amber? Where are you going?'

Amber broke from her position in the garage and raced through to the kitchen.

Josh followed her. 'What are you doing now?' He stopped moving and glanced at the dust on the kitchen counters. Peered at the floor, noticing the grey balls of dross.

Ryan had been inside the garage. Twice Ryan had been outside her room but he had returned here – down here where they were all stored. She recalled the night she'd opened the door and there was nothing inside the garage, nothing but an impenetrable darkness that slipped inside her and turned her mind inside out. In *here*, every time, right in *here*, inside the garage. The garage and the ground floor flat of 82 Edgehill Road: the black room. Both close to the earth she blessed, where she *wintered*.

Amber swept up her phone from the kitchen counter. 'Fergal broke in here. He did not take anything. Why?

Why was he here then? If he was still around he could have got to me any time I left the property in the last two weeks. What is he waiting for? You think alarms would put him off? Because he's not waiting any more, Josh. He's arrived. Got here months ago, before I even opened the bloody door. He wasn't looking to steal anything from the building site. He came here to leave something behind. That is why he was here. The box. The wooden box was not inside that caravan. Nor was it inside number eighty-two when they found me. Think, mate, for God's sake help me!'

'Amber, Amber, calm down. Kid, please, calm down. Take it easy. Water. Sip some water. Catch your breath.'

'His last words to me, Josh: "You're not having her". Not *having her*. He wasn't talking about Svetlana. He was talking about *her*, the bloody Maggie. He went downstairs with his face covered in acid. He was burning alive, Josh, but he still made it down those stairs to the ground floor flat. To get her. To collect her. That's why he ran. To pro-tect her. To get her the fuck out of that house. There was enough of her in me to know where I was, where I'd go, maybe she even made me come here, where she wanted to be. But for her to start this again, she needed to be here in person. Needed to be hidden here . . .'

Because she chose you.

I will come unto thee. For I have determined there to winter.

Amber slumped against the kitchen counter, her face pressed into the cold surface. Josh placed a hand, gently, upon her back and said consoling, comforting things that she could hear but never registered. She slowed her breathing, her heartbeat, and tried to clear her mind so she could think of the next step; the one she had to take today.

Josh's voice eventually drifted back to her as if a radio had found its signal. '. . . and we can see someone. OK. Relaxants. Couple of tranqs and a cup of tea, kid. Let's call the doc, and then I'll call the police. But don't worry, I won't let you out of my sight. We will find him. I promise you. I'm not leaving this bloody county until we have him banged up.'

Amber turned her head to one side, rested it against her forearm. 'Josh. If you really want to help me, you'll come with me to a DIY store and then help me get that floor up.'

His face and shoulders seemed to slump. He removed his hand from her back. 'I can't. I can't help you be crazy, kid. And that floor's got to be six inches thick. You start breaking into the foundations and the whole thing could come down on you. This is just nuts.'

'Then I will break this place apart myself.'

Amber leant on the kitchen counter, supporting her weight with her elbows, her phone pressed to her ear. Josh was still outside. He'd said he wanted to check the grass and flowerbeds under the walls for footprints. He had remained committed to the lines of inquiry and detection and protection he felt comfortable with; he'd stuck with what he could accept. And so had she. Occasionally she watched Josh's head pass the kitchen windows as he made his inspection of the grounds, as much, she suspected, as an excuse to remove himself from the presence of a crazy woman as to establish the security situation at the property.

The man she had spoken to, at the third local building firm she had called, came back to the phone. 'Today, you say? Garage, yeah?'

'Yes, today.'

'We can get someone round to look at it Friday. But we can't start 'til next week earliest.'

'No. It has to be today. Do you know anyone else who can do this for me?'

'You can try Wellings.'

'Already tried . . . Tools! If you can tell me what tools I will need, then I will buy them. Hire them. Do it myself.'

'I wouldn't recommend that, miss. Garage floor, you say? Well, most of 'em need chipping drills. Jackhammer too. Cus the concrete will be thick, see. Plus you might have wires running underneath the cement. Pipes you don't want to break either. You'll need to find that out first, then cut a section round 'em with a breaking chisel in a rotary hammer. Whole floor will need a saw, grinder too. It's a big job, love. There's only the lad and me here, and we both gotta get up Shaldon way.'

A cold disappointment seemed to press her weight harder and further into the surface of the counter. The idea of demolishing the garage floor suddenly seemed ludicrous after this sudden intrusion of technical information, this insertion of reality into her frantic, irrational thoughts. She swallowed the despair that wanted to surge into her mouth; the prickly frustration that electrified her fingers, made her want to scratch her face and tug her own hair. She was so thwarted she wanted to hurt herself.

'Sorry, love. Nothing we can do today. But if you give me the address, I'll get the lad to come up Friday.'

'No. Not Friday. I'll give you two grand each, today. If you can get here today and smash that floor out, I'll give you two grand each. Just the floor. Today. The floor, that's all.' *Right down, right down deep.*

There was a long silence at the other end of the phone, which she accounted for as the time required for the builder to decide on her mental health. 'Something was lost in there, you say? In the garage floor when it was laid?'

'That's right.'

'Jewellery or something like that?'

'Not exactly, but something that needs to be found. And fast. Today, while it's still light. Will I see you later, Mr Finney?'

'I suppose I could shift things around a bit. If it's that important.'

'Matter of life and death. That's how I see it.'

'There'll have to be a deposit.'

'I'll pay you up front. Right now with a credit card. Or today in cash if the bank authorizes that amount. I'm good for it.'

'Cash is better for this kind of job.'

EIGHTY-NINE

Josh remained quiet. He sat at the kitchen counter, staring into the coffee cup between his hands. Amber could see him through the window from where she stood beside the dusty, gritty paving stones on the driveway, where the pile of rubble had built up throughout the day: a mound of broken concrete, gravel, sand, crushed rock, wooden boards, wire mesh from the vapour barrier, disconnected PVC pipes and severed wires that had been drilled, hammered, chiselled, and cut from the floor of her garage. The builders had kindly taken most of the debris with them.

Before the remains of a perfectly good floor had been shipped off, she had raked through the rubble as it built up from noon until seven p.m. Even wheeled the barrow from the excavation to empty it onto the drive. In between making endless cups of tea for the two men who dug out her garage two foot deep, and then as far into the soil as was safe before subsidence became an issue, she had sorted through and sifted the rubble until her fingers bled. Picked up each grey or discoloured stone to make sure it was not bone – a metatarsal or finger joint encased in cement – while the ache in her head had gradually grown to match, and then exceed, the pain in her lower back from being stooped over for hours. She had cuts on her knees from crawling around in the wreckage while checking all the white bits she could find to make sure they were not premolars.

Occasionally, her frantic antics were watched by the workmen. Jeff Finney, the older man she had spoken to on the phone, and whom she had paid, had often caught the younger man staring at Amber while she scrabbled about on all fours, and sometimes attacked the larger chunks of concrete to break them apart with a hammer they had loaned to her. And when the builder noticed his young assistant gawping at the crazy, dirty girl, with cement dust wiped through the sweat on her face, he would whistle quietly and nod his head at the ground to draw his lad's attention back to the job in hand.

Unable to watch the destruction of her garage, Josh had gone back to the caravan site to meet the police. Then returned to the farmhouse and sat in the garden with a newspaper, or more often than not, staring across the maize field beyond her garden. Amber guessed he had been thinking of what to do with her now that she had gone crazy – or crazier.

The sun was sinking. The security lights on the front of the house illuminated the front drive for as long as Amber remained there, like a flood-lit fool. She moved slowly to her car and sat down with her back resting against the side and looked at the paving between her feet.

She didn't hear him approach, but Josh came and sat down next to her. His knee joints cracked. For a long time he never said anything, just tapped the back of her hand with the base of a cold glass bottle. Beer, and probably the best beer she had ever drunk; half a bottle of chilled, fizzing, hoppy loveliness taken in a long draught that slipped down her throat and made her burp. 'Excuse me,' she said, as an afterthought.

Josh smiled. Then sipped from his own bottle.

Amber gazed at the house. 'I'll have to get a bag together. Find us a hotel.'

Josh turned his head to look at her but never spoke.

'I can't stay here.'

'This a temporary measure?'

Amber shook her head. 'Permanent.'

'Once the garage has been put back together, you'll get a good price. Far more than you paid for it. Sell it to a rock star.'

'No one can live here. Not any more.'

'You are kidding, right?'

'Can't risk it.'

They sat in silence for another ten minutes and finished their drinks.

Josh swallowed a mouthful of beer. 'No body. No box.'

Amber shrugged. She didn't even know how Fergal might have planted the relics, the trophies. She'd assumed they were inside the curtained wooden box, that it was some kind of shrine she was unable to imagine in too much detail because it upset her so much. But as the rubble mounted up and the soil revealed itself to be harmless, she'd begun to think that he might have scattered the hair and bones like seeds, for some hellish crop to germinate later, fertilized by her own presence inside the house; scattered bits of dead women, and her boyfriend's missing teeth, all through the house's foundations or inside wall cavities. It was possible. She didn't know for certain, but if her hunch was correct about the trophies carrying the presences of their former owners to the farmhouse, the entire house could be contaminated.

Or perhaps the remains were out there, in the fields. Or under the driveway. Or buried beneath the garden; hadn't she dreamed of an excavation? They could be anywhere. She could spend a lifetime digging, but she did not have a lifetime. She had little idea of what was coming next, coming for her, but she doubted she would last more than a couple of nights at the farmhouse. Too much more of this and her mind would go out with a flash anyway, like a wet circuit. And if she were wrong about how the influence reanimated, and it all started again someplace new . . .

She looked up at her beautiful home. The whole thing would have to come down. Amber felt her head swim at the thought of it, then thought she might throw up; she had drunk the beer too fast on an empty stomach.

Josh got to his feet and went and stood at the lip of the driveway, looked down into the foundations of the garage. 'The builders who poured the concrete. They would have seen the box.'

Under the strong overhead light, the scene reminded her of the garden in Edgehill Road, revealed under the portable police lights as detectives sifted through every inch of soil looking for more evidence, more bodies.

'How much soil came out?' Josh asked without turning his head.

'Loads. As much as they dared. A few feet down. Any more would have created subsidence.'

Josh nodded his head, whistled. He said, 'four grand'

under his breath, but Amber still heard him. He picked up a length of copper pipe the builders had left behind, and even dismantled carefully so she could reuse it.

'I'm going to get a shower, mate.'

Josh nodded. 'Right.'

'Then I'll call a place in town. Pack a bag. Find us somewhere to stay. I'll spring for dinner.'

Josh stared into the garage, but didn't answer.

NINETY

Amber was never sure what happened first, because everything was so unexpected and seemed to happen at once.

She was standing with her face thrust into the shower's hot cascade, to blast away the cement dust and sweat from her skin and hair. And only while under the vigorous beating of the hot water did she notice the brief dimming of the white electric light inside the wet room. At first she assumed the spotlights in the granite walled room had flickered.

A swift glance over her shoulder convinced Amber there was nothing wrong with the ceiling lights, because they were bright enough to briefly outline the silhouette of the second occupant inside the wet room.

Without making a sound, whoever had just stepped into the room had curled the steam behind them into a slipstream, like the tail of a large serpent. So the dimming had been caused by the passing of a shape, or a person, into the shower; a swift entrance that had interfered with the light that fell into the space from the bathroom proper. And the realization she was no longer alone in the confines of the stall nearly shut her heart down.

The dark walls of the wet room were obscured by clouds of steam; the far wall behind the shower head that housed the black marble toilet was invisible. What part of her mind that panic left available was filled with the image of poor Kelly Hughes's polythene-draped, near weightless bones being carefully raised from the darkness of the bathroom floor of 82 Edgehill Road.

Amber turned around and crossed both arms over her breasts. Hot water continued to batter her head and shoulders, and now dispersed an aerosol of water over her face. Within the swirls and billows of steam that filled the narrow rectangle, she thought, and then was certain, and then relieved that she had been mistaken, but then dreadfully certain again, that she could see a shape. A silhouette stood no more than four feet in front of her, in line with the door she would need to escape through.

'Josh,' she whispered. She hoped it was Josh, despite the terrible discomfort his presence would create in the unlikely event that he had intruded upon her shower.

The figure vanished, or seemed to melt in a torrent of vapour, and then the tatty outline of a head remerged from out of the steam. What she thought, or imagined, was a pair of large spectacle lenses glinted. And even in this place of cleanliness, of fresh water, a space redolent with the scents of gels, lotions and shampoos, she was struck by the hot odour of the thing that had come into the wet room, which was not Josh.

The dimming of the light, the suggestion of the male presence inside the dark, steamy room, and the distant calling of her name from below, which she only realized later was Josh calling for her attention downstairs, all transpired within a few seconds.

And then Amber was coughing to clear her sinuses of

the fungal stench of unclean male flesh that polluted the steam and billowed about her face. It was as if the decomposing clothes of a long unwashed vagrant had just been scissored from pallid flesh in a hot, unventilated room: cattle hormone-harsh, the sulphur of swine, the vinegar of vomit, before the first gust was penetrated by the sharper bite of the halitosis of blackened gums. Under such an assault against decency, Amber's stomach convulsed and she bent over to spit sour beer suds from her mouth as she stumbled for the entrance of the room.

She regained consciousness lying on her back.

The floor tiles were cold against her shoulders and buttocks, the shower water smacked her face and blinded her. A moment was needed for her eyes to right themselves. The impact against the side of her head had made it appear as if her vision had been knocked out of her head, to remain in the air once her body dropped to the sodden tiles.

The mists parted and curled up like waves as something thrust through the steam. A hand clutched one of her thighs with a grip so cold it made her scream. She tried to roll over, but a second contact, and one chilled enough to convince the flesh of her knee it was being burned, kept her down by pushing her legs apart.

She screamed. Screamed and swiped the air above her body. Cut her nails through warm steam, made vapour and air writhe and surge and dance about her frantic hands that swatted the nothingness above her opened thighs.

'Amber!'

Josh ran into the bathroom beyond the shower room.

His booted feet thumped and slid on the tiles. Above her, in the thick white veil, she saw his silhouette appear in the doorway of the wet room, then thrust through and into the steam. 'God, Amber. Here, let me get you up.'

He paused when he saw her glistening nakedness. 'Christ's sake,' he muttered. 'Sorry. Didn't know. You slip, kid?'

She couldn't speak, and even though the wet room was hotter than a greenhouse for tropical plants, the muscles of her legs and arms shook and jumped as if she had been placed inside a walk-in refrigerator.

Back on her feet, out of the wet room and inside the bathroom, with a towel covering her front, she fell against Josh and sobbed into his shirt.

Out of awkwardness, shock, or just an intuition that she was in no shape to explain why she had been lying on the floor, screaming and thrashing her arms in the air, with her legs thrust open, Josh remained silent until her sobs subsided.

'He was in there.' She swallowed. 'Bennet. In there.' She pointed at the wet room, peeled herself off Josh's wet front, rearranged the towel and moved to the door of the bathroom. 'He's here. That pig. That stinking pig. That rapist!'

She screamed so loudly, Josh flinched and winced before quickly moving to her. He caught her wrists and lifted her out of the bathroom by her tensed forearms. 'Amber! Amber! Kid! Listen to me.'

'That pig! That bitch!'

'Amber! I found something.'

'That bastard . . .'

'I found something. I think I found our man.'

Amber stared into where she thought Josh's eyes might be; his glasses were opaque with steam. She swallowed and from a throat that hurt she whispered, 'Here?'

Josh nodded, then turned his head to look at the steaming doorway of the bathroom. 'We'll need a spade.'

NINETY-ONE

'That all you've got?' Josh looked at the implement Amber held out to him. The price tag was still fixed to the handle. 'A trowel?'

'I never bloody thought I'd be doing more than potting plants here.'

'We'll have to wait until tomorrow. Get the right tools to get that earth up. Maybe get the police in on this.'

'No. Now. It has to be done now. We're so close.' Amber turned her attention back to the copper pipe that still stood upright in one corner of the earthen floor; the portion of soil that Josh had hacked and dug at with an offcut of wood while she showered.

If they found *him* down there; if they found *anything* down there connected to the house in Birmingham, she would burn it herself. She would not allow such artefacts to curse or contaminate another place, or continue to project their influence at her. That was something she would not risk. Whatever was brought up would be summarily destroyed, with or without Josh's blessing. This was not a matter for the police. They'd had their chance.

The entire surface of the soil floor bore the scars of Josh's recent prospecting. He had moved systematically, one square foot at a time, and pushed the hollow copper pipe as deeply into the soil as he could, before the earth became too dense, or the end of the pipe impacted against a broad stone or hard object beneath the surface. After each insertion into the ground, he had withdrawn the pipe and placed the wet end beneath his nose, and sniffed. He had shown her how it was done; how buried bodies in waste ground, in woods and grassy fields, used to be found by policemen. He had told her this was how they found the children under the moors.

He also told Amber that though he did not initially believe her about Fergal being buried under her garage, he could see that she believed her own theory, and passionately enough to spend four thousand pounds to have two builders smash it up that very day. Josh conceded that his theories about Fergal Donegal were not adding up either. So he'd had a hunch: if someone was to bury something incriminating beneath the ground of an unprotected building site at night, while the workmen were not present, they would have needed to hide their evidence shortly before the cement was poured, otherwise the builders would have seen a foreign object in the foundations when they came in to work. Such an implant would also need to be inserted far enough beneath the earth, and artfully too, to deter an investigation into broken ground.

Fergal was in Devon, he knew that, and had most likely broken into the building site ahead of her relocation to the farmhouse: entered a site only four people, including him, knew about in connection to its future resident. As much as anything else, Josh had confided to Amber that he wanted to know what 'that bastard was doing in here'.

'I'm not going to ask you to sniff the end of that pipe,

kid. But trust me, there's something dead down there,' Josh had said, and nodded at where he had dug at a corner like a dog after a buried bone. 'I've scraped as much of the dirt off a small portion as I could, and I found polythene. Something wrapped in plastic. Something rotten. And it's too big to be a cat.'

Following her interrupted shower, Amber had summoned the wits and presence of mind to change while Josh stood outside the door of her bedroom. Out of his sight, she had buried her face in a towel and smothered the sobs and tears that came as an aftershock; the residue of a sexual assault by a dead man who had followed her to Devon from Birmingham: Arthur Bennet. 'That old perv' had not yet made an appearance at the farmhouse, and she had wondered why. But he was here now. Perhaps he had saved himself for a special occasion. Maybe the Praetorian Guard was being summoned from the earth and the darkness now that she approached the source: *Old Black Mag.* Black Maggie. Whatever was here was growing in strength and intensity day by day; had built and was showing more of its black hand. Messengers were revealing themselves to her. She sensed an eagerness for her capitulation.

'I don't know if you should stay, Josh.'

He looked up at her, surprised and seemingly disappointed at her remark. 'Eh?'

'I don't think that what is down there is something within your remit, mate. Beyond the call of duty and all that. It might seem funny coming from me, but I don't think I can guarantee your safety if you stay any longer.'

Josh smothered a smile and attempted to inject some levity into the half-demolished garage they stood inside.

He tapped the pocket of his jacket. 'I've got your little friend.'

'Won't do much good in this situation. And I'm a bit concerned I might not be safe from you if you're susceptible to what might be down there.'

Josh stopped smiling. 'I'm not leaving you. Not like this, kid. Not here. So you want to take the first shift with that?' He nodded at the trowel. 'Or maybe we'd both be better off using spoons to get this dirt shifted. But let's get cracking. I feel like it's going to be a long night.'

Amber nodded her assent. 'Before we start, how are you at siphoning petrol?'

NINETY-TWO

Josh was the first to break the silence. 'What the fuck?' He was asking himself the question as much as directing the query at Amber.

They stood together, a few feet back from the lip of the crude crater they had dug into the soil of the garage floor; stood side by side, their shoulders not quite touching, in the place they had withdrawn to after Josh had used a broom to knock and brush the last chunks of soil, and the last scattering of stones, off the polythene-wrapped lump they had exhumed.

It had taken them a long time to get used to the sight of so many earthworms as they worked the soil. Some of them had bled as they were severed by the trowel. Thick, coiling, undulating, meat-rich earthworms; a few as long as small snakes that seemed to suck themselves back inside the holes uncovered by the trowel. 'You ever seen so many bloody worms?' Josh had asked her. At that point Amber had decided against explaining why she thought the worms were present in such great numbers.

Nearly two hours passed in the time it took them to dig deep enough to isolate the full length of what the plastic coated; they had used the trowel until their hands were blistered, and a rake from the garden, and a piece of wood to break up, to dig, scrape, scatter and expose what lay beneath. By the time they had finished digging they were filthy, their jeans smeared with brownish red stains from the clay, their hands dark and encrusted from pulling up lumps of earth and scooping out handfuls of moist debris.

The wreckage was lit up yellow from the lights in the ceiling; the room smelled of damp mud, concrete, timber, the cool evening air that had settled over the exposed ground as if it were now coming inside to reclaim what was no longer concealed.

Amber's entire body ached, her head throbbed. She felt slack from head to toe, and weary enough to lie down and pass out. The only thing keeping her exhaustion at bay was the shock and horror of revelation – perhaps the final revelation that went some way to making the impossible seem less implausible, and maybe even less preposterous to Josh now too.

He was struggling with this, though not physically. Fatigue was not his problem. He wasn't young, but he was fit and strong, his capabilities discreet, carefully hidden; he had nothing to prove, which she had always liked. Instead, Josh was wrestling with the ideas she had introduced into his world; the notion that not only did spirits exist, but in some instances they had not entirely separated from their physical remains after death. If that wasn't enough, she'd also claimed the absurd, the improbable and the ludicrous: that something much older and more powerful than these spirits had kept them in a form of tormented captivity, while using their suffering for malicious purposes against her.

Beneath the polythene that was heavily stained on both

sides, the man-sized contents were obscure. The enclosed object was as long as only the tallest of men could be when lying prostrate. At the sides of the tomb, the long arms seemed to have broken free of the polythene.

'There's more down there than just the body,' Josh added, while squinting into the cavity.

Amber had thought the same thing as she had watched Josh wipe away the last of the object's covering of dirt. There was another, smaller lump beneath the feet of the figure in the grave, also wrapped in polythene, though more carefully and tighter than the body was parcelled.

'Come on.' Josh stepped back to the cavity. 'Scissors. I'll need scissors. Or a knife. Let's get this over with.'

The idea of opening the man-sized package filled Amber with nausea; she had forced Josh to dig this thing up, but now lacked the strength to see the occupant of the makeshift tomb revealed. If the inhabitant of the grave was unwrapped then what else might be disturbed along with its unstable vigil beneath her home?

'Should we . . .'

Josh looked over his shoulder. 'What? Call the fuzz? I think we should. That's a body, kid. A body. We think we know whose it is, but we need to know how it got here.'

By itself, she nearly said aloud. The idea that she was looking at some kind of deranged self-sacrifice and self-imposed interment was making her feel faint with a disgust and dread that would not abate through prolonged exposure, but only grow. Concepts such as familiarity could not be experienced before such matters; her entire experience with the Maggie was one layer of ghastly disbelief and shock laid over another, again and again, *until you lost your mind or took your own life to escape . . .*

'Go on. Josh. Get it open.'

Amber looked at the red petrol canister that Josh had placed on the driveway beside her car. Burning a body, even *his* body, after all Fergal had done to her and to others, seemed as barbaric and savage and demented as the impulses that had driven Fergal Donegal in life, in death, and beyond death. Torching his remains might even be beyond her.

Josh nodded and knelt down beside the polythened corpse. 'Better fetch those scissors, kid.'

Amber went back to the kitchen, all the time wanting to shout, *Please don't get so close.* But how else could Josh open the plastic casket? She returned with her Wusthof scissors, their razor sharp blades only thus far used to cut a string of sausages and the tops off a few packets of pasta, a usage they would never know again. She handed them to Josh and he took them like a preoccupied doctor might take forceps from a nurse in theatre.

'Jesus,' he said with a gasp after the first incision, and leant his buttocks back onto his heels while he covered his nose and mouth. 'Jesus Christ. He fucking stinks.'

Amber winced and pulled her hooded top up to cover her own mouth and nose as the brain-deep stench of putrefaction filled the garage.

Hurriedly, Josh pushed the scissors along the length of polythene, his balance almost gone, his actions ungainly as the smell interfered with his concentration. When the plastic shroud was cut from bottom to top, he stepped away from the grave, coughing like a bear, with the end of his barks almost breaking into regurgitation. 'Torch,' he gasped more than said.

Amber handed Josh his black Maglite. 'Baghdad. Basra. Last time I smelled that,' he whispered. His face was white. The dirt smeared across his jaw made the bloodlessness of his face appear more vivid. And Amber's heart cracked for him. He was doing this for her: being confronted by things he would never forget; things that collaborated with other vile memories he'd tried to bury at the back of his own mental garage.

Please, please, please let this end here.

'This our man?' Josh said, his face a grimace as he trained the torch beam onto the head of the thing in the grave. Amber moved up beside Josh and stared down at what the torch beam lit up.

The remains of the blackened head reminded her of a photo she had seen years ago, of a long-dead explorer mostly preserved by snow and ice. It was hard to tell whether the remaining flesh of the face had withered tight to the skull after death, or whether the half-starved wreck of a body had been laid down in the crude plot.

Not much of the face was left for examination. One eye socket was mostly bone and one cheek was entirely missing. Long teeth were exposed through the missing flesh of the cheek and jaw, as if they were staring at a cadaver post-surgery. The mouth had dropped open and the face issued the unpleasant aspect of a whinnying horse with blackened teeth. The damaged side of the narrow head was smooth and earless.

'Strangled,' Josh said, his voice subdued. 'You can tell by the tongue.' That was visible at one side of the lower jaw, bulging and blackened like a plump fig found in some forgotten king's barrow. 'It's still there.'

'What?' Amber's voice was a ghost.

'Ligature. Looks like string. We've seen it before, kid.'

And so they had; a length of what looked like the same gardening twine that the Bennet family had used to throttle young women in their terrible house was still wrapped around the corpse's pinched throat. 'Fuck sake,' Josh added, and gripped the back of his own head.

Amber didn't have the wherewithal or strength to ask Josh to elaborate on what he was feeling. She just stared into the pit, mute with the personal horror of what she had done to Fergal's face with the acid. Because she had dissolved an eye, a cheek, the flesh of one side of his jaw; she had even rinsed away an ear. His agony must have been monumental, the lingering, long-term pain insanity-vast; this was screaming in the night, every night, begging for death pain. And he had carried that suffering for three years. *Three years.*

'Suicide.'

'What?'

'He did it to himself. Look at his right hand.' Josh shone the torch onto the visible blackened and skeletal hand. 'He's holding the end of the twine. He made a slip-knot and put it round his own bloody neck and pulled it tight. Jesus wept. Jesus Christ Almighty. He buried himself alive and then strangled himself . . .'

Amber wasn't sure why, but she started to cry, maybe even for the long, emaciated and blackened shape that lay upon its bed of filth. And in some unexpected turn in her emotions she remembered his face in Svetlana's prison cell, when Fergal had tried to kill the girl with his battering fists, that punched and punched her face through a thin, cheap pillow on the bed that he had tied her to. And in those final moments, his expression had briefly changed and she thought she had seen a boy, a child, deranged by fear and grief and suffering.

What lay beneath.

Josh either sank to his knees, or volunteered to squat in the interest of comfort, Amber did not know which, until he shook his head and said, 'Look at the edges of the soil. The stuff we took out.' Josh picked up a clump of mud. 'The edges are straight. He dug the hole. He cut a layer of clay into deep, thick slabs. So he could neatly lay them back in place over his body from inside the grave. So they would fit together without leaving gaps. Covered himself up from his feet to his head in polythene and then added a thick layer of soil, block by block. Started with his feet and then worked his way up to his head. Meticulous. And after he'd covered his face, he must have pulled that cord . . . Jesus wept. He even made arm holes in the polythene so he could wrap himself up before he placed the slabs of clay on top of himself. He must have spent ages preparing his own death. Lain very still, in that polythene, in the darkness, under a layer of soil, and just . . . bloody topped himself. Why? Jesus Christ, why?'

To set her free. He gave himself so she could reign again, so the corn would grow high.

They remained silent for a moment. Amber crouched down and took the torch from Josh because he was no longer shining it into the excavation site. She straightened her back and moved the light onto what lay below the corpse's feet. The polythene object, buried beneath the soles of Fergal's decomposing trainers, suggested the right angles of a square: the top of a box. She swallowed. '*Her*. It's *her*. Inside that. The box – it has to be the box from number eighty-two.'

Josh looked up at her with his tired, pale, dirt-streaked face. The expression of revulsion and fear in Amber's expression must have registered, because he turned his head back to the grave so quickly he lost his balance and fell onto one hand. Then stood up. 'What the fuck is this?' He clambered down into the cavity and felt around the top of the box. Then pulled it upwards. The polythene rustled and soil slid from the wrappings. Through the cloudy and dirt smeared plastic, Amber could see wood.

On the soil floor beside the grave, Josh cut the polythene and the parcel tape that had been used to protect and preserve the box and its precious contents. Once the box was unwrapped, Josh placed it upright before them and drew the little purple curtain to one side, as if he were revealing the stage of a small, portable puppet theatre.

It was not possible to fully see the second occupant of the grave. But impressions and details did drift out of what Amber initially revealed with the torch light.

'Oh God. It's a child,' Josh said, as if to augment her shaky comprehension.

The brown leathery flesh of the tiny arms of the thing in the box suggested they were dry, and had been preserved at some time. Sticklike arms either side of elbow joints no bigger than dried dates, ended in hands too finely detailed with little digits and fingernails to be fake. A round wooden object, like a wooden bowl, was clutched by the small, withered hands: a drum skinned in dark leather or hide. The little body was clad in what looked like a once-white but now filth-smeared dress of calico or lace, made for an infant, like an old-fashioned christening dress.

The small withered head was entirely black, almost black enough to obscure the features. But the skull was covered thickly with more hair than such a tiny scalp could ever feasibly produce. A wig. A wig of various tones and hues revealed as the light moved across it. Donor hair.

The mouth was open, or what remained of the lips were parted, and a small row of yellow milk teeth were revealed in a grin. The head's tiny eyes were closed, something for which Amber was deeply grateful.

A long satin sheath covered what served for legs and feet and protruded from beneath the hem of the gown.

'Don't . . . don't touch it. Please,' Amber said as Josh reached inside the box. *Just let me destroy it.*

His hands paused in their descent. 'I don't understand . . .'

Amber waited for Josh to finish the statement, but he seemed disinclined or too preoccupied to follow his own train of thought.

'The body,' he eventually said. 'I can see it.'

Amber tried and failed to swallow the bolus of dread and anxiety that clogged her throat like putty stuffed into a wet pipe. She wanted to tell Josh to get away, to just get the fuck away from the thing in the box, but she could not find her voice.

'It's . . . It's stuck to . . . The head is stitched onto the body . . . It's a snake. A black snake. The hair is real too.

The dress. Jesus, the dress . . . Look at the dress . . . Torch, here, shine it here.'

Amber could barely move her arm, let alone direct the torch beam onto the front of the small, tatty figure's dress, partly obscured by the leathery drum that hung about its neck and nestled into what she had thought was a lap, but must be a coil hidden by the dirty calico gown, the satin sleeve made for a tail.

Josh took the torch from Amber's hand. 'Look.' That was all he said as he directed the beam onto the front of the dress, at what resembled childish, beaded necklaces festooned about the doll's neck. But under closer examination the stiff, brown, petal-shaped objects, that at first appeared like dried fruits or spices, were revealed to be ears: shrivelled human ears. And between such ghastly decorations, what, at a casual glance, may have looked like dirty sea shells or unpolished stones strung on a thong, grew large in her comprehension as teeth. She was looking at human teeth. Some were black with a great age, others a mere ivory-yellow because they had been harvested in more recent times.

'Fingers. God, there are fingers stitched into the fabric. Toes. Amber, we need to—'

Josh failed to finish another sentence. Instead he stood up quickly, his hand dipping in and out of the pocket of his jacket in one smooth motion, and he barked in a voice she had never heard before, 'Stop right there!'

Amber flinched and issued a small shriek. Then she noticed Josh's eyes, and how inside those brown eyes disbelief fought with horror and the honed expertise of a man of war, who now pointed a firearm at an enemy. She turned to follow the direction of his gaze and found herself staring into the gaping mouth of the garage.

She screamed.

And the thin, dirty figure that Amber saw clearly, before it moved past the front of the garage and out of sight into the darkness of the driveway, she managed to ascertain was female.

Female and naked, with blood-blackened ankles and wrists, and something pulled tight about its throat, like a dog leash. What little she saw of the trespasser's face that was not concealed by filthy, tangled hair was bloodless, and so white it could have been blue. But the dark mouth had hung open in imbecilic wonderment. And such eyes as it had were colourless.

The figure had moved its head in their direction, rather than directly at them, and then staggered away in confusion. As it stumbled out of sight, the piteous breaking voice of a distressed young woman filled the otherwise silent air of the night. 'I . . . don't . . . where . . . where . . . this . . . am I?'

Amber turned her face to Josh, as if in need of some acknowledgement that what she had just seen had indeed been seen by her friend too. But her eyes moved past him to what lay behind, and to something that had recently altered within the broken earth at his heels.

Inside the little box, and within the small black head, a pair of marble-white eyes had opened.

NINETY-THREE

It was time for her to take control and to protect Josh, because she did not like the way his hand shook; a hand that gripped a gun that was connected to an arm that also trembled, directed by a traumatized mind behind a bloodless face that jumped with tics.

'Josh. Josh, mate. She's making us see them. Her. In the box. They're not really there. And there will be more of them. Please, Josh. Look at me. We've got to get rid of it. Outside. And burn it. A gun is no good.'

And while she tried to talk Josh down from wherever his senses had climbed, so taut and trembling, Amber kept her eyes on the wooden chest behind his heels. She gently and carefully eased herself around his body to get closer to the crate that carried the tiny black queen, because Amber felt as if her life depended upon the shutting of the purple velvet curtain, and the concealing of those small white eyes, that were no bigger than pebbles but now shone horribly from the dull black leather of the face.

Slowly, almost unable to move her feet in fear, Amber inched towards the box and then quickly flicked the curtain across the figure inside the crate. She bent her knees and raised the heavy vessel from the earth and instantly hated the idea of the chest's occupant being so close to her throat. Such was her revulsion of what she carried, she nearly dropped her cargo, twice.

Her passenger stank of earth, of death, and of the reeking dusty darkness it had resided in for a century. About the box hung the fragrance of 82 Edgehill Road, and the scent of those who had lain so long beneath its floorboards and crouched inside its walls. And so powerful was the odour of a history black with murder, she could have been inside that old house in Birmingham again.

Tears welled over her eyes, and then those tears rolled down her cheeks. 'Petrol,' she barely managed to say. 'Josh, petrol. Quick. Quickly. The fucking petrol!'

She wasn't sure he heard, because he did not move for the petrol can, but stood immobile, an arm raised, as he stared at the mouth of the garage, perhaps wanting to unsee what had so recently staggered across the driveway.

Amber stooped and hooked a finger around the plastic handle of the can. Out into the darkness on unsteady feet she carried the Black Maggie, and her sloshing can of fuel, out of the garage and across the rear of her car, down the side of her house, headed for the rear garden.

Instinct demanded she take *it* away from the house, get it outside, out of the lightless confines it seemed to favour, off the property, and out of the back gate, so it could burn in the very fields that had been blessed by the sacrifice of its most devoted disciple.

Josh came after her, in silence. At least she hoped it was Josh so close to her heels, but she was too afraid to look behind to make sure.

The security lights clicked on around the farmhouse when she stumbled beneath the sensors on the walls. But beyond the boundary of her property, the night and the fields of night were obsidian black, and more silent than she had known any place on earth.

And she only slowed and then stopped mere feet from the aperture between the side of the house and the perimeter wall, that opened onto the lawn of the rear garden, when it appeared to her that another visitor was down there, waiting somewhere upon the orange-tinted grass. A visitor with a voice that was all too familiar.

'And then you said . . . I said . . . I wouldn't . . . unreasonable . . . but who was I . . . you, you told me . . . you swore . . . it was . . . meant something . . . a sign . . . frightened, the more I . . . and now I know . . .'

'Don't look, Josh! Please God, don't look at it! We've got to get this lit. Burn it. Now! Burn it. Burn it. Burn it. Burn it.' And she kept on repeating the phrase in this unreal night to remind herself of her purpose and the sole intention of this rickety journey she had made into the flood-lit garden.

Another stood on the patio, but Amber refused it her attention. 'Don't look, Josh. Please don't look,' she shouted again into the cool air, as if to press an oversized lid onto the tin of her own red madness and the white lightning of hysteria that sparked and flickered amidst her disintegrating thoughts.

What she saw in her peripheral vision, this pale and wasted and unclothed thing with its bony arms raised to the black sky, Josh must have seen in greater detail, because he began to say, 'What? Who? Amber?' in a voice like a little boy.

A fourth intruder spoke, but Amber turned her face

away the moment she saw the brown, bandy legs of a silhouette, too thin to be alive, that skittered more than
walked across the ground on the far side of the garden, as
if it were circling them on the terrible shanks that serviced
as legs. 'Involved . . . you are . . . you said . . . not that
simple . . . must understand . . . Not going . . . refuse. I
said it. I said it . . . wouldn't stop . . . and look . . . what
happened . . . the lights . . . even listening.'

'Stop! Right there. Stop!' It was Josh shouting behind
her.

Amber left him and headed to the garden gate that
stood before the acres of night-drowned maize. She did
nothing more than flinch when the handgun began to pop.

'Donegal, you bastard!' Josh shouted from a position
closer to the house, before his voice seemed to continue
from a distance as if the plain they stood upon had
expanded, stretched impossibly. 'Stop, Donegal. Or I'll
drop you.'

She kept her eyes down, on the grass, on her feet upon
the grass that was real, tinted amber by the lights that
were real, attached to the house that was real. She was
moving, she was breathing, she was carrying something so
heavy her arms screamed in pain and resistance, and her
hands began to numb, which meant she could feel and that
this was all real.

At the edge of the orangey light that lit up the inside of
the treeline and the stone of the perimeter walls, and in a
fashion that inappropriately suggested a nocturnal celebra-
tion was about take place, Amber detected fresh activity
that brought her to a stop. There was a bustle of vague
silhouettes gathered about the rear gate. Their faces were

indistinct, but their thin arms were raised in the darkness. But whether in awe or from some mute and desperate plea for mercy she did not know. She looked away. Out of the bustle she heard Ryan call her name once: 'Steph!'

But from the old oak tree in the bottom corner of her garden, others demanded her attention.

She steeled herself and did not look again at the four women who kicked their little booted feet, as they swayed and buffeted each other beneath the limb they hanged from. They were as real as the blanched bark of the tree they swung below. A mere glance had informed her that the eyes of the hanged were open and bright and that their dark mouths were moving and mouthing things she could not hear.

It was a dream. She was seeing things from a dream. Being made to see things from a dream.

'Dad, help me now! Dad. Please, Dad. Josh! Help me now,' Amber shouted as she cried, and turned her head to find Josh.

There he was, on his hands and knees, his glasses gone. He had taken some of his clothes off, his jacket, his shirt. His pale, freckled torso shone like a grub as he went round and round on his hands and knees, in a circle on the amber grass, blind but talking to himself. With each hand he slapped the earth in some demented rhythm.

A tall, blackened silhouette, a scarecrow vestige of a freakishly tall man, now stood upon the patio. Beside the lanky figure, a smaller, withered creature wearing glasses and a dirty coat grinned at Amber. It cupped its shrivelled genitals inside a thin, brown, four-fingered hand.

And in her panic and disorientation her vision skimmed

616

the upper floor of the farmhouse. Indoors, all of the lights burned brightly. Thin, naked shapes draped in polythene clattered their fingers against the window panes. Amber tore her face away from the house and looked at her feet.

Beyond the line of trees on her left, a little boy she could not see broke into song:

'All around the Mulberry Bush, The monkey chased the weasel. The monkey stopped to pull up his sock, Pop! goes the weasel. Half a pound of tuppenny rice, Half a pound of treacle. Four maids to open the door, Pop! goes the weasel.'

Ryan called to her again, from behind her back this time, from nearer the house. His mouth was no longer full of blood. His voice was clear. 'Steph. Help me.'

She used all of her will and concentration to prevent herself turning her head.

Inside the wooden box a small drum began to beat a rhythm she had heard before. The sound tried to put an end to her heartbeat.

Josh's hands fell upon the grass in time to the beat of the tiny leather drum.

She stumbled to the bottom of the lawn, before that backdrop of so many blackened and piteous figures, half concealed by darkness. A scant-haired congregation of stained bones was waving; their gaunt postures quivered as with the ecstasy of having risen.

Thine honour, these maidens, thine honour, the corn doth rise like grass.

Then silence came, and darkness, total darkness, as if all of the security lights and the lights inside the house had failed. This was followed by a distant scream that made

Josh sound feminine. And into the black came the noise of a pack of dogs fighting each other, snarling, scrapping over something on the ground, somewhere far off. She thought she heard the gun again.

Amber closed her eyes on it all.

Behind her closed eyes, deep within her mind, the red-black night leapt and was alive with movement. At the gate, even with her eyes shut tight, she plainly saw that more and more of *them* had come to stand like piecemeal relics risen on judgement day, their genders and identities erased by an age of suffering and decay. So many arms as slim as bamboo wavered in the air as far as she could see. So many fingers reached for the blooded sky, like corn waving in a breeze, like the crucified, the gibbeted scarecrows left to the elements, to linger in suffering.

The end of the world.

Matches. Petrol. Burn it.

She opened her eyes to find the matches and remembered there was no light. Amber wasn't sure if she was even awake. Was no longer certain where she was.

She placed the box upon what she hoped was grass, but the connection of the wooden chest upon the ground made a hollow knocking sound, as if it had fallen upon a stone floor.

She fumbled for the box of matches inside the pocket on the front of her hooded top. Her hands were real. The cardboard matchbox was real. She was real and warm and solid. 'I'd rather burn. You hear me, bitch? I'll burn before you have me.'

A moving susurration, with a suggestion of a great weight and girth, began to circle her.

Amber slipped to her knees.

From inside the wooden box, a baby began to cry in a way that pierced her heart.

From the sides of the surrounding absence other unseen figures crawled across whatever she now sat upon in complete darkness. The crawlers wheezed, sucked at the air.

The baby cried with a consuming, engulfing distress; a sound from the beginning of time.

The circling movement about her position drew nearer.

Once the match was lit, at first it illumined nothing but her legs and the box. But then, beyond the flame, the air above the maize field appeared to lighten. She wondered if a red sun was rising from the sea, up from the horizon to spread this hideously beautiful fire of crimson across the sky.

With her other hand she uncapped the petrol canister.

What is the time? Is dawn here for me?

Someone spoke, next to her ear. And she stifled a scream but dropped the match into the cold darkness where it doused. She did not turn her twitching head to see the face that had drawn so close to utter, 'Involved . . . you are . . .you said . . . not that simple . . . must understand . . . Not going . . . refuse. I said it. I said it . . . wouldn't stop . . . and look . . . what happened . . . the lights . . . even listening?'

Her arms were shaking so violently now, but her fear-weakened fingers managed to seize the handle of the can and then upend the nozzle over the purple curtained front of the box she had dropped to the ground. The stench of petrol seemed to revive her, then make her nauseous.

'I'm cold . . . I'm so cold . . . Hold me. I'm cold . . . I'm so cold . . . Hold me. I'm cold . . . I'm so cold . . . Hold me.' The breath of the girl was cold upon the nape of her neck.

The infant inside the box wailed anew. The newborn kicked and struggled for life behind the sopping purple curtain.

Black scales writhing in chitin. Black teeth on a thong. The arms of the bereaved raised to the ceiling of a black chapel. A withered man upon a pink bed, his eyes are open. A mother stands up in polythene, her bulk mottled like the skin of a pudding.

What is the time?

Amber joined the babe in its misery and distress and horror, and she wept and felt her own mind sink away and give up its space to an urge that needed to scream until an artery popped and sprayed behind her eyes.

The tightening coil, and its rasp across wet stone, was all but around her.

Her frail hands lit a second match. Dropped the flaring stick upon the tiny regal curtains of hell.

The fire licked petrol blue. Swayed and danced orange tips. And flared so fiercely she thought she was inside an explosion. The hair of her fringe crisped away with a crackle. Fire licked her eyebrows. One leg caught fire. A sun's warmth cupped her face.

A hissing of something dry and hollow followed the implosion of the spitting fire. Liquid dripped and fizzed in the grass about her legs. She slapped at the flames on her thigh.

Burning hair smoked the air.

Light.

She heard animal cries, bestial grunts, as if every field bordering the farmhouse were crowded with panicking livestock.

She slapped and slapped at her legs.

The small petrol-fuming pyre lit up the lawn nearby, but she refused to look into the crude shallow holes in which the black-boned crouched foetal and yawned. The land beyond was charred and red with embers into forever, devastated like a great battlefield. She saw it for a moment. Distant stick figures tottered blind, felt their way through ruin.

Amber recoiled from the fire, and away from the activity in the flame-smothered box, from the small black head that rose to briefly gulp at the flames, as if in ecstasy. She fell to the ground and rolled into the darkness to put out the flames on her legs.

EPILOGUE

'Ashes in the water, ashes in the sea. We all jump up with a one, two, three.' Amber didn't know how long she had been singing to herself, but stopped when her throat was dry enough to reduce her voice to a whisper.

Once the sun had gone down, the blue-black tumult below the passenger decks faded to black. Of the ocean she could see nothing, but the great heaving and occasional wallops against the hull of the ship, so far below Deck 12, remained constant. Above her, the same infinite dark stretched, only pinpricked by stars so distant her dad had once told her that they were already dead. At the time she had found the idea both awful and sad.

Despite her jumper, coat and the blanket she had wrapped around herself, the mid-Atlantic night air still beat against her body, bit her nose with cold, and stiffened her joints. But she continued to sit alone on the balcony outside her cabin, content to stare into the darkness out there and inside herself. Only here, in such a cold and lightless place, did her thoughts find the right space in which to expand and to cope with what had happened.

From the newspapers that had been brought on board in New York, she could see the story had now vanished from every tabloid and broadsheet. And for that she was glad. The story had never made the front pages anyway. To her satisfaction, the fire in her home had only been treated as a novelty piece. Greater scandals and tragedies occupied the more prestigious and significant column inches. *The Times* had shown a photograph of the blackened ruin of the farmhouse, the old picture of her walking into the inquest, and a still of the actress who played her in *Nine Days in Hell*. The photographs were augmented with the headline: TRAGEDY CONTINUES FOR EDGEHILL ROAD GIRL. FIRE DESTROYS LUXURY HOME.

The articles mostly mentioned her success as a film producer, bestselling author, her reclusive existence following her escape from the notorious North Birmingham house, and the tragedy that befell her plans to settle in South Devon. For once the media didn't know anything else and appeared disinclined to just make things up.

Her representatives had said little and the journalists were probably too fatigued by her story to revisit her life in any great detail over a house fire. Online trolls had claimed the fire was an obvious publicity stunt now that the theatrical run of her film was over, and that her exploitation of her story was exhausted. Others remarked upon the evidence of a curse without ever knowing how close to the truth they were.

Remnants of what she and Josh had burned before the farmhouse would never be found. The ashes of her nemesis and its acolyte they had scattered in the Teignmouth Estuary to wash out to sea. It was a measure they had devised in the hope that they could prevent such foul seeds taking root on land again. Perhaps they had even buried a

God at sea. When she'd shared this thought with Josh, he'd not said anything.

Josh had only begun to speak again two days after the sun had risen and bleached away that last night in the presence of the Maggie. And when he began to communicate he hadn't questioned Amber's wishes to destroy the property. Instead, he had rediscovered those concealed resources that had performed so well for him in service, and had committed himself to a silent, methodical, critical path that began with the disposal of an unnaturally long human body, and what was left of the effigy that had been obeyed so faithfully. The miserable trophies of the thing's constituency, that they had separated from the blackened effigy, they'd concealed inside a shoebox and buried the box in the corner of a local churchyard.

She and Josh had burned Fergal's emaciated remains, and the charred remains of the idol of old Black Mag, in a metal skip. Josh had located the skip inside an empty feed barn near Newton Abbot. Amber had not watched the cremation. Nor had she been expected to watch Josh's smashing of the bones and teeth of the effigy that had survived incineration. Because it was not sawdust or stuffing that they had found inside the burned idol. Amber had assisted Josh, with her face masked throughout the operation, with the sweeping of the ashes of their foes into dust pans, and then into the plastic bags that they had later emptied into an outgoing tide from the end of a deserted jetty.

They left nothing behind.

Josh had then made sure that the fire in the farmhouse began in the kitchen, close to where *she* had lain. The incineration of Amber's home was not viewed as suspicious by the police; Josh's expertise in such matters ensured the subtle tracks were covered. Amber's solicitor was dealing with the insurance company over an electrical fire.

She had briefly wondered whether a priest could be paid to bless the ground, but had then realized that what had been buried in her home was probably much older than Christ and had been served before the first Roman footfall on British soil. She was left hoping, desperately, that her salvation had been determined by something as crude as the exhuming and incineration of the relics and remains that had followed her to Devon.

After they'd finished off her home and its unsightly intruders, Josh began his leave of absence from work. He'd didn't know whether he would return to security duties, or what he might do instead. Neither of them had been sure what they would do next. They had resided, mostly in silence and away from each other, in neighbouring hotel rooms for one week, and they had waited, and waited, each dreading the fall of night to see what might happen in the darkness about their beds.

Nothing had happened. No nightmares had opened inside Amber's dreaming mind, no desolate voices had called from beneath her windows, and no long, grubby figures had stood upright and raised their blackened faces to grin at her. On the first night she'd slept eighteen hours. Only waking once when Josh checked on her.

Josh had struggled to communicate what he had experienced in the garden of the farmhouse. He had tried, but Amber realized that he was currently being forced to do what she had been forced to do many years before: to question everything he had taken for granted, and believed, in life. And he too had been driven to wonder what else was out there, around them; where this torrid and uncoordinated journey through life was headed, and what lay at the end of it. A man's thoughts could not get much bigger.

But Josh had admitted that after they had left the garage that night, he had seen Fergal and Arthur Bennet, and other things that may have once been people; forms that no handgun offered any protection against; things that were not there after the garden and sky had been briefly lit with a false red dawn.

Nothing had ever frightened him as much as what came to them within the darkness outside the rear walls of her house; nothing in the call of duty had shaken him in the same way before. His presence had enraged Fergal and Bennet, he knew that much. And he had been sure that he had been only a boy when he could no longer find Amber in the darkness. He'd hoped to prevent them from reaching her, but only half remembered being knocked around, then down, and finally savaged by what might have been dogs, or what had once been men, on a stone or cement surface that should have been a grassy lawn beneath his body. He'd told Amber in the only way that seemed available to him, that he had 'unravelled. Lost it. Thought I was a kid at school again. I was dragged around the ground by someone with cold hands. My shirt was ripped off. I thought I was dead. They hit me hard. Think it was with a house brick. But I could still think, but not see. I thought I'd been blinded. It was like hell.'

The bruises and gouges on his flesh had eventually faded. The septic bites she had cleaned and dressed for him had now healed. But Josh did not know where exactly he had been during that night; he was certain he had not been in the garden that they had run into from the garage. Nor did he ever want to visit such a place again, and so he had agreed without complaint to the destruction of the building where such impossible things had reappeared in his client's life.

Eventually, Amber rose from the balcony lounger on stiff legs and sniffed. Brought a tissue to her eyes and nose. And slowly made her way back inside to the light and warmth of her cabin. She would continue to sleep and eat inside there, to pass the time with small distractions, to accept sleep warily as if she was a sentry on watch for an unpredictable, patient enemy, and she would let this ship take her wherever it went before she boarded another. And she would wait, and wait, and wait, until she knew where to go and what to do next.

ACKNOWLEDGEMENTS

It is with genuine fondness that I acknowledge the influence of the encyclopaedic work of the late Peter Haining and the late Dennis Bardens, who both wrote so enthrallingly about apparitions. The absence of their books from my shelves would haunt me. The chilling, and near unbearably ghastly, true crime books of Howard Sounes (*Fred and Rose*), John Leake (*The Vienna Woods Killer*), Stefanie Marsh and Bojan Pancevski (*The Crimes of Joseph Frizl*) were invaluable in my attempts at creating these killers, as were the studies of Martha Stout (*The Myth of Sanity*) and Robert D. Hare (*Without Conscience*). P.V. Glob's classic, *The Bog People*, offered a shrivelled hand in the service of creating Old Black Mag's history.

Many thanks to my editor, Julie Crisp, for her keen thoughts and suggestions, to my agent, John Jarrold, to Kesia Lupo and the Pan Macmillan team, and the teams at St Martins, Minotauro and Braggelonne. Additional gratitude goes out to my beta readers: Hugh Simmons, Mathew Riley, Anne Nevill and Clive Nevill.

My sincerest thanks to the British Fantasy Society and to the community of bloggers and reviewers who continue to check out my books and support them.

Readers: I salute you! You keep me going.

ACKNOWLEDGMENTS